THE
DREAMGUARDIANS

N. R. Matthews

For

Karen

Freddie

Alice

Never stop dreaming...

With love

CONTENTS

CHAPTER 1 - THE ENCOUNTER

T J sat in his small chair, which was tormenting him by its increasing discomfort. His mind was wandering as he struggled to concentrate on the last lesson of the morning.

The young man gazed out of the first-floor window towards the glimmering sea in the distance. He longed for the bell to confirm his escape into the hot midday sun. It was mid-July and just a few hours now separated TJ and his fellow classmates from escaping their last ever day at Whitecross primary school.

Truth be told, TJ had enjoyed the challenges and invariable ups and downs of school life, but even he couldn't wait for their impending release into the freedom of another long and well-earned summer holiday. The fact that their holiday parole would be followed by another five-year stretch at a new secondary school hadn't been fully appreciated by his friends, but TJ smiled and reminded himself that sometimes ignorance is bliss.

"Thomas Daniel Joseph, are you with us? Thomas... Tom... TJ!"

The rising intensity of Miss Flowers' voice, culminating in the verbal short sharp shock of "TJ!" snapped the young man's attention back into the classroom.

"You're such a dreamer TJ. Now I know we're nearly done for the year, but it's very important to me that you remember these key facts as you transition to your secondary school," Miss Flowers implored, with a little exasperation thrown in for good measure. "I would be heartbroken if you weren't fully prepared for your next chapter of school life. Whatever would your new school think?"

"Sorry Miss," TJ replied, deciding against injecting some light humour that would soften Miss Flowers, as had often proved the case in the past.

"Please pay attention TJ," Miss Flowers continued, "not long to go now and I really want you to remember this as you head off into Year 7."

"Yes Miss, sorry Miss," TJ sheepishly replied for good measure.

After what seemed like an age, the lesson wound down and the bell was welcomed by the usual stampede to the door.

"Walk, go carefully," requested Miss Flowers with a final air of resignation as the class swept out on a tide of excitement for what, after all these years, was their last lunchtime at the school.

TJ and his friends emerged into the sunshine for one final charge around. After lunch there would be a few more hours playing pointless games, counting down the minutes until they all parted company and another of life's chapters closed. He was mindful he wouldn't see some of his class-mates again, which gave him mixed emotions, depending on the people that came to mind.

After working up a sticky sweat, TJ called a game of tag to a halt and headed for the cool of the shade where some familiar faces were gathered around a wooden picnic table under a corrugated structure that was years past its best.

"Are you alright TJ?" asked Rosie with her usual concern for him. Rosie had a soft spot for TJ and found him kind, funny and caring. TJ also liked her for the same reasons and thought she was pretty too, something he was starting to notice more as he was getting older. TJ had enjoyed spending time with her over the past few months, so much so that his reaction was one of em-barrassment whenever his mum cooed sweetly that Rosie was a lovely girl.

"Yes, I'm fine," TJ replied as he perched on the end of the bench next to Rosie. "I'll be sad to leave here, but I'm looking forward to the holidays very much."

Rosie smiled. She felt the same about leaving school but wasn't looking for-ward to not seeing TJ for most of the holidays. But she knew how much TJ was looking forward to going away and how happy he would be to be back there.

"You've really missed him, haven't you?" she asked sincerely. "I hope you have a lovely time away."

TJ nodded and in his mind's eye could picture it already; Mum driving him and his sister up the long carriageway driveway to that huge and imposing grand house where they would spend most of the summer holiday with his most favourite person left in the world.

The daydream ended quickly as a whirlwind struck and a younger girl ran to the table. "Hello, you two love birds," she shouted quickly and excitedly. "What are you talking about? Anything I need to know?"

It was TJ's younger sister Elizabeth.

TJ rolled his eyes. "Nothing that involves you, so go away Lizzy," he said curtly. Even though they were close and enjoyed each other's company at home, there were no public displays of sibling affection allowed at school. Having a younger sister when trying to be a cool eleven-year-old was hard work.

No need to be so rude, *Thomas*," Lizzy said, knowing that the use of his full name, rather than the cooler 'TJ' all his friends used, would sufficiently irritate him.

"Just leave us alone *Lizzy Wizzy*," TJ's friend Charlie shouted from the other end of the bench. Charlie was well renowned for his grumpiness, but he had been a loyal friend to TJ, especially after 'it' had happened.

Lizzy shot Charlie a glare. She didn't mind being called by her nickname, but only by certain people. TJ was allowed, since the way he said it reminded her of someone and stirred some memories buried deep within. If truth be told, Lizzy was quite proud of the middle name she had inherited from her Granny Winifred. Hence the name 'Lizzy Wizzy' was born. But she didn't like her special nickname being used by horribly annoying boys like Charlie.

"What are you looking at me like that for? Calm down *Lizzy Wizzy*." Charlie went for a second dig, knowing full well how much it would wind TJ's little sister up.

"Shut up Charlie," Lizzy Wizzy shouted back. "Just leave me alone, you're so *boring...*"

"Oh, give it a rest you two," TJ interjected. "Can't you just be nice to each other for just one more lunchtime? After today you won't see each other for ages."

Reluctantly, Charlie heeded the advice and turned his attention to chatting with the others around the table. Rosie took pity on Lizzy and beckoned her over to sit down next to her.

"Thank you," Lizzy Wizzy said as she gave Rosie a big cuddle. "I really wish I had a big sister like you. I mean, don't get me wrong, TJ is a good brother but it's not quite the same."

Rosie laughed. "I know what you mean," she replied compassionately. "I was just asking TJ about your holiday and whether you were looking forward to it." Lizzy Wizzy nodded furiously and her eyes began to well up. She too couldn't wait to spend her summer holiday with her most favourite person left in the world.

Things hadn't been quite the same since 'it' happened and life had changed so abruptly and brutally. Even now, whenever TJ or Lizzy Wizzy thought about 'it' they would get upset, as it triggered so many bittersweet memories. TJ also found that whenever he started to talk about 'it' with others, they got upset too. So over time he had tried to suppress those thoughts and carry on 'as normal', as he was often flippantly advised by people who didn't fully understand.

As Rosie and Lizzy Wizzy continued their conversation, something caught TJ's attention. On the other side of the playground, hiding within the climbing frame was a little girl crying. Being a kind, thoughtful and sensitive young man, TJ was concerned, but also somewhat puzzled: in all the years at the school he had never seen or noticed this little girl before. It struck TJ as unusual since she had striking red hair and pale skin. It made her look something like a ghost, even though he was convinced they didn't exist.

Intrigued, TJ left the table and made his way over, carefully threading his way through the chaotic speeding traffic of younger pupils unwilling to stick to any particular lane or route as they darted around randomly to avoid being tagged by one another.

"Hello, are you alright?" TJ asked the upset little pale red-haired girl in what he hoped was his best caring voice.

"Yes, I'm fine," came an unconvincing reply, snuffled through tears.

TJ tried again. "Doesn't really sound like you're ok. What's the matter? Are you hurt?"

The girl shook her head but offered nothing further.

"So, what's up then?" TJ continued. "My Mum always says that a problem shared is a problem halved." If nothing else, TJ was persistent.

The little girl looked away to try and hide her red eyes as tears threatened to cascade down her pale delicate face at any moment.

"It doesn't matter, you won't understand," she managed to say as she struggled to regain her composure. "Nobody can understand."

TJ refused to be brushed off easily. "Come on, try me, you never know," he cajoled.

The girl looked at him suspiciously, doubting how and why he could help her, but she saw kindness and a sympathetic face which made her feel a bit better.

Tentatively and hesitantly, she began to speak. "I keep having this bad dream. A really horrible nightmare that keeps coming back." TJ noticed her body tense the more she spoke. "It keeps me awake and I'm scared. I don't know what it means, and I just want it to stop."

Her tears burst forth and she sobbed again, her shoulders juddering.

"There, there, I know it's not nice, but there's no need to cry," pleaded TJ, although he wasn't very convincing. He tried a different approach. "What is this nightmare? Tell me and then maybe we can work out what it's all about."

TJ wasn't convinced he could help, but he felt sorry for the little girl who looked even younger and more vulnerable than his little sister.

The upset little pale red-haired girl nodded her head and, after composing herself, began to describe her recurring nightmare. As she did so, TJ closed his eyes.

Without warning, he was there.

*

They were both in a small dingy stone room at the foot of a narrow stone spiral staircase that snaked up ahead of them. A flickering orange light emanated from a burning torch flame mounted on the wall.

Somewhere behind them, TJ heard the clomp of what sounded like heavy footsteps and the clinking of an iron chain being dragged along. His heart leapt in his chest and he felt his blood run cold.

What was that he thought, careful not to speak aloud for fear of scaring his companion.

TJ turned. He could make out a narrow corridor that led to a thick granite wall. It wasn't the dead end it appeared, but neither TJ nor the upset little pale red-haired girl could fully see the passageway leading to the left. If they could, they would have seen a longer corridor lit by flaming torches. All they knew was that once something turned that corner, it could go nowhere other than the staircase where they both now stood.

Then TJ heard it again. Another clomp that echoed somewhere down the hidden corridor and another clink of chains. Although scared, TJ thought he should be brave.

"Who... who's there?" he called out in the direction of the end wall in as strong a voice as he could muster. It wasn't very convincing.

'Clomp,' 'Clink,' echoed the reply.

"It's not funny," TJ said in a faltering voice. "Who is it? Who's there?"

He shot a glance at the little pale red-haired girl who stood motionless, her face frozen with fear.

'Clomp,' 'Clink,' 'Clomp,' 'Clink'. The sounds were moving closer.

"Stop it, you're scaring me," the little girl pleaded in a small shaky voice.

'Clomp,' 'Clomp,' 'Clomp,' 'Clink,' came the reply. Then it stopped.

TJ dared breathe. Had it gone away, whatever it was?

Then another noise filled the corridor, even more terrifying than the banging and rattling. A deep moan that sounded barely human.

"Mmmwwwaaaahhhh."

They saw a shadow loom on the wall, confirming something was approaching down the corridor.

The little pale red-haired girl emitted a piercing scream, which took TJ by surprise and scared him even more. The girl turned and started to run up the spiral staircase as fast as she could. But the treads were different sizes and heights and it was impossible to make quick progress. She put her hand on the wall of the staircase to steady herself; it was thick stone and cold to the touch.

'Clomp,' 'Clink,' "Mmmwwwaaaahhhh," rang out again. It was getting closer.

TJ turned to see if whatever it was had come around the corner yet. It hadn't, but the shadow was closing in. The little pale red-haired girl screamed again as she lost her footing and fell onto the thick stone steps. There was no time to cry as an even louder moan erupted from behind them.

TJ moved quickly and helped the girl up. She continued to scramble as quickly as she could, followed closely by TJ. They reached the first twist in the staircase and were relieved they could no longer see what was about to come around the corner below.

The respite in their panic proved brief. The clomping and clinking resumed. It started to quicken. Then it got louder.

By now, whatever it was had reached the bottom of the staircase. It started climbing the stairs. It was gaining.

'Clomp, Clink,' 'Clomp, Clink,' 'Clomp, Clink,'...

TJ's legs started to hurt as the muscles in his thighs burned. They kept scrambling and climbing the staircase, which was getting narrower the higher they climbed. They were both now out of breath and struggling to make progress up what seemed to be a never-ending staircase.

Down beneath them, whatever it was continued to clomp. Whatever it was continued to clink. Whatever it was continued to moan. Whatever it was continued to climb. Whatever it was continued to chase. Whatever it was continued to close in.

"Please stop!" the little pale red-haired girl cried. By now she was struggling to catch her breath as she desperately kept climbing. Over her huffing, puffing and crying she could still hear the noises get ever closer. "Stop it, I'm scared," she whimpered, ready to give up.

As she rounded another twist in the now very narrow staircase, she saw a wooden door a short distance up ahead of her. "At last!" she gasped, "time to escape." With renewed hope, she dragged herself up the last couple of steps to the door.

She grabbed the large black iron handle ring, turned it and pushed. Nothing happened. She tried again, but the door didn't budge.

"No!" she wailed. "Please open!"

TJ made it to the door and took hold of the iron ring himself. He turned it and pushed, but the door remained firmly closed.

He rattled the handle again and pushed with all his might. "Come on, open," he pleaded desperately.

But it didn't, and the noises below them got closer and closer. They turned and saw the shadow start to come around the last of the twists in the staircase.

Whatever it was had almost reached them.

TJ rattled the black iron handle harder and harder and the little pale red-haired girl pounded the door with her sweating palms.

But still nothing happened.

Then they saw it; a grotesque hand reached up to grab the little girl's foot. There was no other option left but for them both to scream...

*

TJ jolted back to life and became aware of his surroundings in the playground again. He was dazed and confused. What had come over him and how was he able to experience, right then, the little girl's nightmare?

It was as if he was there in her dream with her. Not only observing it, but living it and feeling it too, in all its terrifying detail.

At that moment he realised the little girl was staring at him hard through her tears. Then, as if in a trance and in a deep voice that didn't seem to belong to her, she exclaimed, "you're one of them..."

A shiver went down TJ's spine. He was frightened, even if eleven-year-old boys were not meant to scare easily. "What do you mean, one of them?" he asked the girl quizzically as she seemed to stare straight through him.

Suddenly, a whistle blew sharply, piercing the air. TJ turned momentarily to see what was happening, but it was nothing other than a teacher stopping a game from getting out of hand on the other side of the playground. Satisfied it had nothing to do with him, TJ turned back to the girl, repeating his question as he did so.

"What do you mean, one of them?"

But there was no reply. The mysterious upset little pale red-haired girl had gone.

***

The afternoon dragged on and finally the end of the school day, term and year arrived. It was a mixture of emotions; the excitement of the start of the holidays and promise of a new school, tinged with the sadness of departing friends and hard realisation that life had suddenly changed and would never quite be the same again.

TJ had spent the afternoon mulling over his strange encounter at lunchtime with the upset little pale red-haired girl. He was still struggling to understand what had happened and what "one of them" was.

When he arrived home, he was so lost in thought that Mum was immediately worried about him.

"TJ, you don't look right, what is it?" she asked compassionately. "Are you upset about leaving school and your friends?"

"A little," TJ replied, "but not just that."

"Come on then, tell me what's bothering you," Mum said reassuringly. "Don't forget, a problem shared is a problem halved."

TJ offered a weak smile at Mum's familiar saying.

"There was this little girl today at lunch," TJ started. "It was really strange."

He then recounted what had happened with the mysterious upset little pale red-haired girl. As he did, he could see Mum begin to tense. When he explained about the dream and what he had himself seen and felt, her hand slowly covered her mouth.

She slowly shook her head and began to get agitated. "Oh please, no. Not you...," her voice trailed off.

TJ stopped and looked puzzled. "What do you mean Mum, not me? Do you know what this is all about?"

"No, don't be silly, of course not," Mum snapped, "I really don't know what you're talking about." She was getting angry. "It's nothing. I think you must be making it up."

TJ was startled and hurt by her reaction. "But Mum, I'm telling you the truth," he protested. "At the end the little girl said I must be one of them, but..."

"That's enough!" shouted Mum, shocking TJ into silence.

"You don't know what you're saying, and I don't want to hear anything more about it. Do you understand?" By now, Mum was not only shouting but upset too.

TJ's inclination to protest immediately gave way to a sad nod of agreement. He had never seen Mum this angry before and it frightened him. Especially because he knew he was telling the truth and, deep down, TJ knew his Mum believed he was telling the truth too.

He was sure Mum understood something about what the little girl had meant, which heightened his sense of curiosity. Although clearly angry and upset, TJ could detect something else in his Mum's eyes and voice: genuine fear.

CHAPTER 2 – LET THE ADVENTURES BEGIN

He was still thinking about the whole incident with the upset little pale red-haired girl as he looked out of the car window. Even now, a couple of days later, TJ was still intrigued and a little scared. Out of his rear window he watched the landscape change from suburban sprawl to the beautiful countryside that increasingly embraced them as the miles sped by and they homed in on their destination.

Mum slowed the car as they drove through another quaint village with more ancient twisted cottages within a whisker of the road. TJ wondered how these cottages remained standing as the traffic continuously brushed past them. He dared think what might happen if he leant out of the window and gave the most vulnerable cottage a little push. He could see the headlines now: 'Boy Pushes Over House', and he grinned to himself at the ridiculousness of his daydream.

While TJ engaged with his ever-changing surroundings, Lizzy Wizzy was asleep next to him. She had drifted off some miles ago. Her long immaculate blonde hair at the start of the journey was now all ruffled. Her cheeks were as pink as the headphones skew-whiff on her head, although they were missing the fake-diamond studs that gave the headphones that extra special bling so essential for an eight-year-old girl.

Up front, Mum was concentrating on the road and tapping the steering wheel gently in time to the music on the radio. She relied upon the relaxing classical music oozing from the speakers to get her through long lonely journeys in the driver's seat. The radio was trying hard to play its part in eradicating yet another reminder of how life had changed since 'it' happened.

TJ leant forward as far as his seat belt allowed. "Can't we listen to something else Mum?" he pleaded, already knowing the answer.

"Sorry TJ, you know how it is. Classic FM all the way. I can't have all those songs that you and Lizzy Wizzy listen to playing in here. Can you imagine two hours of that?" She rolled her eyes jokingly.

"Oh Mum, don't be so boring, you're in your forties, not your seventies," TJ groaned.

"That's enough of that, thank you TJ," Mum retorted, with the half-serious, half-playful tone he both appreciated and respected.

TJ would never admit to his Mum that deep down he appreciated the beauty within the music that had been playing: Carnival of the Animals by Saint-Saëns', Chopin's Nocturnes and the haunting serenity of Mum's favourite, Clair de Lune by Debussy.

TJ loved his Mum very much. She didn't smile or joke as much as she used to, but then again, none of them did. He was just grateful Mum was still able to show her more light-hearted side despite everything that had happened. It can't have been easy he thought, as he reluctantly started to remember what life used to be like.

"Anyway, not long to go now," Mum called over her left shoulder, "give Lizzy Wizzy a nudge as I want her to see the Old Girl come into view". TJ obliged, as it was indeed the most glorious sight he'd ever seen.

Mum hushed the protests from a rather grumpy Lizzy Wizzy as TJ gave her a few brotherly nudges in the ribs. Then, as they came over the brow of the hill, a familiar sight came into view. Up ahead, as far as the eye could see, lay three hundred acres of Suffolk park land, broken into an uneven patchwork of smaller paddocks by a seemingly random combination of rustic wooden fences and hedges. A huge majestic Oak tree - one of many to dominate the landscape - stood proudly in one field, lazily surrounded by a herd of brown cows while some sheep grazed industriously in an adjacent field.

"There she is," TJ pointed excitedly, as an expansive rooftop littered with chimney stacks began to poke through the treeline. "Hello Old Girl," said Lizzy Wizzy sleepily waving as more of the huge stately home came into view in the distance. Mum started to slow the car, and after a little while longer diligently indicated and turned right off the road, steering through the imposing stone gate posts and past the old coach house that had seen better days. The perspective changed and ahead was a long tree lined carriage drive.

They all paused as they took in the breath-taking sight. In the distance ahead was an Elizabethan stately home, built in the 1500s, with an impressive Georgian façade that had been added a couple of hundred years later. To the occupants of the car, however, she was more than just an old house. She was known and addressed lovingly as the Old Girl.

Mum broke the silence. "Here we are again," she said. "She just gets more beautiful the older she gets, doesn't she?"

It was hard to argue with that thought TJ. The sight of the vast estate never ceased to amaze him. But it wasn't just that he loved. It was the small figure he could see coming into view the closer they got, standing outside the front of the Old Girl that made this place so special.

Lizzy Wizzy spotted it too. "There he is!" she called out excitedly. Outside the huge doors, dwarfed by the imposing building, was an old man with immaculately swept back grey hair. As they got closer, they saw he was impeccably dressed in a checked shirt, trusted tweed jacket and brightly coloured corduroy trousers. The trousers were a strong clue of the fun and youthful personality that lay concealed within a body that was increasingly showing the ravages of time.

Mum drove the car partly round the stone fountain opposite the huge thick wooden doors and brought the car to a stop. TJ wasted no time. He flung open his rear door and jumped onto the gravel driveway.

"Dear boy!" the old man called as TJ ran over to him and embraced him as hard as he could. In doing so he almost knocked the old man over, reflecting as much TJ's developing strength as the increased fragility of the old man since they had last been together.

"Grandpa Mal!" TJ said as he nestled into his chest. "I've missed you so much."

"I've missed you too, dear boy," Grandpa Mal laughed as he ruffled TJ's hair. "My, how you've grown since I last saw you. Let me take a look at you." His voice sang with delight at seeing his grandson again.

TJ reluctantly released his hold and stood back; his eyes slightly glassy eyed from the emotional reunion.

"There, such a good-looking young chap," confirmed Grandpa Mal, nodding his approval and lightly patting his cheek.

An impatient Lizzy Wizzy seized the initiative and dove in for a welcome cuddle of her own.

"I've missed you so much too Grandpa Mal," she cried, the reunion proving too much for her too.

"Indeed, dear girl, likewise. You get prettier by the day, just like your mother," he said with a little grin and a welcoming nod towards Mum.

"Hello Mal," Mum said as she gave him a kiss on both cheeks, "it's really good to see you. How have you been?"

She knew her father-in-law well enough to know she would never get an honest answer to her question. The reply was delivered with Mal's typical politeness and lack of self-centeredness and self-concern.

"Oh, not too bad thank you, Emma dear. Ticking along just fine. Mustn't complain. Now, do come on in. I've not long boiled the kettle and have some rather splendid homemade lemonade and biscuits that I need help consuming."

He winked at the children, then turned and carefully made his way back towards the imposing house, slow but steady as he went.

Lizzy Wizzy rushed past and through the giant doors, welcomed by the cool of the impressive interior. TJ chose to wait for Grandpa Mal to make his way inside. Before entering himself, he looked up at the magnificent house, his eyes drinking in the splendour of the brickwork from one wing to the other, and the endless windows. He remembered once trying to count them, before impatiently admitting defeat.

"Good to be back Old Girl," TJ whispered. "The summer holidays are finally here. Let the adventures begin."

***

After some refreshing lemonade, multiple cookies and sharing all the news of the past few months, TJ made his way up to his room situated on the second floor of the East wing of the house. He liked it up there as it was well away from Mum's bedroom and gave him a sense of freedom.

The room was littered with antique furniture, but also a modern buttoned armchair to snuggle into with a good book. There was ample room to accommodate the numerous belongings he had brought with him. The plan was to spend most of the summer holiday here, visiting the usual haunts and making the most of the Old Girl and her three hundred acres.

This year the holiday would be better than ever. TJ's younger cousins were arriving tomorrow, and he couldn't wait to catch up with them. They had moved away not long after 'it' happened. But they were all still incredibly close. As 'thick as thieves' as Grandpa Mal affectionally described them.

In keeping with the family tradition of combining and shortening names, TJ's cousin Charlotte Harriet Willow was affectionately known as Chatty. She was just one year younger than TJ but now spent most of her time with

Lizzy Wizzy, the younger sister she yearned for, whenever they all met up. The two girls would spend hours together, talking, dancing, drawing and listening to music, but also happy to join in with the boys whenever they saw them doing something exciting, often beating the boys at their own games.

There was no such clever nickname for Chatty's younger brother, Benjamin. He was quite simply and fondly known as Benjy. At just seven years old Benjy was two years younger than Lizzy Wizzy and the baby of the group. Even though Benjy was quite a bit younger than TJ, they both loved spending time with each other. Once reunited the two boys would spend nearly all the summer climbing trees, playing cricket, throwing a rugby or tennis ball to each other and digging furiously on the beach.

TJ wished the day away quickly so the holiday with the four of them could begin. In the end it passed slowly, as it often did when waiting for something to happen or someone to arrive. The highlight of the afternoon was playing chess with Grandpa Mal. Even though TJ had never beaten him fair and square, he loved spending so much time alone with Grandpa Mal. The old man continued to take pity on TJ and still offered him the chance to replay a move whenever he missed an obvious chance to either take a piece or save one of his own.

"Are you sure, dear boy?" Grandpa Mal would enquire whenever TJ made a questionable move, allowing him to reassess the situation and discover what he had missed. Even though TJ hadn't won again today, he knew he was getting better. It would only be a matter of time before he would finally beat him.

Grandpa Mal acknowledged the fact today when he shook his hand after the last game. "Well played, dear boy," he had said. "Nearly had me there. Won't be long." TJ had beamed at the time and he did so again as he thought about the day's events.

It was certainly good to be back with Grandpa Mal again and it would be even better tomorrow when Benjy, Chatty and Auntie Katherine arrived. Even though they were only sisters-in-law, TJ knew Auntie Katherine was good company for Mum. He hoped Mum would be sufficiently distracted so as to not stop all the mischievous fun he was planning to have with the others.

TJ was tired after the journey and Grandpa Mal's hearty dinner, so he made no protest when it was bedtime. Lizzy Wizzy had gone up even earlier. Despite her obvious excitement about getting to see Chatty and Benjy in the morning she had gone off to sleep quickly in another smaller bedroom down the corridor from TJ.

Lizzy Wizzy preferred the smaller bedroom as it was cosier and safer. She struggled to get to sleep sometimes and would occasionally still wake suddenly in the middle of the night, petrified and unable to get back to sleep on her own. Mum would have to calm her by stroking her hair and singing a lullaby. It hadn't always been this way but had started after 'it' had happened. Thankfully, it seemed to be getting better as time passed and her older brother was proving sufficient comfort these days.

TJ had been affected by 'it' in other ways, but trouble sleeping was not one of them. Mum often joked he'd reached his teenage years early and could sleep for prolonged periods of time through anything. If there was one thing TJ really liked it was being tucked up in bed with a book and then snuggling deep down into the duvet for an uninterrupted night's sleep.

Tonight, however, was different.

TJ drifted off to sleep soon enough. The last thing he remembered was thinking it was less than twelve hours before Chatty and Benjy arrived.

Then it started…

*

The Portuguese sun was high in the royal blue sky, yet its heat was tempered by the cool refreshing water. TJ was stood on the side of a swimming pool within the villa garden.

"My turn! This will be the best one yet!" he shouted excitedly to Lizzy Wizzy and his two cousins who were already in the pool.

Beyond the garden wall was the lush green fairway of the 15th hole that led seawards towards the green. Beyond that, a winding cart path led up to the iconic 16th hole that ran along the cliff-edge. One wayward hook and the golf ball would be consigned to a sandy death after quite a free-fall. To the side of the golf course, a road ran down a long hill towards the *Praça* where thick creamy milkshakes were waiting.

The villa was a familiar home from home where they all came to relax and enjoy a holiday together. It had started as just four adults all those years ago, hanging out at their favourite beach bar. But even though the numbers had now doubled, the location was a firm favourite and had stayed the same.

TJ looked over to his Dad, who was happily multi-tasking on a sun-lounger: sunbathing, drinking an ice-cold beer and acting as Head Judge for the children's diving competition. Next to him, the two Mums glanced over the top of their books to watch yet another attempt at a spectacular dive. They had already seen Lizzy Wizzy perform a balletic spring into the water, Chatty a vertical feet-first entry they had named the 'pencil dive', and a typically daring and crazy summersault from Benjy. Although he hadn't got it quite right and slapped the water hard, he came up from beneath the water grinning from ear to ear, eliciting loud laughter and cheers from the others.

On the other side near to the pool, Uncle Bertie lay oblivious in a self-induced comatose state, absorbing as much sun as possible.

"Are you ready, Judge?" TJ called over excitedly to his Dad, who nodded and motioned something back to TJ. He instinctively knew what he meant. They both grinned and gave each other the thumbs up.

On the count of three, TJ leapt into the air aiming for the side of the pool closest to Uncle Bertie. His elaborate dive had been ditched at the last minute. Instead he clutched his knees tightly and executed the perfect "Bomb", displacing a large wave of water out of the pool. It cascaded over the unsuspecting Uncle Bertie, who woke instantly and jumped up with a great cry akin to that of a fatally wounded animal.

Everyone laughed. Even Uncle Bertie, eventually...

*

Without warning, the scene changed. TJ was inside the villa, late at night. He was aware that Mum and Auntie Katherine were chatting in the kitchen behind an almost closed door. Outside, TJ could hear the crickets provide a soothing and gentle soundtrack. He heard the sprinkler system kick in, offering the parched garden much needed refreshment after another hot day on the Algarve.

There was music playing softly outside on the terrace and the unmistakable voices of Dad and Uncle Bertie. They were deep in conversation, punctuated with laughter and the clinking of wine glasses. TJ smiled and decided to get closer, so he could hear what they were up to. He longed for the time when he would be old enough to stay up and join in with the men.

He crept stealthily past the kitchen door and into the lounge, towards the half-open patio doors. The frivolity outside had subsided, and the volume of the conversation was now low. TJ ducked down behind the sofa closest the doors and peered around the arm. Amidst the candlelight around the terrace, TJ could just about make out the backs of Dad and Uncle Bertie, seated at the patio table, with a discarded backgammon board on the floor.

TJ strained to listen to the conversation that by now was almost inaudible. Then voices began to be raised. TJ smiled as he expected another bout of laughter to follow shortly. He loved hearing his Dad laugh; a sign that all was well with the world. But no laughter came. It quickly became clear that all was not well.

TJ was used to hearing arguing, but between young children like him and Lizzy Wizzy, or Chatty and Benjy. He had never heard anything like this between two adults and it made him feel uneasy. For sure, Dad and Uncle Bertie had a competitive relationship, particularly when sport was involved. But he thought they were as close as brothers, even if in reality they were brothers-in-law.

The argument became heated and TJ began to wish he wasn't eavesdropping. However, he now couldn't help but overhear the parts of the conversation spoken harshly and with some intensity.

"But what entitles you to it?" Uncle Bertie shouted angrily.

"That's just the way it is and must be," Dad responded defensively.

Uncle Bertie made another interjection, but it was lost as he knocked over his chair as he stood up.

Dad got quickly to his feet too and the two men squared up to each other. Jabbing a finger at Uncle Bertie, Dad responded in a controlled but firm manner.

"I'm not having this again," he said. "It's about time you accepted it and moved on. That's the end of it. And if I find you in there again interfering and prying, then that'll be the end of it for you."

With his heart in his mouth, TJ scurried back past the kitchen where the conversation was still flowing in a much friendlier fashion.

TJ didn't understand what had just happened, but he had heard enough.

CHAPTER 3 – REUNITED AT LAST!

S unlight flooded the room through the thin curtains and TJ woke feeling tired. For some reason he hadn't slept well, which was unusual for him at the Old Girl. Then he remembered the vivid dreams that ambushed him in the night. He had long forgotten about that incident some time ago on their summer holiday.

TJ was at a loss to explain why that dream had suddenly appeared last night. Perhaps it was because Chatty and Benjy were arriving today. After all, it had started off as a happy memory of their holiday. The warmth of it comforted him, before it quickly faded as he remembered the second part of the dream. Even now he was not able to explain what he had witnessed that evening between Dad and Uncle Bertie. Ordinarily they were the best of friends; as close as brothers ever since they met at secondary school all those years ago, before Bertie had fallen in love and married Dad's sister, officially cementing his place within the family.

TJ couldn't remember whether the atmosphere was frosty for the next few days after the incident he wasn't meant to witness. Certainly nothing more was ever said, at least not in front of him. TJ wasn't even sure if Mum or Auntie Katherine were aware what had taken place.

As it turned out, that was the last holiday they all went on together. A few months later 'it' happened, and life changed. So cruelly, certainly unfairly and definitely permanently.

TJ started to feel a bit better as he made his way into the kitchen and the delicious breakfast being cooked on the old Aga began to attack his senses.

In the breakfast room at the opposite end of the kitchen, Grandpa Mal was shakily pouring orange juices into glasses when he noticed TJ enter the kitchen.

"Good morning, dear boy!" he exclaimed chirpily. "Did the Old Girl provide you with a lovely deep sleep, as usual?"

"Not really," a subdued TJ replied, "I had a strange dream."

Grandpa Mal's demeanour changed instantly and he looked away.

"Oh really, what was it?" Mum enquired over the sound of sizzling thick-cut bacon from the local farmer's shop.

"Can't remember," TJ lied, "but it was strange." He didn't lie very often but didn't want to embark on a trip down memory lane that would only upset them all. It still felt too soon to go there.

"Oh well, never mind. Early to bed if you're tired tonight," was Mum's typical response. TJ groaned, but Mum ignored him. "Go and fetch your sister please. Breakfast is nearly ready, and the others will be here sooner rather than later."

TJ obliged and retraced his steps to Lizzy Wizzy's room, now with a spring in his step following the reminder that his cousins Chatty and Benjy and Auntie Katherine would soon be here.

They tucked into a fine hearty full-English breakfast, with the exception of Mum who was content with granary toast liberally covered with marmalade. The discussion turned to plans for the day, week and whole holiday, as it often did with Mum. She was happiest when they were all properly organised; as if regaining control over the here and now would somehow make up for the complete loss of control, helplessness and despair that had unwelcomingly arrived when 'it' had happened. TJ and Lizzy Wizzy knew to just let Mum get everything in order in her head, but at least try and influence the intricate timetable that was being assembled.

The conversation was interrupted by a couple of loud bangs in the distance that echoed around the Old Girl. TJ and Lizzy Wizzy looked at each other, then in a flash their wooden chair legs were scraping furiously on the flagstones of the kitchen floor and they were off. They raced down the corridors towards the front entrance, jostling, laughing and ignoring the "be careful" shouted by Mum from the kitchen.

They slammed into the front doors and then, with each other's help, heaved the huge wooden door open. Sure enough, outside stood the long-awaited visitors. The children shouted and jumped excitedly when they saw each other. Reunited at last!

Mum and Grandpa Mal eventually joined the reunion that was not short on hugs, kisses, tears and a number of exclamations of "dear boy" and "dear girl" from an emotional Grandpa Mal.

***

After bags had been unpacked and a quick catch-up it was time to get the holiday events underway. As the weather had remained good, the unanimous decision was a short car ride to the coast. They bundled beach bags full of towels, as well as a rather elaborate picnic into the boots of two cars. TJ sat up front with Mum this time and set the destination into the Sat Nav, more out of habit since this was a familiar and keenly anticipated trip undertaken each time they visited Grandpa Mal.

After a short while, fields golden with wheat proudly reaching for the sun turned into heathland. As the landscape changed to heather and fern, they passed a sign warning them to watch out for stray deer. Finally, they entered a picturesque village and after passing the village green turned right towards the beach car park.

The convoy slowed as the road turned into a gravel path and then they all breathed in as they squeezed over a narrow bridge that took them over the river and even closer to the beach. Down below on either side of the bridge, families were peering over the riverbank into the water, jigging strings up and down. Every now and then a line was drawn up and any unsuspecting crabs clinging to the bait were quickly dispatched into buckets.

Mum and Auntie Katherine parked in a small car park quickly filling up with holidaymakers. In the middle was a forlorn cabin selling essential wares for this part of the world: kites, fishing nets and crabbing bait. The troops disembarked from the vehicles and took an item of kit from the boot ready for the short march ahead.

They trudged carefully over an uneven wooden footpath that threaded through the dunes to the beach. The sea breeze was stiff but refreshing and took the edge off the sun that was unusually threatening for an English summer's day. People had nestled into the sand dunes amongst the wispy grass to escape the wind, while others sheltered behind colourful windbreaks dotted along the beach.

Pop-up beach tents exploded out of their cases and the four children quickly filled the side pockets with sand to anchor them into place. Failure to do so would have added two more large and awkward species of kite to the many that were already airborne.

Both Emma and Katherine dutifully laid out beach towels and arranged the bags in the tent as only Mums could do. The children had little interest in home building and wasted no time in charging the short distance down to the sea, slowing only to navigate carefully strips of pebbles.

After a bout of wave jumping and much hilarity, the boys began to dig furiously in the sand, eagerly creating a fortress to keep out the sea. After a while they were suddenly overwhelmed by an ambush from a wave that severely damaged the ramparts. The boys' hard work had paid off though as the castle walls captured a small pool of water. Quickly the slimy sand was used to rebuild the wall, hands frantically shovelling and patting before another wave infiltrated and dissolved the freshly reinforced remnants. The emergency barricade work carried on a little longer before the futility of trying to keep out the waves became clear.

Further up the beach, the girls were happily creating a sandcastle city upon which to display the designer shells, stones and cuttlefish they had diligently collected in their buckets during a productive beach combing session. Once complete, they waited for an unsuspecting client to wander past and fall in love with the latest beautiful summer beach collection. The wait was ended when the marauding waves began to attack their fashion outlet.

At that point the two separate groups joined forces, both driven by the disappointment of seeing their creations damaged by the tide. Hands were once again put to work, the combined effort creating an even larger defence against the enemy. Damage from several waves were swiftly repaired, resulting in a more prolonged battle now that the defending army had doubled in rank. The shouts and squeals of despair and simple delight increased in volume with each attack from the waves.

Finally, it was time to surrender as a huge wave crashed through, submerging and consuming everything in its path. The impressive walls and deep trenches that had been lovingly forged were overwhelmed for the last time. What little left standing after the initial sweep in of the tide was demolished by the drag of the wave as it rushed back out to sea.

Not for the first time in their lives, what had seemed to be well defined and stable structures had been wiped out in a matter of seconds by a force that respected nothing and no-one.

***

It had been a fun but tiring first day all back together. They reflected on it as they lay sprawled amongst heavy cushions on the large sofas in the Great Lounge. The panelled room was beyond impressive. The high ceiling and cornice were intricately decorated, and a huge elaborate fireplace and mirror dominated one of the walls. The remaining walls featured large portraits of seemingly important people through the ages, captured in time by artists of great skill and anonymity.

Most of the day had been spent at the beach. A dip in the sea had built up an appetite for the picnic, which was then followed by a lively game of French cricket and yet more digging in the sand. Eventually they had trudged off the beach feeling windswept and clambered wearily, but happily, back into the stifling cars.

Benjy was curled up in his pyjamas drinking a cup of warm milk. The journey and exertion at the beach had used up almost every ounce of his energy. Even though he was still little in both age and stature, he was desperately trying to stay awake and keep up with his older sister and cousins. His strawberry blonde hair was damp from a bath and the sun had brought out the freckles on his face.

Chatty and Lizzy Wizzy were sprawled out together, resting their heads together. Chatty had grown since they last saw each other and was now the tallest, much to TJ's displeasure. Chatty had also matured since they last saw each other, which wasn't surprising in light of what had happened. Her newly styled brown bobbed hair also gave her an air of sophistication beyond her years and was yet another reminder of change and how quickly the children were growing up.

TJ intermittently sipped a mug of hot chocolate. His legs and arms ached after so much digging and running in and out of the sea, but it had been a good day.

Grandpa Mal sat reading a story to them, his soft tone helping calm them all further. They loved it when Grandpa Mal read to them as he brought the stories to life, alternating voices for all the different characters.

Eventually, the children made their way up to bed. Each of them looking forward to a restorative night's sleep and what the next few weeks would have in store for them.

Even though circumstances had changed, it was good to be back together again. The four of them, ready for anything.

CHAPTER 4 – SOMEONE IN THE SHADOWS

TJ was pleased to tuck down into bed. The best parts of the day were running through his mind, but they soon gave way to his weariness. He drifted off to sleep thinking about Grandpa Mal's bedtime story, how good it was to spend time with Grandpa Mal again and how much he'd missed Grandpa Mal.

*

The wooden cabin was tucked away on the hillside, the town some way down below in the valley. From this vantage point it looked like a model village, with the spire of the church poking out above a patchwork of wooden pitched roofs.

The old man looked out of the window in the direction of the mountain range. Snow was dusted on the top and in the distance was the unmistakable sight of the Matterhorn, separating Switzerland from Italy. Its angular peak stood majestically overlooking all that it surveyed. Streaks of wispy fine white powder swirled around the peak in the wind, giving it a mysterious aura against the clear blue sky. Then, as the sun rose for the day over the Alps, the tip of the Matterhorn glowed orange as if about to erupt. A few minutes later and the whole eastern side of the peak would be bathed in sunshine, and another day on the slopes would begin.

The old man smiled at the view and turned away from the window back into the small room. In the corner the woodburner was already well lit, generating plenty of heat to warm the cabin as well as providing a lovely glow. On the top stood a well-worn copper kettle that had clearly seen better days but was still diligently and faithfully boiling water for the breakfast tea.

A wooden table took up most of the room and was already laid for breakfast. An array of cereals, muesli and preserves had been placed in the centre of the table well before sunrise. He didn't sleep so well these days, especially since something – or definitely someone - was increasingly troubling him.

The old man took a seat at the table and shakily poured some muesli and some milk into a bowl. He then turned his attention to pouring three glasses of orange juice as carefully as he could manage. He spilt some. In the room next door came the clatter of a frying pan and the sound of two younger male voices. They were jovial, reconfirming the plans for the day ahead.

Last night the red wine had been flowing freely as the two men made provisional plans for the day: take a cable car up to Trockener Steg, then onto another - the highest in Europe - to the Matterhorn glacier paradise. From there, they would ski down piste after piste, the harder and steeper the better.

The agreement was to stop only to admire the stunning views along the way and for lunch in a restaurant off the beaten track. As it was, they would probably also end up stopping mid-morning for a hot chocolate and then mid-afternoon for a Glühwein. Nevertheless, they planned to stay out on the slopes for as long as they could before the sun went down and après-ski started in earnest. But they would not fully indulge as they had the old man to think about. He didn't mind being on his own during the day whilst they skied, but he appreciated their company in the evening when the cold and darkness set in.

The smell of frying bacon and sausages began to fill the room and before long the two younger men entered the room carrying plates of cooked breakfast and thickly sliced buttered toast. They joined the old man and tucked into the hearty breakfast in high spirits.

The old man shifted uncomfortably in his chair. He knew what he was about to say would change the atmosphere.

"Do you want to explain what happened last night?" he said. "I'm not completely sure, but I think it was you." He stared at the larger of the two men. "Whatever it is you think you're looking for and trying to discover, you won't find it. Not in that way."

Despite his advancing years and frail appearance, the voice was steely and defiant.

The larger man responded defensively. "Now hang on a minute, I have no idea what you mean."

The third man dropped his knife and fork onto his plate, but nobody jumped at the noise.

"I hope that's the case," the third man said. "I've warned you before about this." He turned to the older man. "Are you sure it was him?" he asked.

The old man shrugged. "I think so, but I'm not so sure. It's getting harder to tell these days. He's getting better and more powerful each time and I'm getting weaker..."

The larger of the younger men looked at them both. "I'm sorry, but I just don't understand what's going on. I've not been up to anything, I promise," he pleaded. "I would never do anything to upset you both. I mean, after all we've been through Daniel, and especially you Mal. I don't know what I need to do or say to convince you." He began to sound agitated. "You're family. The two of you, Katherine, Emma and the children, you all mean the world to me."

As Daniel was about to say something, Mal suddenly grabbed his arm.

"Stop," he cried. He pointed over Daniel's shoulder in the direction of the stairway. "I think someone's there, in the shadows. Look." His eyes widened with fear. "No, it can't be, oh please no," he exclaimed. Then he shouted loudly towards the stairway, "quick, go, before it's too late..."

*

TJ woke suddenly in a cold sweat. There were many things he didn't understand about what he thought he'd just experienced and seen. All he knew for certain was that he felt confused and fearful.

The clock confirmed it was almost 3.30am, but despite the early hour he knew he wouldn't be able to get back to sleep. Rather than toss and turn TJ fumbled around for his slippers and retrieved his dressing gown from the hook on the bedroom door.

He crept along the corridor so as not to wake the others. The last thing he wanted right now was to get into even more trouble if Mum caught him sneaking around in the early hours. Especially when he wouldn't be able to explain the reason why. How could he?

He found it hard to accept that his Dad wasn't around anymore. So how could he bring himself to talk to Mum - or even Grandpa Mal or Auntie Katherine for that matter – about the things he thought he'd just seen or heard?

An increasingly upset TJ tiptoed stealthily to the Snug, taking care to avoid any staircase or corridor near Mum that might creak and reveal his presence. The Snug was another of his favourite rooms; a place to hide away from the cares of the world. However, he began to doubt it would be possible to achieve that this time, as his troubles were proving difficult to outrun.

The room was oak panelled and dominated by an impressive bookcase stuffed full of old books. There was a small section reserved for books and games for the children for when they came to stay. TJ shut the door behind him, turned on a small lamp that emitted a soft glow and slumped into the Victorian square back armchair he loved to hide away in, comforted by the feel of the purple velvet fabric.

He began to sob quietly, burying his head into his knees as he simultaneously burrowed sideways into the chair. Even though he was tired, his mind was racing and there was no chance of getting any sleep now. TJ decided there were just too many questions for a boy like him to cope with; just eleven years old and very, very ordinary.

The events of the past eighteen months finally caught up with him. His quiet sobs turned into louder cries as the tears came uncontrollably. The dreams over the past couple of nights had been a harsh reminder of just how much he missed his Dad.

How were they expected to live without him? Why did he have to die? How would they cope in the years to come without him?

In his inconsolable state TJ didn't hear the footsteps come down the hall or the door creak faintly as it slowly crept open. A hand reached out and grabbed him.

TJ jumped at the sudden shock and screamed...

CHAPTER 5 – PATIENCE, DEAR BOY

The screaming continued. TJ had neither seen nor heard anyone come in and the touch had given him the fright of his life.

"Dear boy, shhh, it's me," came a reassuring voice.

TJ stifled his scream and looked up, although he couldn't quite focus through the shadowy light and his teary eyes.

"It's alright dear boy, it's Grandpa Mal," he said tenderly as he leant over his grandson. "There's no need to be afraid."

"Grandpa Mal!" TJ spluttered through his tears.

"I'm sorry dear boy, I didn't mean to startle you," Grandpa Mal said apologetically.

"Startle me? You scared the life out of me, Grandpa Mal." It was all too much for TJ to take and a fresh flood of tears came all too easily.

Grandpa Mal perched on the edge of the chair, ruffled his hair and continued to reassure TJ. "I'm sorry. Go on, let it all out, dear boy. You've been through so much."

Grandpa Mal just about managed to get his own words out as tears welled in his eyes and he too began to choke up.

TJ's sobs eventually began to subside, and Grandpa Mal handed him a white cotton handkerchief from the pocket of his rather splendid paisley dressing gown.

"I think it's time we talked, dear boy," Grandpa Mal started. TJ nodded, although he didn't know how he would even begin to put into words what had been happening, as he didn't really know himself. "But not here," Grandpa

Mal continued, "we need to go somewhere very special and private. After all, you can never be too sure who might be listening or watching."

With that they got up from the chair and made their way from the Snug. Grandpa Mal led the way into one of the corridors that led from the East Wing of the house towards the West Wing of the house.

TJ was much less familiar with that part of the Old Girl as it had always been off limits to the children. Dad had surreptitiously reinforced that point over the years they had been visiting Grandpa Mal by making them repeat after him a silly rhyme he'd made up:

'I must not sneak or take a peek in the West Wing of the Old Girl
For if I do, dreams won't come true and my mind will be a whirl
So I must be good, like I always should, and never ever care
About what goes on in the old West Wing and venture over there...'

Dad's rhyme went through TJ's head as he was creeping towards the West Wing. However, he didn't feel any guilt because he wasn't properly sneaking. This time he was with Grandpa Mal. If anything, some of his dreams were about to come true: he was about to discover a new part of the house, get to spend some quality time with his most favourite person left in the whole wide world and talk about something that was clearly quite important.

After many twists and turns around the Old Girl, TJ was completely lost. He thought he would never find his way here again or his way back to the main living quarters in the East Wing without Grandpa Mal's help. Finally, they approached a door, much like any other in the house. Grandpa Mal stopped and looked from side to side. Then he fumbled in the pocket of his dressing gown, pulled out a key and after a couple of shaky attempts put it in the lock and turned it.

He pushed the door open gently and whispered to TJ. "Nearly there, in you come dear boy." TJ's state of mind had now changed, and he was feeling less upset and more intrigued. What was special about the room he was about to enter and what was it that Grandpa Mal wanted to talk to him about?

Grandpa Mal flicked on a light switch and they made their way into the room. TJ was immediately confused. The room was small, sparse, windowless and illuminated by a single bulb hanging from the end of a long-woven cord. In the middle of the room was a wooden desk, inlaid with leather, with an uncomfortable looking wooden chair tucked under it. In contrast to the rest of the house the paint was dull and peeling. On the far side a tapestry covered an entire wall. The decoration on it was fading and it had clearly seen better days.

"I thought we were going somewhere special, Grandpa Mal?" TJ asked quietly. He was a little crestfallen at the blandness of the room. "There's nothing here."

Grandpa Mal closed the door quietly and turned to TJ. "Patience my dear boy," he said. "We are so very close. You have no idea, but soon you will."

Grandpa Mal walked up to the desk. He took another key from his pocket, opened the top drawer and slipped his hand inside. He brought out an ornate iron key that looked to TJ as if it still belonged in another century.

"I must warn you, dear boy. This key will unlock a whole new world of mystery and wonder, but also great danger that I hoped I would never have to reveal or expose you to. I have to say your mother will be very upset with me for what is about to happen, but things are much more serious and developing far quicker than I could ever have feared."

TJ's eyes began to widen, but he didn't know whether it was from excitement, nervousness or fear.

Grandpa Mal made his way slowly over to the corner of the room. He slipped behind the tapestry without any effort or sign he was there. Finally, TJ heard the rattle of the iron key in an iron lock followed by a creak and loud bang as a heavy door swung open.

"Come, dear boy," TJ heard Grandpa Mal call out from behind the tapestry.

TJ tentatively made his way around the back of the tapestry towards Grandpa Mal. As it turned out it was not against the wall, but about a foot in front of it. TJ could just about make out that Grandpa Mal was halfway through another doorway, at the top of a stone staircase that led down into what looked like a bottomless black hole.

Before he started to descend, he turned to TJ. "There's no going back from here, dear boy. Are you sure you're ready for this?" he asked.

TJ took a deep breath as so many thoughts were currently running through his mind.

"I'm ready," he said and followed Grandpa Mal down the stairs.

CHAPTER 6 - WELCOME

G randpa Mal slowly made his way down the steep stone steps. He held on tightly with one hand to an iron rail fixed to the stone wall and with the other shone a small torch he had retrieved from his dressing gown pocket.

"Careful now dear boy, these steps are quite steep and could do you something of a mischief."

"I'm fine Grandpa Mal," TJ replied, thinking that he should be the one saying that to Grandpa Mal.

They reached the bottom and the torch shone down a tunnel so long that the light didn't seem to reach the end. All TJ could make out was stone on the walls, ceiling and underfoot. No wonder it was cold and smelt damp. He began to wish he was safely tucked up in his warm bed again rather than wandering around a cold damp tunnel somewhere beneath the West Wing.

"Help me count, dear boy, we want to get the right one," Grandpa Mal requested as he started on down the tunnel.

"But what are we counting?" TJ asked as he caught up with Grandpa Mal.

"Doors," he replied with a sigh. "Of course, of course. Sorry dear boy, I forgot I've never been down here with you, just your..." He abruptly checked his sentence. "One!" he exclaimed, his voice echoing down the tunnel.

TJ looked to his left and could just about make out a wooden door in the shadows. It didn't look as if it had ever been opened, although as TJ was beginning to understand sometimes appearances could be deceptive.

They walked a little further and TJ called out "Two!" as they passed another door on the other side. They continued, passing three and four, then five and six. TJ noticed the floor was increasingly sloping down and they were slowly descending further underground. "How many more doors to go," wondered TJ to himself?

"Nine... ten!" TJ called out, expecting them to stop at door ten. But Grandpa Mal kept on going.

Then at door eleven he stopped. TJ looked carefully. By the limited torch-light he could make out that this door was different to the others. It was made of steel, not wood, and was devoid of any cobwebs. This door has been used, thought TJ, and quite recently at that too.

No more keys were produced from Grandpa Mal's dressing gown. Instead, he flicked up a cover camouflaged on the door just above where a handle would ordinarily be. The soft glow of a keypad was revealed. TJ let out a little gasp and Grandpa Mal smiled. "You haven't seen anything yet, dear boy," he said with a glint in his eye.

He punched in a long stream of numbers. His reward was the sound of steel bolts sliding. They clunked as they fully retracted, and a beep signalled that the door was now unlocked.

"Welcome to my special place," he said as he swung open the door and flicked a switch. This time TJ really gasped.

***

Back in the East Wing of the house, Lizzy Wizzy had been dreaming. It was a dream that she was sure she had experienced before. It felt so warm and happy that she wished it had lasted forever.

But, not for the first time, something had disturbed her. Now she was awake and crying and she couldn't properly explain why. Her pyjama top was wet from sweat and she felt upset as well as cold. She felt so lonely. So *alone*. In fact, she felt sad to the very core of her being, as if nothing would ever be right in the world, ever again.

As she sat upright in her bed, Lizzy tried hard to remember the dream that had taken her to that warm and happy place, but as usual she couldn't re-member it. She scolded herself as she said "think, *think*," and then despond-ently cried, "why can't you remember?"

Lizzy decided that being upset and alone in her bedroom was the last thing she wanted. Sliding her legs out of bed she felt for her slippers with her feet and kicked them round into place, so she could put them on. She picked up her warm fluffy pink dressing gown with bright polka dots and slipped that on too. It offered a bit of comfort, but she still felt upset and alone.

Opening the door quietly, Lizzy tiptoed down the corridor towards TJ's room. She needed the company and a listening ear from her older brother.

She found he had helped take away her feelings of loneliness. However, TJ had yet to help her remember her warm and happy dream despite all his efforts to jog her memory and the number of times she had had the dream.

TJ's bedroom door was slightly ajar which Lizzy thought was unusual. She crept in and made her way carefully over to his bed, her path helped by the full moon shining through the thin curtains. "TJ," she whispered as she approached the lump in the bed, "TJ, it's me! Are you awake?" The lack of response told her TJ was in one of his deep sleeps. She changed her approach. "Wake up, TJ," she said a bit louder as she shook the lump in the bed. But something wasn't right. The lump was soft.

Lizzy leant over to the bedside cabinet, turned on the bedside lamp and heaved back the covers. The form of a sleeping TJ had been quite professionally replicated by an array of carefully placed pillows, cushions and teddies.

"Oh!" exclaimed Lizzy, disappointed not to find TJ. "I wonder where he's gone?" she asked out loud, then immediately felt silly for talking to herself. Ordinarily her curiosity would have got the better of her and she would have gone on an adventure to hunt him down. However, she didn't feel much like wandering around the Old Girl in the middle of the night, particularly as she was still feeling very unsettled.

She made the decision to stay put and wait for TJ to return. Throwing the surplus cushions to the floor she placed a pillow under her head and snuggled down into TJ's bed. This will give him quite the fright when he returns, she thought, and that immediately made her feel a little better. But not by much. Her interrupted and now forgotten dream was still troubling Lizzy. Why couldn't she remember?

***

TJ was expecting a stone cellar room with low ceilings behind the steel door. How wrong he was. As they entered the room, he was completely awestruck by what he saw.

Grandpa Mal's flick of the switch had summoned a soft glow from lamps, uplighters and elaborate wall lights. They must have travelled quite deep underground as the ceiling in the large room was high. There was too much for TJ to take in initially, but his eyes began to widen as he took in the splendour and richness of the room.

The first thing that struck him was the ceiling, covered with intricate paintings and ornate gilded cornicing. Immediately above his head was a night sky, painted a rich deep midnight blue and studded with silver and gold stars. This covered the first quarter of the ceiling before it seamlessly blended into different scenes, each with different characters, telling a story.

The first scene TJ noticed in the centre of this section was a man and a woman lying asleep next to each other on a bed. The silk sheets draped over them had failed to completely cover up one of the lady's breasts and TJ blushed at the sight. To one side of them stood figures dressed in white, almost angelic looking, while dark shadowy figures loomed menacingly on the other. To the left of this scene was another. This time a lady was sleeping alone. Standing over her was another figure in brilliant white, as if protecting her from a dark figure that this time was fleeing.

As Grandpa Mal made his way further into the room, TJ stopped and continued to cast his gaze at the pictures on the ceiling. He noticed the next scene depicted a man sleeping in a four-poster bed. This time there was just a dark shadowy figure in the scene. It was crouched over the sleeping man, its arms reaching out threateningly as if trying to claw at the man's head. TJ felt himself go cold as he looked at the nightmarish scene and the scared and pained face of the sleeping man.

TJ looked at the opposite side of the ceiling. One scene pictured a distressed sleeping woman being tormented by a sole shadowy figure. Another featured a man sleeping peacefully, watched over by a figure of light whilst another shadowy figure was in full retreat.

The remainder of the ceiling furthest from him was covered with resplendent painted scenes. Five were larger and more prominent than the others. The first contained an older man sleeping at the foot of a rising spiral stairway, which snaked its way through a starry night sky into golden rays above. Figures of light surrounded the man and were ascending and descending the stairs.

The second was of a young man asleep in a farmer's field. Next to him, a wheat sheaf stood proudly as all the others around it were bowed down. Above the sleeping man the sun, moon and eleven stars were bowing down to him.

The third prominent panel featured another man standing on the ramparts of a castle. His eyes were open, and his face looked unsettled, as if wrestling with uncomfortable and almost unfathomable thought. In one hand he held a dagger, with the tip of its sharp blade faced inwards towards his neck. TJ wondered what torment was captured in this moment.

The fourth panel was the most vivid: a figure of intense light on its knees, trapped in a cage. The cage was surrounded by many shadowy figures. Some were reaching through the bars trying to touch the figure trapped inside. Others appeared to be dancing, celebrating the entrapment. As TJ looked at it he felt an overwhelming deep sense of sadness in his soul and tears began to well up in his eyes.

He turned his gaze to the fifth panel. There was one figure surrounded by intense light, looking down from on high over all it surveyed. Beneath it were many cages, similar to the one in the other panel. However, the cages were opening, allowing figures of light to escape towards the intense light. Next to the cages, shadowy figures were falling or trying to turn away and hide from the light that was shining down. TJ felt himself taking a deep breath as he took in the scene and felt a warmth and strange strength enter his body.

"What is this place?" he whispered, almost rhetorically.

Grandpa Mal spoke from the middle of the room. "I see you're rather taken by the artwork on the ceiling. So beautiful and so very old. And also revealing. Yes, definitely. There is so much to tell you dear boy. We must get started. Please, do come and sit."

He beckoned TJ towards two large wingback chairs that sat in front of a primitive stone fireplace. TJ was surprised to see a fireplace deep underground, but there were so many chimney stacks on the house it would be impossible to trace one specifically back to this room. In any case, nothing about this house surprised him anymore. A fire had already been prepared, so Grandpa Mal struck a match from the firebox and lit the kindling under the logs in the cast iron grate. The smoke began to draw up the chimney and the comforting sound and smell of a crackling fire began to emerge.

Upon Grandpa Mal's invitation to sit, TJ's attention turned away from the ceiling. His eyes started to drink in the rest of his surroundings as he made his way into the room. It was the most amazing combination of curiosity room, library and study. The wall on his left opposite the fireplace housed a library like TJ had never seen before. Row upon row of old books of all shapes and sizes were packed into glorious order on the shelves. Two sets of wooden library stairs reached invitingly heavenward at different levels. They were on castors and able to slide along the bookshelves, ensuring no book was out of reach and no boundaries to a reader's quest for knowledge.

Old books were also piled high around the room on various tables from different periods. TJ also noticed a number of stuffed animals. Some were in glass domes or glass tanks. Others were ironically liberated from such cages but still unable to escape their state of taxidermy. TJ could make out pheasants, partridges and other birds, as well as a cunning fox and more sinister wolf brandishing sharp teeth. In front of one of the bookcases, a peacock proudly displayed its patterned plumage in a permanent courtship ritual. Each 'eyespot' watched TJ carefully as he made his way towards the chairs.

A beautiful stag's head was mounted on the far wall opposite the door, its strong antlers branching out, casting angular shadows over the painted wall. Further along was a wild boar's head, complete with moustache-like tusks, as well as an array of mounted animal skulls. TJ could make out the skulls of rams with their ribbed horns as well as the skulls and less developed antlers from young stags, the local muntjac in particular.

In front of this wall were various display cabinets, a large wooden library wardrobe with brass-fronted drawers and banks of stacked Globe Wernicke barrister bookcases. The bookcases and display cabinets housed a collection of anatomical models and figures. An anatomical arm hung down from a chain in one of the cabinets, its muscles and raised sinews well defined through the plaster flesh.

A wax anatomical head and torso was also visible. It was quite ghoulish as the top part of the skull was missing revealing sections of the brain. One eye was closed and the other missing, allowing the eye socket to be studied. The remainder of the face was a mixture of skull and the fabric of the body normally concealed by flesh. The rib cage was visible but empty, the heart and lungs not the focus of this particular model.

On top of the library wardrobe were a couple of plaster busts. One was of a striking bearded gentleman in the armed forces on a wooden plinth. He looked serene and peaceful as he gazed out into the room. His plain grey appearance was broken in places by white where the plaster had suffered damage over the years. The other bust was of a rather ugly looking man. Although part of his nose was damaged, TJ was convinced the man's face would remain ugly even if it had been complete.

Slowly, TJ reached the chairs. The one facing the door was large and covered in leather, the other was smaller and upholstered and faced towards the stag head on the wall. The chairs looked like thrones to TJ given their size. Grandpa Mal sat down in the smaller chair and invited TJ to sit in the large leather chair. In between them was an ornate games table inlaid with the squares of a chessboard as well as a backgammon board. However, there were no chess pieces ready to do battle or backgammon checkers to get a game underway.

Next to each chair was a side-table. Upon each stood a lamp and more books. On the table next to TJ stood one of the most striking objects in the room. It was a ceramic phrenology head, although TJ neither knew what is was or what it was for. But it was certainly distinctive. Black lines marked out different areas of varying sizes around the cranium and over the left closed eye of the ceramic head. These areas had been labelled in a language that TJ neither recognised nor understood. The crackled glaze and ornate writing on the ceramic head suggested the piece had some age. Like nearly everything in this room, it was old, mysteriously odd and strangely beautiful.

TJ sat, his eyes continuing to dart around the room as he tried to take every-thing in. To the left of the fireplace lived a large antique globe, continents shaped as they were understood to be centuries ago and countries labelled in thinly scrawled Latin writing. As TJ looked ahead, he noticed that the wall housing the door he had come through was also painted midnight blue and decorated with stars. Dozens of mirrors of different sizes and types of frame hung on the wall, giving the illusion that the room was even bigger than it already was. Some of the mirror plates looked very distressed, but still retained an air of beauty and would still reflect the truth when asked to.

"So, my dear boy, what do you think?" asked Grandpa Mal.

"It's the most amazing room I've ever seen Grandpa Mal," TJ replied. "I think I could spend forever in here, just reading all the books, looking at the paint-ings and admiring all this, this, stuff…"

Grandpa Mal smiled and nodded. "Indeed, dear boy. That's exactly what I thought when I first set eyes on this room many, many years ago. Such happy times…" He trailed off wistfully.

"Grandpa Mal, what is this place?" TJ asked. "What does it all mean?" TJ's head was starting to spin with all the questions his eyes and mind were gen-erating, and his heart beat faster with the excitement of it all.

What TJ didn't realise was this was just the beginning. What Grandpa Mal was about to tell him would turn his head and thoughts upside down. It would challenge and stretch his understanding and change life as he knew it.

Grandpa Mal leant forward and said in a quiet voice, "my dear boy, we have so much to get through. All will be revealed."

He opened his arms out wide and continued.

"So, my dear boy, welcome to The Great Room, the home of the Brethren of the Dreamguardians…"

CHAPTER 7 – THE GREAT ROOM

C onfused, TJ struggled to understand what he had just been told. "The what, Grandpa Mal?" he asked.

Grandpa Mal raised his hand as if to signal quiet. "I know that doesn't mean much to you now, dear boy. But we have a lot to get through and even then, you still might not understand fully. So have patience, dear boy, and try your absolute best to keep up." He smiled, knowing that the challenge would be fully accepted by young TJ.

"First things first, though. I am obliged to say that what I am about to tell you is known by very few people. That is both the case now and has been so throughout history. I must ask you once again to promise you will never reveal what I am about to tell you. Never, to anyone."

TJ nodded furiously, "I promise."

"Good, lives depend on it, dear boy," replied Grandpa Mal, reinforcing the gravity of the promise.

"I will take you now on a journey, dear boy, across many centuries. You must not interrupt, for fear I will miss something important. You must keep up, for fear you will miss something important."

TJ nodded. He vowed to himself he would concentrate like never before. He did not want to let Grandpa Mal down.

"The Brethren of the Dreamguardians has been in existence since before even the birth of Christ. Some of its earliest members are identified and honoured in this room. But of course, although possession of the gift by the earliest Dreamguardians has been publicly documented in prominent places, we have been very careful to remove any reference to the Brethren even in those accounts. This was done for a very good reason, my dear boy, in order to protect us from *them*."

TJ was about to ask Grandpa Mal who 'them' was, but then remembered his promise and quickly held his tongue.

"But before I explain all this, dear boy, we must start at the basics," Grandpa Mal continued. "Let us assume that, on average, a person will sleep for eight hours. Or in other words, a person sleeps for one third of a day." TJ nodded his agreement. "Consider this then dear boy. I have been fortunate to have lived a very good life and during my seventy-five years on this earth I have seen many marvellous things. But I must also have spent about twenty-five years of my life asleep. Twenty-five years!" Grandpa Mal chuckled at the fact. "That's a long time, my dear boy. More than twice your age!" and he shook his head in disbelief as he smiled ruefully.

"So, what happens when you sleep is very important and not just because we spend so much time doing it. You must also consider its benefit to us as human beings of simple flesh and blood." Grandpa Mal paused for a moment. "Ah, I will try and keep this part as simple as possible for you, dear boy. But as you get older you will no doubt take the opportunity to delve deeper and find out even more with the help of this room.

"You will find plenty of research amongst the books in this very library here, dear boy, about the importance of sleep for our health, minds and the way we live. I think we must all know anyway that good sleep is essential for a healthy mind and body." TJ nodded his agreement and Grandpa Mal continued. "Indeed, research by some scientists has shown your memory can actually be strengthened and improved whilst you are asleep. Others suggest our dreams can help us process emotions and therefore reduce worry and anxiety. Perhaps more well known is that a lack of sleep can obviously affect your attention and learning. I'm sure your mother has said that many times before". Grandpa Mal chuckled. "And all this at some unearthly hour of the morning. How ironic!

"Now you may not understand fully this next bit, dear boy, but studies by other very knowledgeable and clever scientists also suggest that a lack of sleep can result in higher levels of inflammatory proteins in your blood. They believe these are linked to conditions such as heart disease, strokes and arthritis. So even stress levels can be lower with more sleep. I'm sorry, are you still with me, dear boy, I realise this is perhaps not easy to understand?"

TJ blinked and nodded eagerly. He had just about understood most of it and so desperately didn't want to let Grandpa Mal down.

"Excellent, there's a good chap," Grandpa Mal said smiling. He stopped for a moment and pointed at a wicker log basket next to the right of the fire. "If you wouldn't mind doing the honours dear boy, before we really get into the other exciting benefits."

TJ left his chair momentarily to pick up some larger logs and place them on the fire which had taken nicely by now but was glad of the additional fuel.

"Now we could spend many hours talking in much more detail about the health and wellbeing effects of sleep. Having been to so many meetings and conferences about such things, believe me I should know. However, I want to move on to the really exciting part. But before I do, let me ask you a question, dear boy."

This took TJ by surprise and he tensed and shifted uncomfortably in the grand chair. "Sure, Grandpa Mal," he replied hesitantly. Grandpa Mal reassured him. "Don't look so worried, it's not a difficult one." TJ relaxed a little but smiled awkwardly.

"Whilst a good night's sleep is undoubtedly good for a healthy body and mind, what else do you do when you are asleep, dear boy?" Grandpa Mal asked.

TJ thought for a moment. Then a smile broke out on his face as he realised it wasn't really a difficult question and he knew the answer. "You dream, Grandpa Mal" he replied.

"Yes, exactly," exclaimed Grandpa Mal, "right first time. We dream! Which means we should now talk about creativity, dear boy.

"If you care to take a look at the evidence – most of it included in the books in this room - you will indeed discover that some of the world's greatest inventions, music and art were conceived within a dream. It is quite wonderful to consider the power that is contained within the subconscious mind.

"Even in your lifetime, dear boy, we have read testimony of how modern popular music has been inspired by, or indeed written in a dream. Although I'm not too familiar with such modernity, some of the Brethren have shown me articles on that internet-thingamajig about songs that have come from dreams. Even songs from some of the biggest bands in the twentieth century."

TJ smiled at Grandpa Mal's description of the internet, although he wasn't too sure if Grandpa Mal was as ignorant about such things as he let on. There were clearly lots of things he didn't know about the real Grandpa Mal. What other hidden secrets did he have?

Grandpa Mal paused for a moment. "Seeing as you did so well just now, dear boy, let me ask you another question. Do you know the artist responsible for the painting on the wall over there?" He pointed towards the corner of the room over TJ's left shoulder.

TJ leant to his left round the huge chair and peered to the end of the room. He had not noticed the frames on the wall in that corner, which was hardly surprising given how much there was to see in the room. TJ got up from his chair, walked over and stood in front of the collection of frames on the wall. Before he studied the painting in detail his eye was drawn to three separately framed drawings beneath it.

Each looked to have been drawn on faded parchment. One was of a naked man who seemed to have four arms and four legs. He was simultaneously standing in the shape of a cross and as if performing a star jump, drawn within both a square and a circle. Tiny writing was above and below the picture, but the words were ineligible, at least to TJ.

The second contained three smaller drawings related to the study of brain physiology. The largest was the side profile of a man's head, with sections of the brain labelled again in an unfamiliar language. The medium-sized drawing was of another head that had been split into two sections. The top third of the head had been lifted off and sandwiched in between the two parts of the head was the brain. It looked like a jellyfish with tentacles hanging loosely down. TJ wasn't sure what the smallest drawing was but guessed it might have been a top down view of the brain. Again, he couldn't read all the annotations to the sides of the three drawings.

The final drawing was a close-up drawing of a skull, with yet more ineligible writing beneath it. Half of the top of the skull was missing, and TJ was struck by the artist's apparent obsession and fascination with the head and brain.

The painting that Grandpa Mal was referring to was completely different. It was landscape in its orientation and featured a long white table that ran from left to right. Thirteen people were on the far side of the table, facing the artist. A figure in the centre had both arms outstretched, pointing towards a small roll of bread with their left hand and a small glass of wine with their right hand. There looked to be great consternation amongst the other twelve around the table.

TJ turned towards Grandpa Mal who was still sat in his seat. "I think I know what the painting is Grandpa Mal. I think it shows The Last Supper, but I don't know who painted it. The man in the middle must be Jesus and the others are the twelve apostles".

"Very good my dear boy. Your mother would be proud. Yes, indeed, the painting is The Last Supper. Jesus has just told the twelve apostles that one of them will betray him and the painter captures their different reactions. You can see Judas, the fourth from the left, clutching a bag that is probably full of the silver he earned from betraying Jesus."

TJ admired the painting a few moments longer then returned to his chair. "The painting and the drawings are by Leonardo da Vinci," Grandpa Mal continued. TJ said to Grandpa Mal that he had heard of him. "Not only was he a world-famous artist, but da Vinci was a polymath," Grandpa Mal added. TJ pulled a puzzled face and so Grandpa Mal explained. "A polymath is someone who has expertise in a wide range of disciplines, dear boy. Da Vinci was also an inventor, a scientist, an engineer, a mathematician, in fact an interest in so many things. Now did you know that some credit him with inventing the helicopter and the parachute, centuries before the technology existed to build them?" TJ shook his head from side to side and let out a quiet "Wow".

Grandpa Mal got up slowly from his seat. He made his way to the other side of the room and looked along one of the bookshelves. He was muttering under his breath as he looked up, down and across the rows of books. TJ heard him ask himself "Now, where is it?" Satisfied he had found what he was looking for, he reached up and heaved a large, old and dusty book from the shelf. "Oh, help me please, dear boy, it's heavier than I remember".

TJ jumped up and helped Grandpa Mal carry the book to the nearest table. Grandpa Mal adjusted the anglepoise lamp on the desk so that it was concentrated on the book, illuminating the brown musty pages. TJ stood to Grandpa Mal's side as he turned to the index at the back of the book. He then carefully made his way through the thick heavy pages to a specific one. His finger hovered over the words as he made his way down the page and then stopped. "Just what I was looking for. Here we go, dear boy".

TJ leant in closer. Amongst the text he could make out the picture of an old man with long hair and a long beard. "That's da Vinci himself, a self-portrait from 1512," Grandpa Mal said authoritatively. He pointed at a particular line of text. "I know it's old handwriting, but can you read this?"

"I think so," said TJ. Slowly he read the words:

" 'Why does the eye see a thing more clearly in dreams than the imagination when awake?' "

"Exactly, dear boy!" Grandpa Mal said excitedly, ruffling TJ's hair. "The words of Da Vinci himself. One of the greatest minds the world has ever known and a member of the Brethren of the Dreamguardians when he was alive."

TJ stood open mouthed as he took in Grandpa Mal's words.

"One of the finest exponents of art and invention through the power of dreams. It's all exciting stuff, isn't it dear boy!" Grandpa Mal said returning the book to its home in the bookshelf.

"I should say!" TJ replied excitedly.

"Up for some more?" Grandpa Mal asked.

"Absolutely!" TJ said.

"How about some literature this time?"

"Why not!" TJ replied, his heart now beating quickly with excitement.

"Then look up, dear boy, look up!" Grandpa Mal was now in full flow. TJ was sure he hadn't seen him this animated, at least not in his own short lifetime.

"Up there", Grandpa Mal said, pointing to the man painted on the castle ramparts, "is Hamlet..."

TJ interrupted and proudly finished the sentence, "...Prince of Denmark, by William Shakespeare." Grandpa Mal raised his eyebrows in surprise. "We read some abridged classics in Year 6 Grandpa Mal," TJ explained.

"Ah, very good, dear boy!" Grandpa Mal chuckled. "Do you remember Hamlet's famous soliloquy then, when he thinks he is alone? Act 3, Scene 1".

TJ thought for a moment. "I'm not sure, is that the part that goes 'To be, or not to be?' "

"Very impressive, dear boy," Grandpa Mal continued. "Here, let me help you," he said, "but remember to listen carefully". He then closed his eyes and passionately recited from memory Hamlet's soliloquy:

' "To be, or not to be? That is the question—
Whether 'tis nobler in the mind to suffer
The slings and arrows of outrageous fortune,
Or to take arms against a sea of troubles,
And, by opposing, end them? To die, to sleep—
No more—and by a sleep to say we end
The heartache and the thousand natural shocks
That flesh is heir to—'tis a consummation
Devoutly to be wished! To die, to sleep.
To sleep, perchance to dream—ay, there's the rub,
For in that sleep of death what dreams may come

When we have shuffled off this mortal coil,
Must give us pause. There's the respect
That makes calamity of so long life. " '

"Beautifully done Grandpa Mal," TJ said, "but I'm not sure I understand. Sorry."

Grandpa Mal smiled. "It's fine, don't worry. Indeed, beautiful but always difficult to decipher. But then, that was the intention. Let me try and make it easier for you:

"To die, to sleep.
To sleep, perchance to dream—ay, there's the rub,
For in that sleep of death what dreams may come"

TJ's eyes widened as he began to notice the focus on the words 'sleep' and 'dream'.

"Dear boy, Hamlet is asking whether it is better to die rather than address his troubles. But he is fearful. Of what you might ask? Well, that even when he is dead, he will dream and never get any peace from his troubles."

Grandpa Mal walked over to TJ and placed his slightly shaking and frail hand upon TJ's shoulder. He looked at him intensely and then spoke carefully.

"You see, like Da Vinci before him, Shakespeare was one of us, dear boy. He understood the power of dreams: their ability to unlock such creativity, beauty and good, but also the grave risks involved and their destructive potential."

He walked back to his chair and gently sat back down. His excitement seemed to have worn off and he was looking more serious. He motioned for TJ to return to his chair too and he obliged.

"Our dreams have furthered the discovery, progression and enjoyment of mankind. They have pushed us on in our understanding and fulfilment of life. However, my dear boy, the sad truth is that many dreams have been lost over the centuries. Who can tell what beauty, progress and enlightenment has been lost... no, not just lost, but *stolen* from us?" A righteous anger and resentment emanated from Grandpa Mal as he spoke. "Such loss, dear boy. Such tragedy. Such *theft*..." He clenched his fist and banged it down on the arm of the chair. TJ jumped at the uncharacteristic action.

Grandpa Mal composed himself. "Thankfully, more have been saved than lost; extremely important ones at that. But the battle is real and proving harder as each generation passes." He looked intensely at TJ.

"This is why we exist, dear boy. We must ensure dreams remain for the continued development of good. We must ensure they are neither stolen nor turned against us so that they become a destructive force for evil."

Grandpa Mal leant forward and TJ reciprocated.

"I am one of the last remaining Elders of the Brethren of the Dreamguardians. But as you can see, dear boy, I am getting old. My health is sadly fading and at an increasingly rapid pace. I need to pass on the history, tradition and secrets of the Brethren to a new generation before it is too late."

Grandpa Mal's voice began to crack. He rubbed his eyes with his boney index fingers and tried coughing away his emotion. At the same time TJ tried to swallow back the lump in his throat.

"But we are facing an even greater challenge than this, dear boy. The Elders can sense a deepening and intensification of darkness and lost dreams. This is a worrying development, dear boy. Most worrying. If this is allowed to continue, then the Dreamguardians are in grave danger."

TJ couldn't quite follow but knew that Grandpa Mal would explain it all in due course. Grandpa Mal looked determinedly at TJ.

"My dear boy, I will teach you the ways of the Brethren and what it truly means to be a Dreamguardian. There is no greater life you can live, or gift you can give to humanity than to be a Dreamguardian: a dream protector, risking your life and fighting for the safe passage of dreams."

Just then the clock on the mantlepiece of the fireplace broke into life, breaking the tense atmosphere with five consistent chimes. TJ jumped.

Grandpa Mal looked anxiously over to the clock. "Oh, dear me, time has beaten us tonight, dear boy. Come now," he said getting to his feet, "we must get you back into bed before anyone notices you are gone and starts to ask questions."

TJ started to protest. "But Grandpa Mal, I don't fully understand. What do I need to do? You also mentioned 'them' earlier. Who are they? And what do you mean risking your life?"

"TJ," Grandpa Mal said sternly, "we will reconvene another time, but we must go. For now, just remember to be very, very careful in your dreams." With that he turned and made his way to the door, ready to retrace their steps back to the East Wing of the Old Girl. A very confused TJ followed with so many questions running through his head.

CHAPTER 8 – PLAIN SAILING

The journey back through the maze of corridors within the Old Girl was undertaken in silence. Grandpa Mal was lost in thought and TJ was struggling to take in and comprehend everything he had just seen and heard.

After many twists and turns, including up and down different staircases, they finally returned to the corridor that led to TJ's bedroom.

"Remember, TJ, be careful. And once again, not a word to anyone. Not to dear Elizabeth and certainly not your mother. Is that understood?" Grandpa Mal whispered.

"Yes, I promise Grandpa Mal," TJ solemnly replied. Although he was still unsure about many things, he recognised the importance and gravity of what Grandpa Mal had started to share with him. In any case, he wouldn't know where to begin even if he did want to share the events of tonight with anyone.

"Very good, dear boy," Grandpa Mal continued. "All being well we will reconvene tonight. We need more time, so meet me in the shadows of the Grand Hall at 2am. Nowhere else. I think this is the safest way to proceed."

TJ nodded his approval and made his way along the corridor to his door, which was slightly ajar. He crept back into his room and was about to slip back into bed when he noticed the blonde hair splayed out on the pillow.

"Oh no Lizzy Wizzy, not again," he muttered quietly to himself. It had been a while since Lizzy Wizzy had one of her 'lost' dream episodes as they called it; where she had woken up feeling so alone and needed someone to be with. In the early days after 'it' had happened they had been a regular occurrence. Poor Lizzy Wizzy would wake almost nightly in the early days, often hysterical followed by an intense sadness. But they had become less frequent as time had passed, in the same way that some of their memories of Dad were beginning to fade. Time is a great healer people had told TJ. But he knew that at best Time was simply good at fooling you and making you forget, while at worst it was an unscrupulous thief devoid of any healing or restorative powers.

TJ settled down into the buttoned armchair with a blanket. Any decent sleep now would be impossible he decided, especially as daylight was beginning to attack and infiltrate the thin curtains. He closed his eyes and pictured again the amazing room he had just visited, with its incredible ceiling, artwork and curiosities. Some of Grandpa Mal's words were now a blur, although others including the incredible stories about Da Vinci and Shakespeare he could remember vividly. They were all Dreamguardians and now, somehow, he was about to become one too under Grandpa Mal's teaching. Incredible! His mind continued to race as he dozed off, still a little confused but blissfully intrigued.

***

TJ was forcefully shaken into life. "TJ, wake up! Where have you been?" Staring hard at him was Lizzy Wizzy, her arms now folded neatly and her hair very much the opposite. "What do you mean?" TJ replied defensively through half-opened eyes. His headache reliably informed him he hadn't been asleep for that long since returning from his unexpected adventure with Grandpa Mal.

"I had another of my horrible 'lost' dreams. So, I came to see if you could help me find it. Or at least keep me company. But you couldn't do either, because you weren't here." She stared at him again suspiciously. "Where were you?"

TJ tried hard to think on his feet as his accuser stood over him. "The toilet" he said, a bit embarrassed and disappointed at his lack of imagination in coming up with an excuse. In any case he doubted she would believe him even if he had told her the truth.

"Rubbish," Lizzy shot back. "I waited up ages for you to come back, but you didn't."

"Well, when I came back, *from the toilet*," – he emphasised the lie again to try and further legitimise it – "you were asleep in my bed. So, being the kind brother that I am, I let you stay there and took the chair. And now here I am with a pain in the neck, in more ways than one..." He smiled smugly as Lizzy Wizzy slowly digested TJ's barb.

"That's unkind," she protested. "So now you're being horrible as well. I know you're lying and that you were up to something. I'm going to tell Mum, especially if you were being silly with Benjy," she threatened.

TJ tensed a bit but hit back immediately. "Well I wasn't. But if you do, I'll tell Mum you were in here in the middle of the night, bothering me again about this stupid 'lost' dream of yours that apparently makes you really sad." He was now in full flow and couldn't help himself. "Mum knows you make it up to get attention and she'll be a lot crosser at you for that, than at me for having to go to the *toilet* in the middle of the night." Attack was the best form of defence he had thought, but he immediately felt bad for accusing Lizzy Wizzy of making up her 'lost' dream. He knew from witnessing its aftermath that whatever it was that kept disturbing her in her sleep was very real and affected her deeply. In the early days the hysteria was quite distressing, while even now Lizzy Wizzy's description of her loneliness upon waking was painful to hear.

"That's not fair, you know it's real." Lizzy Wizzy's head dropped and her lip began to quiver. "You can be so horrible sometimes TJ," she continued. "If that's how you're going to be, then I don't want to be in here anymore. I'm going back to my room."

With that she turned abruptly, stomped loudly to the door and closed it rather noisily behind her. TJ sighed. He didn't feel proud of himself for upsetting Lizzy in that way. While he tried to convince himself, he had done what was necessary to keep the events of the past few hours secret, he vowed he would need to get more adept at protecting his newfound knowledge. After all, that's what Grandpa Mal required of him and had made him promise.

TJ rubbed his eyes. It would be a long day ahead, especially coming off the back of a broken night's sleep. But already he couldn't wait to spend more time with Grandpa Mal in the special room of the Brethren of the Dreamguardians.

***

The large wooden table was laden with provisions as the children took their seats for breakfast. Lizzy Wizzy and Chatty sat together at one end, while Benjy and TJ sat diagonally opposite at the other. Lizzy was still upset with TJ and Chatty had instantly sided with the younger sister she had never had. Chatty was fiercely loyal.

The girls were whispering to each other and looking over slyly to the boys. TJ and Benjy were oblivious to the girls' attention and were happy larking around at the end of the table. Auntie Katherine made her way over to the table with a couple of plates, one piled high with bacon sandwiches and the other with freshly buttered toast. Mum followed with a large bowl of freshly sliced fruit of all kinds.

"Thank you, Auntie Emma," Chatty said politely and Auntie Emma smiled back. "You're welcome Chatty," she said, "now tuck in everyone". Both Aunties sat down behind the steaming mugs of tea that had already been placed on the table.

There was one noticeable absence as breakfast began to be distributed around the table. "Where's Grandpa Mal?" TJ asked. Auntie Katherine finished a sip of her tea, put down her mug and turned to TJ. "I caught him just as he was about to leave this morning," she answered. "He said he had to go out for the day. He asked me to tell you all that he was very sorry he was going to miss the big regatta this year, but he needed to take care of something." Chatty and Lizzy groaned at the realisation that Grandpa Mal was going to miss out on the big race, while TJ was more intrigued by where Grandpa Mal might have gone. Was it something related to him and the Dreamguardians, TJ wondered?

"Do you know where's he gone?" TJ asked. Auntie Katherine shrugged her shoulders. "No, afraid not. They were in quite a hurry when they left. Actually, you would have loved it children," Auntie Katherine continued, "Grandpa Mal being driven off in a beautiful dark grey Aston Martin DB4 - at quite some speed I should say too! It was quite a sight."

An inquisitive TJ latched on to the comment immediately, ignoring for now the thought of missing out on seeing such a magnificent and expensive car. "They? Who was Grandpa Mal with then?"

"I think it was one of his very close friends, TJ," Auntie Katherine responded. "They go way back, but I'm not exactly sure how." She paused while she tried to remember. "It might have been through work, or perhaps through that club he's a member of." TJ's eyes widened, and he took a big breath in. He thought it was meant to be a big secret. "Yes, probably through work or maybe the golf club," Auntie Katherine said. "Anyway, let's hope he's in a better mood when he returns. He didn't seem his usual self this morning and he certainly didn't want to talk about it when I asked what seemed to be bothering him."

TJ let out a sigh of relief. He had a good idea what it was about, but no idea where Grandpa Mal had gone or who with. Maybe he would find out tonight he thought, sincerely hoping that Grandpa Mal would indeed return as he said he would. TJ looked across at the clock on the wall. Its old hands reliably informed him that tonight was indeed still a long way off.

***

After breakfast was cleared away somewhat chaotically, they took a short drive to a different part of the coast. This time the boys rode in Auntie Katherine's car and the girls in Auntie Emma's. They entered the main street of the town and found two parking spaces close to each other in front of the shops and cafes. It was already starting to get busy as tourists flocked to the Suffolk Heritage Coastline.

The boys were parked outside the ice cream shop, which Benjy and TJ thought was a very good omen. Their enthusiasm was slightly curbed by the fact that the girls had parked outside a clothes shop, which would no doubt please Chatty and Lizzy Wizzy.

The children congregated together on the pavement as both Mums grabbed some large canvas bags from the boot. A friendly Labrador sniffed at them as it went past, pulling behind it an equally jolly old lady. They all made their way through an alleyway to the wall separating the crag path from the beach. Turning left they walked along the sea wall past little wooden huts selling locally caught fresh fish and some offering smoked fish.

Not long after passing the Lifeboat station they arrived at the destination for their regatta. The boating pond was about the size of a small swimming pool with its small brick wall sides allowing children of the right age to safely lean over and launch their model boats. The pond was surrounded on all sides by park benches for weary parents and grandparents. Within a stone's throw was a war memorial, as well as a peculiar ancient building with an unusual double chimney. It was made from stone and red bricks and an ornate sundial adorned the wall facing the boating pond.

The children carefully retrieved their wooden sailing boats from the bags Katherine and Emma placed on a bench. They were of simple construction, with two sails held in place by small pieces of nylon rope. TJ, Chatty, Lizzy Wizzy and Benjy lined up at the far end of the boating pond and counted down from three. On the shout of "Go!" they pushed their boats off and started frantically blowing into the sails, as if that would make all the difference and propel their vessels to victory in the main race of their annual regatta.

Benjy's boat veered to the left straight into the boat next to it, eliciting shrieks of laughter from Benjy and cries of mock despair from TJ. They hugged and jumped together as the excitement of the race took hold. On the other side, Chatty's boat was pulling ahead of Lizzy Wizzy's. The children ran around the side of the pond as the boats tacked their way slowly down towards the other end. The children leapt up and down as excitement reached fever pitch and the boats neared the finish line. Chatty threw her arms up in the air as her boat hit the other end first, closely followed by Lizzy Wizzy's. The girls hugged each other as they celebrated their victory over the boys. Benjy fell to the ground laughing as his boat capsized just shy of the finish line, sending TJ into further fits of giggles.

The children carried on skippering their boats while Emma and Katherine sat drinking cappuccinos ordered from the little wooden kiosk next to the boating pond. TJ was first to come over to request time be called on the regatta. After some protestation from Benjy, who could have stayed there all day, they eventually moved back up the crag path for an open-day tour around the 'Freddie Cooper' lifeboat, majestically dry berthed in the station. Benjy beamed as he sat in the captain's seat pretending to steer. For one of the first times in his life he felt important and that he was in charge of something. At the same time TJ was given a brief introduction to the radar and radio. Further inside the boat, Chatty and Lizzy were having fun trying on some of the lifeboat gear.

After the typical long queue at the fish and chip shop, lunch was eaten down on the beach. They bravely fought off the seagulls to protect their rations that had been expertly drowned in salt and vinegar. TJ's fish and chips looked as though they had been brutally murdered, such was the volume of red ketchup that had been squirted over them.

The highlight of the day was a display launch of the Freddie Cooper as they sat on the beach. The giant boat was slowly towed out to the cusp of the waves before being launched down a row of wooden beams that had been carefully laid into the sea. A rigid-inflatable boat was also launched, and the children watched fascinated as a rescue was simulated just off the breakers.

The end of the display ushered a move back to the high street. The day was topped off by mountainous ice creams from the small parlour in the high street. The heat of the day took its toll quickly and Benjy ended up with a chocolate beard and ice cream all down his t-shirt. They all found it extremely funny as Benjy looked at his newly found facial hair in the shop window and pretended to talk like an old man. Katherine failed to see the funny side initially and she rolled her eyes and accosted him with a dampened tissue. Benjy found his quick shave even funnier. His giggle was infectious and by the end of the big clean up even his Mum could see the funny side. Benjy was indeed a sweet and lovely little boy, with a great character. Everyone who came into contact with Benjy loved him and his brilliant personality.

Despite the protestations of the two young men it was time to do some shopping before they left, much to the pleasure of Chatty and Lizzy Wizzy. After what seemed like an eternity to TJ and Benjy, their torture was over. They all made their weary way back to the cars and took the short drive back to the Old Girl.

The house was empty when they returned. The children amused themselves playing board games in the snug as Katherine and Emma prepared sandwiches for supper. Spirits remained high even though energy levels were flagging. As the sun began to set, producing the most glorious sunset over the West Wing, the children were packed off to bed one by one. TJ began to look at the clock anxiously as Grandpa Mal had still not returned.

TJ was glad to finally settle into bed as the activities of the day and the previous night finally caught up with him. He carefully set his alarm clock for 1.50am and hoped Grandpa Mal would have returned by then. It was time for more answers to the many questions he had pondered during the day. While the day was drawing to a close for everyone else in the house, in many respects it was just about to begin for TJ. He smiled and turned his light off, excited but also a little nervous about what lay ahead. Only Grandpa Mal knew what was in store for them later tonight. It took a while, but TJ eventually dropped off to sleep.

To sleep, perchance to dream...

CHAPTER 9 – IN THE SMALL HOURS

D own the corridor from TJ's room, Chatty was curled up in bed. It had taken her quite a while to drift off, but she had now been asleep for about an hour and a half. The clock showed midnight was within touching distance.

Chatty was enjoying a dream about the four of them sailing their small boats on the boating pond. The sun was shining, much like earlier today, while the smell of the sea air and call of the seagulls was tangible to her senses. On the bench at the far end of the boating pond sat Mum, Auntie Emma and Grandpa Mal. He gave the children a shaky wave and they waved back excitedly. "Are you ready?" he shouted weakly over to them and held his handkerchief above his head ready to start the main race of their annual regatta.

On the shout of "Go!" they pushed their boats off and started frantically blowing into the sails, as if that would make all the difference and propel their vessels to victory. After a short while, TJ's boat veered to the left into Benjy's boat, causing the latter to capsize.

"Ha ha, yes!" TJ laughed, punching the air with his right fist. "You're finished Benjy, you *loser*," he shouted. Benjy was crestfallen and began to cry, more the result of TJ's callousness than the loss of his boat.

Chatty was incensed at what she'd just seen. "Leave him alone TJ, don't be so cruel," she shouted at him. TJ ignored her and turned back to his boat. "Go on!" he shouted, egging his boat on towards the finish line. Chatty could feel her anger rising as her boat slowed and TJ's powered on towards the end of the boating pond.

TJ yelled triumphantly as his boat won the race. "Champion! Winner!" he shouted as he scooped his boat up out of the water and raised it above his head.

"That's not fair, say sorry to Benjy," Chatty shouted at TJ. "You're no champion, you're a cheat," she continued.

TJ looked at her and smiled smugly. "Shut up Chatty. I won, fair and square. I'm the best," he said arrogantly. "You're a *loser* too, just like your brother". Chatty bristled with anger and looked over at Grandpa Mal who had left the bench and was making his way over to TJ.

"Grandpa Mal, you saw what he did," Chatty said. "Tell him he's disqualified. You're the umpire after all."

"I will do no such thing," Grandpa Mal said sternly. "Don't be such a sore loser Charlotte. TJ won, fair and square, just like he said". He turned to TJ and his face and voice softened. "Quite right and a well-deserved victory too. Well done my dear boy," Grandpa Mal said proudly, now with one arm around TJ's shoulders. "You are my favourite after all," he said tenderly, ruffling TJ's hair with his free hand.

In her dream, Chatty burned with a rage she had never felt before. At that moment in time she felt an intense dislike for TJ. Who did he think he was? For the first time in her life she felt like she wanted to do something to hurt him. Just like he had hurt her and her little brother a moment ago.

It was all too much and Chatty woke suddenly, confused and scared by what had just happened. She had never experienced anything like that before, she thought. "It was just a dream, right?" she asked herself. "That wouldn't really happen would it? I mean, is that what TJ's really like and does Grandpa Mal really love TJ more than the rest of us?" Deep down she thought she knew the true answers to her own questions, but the dream had unsettled her more than she could ever have imagined. Now she wasn't quite so sure.

*

Next door, Lizzy Wizzy was also having a vivid dream. It started as it always did, in the back of a car. She was much smaller and younger than she was now, sat on a booster seat looking out of the window. She watched the City landscape pass by and in the distance saw three huge towers reaching towards the clouds. As they sped along, they passed people of all shapes, sizes and colours, all with different places to go and things to do.

Then they were driving down quite a steep slope, with big houses to the left. In the front seats two men were talking. But she could never quite see who they were. She could always remember though the old leather seats and the radio playing very dramatic choral music.

The car went through some large iron gates and pulled up amongst some grand old buildings. All around her she could see grey stone, columns, a square of grass, a statue and then two big domes as she looked up. Some way away in the distance she saw a big hill. On top of it was another statue, and then off to the right something big and round, poking through the trees like a giant tethered balloon trying unsuccessfully to escape.

Once out of the car she held the hand of one of the men. If only she could see his face in her dream. The other man pushed open a huge wooden door revealing a flight of marble steps and two huge columns in front of them leading into an enormous room. As they made their way inside, Lizzy Wizzy gazed up at an elaborately painted ceiling. There was far too much for someone so little to take in.

Just then the man holding her hand bent down and turned to speak to her. Behind her, unbeknown and unseen, someone made a move in the shadows. The dream suddenly went black and Lizzy Wizzy wouldn't remember any of it when she awoke.

*

Back along the corridor, TJ's alarm burst back into life. He stirred, silenced it clumsily and forced himself to sit up. He didn't want to risk falling back asleep and missing out on his time with Grandpa Mal.

"It had better be worth it," whispered TJ, but he knew deep down it would be. He sleepily put on his dressing gown and slippers and carefully opened the door to the corridor. It creaked loudly as it opened, shattering the dark silence. TJ winced and paused. He carefully poked his head around the doorframe and peered down the corridor to see if anybody had heard. No one came.

TJ carefully closed the door behind him and made his way down to the Grand Hall as stealthily as he could. The Old Girl was too good for him though, and some of the floorboards creaked slowly and noisily as he passed, as if deliberately trying to give him away. Every time it happened, TJ paused, waiting again for someone to discover him wandering the Old Girl at the dead of night.

He quickened as he passed the rooms where Benjy, Chatty and Lizzy Wizzy were sleeping. If only they knew, he thought. Part of him wanted to share the excitement with them, but it was only a very small part. He was more than happy to selfishly keep everything that was about to happen to himself.

His watch glowed in the dark and showed 1.57am on its sleepy face. Not long to go. TJ made his way down the staircase so grand it had three twists in it. The eyes of the people in the large oil paintings who might have been his ancestors seemed to follow him down the stairs, keeping watch to see who was descending the grand staircase late at night. TJ wondered if any of them knew where he was headed and whether any of them were also Dreamguardians, whatever that fully entailed?

TJ made it to the Grand Hall. It was quite eerie at this time of night with the darkness overcome in places by the moonlight infiltrating the window. TJ could make out the mahogany Steinway piano by the window. Its lid was open invitingly, the keyboard exposed and poised ready to play. But no one ever did. Not anymore. Not since 'it' happened. TJ shivered at the thought. Towards the other end of the room were four-large floor to ceiling columns that offered some privacy from the front door just on the other side.

Beyond the columns, TJ could just about make out the huge sideboard running along the far wall. On it was an impressive collection of large Oriental vases and yet more taxidermy. A ghostly white barn owl looked almost alive at this time of night, ready to strike its prey at any moment. A majestic stag's head was hung on the wall, one of the finest stags to have roamed the estate according to Grandpa Mal. Two stag skulls on either side of the great stag provided a sober reminder that even though they were less worthy of full preservation, they were no worse off than the great stag. Death was a great leveller after all.

TJ made his way towards the sideboard, treading as lightly on the wooden floor as he could although it was largely academic as the living quarters were a long way away. He looked over to the Grandfather clock that was about to chime 2am, for once in front of an audience in the early hours.

TJ couldn't see Grandpa Mal and his heart began to sink. Perhaps he wasn't back, and something had happened to him, TJ worried. Or maybe he had changed his mind and he would never speak to TJ about it ever again. After all, it would be very difficult for TJ to convince anyone about what he had seen, especially a deliberately well-hidden room.

As TJ walked past the columns he jumped. Hidden behind the second column in the shadows, just as he promised, was Grandpa Mal. "My dear boy," he said, "so pleased you remembered." TJ smiled at the thought that he would ever forget to show up. He hugged Grandpa Mal tightly.

Together they retraced their steps from the previous night. Once again TJ tried hard to commit the route to memory. They entered the small sparse room but this time Grandpa Mal walked straight past the desk towards the tapestry. He turned to TJ and held up the ornate iron key. "No time to waste, come on dear boy."

The heavy door was open in no time and they made their way carefully down the stone staircase, both holding tightly to the iron rail as Grandpa Mal shone the torch at their feet.

As they made their way down the stone tunnel Grandpa Mal broke the silence. "So, let's see how much you remember, dear boy. Which..." TJ interrupted immediately. "Door number eleven," he replied confidently. Grandpa Mal chuckled as TJ both guessed and answered correctly his unasked question. "Such a clever chap." He paused. "So much like your father," he said wistfully.

TJ smiled. If he could no longer be with Dad, then the next best thing he could do was to be as much like him as possible. But if only he were still here, TJ thought.

"Did Dad ever come down here?" TJ asked as they approached door eleven.

"All in good time, dear boy," Grandpa Mal replied evasively.

Grandpa Mal revealed the keypad, punched in the code and waited for the beep to confirm the steel bolts had fully retracted. He swung open the door, illuminated the room and TJ couldn't help but gasp again as he set his sights on the room for a second time.

It was even more beautiful than he remembered from the previous night.

Grandpa Mal made his way to the smaller chair and motioned for TJ to once again sit in the large leather chair opposite. Grandpa Mal groaned as he fell back into the chair and rested for a moment. He looked very weary. The fire was already well alight, and they were both glad of the warmth emitted. TJ wondered how long Grandpa Mal had been down here before he had come up to the Grand Hall to collect him. There was a fresh pile of books on the side table that were not there yesterday.

"So, my dear boy, as you know I had to take an unexpected trip today. I am very sorry to have missed the regatta. Who was the victor in the big race this year?"

"Chatty won, by quite some distance. It was a good race," TJ replied and filled Grandpa Mal in on all the details. "Excellent, well done Chatty, dear girl. She's a treasure you know dear boy." TJ smiled and agreed, he loved spending time with Chatty as well as Benjy. "Young Chatty takes just after her mother," Grandpa Mal continued. "She was a lovely girl too when she was Chatty's age. Anyway, we digress. Let us stay focused on the job in hand.

"It might not come as a surprise to you dear boy that I went to a rather hastily convened meeting of the Eldership of the Brethren. I had to ensure that the rest of the Eldership was fully aware and informed of what transpired last night. Do you remember last night TJ?"

TJ nodded. "Of course, Grandpa Mal, I haven't really been able to think about much else."

Grandpa Mal smiled. "Indeed, quite so, dear boy. Now the other reason I needed to meet with the Eldership was to also seek their permission."

He leant in closer to TJ.

"Permission to tell you even more, dear boy."

CHAPTER 10 – US AND 'THEM'

T J sat expectantly as Grandpa Mal continued.

"Now, you'll remember towards the end of our conversation last night dear boy I disclosed some very important things. Let me quickly recap, though I must say this is more to help me organise my own thoughts rather than because I don't think you remember. I think you're far too clever for that, my dear boy."

Grandpa Mal sighed. "There's so much to tell you I must make sure I do it to the best of my ability and in the right order. So, the first point was that we must ensure that our dreams are protected for the continued development of good. Our dreams must not be stolen or turned against us so that they become a destructive force.

"Then I started to introduce you to the Dreamguardians, the protectors of dreams. I also said I needed to pass on the history, tradition, and secrets of the Brethren of the Dreamguardians on to you. In so doing I will entrust the future of the Brethren to a new generation before it is too late."

TJ nodded his agreement.

"Good, good. Although all these are critical, we have decided to leave elements of your discovery to another time. Soon I will take you to see someone who will develop your understanding even more. Is that clear dear boy?"

"Yes, Grandpa Mal," TJ replied. He was immediately intrigued and wondered when he would do this and who he would see.

Grandpa Mal continued. "Last night we spent quite a bit of time on the importance of our dreams and why they require... no, *demand* protection. We only scratched the surface of course, but hopefully you understood the importance of the wellbeing, progress, creativity and enlightenment that can be gained from our dreams."

TJ's heart was beating faster in his chest. He dared not interrupt, but his question was burning inside of him. He couldn't stay quiet any longer.

"But Grandpa Mal, you also talked last night about protecting the Dreamguardians from 'them'. But you didn't say anything more about 'them'. Who were you talking about?"

Grandpa Mal nodded sadly. "Yes, indeed, dear boy. We are now at the point where it is impossible to gain a complete and proper understanding of a Dreamguardian and our importance without recognising to whom 'them' refers.

"My dear boy, an enemy comes to do many things: to steal, harm, discourage, destroy, frighten and to tear down. Need I go on? All these are the complete opposite of what the Dreamguardians stand for and fight to protect. My dear boy, I dare mention their name, as they are not worthy. But when I talked about 'them', I was referring to the *Dreamstealers*."

Grandpa Mal fell silent as TJ digested the revelation. He felt a dark and oppressive atmosphere enter the room as soon as he heard Grandpa Mal utter the word 'Dreamstealer'.

"My dear boy, a Dreamstealer is the reason why someone will wake up remembering just bits of dreams, or none at all. Of course, blaming the absence of a dream on a deep sleep has been a deliberate and convenient way of covering up the existence and power of the Dreamstealers.

"The sad truth is that the Dreamstealers have been around for many millennia, just like the Brethren of the Dreamguardians. In the beginning, the Dreamstealers were very ineffective and weak. Their activities were often justified or downplayed as normally harmless and mischievous 'fun'. There are still some heretics who maintain that view to this day. There are even some who think there is a purpose for the Dreamstealers and a place for them to be brought within the Brethren. What *fools* they are," Grandpa Mal said forcefully, clearly riled and quite animated again.

"With the passing of each generation we find the Dreamstealers becoming increasingly dangerous, sinister and dark. Disturbingly we find them gaining in power and strength..." Grandpa Mal sighed for a moment then shook his head as he continued. "Gaining in power and strength, particularly as they uncover the secrets of the Brethren. Secrets they were never meant to discover and possess."

"How?" TJ asked, his voice trembling a little as he felt the deepening gravity of Grandpa Mal's disclosures.

"A number of ways my dear boy: sometimes carelessness, often deceit and on occasions *betrayal*." He bristled as he spat out a word that had no right to grace his lips. "The last is perhaps the hardest to accept. But you shall learn very quickly my dear boy, to *never* underestimate the enemy.

"You see, dear boy, a Dreamstealer *thrives* on interfering with dreams. The extent to which they are successful will depend on their ability, dexterity, experience and strength. But the very best can - and will - turn the potential for good dreams into bad or even steal them forever. Whatever they believe will cause the most damage or harm.

"Remember in particular what I said last night, dear boy. We can but mourn and lament what beauty, progress, enlightenment and precious things have been lost and stolen from us at the hands of the Dreamstealers."

A tear trickled down Grandpa Mal's cheek as he spoke.

"But why, Grandpa Mal?" TJ asked. As someone so young and innocent he could not understand.

"You shall learn the true origins and specifics in due course. For now, it is perhaps easiest to say that the Dreamstealers have lost such beautiful human qualities as love, charity, hope, compassion, creativity and endeavour. They have been replaced with hate, selfishness, despair, bitterness, destruction, anger and resentment."

They sat in silence for a couple of minutes as Grandpa Mal composed himself. TJ took full advantage of the break in conversation to take in the beautiful room. His eyes flitted from panel to panel on the ceiling, then to all the various curiosities dotted around the room. Grandpa Mal uttered a little cough to recapture TJ's attention.

"I see you admiring the Great Room again, dear boy. This is why we must not become too pessimistic. We should never underestimate the power of the Brethren. So, with that in mind, it's about time I revealed the full extent and glorious truth of the Dreamguardians. Prepare yourself my dear boy. I am quite confident to say that any preconceptions or expectations you might have had are about to be completely surpassed."

He grinned at TJ, momentarily dispelling all the weariness and the effects of his advancing years from his face.

"I'm ready, Grandpa Mal," TJ replied enthusiastically.

"Excellent my dear boy. As you have probably gathered by now, there can be no greater honour and privilege than being a part of the Brethren of the

Dreamguardians and committing your life to protecting dreams.

"It is vitally important though for you to understand the following, dear boy. To be a Dreamguardian is a gift. In fact, the most precious gift. It is a gift that has been bestowed on very few people throughout history. Many have failed to understand that the ways of a Dreamguardian can only be taught if one is in possession of the gift. The gift itself cannot be taught, since it is a function of bloodline, of lineage. But even then, sometimes bloodline and lineage are not sufficient. Do you understand what I mean, dear boy?"

"I think so," TJ replied. "Only certain people have the gift because of their ancestry, but even then, having the gift is not guaranteed."

"Very impressive, dear boy. This is indeed a bittersweet moment for me. I never thought that *I* would ever get to share all this with you. But now that I am, it is so exciting. It is indeed a proud moment for me, dear boy. So here we go. After all, I'm sure you're desperate to know how it all works?"

They both smiled at each other at the ridiculousness of Grandpa Mal's rhetorical question.

"Well, sometimes a Dreamstealer will enter someone's dream. The only way the dream can then be protected is for a Dreamguardian to enter the same dream. The most adept Dreamguardian will do that in such a way that both the dreamer *and* the Dreamstealer have absolutely no knowledge they are there. Furthermore, once awake, the dreamer should also have that same absolute lack of knowledge or awareness that a Dreamguardian has visited their dream or played any role in it.

"It is the responsibility of the Dreamguardian to stop the Dreamstealer from affecting a dream. As I said a moment ago, a Dreamstealer *thrives* on interfering with dreams. There is nothing as demoralising than an unsuccessful Dreamguardian mission my dear boy. I dare not contemplate what beautiful dreams have been lost because of *them*."

Grandpa Mal's pause was momentary. "Now this is the really exciting part, dear boy. Having protected a dream from a Dreamstealer, it is within both the laws and the powers of a Dreamguardian to decide what dream the dreamer will experience."

TJ could feel his eyes widening and his pupils dilating. His bottom jaw fell slightly open too. "That's... that's amazing, Grandpa Mal," he stammered.

"Yes, isn't it just, dear boy," Grandpa Mal agreed. "It is the most amazing and beautiful thing. But it also clearly demonstrates the necessity for us Dreamguardians to exercise righteous responsibility. For as a Dreamguardian, you possess within you the power to do great things, if you so choose. In our lives there is always a choice to make, dear boy. Whether to build up instead of tear down, to fight for truth over lies, to ensure good triumphs over evil, to demonstrate love instead of hate, to be strong rather than weak, and to be just.

"As a Dreamguardian it is also imperative that you keep secret the names and types of dream you can give the dreamer. Knowledge is power, dear boy. This knowledge is precisely what the Dreamstealers seek and require, in order that they may gain the strength and power to *twist* things to their advantage. In doing so it will, of course, be to the extreme disadvantage and danger of both the dreamer and us Dreamguardians."

Grandpa Mal had been in full passionate flow up to now, but TJ sensed an opportunity to clarify a few things.

"Grandpa Mal, just to make sure I heard right, what you're saying is that a Dreamguardian enters the dream of *someone else* to defeat a Dreamstealer who is also in that same dream. But neither of them knows the Dreamguardian is there?"

"Yes, you heard right, my dear boy. Well, almost." Grandpa Mal continued. "I said neither the dreamer nor the Dreamstealer *should* know the Dreamguardian is there, but...". He checked his sentence. "But this is why you will be meticulously trained, dear boy".

TJ's face dropped, and he looked down. "But Grandpa Mal, I don't think I can be a Dreamguardian" he said despondently. "I'm not special in any way. I'm just me."

Grandpa Mal started to chuckle. "Oh, my dear, dear boy. What little faith you have in yourself. What you haven't realised is that have *already* done it, dear boy. Last night, before I came to find you in the snug, you were hiding. Hiding amongst the shadows of a little wooden hut tucked away somewhere high up in the Swiss Alps."

TJ straightened in his chair as he took in what Grandpa Mal had just said. He looked at him quizzically.

"How did you know about that Grandpa Mal?"

"Because I was there," Grandpa Mal replied. "I saw you, dear boy. TJ, *you* were in *my* dream".

CHAPTER 11 – THE GREAT BOOK

The revelation confounded TJ. He sat open-mouthed as Grandpa Mal smiled back at him with a mixture of pride and grandfatherly affection. As the significance of what had been shared began to sink in TJ tentatively spoke.

"But... but how Grandpa Mal?" he said. "I had no idea. I was in your dream?" TJ's eyes widened with excitement. "But how did I get there and how could you see me?"

Grandpa Mal chuckled. "The answers to both your questions are quite simple. The first is because you have the gift my dear boy. You have *the gift!*" Grandpa Mal's face lit up as he made the proclamation.

"The second is because you are inexperienced and have yet to be instructed in how to properly conduct yourself as a Dreamguardian. But that is not entirely fair of course. It was also a big disadvantage that you were in the dream of someone who has been doing the same thing himself for many years, sometimes more than I care to remember dear boy. As a result, I am *very* aware of what is going on in my own dreams. In fact, this is essential if we are to fully protect the Brethren from 'them'.

"But just as I said a moment ago, you will learn all these things and pick them up very quickly I'm sure. As long as you listen carefully, show willing and maintain a pure heart dear boy we can have so much fun learning together."

TJ smiled. He couldn't think of anything better.

Grandpa Mal manoeuvred himself out of his chair, stretched out his back and slowly walked over to the fireplace. He selected a couple of logs from the basket, placed them onto the fire and gave everything a good prod with an old poker.

"That's better," he said, "we need to keep this going a while longer as we've only just really got going. Now is there anything else you would like to ask me, dear boy, before we move on?"

TJ nodded immediately. "Yes, so many things Grandpa Mal," he confirmed. "What exactly is the gift and when did it start? I mean who first discovered it? Then I'm puzzled as to how I actually got into your dream and does that mean I can get into any dream that anyone is having? Then you said a Dreamguardian who had defeated a Dreamstealer could decide what dream someone had. How does all that work? And then..."

"Hold your horses, dear boy!" Grandpa Mal said holding up his hands. "I think you now understand very well the problem I have had dear boy in trying how best to explain all this to you."

He invited TJ to stand. "Let's perhaps tackle them in reverse, dear boy, although explaining precisely the gift, especially its origins, will be the job of the Dreamorian."

TJ pulled a confused and puzzled face. Just as he was about to ask what or who the Dreamorian was, Grandpa Mal left the proximity of the chairs and made his way towards the bookshelves that were bursting to overflowing on the wall opposite the fireplace. Last night he had pulled out the old book containing the words of da Vinci himself: *'Why does the eye see a thing more clearly in dreams than the imagination when awake?'* Ironically even TJ's imagination was struggling to keep up with the apparent reality that was slowly being unveiled by Grandpa Mal. TJ could just about remember the da Vinci saying and he wondered which of the thousands of books on these shelves would be chosen next in order to deliver further enlightenment.

He soon realised the answer was none of them. Grandpa Mal walked to a row of books slightly to the left of the centre of the room and reached his hands deep into the shelf behind the top of the books. He fumbled about for a short while with both hands before TJ heard two wooden clicks and Grandpa Mal turned his left hand anti-clockwise and his right hand clockwise.

He pushed forwards gently and a section of the bookshelf including its undisturbed cargo of books began to move slowly backwards into an unexpected void. The dislodged section of bookcase was now revealed to be in the shape of a previously invisible door. "One moment dear boy," Grandpa Mal said over his shoulder as he slid to the left out of sight.

TJ was taken aback. The doorway had been so well hidden there was no way anyone would have even known it was there. After a little time, Grandpa Mal reappeared and motioned for TJ to follow him.

TJ walked into the recessed doorway and slid to the left in pursuit of Grandpa Mal. He found himself entering a small cave-like room that lay behind the bookcase. Its width was about half the length of the room he'd just left but this time there was no high or elaborately painted ceiling. The walls and ceiling were bare stone. The room was dimly lit by a vast array of candles, some of which Grandpa Mal was still bringing to life.

At the opposite end of the room was a large table covered with a white cloth. It looked like some form of altar. On it stood three large heavy old books, each open and resting on its own bookstand.

Above the table in the absolute centre of the wall hung an ancient robe mounted in a glass frame. Although they had long faded and lost their brilliance, TJ could make out different colours on the robe. Streaks of pale crimson could be seen smeared across parts of the robe and it was tattered in places.

To the left of the framed robe as TJ looked at it hung three smaller pictures. TJ took a few steps closer, so he could get a better view. He recognised them to be smaller copies of the artwork that featured on the ceiling panels in the larger room they had just left. He could make out the man and woman lying asleep next to each other on the bed, with the white figures to one side and the dark shadowy figures looming menacingly on the other. Beneath it was the picture of the lady sleeping alone with a figure in white protecting her from a fleeing dark figure. Below that was the other picture of a shadowy figure in full retreat as another figure of light watched over the man sleeping peacefully.

To the right of the robe were the two pictures that contained the dark shadowy figures in the room. This time TJ was struck by the absence of any figures in white and he felt himself shiver as he looked again at the pained face of the sleeping man in the four-poster bed as the dark shadowy figure appeared to claw at the man's head. For the first time he noticed the distress on the sleeping woman's face as she was tormented by the sole shadowy figure.

Then TJ noticed a strange looking object that was mounted above those two pictures. A long wooden staff had been mounted horizontally on the wall. At the end of the staff facing the robe was a misshaped hoop. The wood it had been made from looked incredibly old and gnarled. A combination of what looked like strips of old leather and rope had been woven across the hoop and now formed elaborately patterned webbing. It struck TJ that it looked similar to a traditional lacrosse stick, but here the hoop was larger and misshapen. The pattern of the webbing looked as though it had been intricately designed and painstakingly crafted, almost as if it was a designer antique spider's web.

Beneath the robe TJ noticed the picture of the figure of intense light captured in the cage surrounded by many shadowy figures. He tried hard not to look at it though in order to avoid the overwhelming deep sense of sadness in his soul that he felt the first time he'd viewed it.

Instead he focused on the collection of largely architectural drawings that hung below it, all of them fanned around one drawing in the middle as if they formed the hub and spokes of a wheel. Around the centre picture TJ could make out a drawing of a grand cathedral with a large imposing dome. Next to that was a prominent column towering above surrounding buildings, followed by a grand palace as well as other separate drawings of various domes as his eye was drawn clockwise round the wheel of pictures. Some of the domes were in cross-section in order to show the interior as well as the exterior. The drawing in the middle was quite different. It was a pencil drawing of a top down view of the human brain. The different parts were very simply labelled with a capital letter. A short while ago TJ thought he was beginning to make some headway in understanding all the secrets of the Brethren. How wrong he was!

TJ's gaze then settled upon the picture above the robe. He felt a warmth and strange strength enter his body as he studied it for the second night in a row. This uppermost picture in the room was of the figure surrounded by intense light looking down over opened cages. Although he didn't understand what it meant or represented, TJ found everything about this particular scene uplifting and exciting: the brilliance of the figure surrounded by intense light; the numerous figures of light escaping towards it; and the shadowy figures falling, cowing or trying to flee from it.

After Grandpa Mal had finished lighting all the candles he turned his attention to TJ.

TJ got in first, however. "What is *this* room for Grandpa Mal? What do all these pictures and objects *mean*?" he asked curiously.

Grandpa Mal chuckled quietly. "Welcome to the *Inner Sanctum* of the Brethren my dear boy. The most sacred and important place for any Dreamguardian. Now you asked me about a Dreamguardian being able to choose a dream for the dreamer once they had defeated a Dreamstealer. Well, they are all listed here, dear boy, in the Great Book."

He pointed and approached the middle book in the centre of the table. "The Great Book also contains the lifeblood of the Dreamguardians, dear boy. Its existence, location, contents and secrets can never, ever, be known or revealed. Not to anyone and especially not to 'them'."

Grandpa Mal started to carefully turn some of the delicate pages. Each page contained elaborately handwritten text, pencil drawn diagrams and occasionally the most vibrant and vividly coloured pictures.

"In the Great Book you will find documented everything there is to know about the Brethren: its origins; the names of every Dreamguardian since 'the beginning'; the most significant and exhaustive research over centuries into sleep patterns and when and how one dreams; enlightenment on the transformative power of dreams; and many sections given over to the enemy that we face and how to fight them." He paused for a moment. "There are other very important sections too. But then we come to the most *wonderful* part." He continued carefully turning the pages until he found the section he was looking for. "The types of dreams a victorious Dreamguardian can bestow upon its dreamer."

Staring out at TJ from the two pages now facing him was a list, written in sloped ancient handwriting. It looked like names followed by descriptions, while small annotations and drawings around some of the words seemed to bring them to life.

TJ got up as close to the book as he dared, as a combination of the candlelight and the elegantly ornate handwriting made it difficult for him to read.

As best he could, he read slowly.

Dreams for a Dreamguardian to bestow upon a dreamer

Advancers
The following dreams are to be used wisely and carefully for the benefit and wellbeing of the dreamer and for the enhancement and advancement of mankind

Chasers – *something or someone will chase the dreamer; gives a very strong chance of the dream being remembered by the dreamer upon wakening; can be used in conjunction with other dreams to increase the potential for positively affecting the dreamer*

Flyers – *takes the dreamer on an amazing flying experience; can be exhilarating or frightening, depending on the dreamer; historical experience has confirmed an exhilarating Flyer can be very effective in cheering up a dreamer and/or building up or restoring a dreamer's confidence*

Levitators - *allows the dreamer to gently float off the ground; possible alternative to the Flyer dream for those with a fear of (extreme) heights but with commensurate reduction in benefits*

Jumpers – *the dreamer will suddenly jump in their dream; can be used to begin to stir the dreamer from deep REM sleep*

Fallers – *principle use is to warn the dreamer and facilitate rapid wakening; use only under* **extreme care***; a Dreamguardian* **must exit** *the dream before the dreamer hits the ground – failure to do so would result in the unbearable consequence… Can also be abused by a Dreamstealer to engineer rapid wakening of a dreamer, in the hope of trapping a Dreamguardian*

Hapsters – *a dream that brings happiness; often involves provoking the experience of something enjoyable within the dreamer or also happy memories if used in conjunction with a* **Rememberer**

Sadsters – *a sad dream; its incidence can sometimes be cathartic to the dreamer and help in regulating and/or defusing emotion; but must proceed and use with caution*

Rememberers - *memory dreams; warning - the effects can be very powerful, depending on the state of mind and personal experience of the dreamer; can be used in combination with* **Hapsters** *or* **Sadsters***; can bring comfort and sometimes emotional healing; beware side effects and possibility for rapid waking with the unbearable consequence…*

Prompters - *important reminder to the dreamer of things to do; do not underestimate the vital importance and role this dream can play; historical evidence proves this dream can make the difference between life and death for the dreamer when awake*

Frustraters – *the dreamer is unable to do something in the dream; use sparingly but can be used to the dreamer's advantage to encourage them to reassess or change their plans or efforts*

Repeater – *the same dream event or activity repeated over and over, for as many times the Dreamguardian feels sufficient to achieve its purpose*

Revealers – *use to impart and reveal some particular knowledge to the dreamer; should only be used by experienced Dreamguardians as can have a regressive and negative effect on a dreamer*

Convincers (Dreamguardian) – *a dream that is able to convince and ensure a dreamer takes a certain course of action or decision; as such use with great care as misappropriation is forbidden and will lead to expulsion from the Brethren*

Creatives – *one of the most beautiful gifts for a dreamer but choose the dreamer and extent of the Creative dream carefully; beware – a* **Creative** *can come suddenly and affect the dreamer in different ways, depending on their inherent* *talents and abilities; historically heightened activity around 3 am-4 am has been reported, especially when involving music and poetry*

Muddler *– an unusual dream which can cause confusion for the dreamer; can be used both positively and negatively and so must therefore be gifted appropriately and with caution*

Encourager *- positively encourages the dreamer or can prompt the dreamer to encourage some other person; this dream has the potential to deliver great restorative power to the person ultimately encouraged; use often, in particular for dreamers who are struggling*

Extravaganza *– an amazingly extravagant and vivid dream; renowned for being one of the best dreams a Dreamguardian can gift; guaranteed to bring immense joy, pleasure and satisfaction to the dreamer, but only if performed well*

Warners *- a dream with a warning of some future event for either the dreamer or some person else courtesy of the dreamer; it is imperative **Warners** are not lost to a **Stealer** or subject to the enemy's **Forgetter**, **Twister** or **Deceiver**.*

Protectives
*The following dreams must **only** be used in the
event of, or real fear of, unexpected
and potentially uncontrollable Dreamstealer activity*

Jumblers *- a collection of jumbled up dreams with various people in strange places; use this to hide evidence from the dreamer of a tussle between a Dreamguardian and Dreamstealer*

Randoms *- really really random dreams! Can be implemented at rapid pace and at short intervals if necessary; use to confuse and distract a dreamer if a Dreamguardian believes they may have been seen or are about to be discovered; alternatively use as a diversionary tactic to allow a Dreamguardian to escape in the unlikely event that a Dreamstealer is too powerful to defeat*

Weirdos *- like **Randoms**, but also really really weird! Only use if at extreme risk of being discovered or if a Dreamstealer may be about to gift one of the following dreams:*

*WARNING: a Dreamguardian is **explicitly prohibited** from gifting the following dreams – doing so will result in immediate expulsion from the Brethren*

Embarassers *– a dreamer is convinced that something embarrassing is happening to them; one common **Embarasser** is a dreamer believing they are being viewed in public without any clothing, another that a certain course of action cannot be performed properly, to the amusement of others; can exaggerate feelings of inadequacy and lead to loss of confidence; a nasty and spiteful trick from a*

Dreamstealer

Stressers – *plays upon signs of stress within a dreamer; has manifest through the ages in various forms such as a dreamer being tricked into believing they are feeling symptoms such as hair loss or crumbling teeth; used by Dreamstealer to unsettle dreams and keep the dreamer anxious and emotionally drained when awake*

Scarers - *mildly scary dreams – evidence that a Dreamstealer has taken some hold of, and power over, a dreamer*

Forgetters – *prevents the dreamer from remembering part of a particular dream; a Dreamstealer is able to use to this to partially prevent or weaken **Rememberers;** explains why the dreamer will wake recalling only parts of dreams*

Stealers – *the fundamental aim of a Dreamstealer; results in the theft and loss of a dream; the only true reason why the dreamer will wake and not remember or recall any dream; often leads to the loss of beautiful and precious things such as progress, creativity and enlightenment; can be harmful to the emotional well-being of the dreamer*

Twisters – *reality within a dream is twisted to the advantage of the Dream-stealer; often used as a precursor to the deployment of the more powerful **Deceiver***

Deceivers – *dream used by a Dreamstealer to trick a dreamer into believing an alternative reality that is not true and does not exist; WARNING: the Deceiver has the potential to cause much damage and harm to the dreamer when awake, especially if the Deceiver has been conducted by a very powerful Dreamstealer*

Multiplier – *dream used by a Dreamstealer to rapidly fill a dream with something or someone feared by the dreamer; extreme versions can cause a dreamer to wake suddenly, with the unbearable consequence...*

Convincers (Dreamstealer) – *exhibits the same properties as the Convincer (Dreamguardian) but in negative form; the Dreamstealer can convince and en-sure a dreamer takes a certain course of action or decision, against the best intentions of the dreamer and in order to satisfy the worst intentions of the Dreamstealer; another dangerous dream if conducted by a very powerful Dream-stealer*

Tamperers - *a more sinister variant of the **Twister** – a dream memory that can be altered or changed to hide or obstruct the truth; only a Dreamstealer in pos-session of great dark power can convincingly alter, change or corrupt a dream memory*

Nightfrights - *more sinister and threatening than Scarers; evidence that a more* *powerful Dreamstealer has taken even more hold over a dreamer; unless stopped could lead to the unleashing of more sinister dreams, to the great danger and detriment of the dreamer and their wellbeing*

Horrors – *extremely disturbing nightmares; a Dreamguardian will torment the dreamer by seeking out and manifesting any weakness and the greatest fear of the dreamer; can only be performed by the most powerful Dreamstealer; the most dangerous dream for a Dreamguardian to enter or be in as the dreamer can wake suddenly, resulting in the unbearable consequence...*

TJ had read the list aloud in increasing amazement and awe as he made his way down the list of dreams. He paused for quite some time as he reached the end as he started to process all the information. Finally, he spoke. "I had no idea Grandpa Mal there were so many dreams and they were all named. I've had some of these for sure. So, I guess I've already experienced the presence of the Dreamguardians, as well as the Dreamstealers." He felt perturbed at the thought.

"Indeed, my dear boy," Grandpa Mal replied. "The Great Book contains many other types of dreams too which you can study over the years to come, but these are the most important ones. You can now see from this passage of the Great Book why it is so essential that certain dreams are protected and allowed to occur. For instance, so many lives saved by Warners and Prompters. An extraordinary number of people comforted and enriched by Rememberers and Encouragers. Incredible events, breakthroughs and inventions foretold by Futures and helped along by Revealers. Amazing beauty and enjoyment from Creatives just as we discussed at length yesterday. This has been the case over many centuries and is still true to this day in our lifetime."

TJ nodded. He began to feel that everything was becoming clearer. He was now beginning to put all the pieces together and understand everything that Grandpa Mal had been sharing with him.

"But it is proving increasingly difficult to protect against 'them'," Grandpa Mal continued. "Scarers and Nightfrights are not uncommon and are usually harmless if a Dreamstealer is kept contained. But throughout history there have been occasions when the Dreamstealers have become more powerful and dangerous. As a result, darkness has risen.

"As I mentioned last night dear boy, the Elders have detected that the number of Scarers and Nightfrights has increased dramatically. They are also intensifying in terms of their darkness. Incidences of Forgetters are also increasing rapidly. Worryingly, Stealers are becoming prevalent, wherever we look. These lost dreams of course represent lost inspiration and so much more, dear boy.

"It also pains me to say, but the regularity and intensity of Horrors are increasing. They are tormenting a growing number of people. I cannot begin to describe how much destruction and devastation they cause. In many ways the Horrors and the sleep deprivation that they lead to are akin to mental torture. It is as if they are sucking the goodness out of people, tearing them apart and unravelling them from within."

He wasn't sure if he meant to, but Grandpa Mal had succeeded in frightening TJ.

"My dear boy, all this points to one thing. Darkness is intensifying. Evil is rising. The Dreamstealers are advancing. The impact this will have on humanity will be severe enough. But the threat it poses to the Brethren is both significant and grave..."

Grandpa Mal looked pale and disturbed amongst the flickering candlelight. TJ sensed the appropriate time had come to ask the question troubling him since last night.

"Grandpa Mal, you said a Dreamguardian was a dream protector who would risk their life to fight for the safe passage of dreams. I think you avoided the question when I asked what exactly you meant by risking your life. Did you really mean to say that a Dreamguardian could lose their life in the process of protecting a dream?"

Grandpa Mal closed his eyes for a moment, as if his mind had been carried somewhere far away. He opened them again and looked seriously at TJ. "Sadly, yes I did mean that. A Dreamguardian can lose their life during their duty." TJ's eyes widened, and he felt his stomach churn.

"We cannot avoid this anymore, dear boy. This is the ultimate price you may have to pay as a Dreamguardian. It is certainly the reason why many have refused to accept the gift and fulfil their true potential and calling as a Dreamguardian.

"You may recall that I spoke to you when you were in my dream?" Grandpa Mal asked. TJ nodded his recollection. "What you didn't realise dear boy is that somebody else was lurking in the shadows too. You didn't know they were there of course, and the consequence was too awful to contemplate. That's the reason I told you to leave, dear boy. Before it was too late."

"Too late for what? Sorry, I just don't understand Grandpa Mal," TJ said.

"Before you were trapped inside the dream," came the sombre reply. "Most likely for good. Lost in a void of dreamless darkness from which you cannot escape..."

CHAPTER 12 – SECRETS REVEALED

For a moment TJ didn't know how to respond. He was stunned. Finally, he found the courage to speak. "Trapped inside someone else's dream?" he repeated. "But there must be some way to escape? Surely you would get back out the following night when the same person started dreaming again?"

"TJ!" Grandpa Mal replied with some agitation. "No! That's not how it works. You must understand. If a Dreamguardian is within a dream when the dreamer wakes, then they become trapped. That particular Dreamguardian will no longer wake themselves and return. An ordinary Dreamguardian could search *forever* through the same dreamer's dream each and every night thereafter but *never* find them to bring them back. You must believe me when I tell you this…" His voice trailed off.

Grandpa Mal put his hands on TJ's shoulder and looked him straight in the eyes. "This is why you need to make sure that you are *extremely* careful when you are in someone's dream. It is imperative. Do you understand me TJ?"

It was more a demand than a question.

"Yes, Grandpa Mal, I understand," TJ replied.

Grandpa Mal heaved a sigh of relief and patted TJ's shoulders. "Good. I just couldn't bear to lose you in someone's dream for eternity. You are far too precious for that. We must also not forget the other serious consequences should a Dreamstealer manage to discover a Dreamguardian, even if they are unable to trap the Dreamguardian in a dream.

"You see if a Dreamguardian is discovered and they are not quick enough to escape, it is within the Dreamstealer's power to convince or deceive the Dreamguardian into joining them. I cannot stress enough to you dear boy that in order to resist a Dreamstealer, particularly one very powerful and accomplished, one must mentally be very strong.

"However, even if the Dreamguardian does manage to escape, the Dream-stealer remaining in the dream is then at liberty to cause unthinkable damage to the dreamer. The Dreamstealer will have taken even more of a foothold in the dreamer's sleep time. Not only will this result in higher incidences of Twisters, Deceivers, Convincers, Nightfrights and Horrors, but these diabolical dreams will persist for longer and with greater intensity in the future. As for more incidences of Stealers, we have already contem-plated my dear boy how devastating it could be if an important dream is lost."

There was a pause as they reflected on what Grandpa Mal had just ex-plained. TJ in particular was disturbed by the awful consequences if things were to go wrong for a Dreamguardian. He was the first to break the silence.

"Grandpa Mal, how exactly does a Dreamguardian get trapped?" he asked.

"The simple answer is if they fail to exit the dream before the dreamer wakes. You might have noticed but the Great Book quite rightly describes this as the 'unbearable consequence'. But equally as important is to ask *why* a Dreamguardian might fail to escape.

"Now dear boy, carelessness and inexperience can be a factor. This explains why we invest so much effort into preparing new Dreamguardians such as yourself. But without doubt, the main reason is because of 'them'.

"The main motivation of a Dreamstealer is to either harm dreams or steal them forever, often for their own benefit and gain. As Dreamguardians stand in the way of them achieving this, a Dreamstealer will stop at *noth-ing* to either remove you from a dream or deliberately ensnare you forever. If they are successful, particularly at trapping you in a dream, then our terrible loss becomes their richest gain. With each precious protector of dreams lost, the Dreamstealers take another step towards the domination of the dreamer's mind and control of the night.

"So, you must be alert dear boy. A Dreamstealer of great cunning can deliberately trap you by suddenly causing a dream so severe - such as an intense Multiplier or Horror - that the dreamer awakes unexpectedly before a Dreamguardian has had the opportunity to leave, especially if the Dream-guardian is not even aware a Dreamstealer is there.

"Alternatively, the most adept Dreamstealer has the ability to turn your *Dreamswick* against you rendering you incapacitated. As you are deprived of strength and power, the Dreamstealer is able to turn this to their advantage which can lead to the unbearable consequence that the Great Book speaks of. So, my dear boy, guard your *Dreamswick* carefully. If it is used against you it is very unlikely you will be able to leave the dream in time. If that is the case then you are lost, forever..."

"A *Dreamswick* Grandpa Mal?" TJ asked hesitantly. He had never heard the word *Dreamswick* spoken of before.

"Yes, one of those dear boy," Grandpa Mal replied quickly, pointing to the wooden staff with the woven hoop mounted on the wall. "The *Dreamswick*. You must *always* remember to carry this when you are in someone else's dream. Used correctly the *Dreamswick* should give you sufficient power to defeat a Dreamstealer in a dream, ensuring both you and the dreamer are protected.

"I must admit there are Dreamguardians in the Brethren much more expert in the origins of the *Dreamswick*. However, it is safe to say that while the *Dreamswick* is a great asset it carries with it big risks. As well as the possibility it can be used against you, it is distinctive and has at various times seen before by dreamers. As a result, its presence has come close to revealing the presence of the Dreamguardians throughout history.

"It is no accident that the *Ojibwe* people's 'Dreamcatcher' looks similar to the *Dreamswick*. However, their 'Dreamcatcher' is simply a web woven on a round willow hoop, with the staff part missing. It is often hung over a baby's cradle to catch bad dreams while it lets the good dreams through. Sounds a bit familiar doesn't it, dear boy?

"This is because at some point in time the *Ojibwe* came very close to uncovering the far-reaching scope and powers of the Brethren. Once, one of the *Ojibwe* caught sight of a *Dreamswick* and remembered parts of it when they awoke. Thankfully, they were never able to completely uncover the full secrets of the Dreamguardians. But certainly, some of the accounts from this time in the Great Book leave us in no doubt that it was a particularly difficult and challenging moment for the Brethren. So, the sheer existence and legend of Native American Dreamcatchers dear boy is an important reminder to us of just how close some people have come to uncovering the Brethren.

"Indeed, you will find that different variations and stories of our existence have appeared throughout history and across cultures. But I am relived to say that despite these near misses we remain undiscovered to this day, dear boy. The Dreamorian will be able to explain such matters so much more authoritatively and eloquently if you so wish, dear boy."

"When will I get to meet the Dreamorian, Grandpa Mal?" TJ asked.

"All in good time, my dear boy," Grandpa Mal confirmed. "We must find the right time to make the trip together. So, it must be arranged very carefully so as not to arouse suspicion on many fronts, especially with your mother."

TJ smiled. Of course, he thought to himself. Mum had become extremely protective of him and Lizzy Wizzy ever since Dad died. A sudden unexplained day trip with Grandpa Mal would need to be handled with care so as not to raise any awkward questions that would require the bending of the truth. One thing TJ was not was a competent liar.

"But leave your mother to me, dear boy," Grandpa Mal continued. "I will find a way to put her mind sufficiently at ease in order for you to take a day trip with your decrepit and increasingly unsteady Grandpa Mal". He smiled, and TJ reciprocated. As for TJ, he knew Mum would never describe Grandpa Mal with those particular words but did know she was getting increasingly concerned for Grandpa Mal's health. Mum could never quite understand why he didn't want to live somewhere more manageable than the Old Girl. In fact, up to now no one had ever really convincingly explained to TJ just how and why Grandpa Mal lived in such a grand house. It was now beginning to dawn on TJ the importance of the Old Girl to Grandpa Mal and the Brethren, and why Grandpa Mal was so reluctant to leave her.

"Now, you have most of the essential knowledge you require to begin your training," confirmed Grandpa Mal. "The only missing thing is the all-important starting point. So, we will work on this first".

"When?" TJ asked.

"When?" Grandpa Mal repeated out of surprise. "Why now of course! Let us return to the Great Room and our comfy chairs. We will need them for the next bit". He ushered TJ towards the small doorway through which they had slipped through and began blowing out the candles nearest him.

TJ stood his ground. "But Grandpa Mal, what about the other things in here: the robe, the drawings of the buildings, the pictures, the other two books next to the Great Book. They all look like they have some particular meaning, purpose or story to tell. You haven't told me about them yet."

Grandpa Mal spoke intermittently as he carried on blowing out candles. "Another time, dear boy... Pfff... We have... Pfff.... more practical things... Pfff Pfff... to explore... Pfff Pfff Pfff..."

Aware he was fighting a losing battle to glean more knowledge about the room, TJ made his way out of the Inner Sanctum behind the bookshelves and back over to the fireplace in the Great Room. He threw another couple of logs onto the fire and gave it a prod with the poker, trying as best he could to replicate Grandpa Mal's technique.

He retook his seat in the larger chair and felt the warmth of the fire take away some of the chill that had started to seep into his bones from the Inner Sanctum. The hour of the day began to take hold of him, and he could feel his eyelids getting heavy.

After a short while Grandpa Mal emerged from the Inner Sanctum. "TJ!" he shouted across the room. TJ jumped back awake in his chair. He must have nodded off. "Dear boy, not yet! Just a few more moments and I will be with you. All the way."

With that he pulled the door back in line with the rest of the bookshelf and locked it into place with a satisfying couple of clicks. The outline of the door immediately disappeared, camouflaged and lost again amongst the thousands of books on that wall.

TJ spoke wearily. "I'm sorry Grandpa Mal, I'm just really tired." He yawned genuinely for good measure as if to reinforce the point.

"No problem, dear boy. It's approaching the time for the talking to stop and for us to spend time on the really exciting part. However, there are just a few more things to cover, although you'll be relieved to know I don't think there is any need to go into too much detail on the really complicated stuff. After all, this will be a process that will continue over the days, weeks and months to come. But, as you will see, it will be worth it dear boy. When done correctly and despite all the dangers, being a Dreamguardian is very exciting dear boy." He smiled infectiously at TJ who smiled wearily back.

As he spoke, he made his way over to the chair opposite TJ, picked up a small alarm clock on the side table and fiddled with the dials at the back. He set it back down on the table and sat down slowly himself, making himself comfortable before resuming.

"Dear boy, we essentially go through five stages when we sleep. The first is very light sleep and is easy to wake from; in some ways it is almost like daydreaming. Technically speaking during this time, we are experiencing *Alpha* and *Theta* brain waves. *Alpha* is like being in a restful place while *Theta* is the period between being awake and asleep. While the research, which I must admit is quite boring, suggests it takes *on average* about seven minutes for someone to fall asleep, we are all different of course dear boy.

"The second stage is a slightly deeper sleep and can last about twenty minutes. The thing to remember here dear boy is that our body temperature starts to drop, our heart rate starts to slow, and our brain starts to produce *Sleep Spindles*. That is, short periods of rapid brain wave activity. Use these as important signposts for what stage a dreamer is in dear boy.

"Our deepest sleep occurs during stages three – which in effect is another transitional period, this time between light and very deep sleep - and four.

During these stages, our brain activity has slowed until we are experiencing what are known as *delta* – or slow - brain waves.

"Stage four is *Deep Sleep* or *Delta Sleep* as it is sometimes documented. This tends to last for about thirty minutes. In case you're interested, sleepwalking often happens at the end of stage four sleep. Quite fascinating dear boy."

TJ nodded wide-eyed, trying hard to take all the information in, as Grandpa Mal continued.

"Now don't worry too much about all the scientific detail and puff, dear boy. However, what is perhaps most important is that about an hour and half into sleep, after this fourth sleep stage, the magic happens. For that is when fifth stage sleep – or REM sleep - begins."

TJ raised his eyebrows and shrugged his shoulders as a clear signal to Grandpa Mal he had no idea what he was talking about. But at least it sounded exciting to him!

Grandpa Mal took the hint. "Let me explain. REM stands for Rapid Eye Movement. During this stage of sleep our eyes are doing exactly that - rapidly moving – because this is when most of our dreams take place. Although dreams can occur during any of the other non-REM sleep stages, you must remember that they are most vivid and intense during REM sleep. So, these are the ones we aim for.

"Interestingly, during REM sleep lots of things change dear boy. Our heart rate and breathing quickens, blood pressure increases, and we cannot regulate our body temperature. Meanwhile our brain activity increases to *Alpha* waves, the same as when we are awake. Yet we are asleep! How marvellous!

"The funny thing is that even though our eyes may be moving rapidly, other parts of us are not. The body is effectively paralysed until REM sleep ends, but it sounds worse than it is! In fact, this is entirely for the safety of the dreamer. They are paralysed so they are unable to act out their dreams. To be honest, dear boy, this is just as well. You can read in the Great Book about some of the dreams that have been gifted by some of the rather extrovert and extreme fun-loving Dreamguardians! The mayhem and damage that could be caused in those circumstances if the dreamer's body was able to fully function is not worth thinking about!"

TJ looked a bit confused and worried.

"Ah, I should clarify and put your mind at ease dear boy. I should have said the paralysis refers to all the *voluntary* muscles of course. Clearly the *involuntary* ones such as the heart are able to fully function on their own. We can't have them stopping of course!" He chuckled to himself at his little joke.

Composing himself he continued. "The somewhat thrilling, yet exhausting, fact is that a dreamer will go through cycles of these stages several times in one-night, dear boy. Although we begin at stage one and progress through to stage four, we often return to repeat a combination of stages two and three before entering REM sleep again. Once that ends, we often return to stage two sleep. And so, it goes on. There can be as many as four or five cycles per night dear boy.

"Each sleep cycle we go through will include more REM sleep and less of stage four deep sleep. By the time morning comes we are likely to be experiencing mainly stage one, stage two and stage five REM sleep."

Grandpa Mal paused to check if TJ was still with him. He was, just, but Grandpa Mal could see he was beginning to drift off again.

"Of course, one should really spend hours and hours going through all the research, psychology and physiology of this dear boy in great detail. But I think that's sufficient for what someone of your age at this hour of day needs to know or could ever wish to know. The main thing is that you have some appreciation of the different stages of sleep and know when the best time is to enter a dream. So, did you work it out yet, dear boy?"

"I think it must be stage five Grandpa Mal, when someone is most likely to be having a proper dream," TJ replied tentatively.

"Yes indeed, very good dear boy! You are your Father's son and your Grandpa Mal's grandson after all!" TJ wondered exactly what he meant but didn't get a chance to interrupt as Grandpa Mal swiftly continued. "Yes, the most important dreams are those that occur during stage five REM sleep. Now the first REM cycle does not last that long, but they get longer over the course of a decent period of sleep. It is perfectly possible for a dream to last from just five minutes in the early stages to as long as an hour later on.

"Finally, practical experience over the centuries has definitively proven there is no effect on a Dreamguardian of the shift from REM to non-REM sleep. It is the shift from REM sleep to being awake that is the most dangerous for a Dreamguardian. You *must* remember the *unbearable consequence* dear boy: never ever get caught in a dream by the dreamer suddenly waking, either through some careless action of your own making or due to the actions of a Dreamstealer."

TJ nodded acknowledgement of his remembrance and Grandpa Mal smiled. "So, the time has come for us to experiment, dear boy. Consider this your first training session. You will now enter one of my dreams again dear boy. Although you have done it before quite by accident, now it will be deliberate. As it will be my first dream of the night it will not last very long. Even though I will know you are in it, dear boy, I will give you control of my dream."

TJ could feel his heart beat faster and his palms start to go clammy.

"What do you mean by control Grandpa Mal?" he asked.

"Dear boy, do you remember from the Great Book the list of dreams that a Dreamguardian may gift a dreamer?" Grandpa Mal replied softly. TJ nodded. "Well you may choose one of those to gift to me. We can then experience it together. However, should anything go wrong you just need to remember to exit my dream before I wake.

"In order to enter my dream, you need to do two things dear boy. The first is that as you yourself drift off to sleep you must be thinking about me and repeat my name in your head at least three times. As you have the gift this will enable you to enter my dream.

"The second is you must visualise the ancient robe and *Dreamswick* that is contained within the Inner Sanctum. This will ensure that within my dream you will have your own robe and *Dreamswick* to protect us both from any Dreamstealer that may – or may not - be lurking. After all, while the presence of a Dreamstealer is unlikely on this occasion dear boy, it cannot be guaranteed.

"Finally, the Great Book sets out very clear instructions and rules about when a Dreamguardian must leave a dream.

"If a dreamer has not given a Dreamguardian prior permission to enter the dream but comes to realise you are there, you must be very quick to exit. You will see this listed in the Great Book as *Dreamer Enforced Expulsion*. You must be quick as the shock of the realisation that someone is in their dream may be sufficient to wake the dreamer *almost immediately*.

"However, if the dreamer has given you prior permission to be in the dream then you have no choice and will automatically be expelled from their dream as soon as they order you to leave. In the Great Book this is called *Ex-Ante Permissionary Expulsion*.

"If the dreamer is a Dreamguardian – and a good one at that - then it is possible for them to automatically expel you from their dream even though you did not have their permission to enter their dream. This process is grandly referred to as *Ex-Post Permissionary Expulsion* in the Great Book. However, this can only be the case if the *dreamer* reacts with sufficient speed and before any possible interference from a Dreamstealer that might be present.

"Finally, if a Dreamguardian does not have prior permission to enter a dream and believes they are at risk of being discovered or trapped inside the dream - either due to carelessness or the presence of a more powerful Dreamstealer - then they must be very quick to exit. This is documented in the Great Book as *Voluntary Non-Permissionary Expulsion*.

"Listen to this next bit carefully dear boy. In the event of *Dreamer Enforced Expulsion* or *Voluntary Non-Permissionary Expulsion*, the only way you can exit safely is to repeat the name of the dreamer followed by 'exit' at least three times. Is that clear TJ?"

TJ thought for a moment. He was starting to get very confused by the descriptions within the Great Book of the different exits but thought he had understood the main thrust of the processes.

"I think so Grandpa Mal. If a dreamer has somehow given me permission to enter their dream or the dreamer is indeed a Dreamguardian then I will automatically exit their dream as soon as they tell me I must leave."

"Very good dear boy," Grandpa Mal responded. "This is what happened last night when I suddenly discovered you in my dream. You were subject to *Ex-Post Permissionary Expulsion* and so in effect you were automatically forced to exit my dream."

TJ was relieved. He didn't want to let Grandpa Mal down at this critical stage. He carried on tentatively. "But if I am in the dream of someone who is neither a Dreamguardian nor given me permission to be there, then if they suddenly realise - or are about to - that I am there, either due to my carelessness or the presence of a more powerful Dreamstealer, then I must exit as quickly as possible.

"I do this by saying the name of the dreamer followed by the word 'exit' at least three times. If I fail to do this quickly enough then I could be subject to the *unbearable consequence*. That means I will be trapped inside the dream, *forever*. Or in other words, lost in a void of dreamless darkness from which you cannot escape..." Unsurprisingly, given their gravity, TJ had remembered Grandpa Mal's description word for word.

Grandpa Mal nodded. "Most excellent, dear boy. The high hopes for you expressed within the Eldership earlier were not misplaced." TJ smiled, and he breathed a small sigh of relief. So far, he felt he had acquitted himself well despite all the shocks, surprises and intensity of the things being revealed to him. This was essential: he didn't want to let Grandpa Mal, or Dad for that matter, down.

"Now are you ready, dear boy?" Grandpa Mal asked.

"Yes," TJ replied with as much confidence as he could muster at this precise moment in time.

"Excellent," came the reply, "your practical training officially starts here dear boy. Don't forget to practice how to exit when you feel the time is right. But don't worry too much because you are, of course, fully invited into my dream. So, I will be sure to keep you safe and perform *Ex-Ante Permissionary Expulsion* if need be."

Both TJ and Grandpa Mal looked each other in the eye and smiled, although both were as nervous as the other. "Now, time for us both to sleep, perchance to dream," Grandpa Mal said as he closed his eyes. TJ did the same, repeating Grandpa Mal's name over and over again as he did so...

CHAPTER 13 – THE FIRST GIFTING

The excitement of the time just spent with Grandpa Mal was rapidly wearing off and TJ felt himself drifting off to sleep quite effortlessly. The fire was warm, and the chair embraced him like a soft leather blanket as he curled up into it. He couldn't fight the early hours any longer and neither did he need to do so...

*

The room was large and quite dark, although it was just about possible to make out row after row of hanging rails, each one stretching into the blackness ahead. From the rails hung robes. Beside each robe a wooden staff protruded from a wicker basket.

For a moment TJ was disorientated. "Where on earth am I?" he whispered to himself as he carefully approached the rail in front of him. TJ took one of the robes and was instantly struck by the intricate carving of the letters 'DG' on the wooden hanger beneath. The robe itself was white and woven from fine soft cotton. Faint stripes had been painstakingly embroidered into the robe with gold and purple thread. TJ slipped on the full-length robe and immediately felt important, reassured and confident. He lifted the wooden staff from the basket and was surprised just how light it was. At the other end was a misshaped hoop with an intricate web woven across it in strips of fine leather. A *Dreamswick*!

A sudden sound from behind startled TJ and a figure quickly rushed past him. It grabbed a robe from another rail and the *Dreamswick* beside it and continued on into the blackness. As the sound of the footsteps faded into the blackness ahead, some way off at the far end of the room a door opened, allowing a great shaft of light to enter the room. As soon as the figure exited the room into the light the door slammed closed, and the darkness returned.

TJ made his way towards where the doorway of light had opened a moment ago. With each step he passed robe after robe and basket after basket of *Dreamswicks*. Finally, he reached the end of the room and after some fumbling found a smooth brass doorknob. With some trepidation he turned it, pushed the door open and walked through.

For a moment the light blinded him, and he closed his eyes. As he gingerly opened them again he found himself standing on lush green grass next to a large expansive lake. He was surrounded on all sides by an impressive landscape. The mountain peaks were bathed in sunshine although in the distance ominous dark clouds looked threatening.

"Hello, my dear boy" came an unmistakable voice from behind him.

TJ spun round, almost tripping over his long robe. In the daylight TJ could appreciate the full beauty and quality of the robe. In contrast, Grandpa Mal had his old walking clothes on.

"Grandpa Mal!" TJ exclaimed. "Where are we? What is all this?" he asked.

"My dear boy, good questions indeed. I believe we are somewhere in Scotland, at one of the lochs. I visited here a few years ago and this appears to be where we have returned tonight."

"Tonight? But it's daylight, warm and the sun is shining," said a confused TJ.

"Indeed, but don't be fooled my boy" Grandpa Mal cautioned. "This often happens and confuses nearly every new Dreamguardian. While we may indeed be somewhere in Scotland during the hours of daylight, in reality it is very much night-time. And you, my dear boy, are well and truly within my dream."

TJ was struggling to understand. "But how exactly did I get here? What was that room I just came from Grandpa Mal and what is this robe for?"

"You were in the Armoury dear boy. That is the place each and every Dreamguardian *should* pass through before they enter a dream. From there you must put on the robe of light, just as each and every Dreamguardian has done since the very beginning. It is an important symbol of our identity dear boy and is a clear signal of our intention to use the gift for *good* and not evil. The *Dreamswick* is of course your weapon against 'them'.

"However," Grandpa Mal continued, "I have deliberately chosen a safe and remote location for this dream, dear boy, one that I have not visited in my dreams for some time. So, we ought to be safe from any Dreamstealer. Therefore, you shouldn't need the *Dreamswick* tonight, but you must *always* have it with you dear boy and be fully prepared to use it, just in case."

TJ recognised the seriousness in Grandpa Mal's voice and vowed he would never be without the *Dreamswick*, even though he still wasn't sure how to use it.

"Now if you remember dear boy, as this is my first dream of the night we don't really have very long for you to practice. So, we must move quickly. I want you to concentrate on *two* things tonight, dear boy. Your first objective is to gift me any of the permitted dreams you can remember from the list in the Great Book. Do this with the help of the *Dreamswick* that you must always hold in your right hand for it to be effective. Turn it so that the hoop is facing the ground and that, combined with a bit of decent concentration, ought to do it dear boy. Your second aim is to safely exit the dream at an appropriate time, at which point we should be able to reconvene in the Great Room. Remember, don't leave it too late to practice dear boy, otherwise I will be forced to intervene. All clear?"

TJ nodded. He looked around at the vast yet beautiful surroundings and took a deep breath. He held the *Dreamswick* in his right hand, turned it so that the hoop faced the ground and concentrated on the dream that had caught his eye in the Great Book.

Almost in an instant they were off the ground. The loch and trees shrank beneath them as they effortlessly gained altitude. Without any effort they were flying through the air in perfect synchronization, TJ's robe enthusiastically flapping behind him like a giant cape as they soared and swooped.

TJ looked across excitedly at Grandpa Mal and shouted loudly to him over the rush of the wind. He managed to force out "Grandpa Mal! This is incredible!" as the wind filled his lungs almost as soon as he opened his mouth. Grandpa Mal nodded and shouted something back although TJ couldn't hear it above the noise.

Without warning Grandpa Mal suddenly started a deep dive, gaining incredible speed as he rocketed like an arrow down towards the loch. TJ followed, clutching his *Dreamswick* tightly. His eyes watered as he tried to catch up with Grandpa Mal who by now was getting close to the water. TJ began to panic as Grandpa Mal approached the water at speed. But Grandpa Mal levelled out just inches above the surface. When he reached the shore Grandpa Mal was off again, gaining height as he flew up into the forest on the mountainside beyond the loch. He weaved in and out of the pine trees with the skill of an Olympic slalom skier, every now and then looking back to see if TJ was keeping up.

"Keep up dear boy!" Grandpa Mal shouted over his shoulder as he performed a 360-degree barrel roll. He had the agility and mentality of a young man again. As he entered a clearing in the forest he went vertical, shooting thousands of feet in the air very quickly. For some reason TJ found he was quicker going up than he was going down and he finally caught up with Grandpa Mal. "Follow me!" he shouted to Grandpa Mal as he overtook him.

TJ was now in the lead and began to gradually arch his back. This manoeuvre would beat Grandpa Mal's 360-degree roll hands down. TJ was going for a big loop the loop. He clung on to his *Dreamswick* for dear life and then felt the forces impact his body. The world below turned upside down as he pushed onwards, upwards and finally all the way over. Grandpa Mal completed his own loop the loop and they gave each other an excited thumbs-up.

TJ continued to lead the formation and shot off again. As Grandpa Mal followed he looked ahead he saw the storm clouds were getting closer and closer. They looked incredibly angry and he could see the rain mist below the menacing dark grey and black clouds.

"TJ, watch out for the storm clouds!" he shouted as loud as he could.

"Keep following me Grandpa Mal, trust me!" TJ bellowed back over his shoulder above the wind.

Grandpa Mal shouted back. "No, TJ, stop! Stop dear boy!"

But TJ didn't. He flew them ever closer to the storm clouds that were looking almost apocalyptic in front of them. Just as Grandpa Mal feared they had reached the point where they would be sucked into the deepest depths of the cloud, they saw it. A most magnificent rainbow arc that stretched for miles from left to right appeared in front of them. Each colour was perfectly layered on top of the other and spectacular against the dark sky. Its beauty took Grandpa Mal's breath away.

TJ slowed his flight and grinned as Grandpa Mal pulled alongside him. "Isn't it amazing Grandpa Mal?" he asked.

"Quite so dear boy!" Grandpa Mal replied.

"Now for the best bit. Hold my left-hand Grandpa Mal and don't let go until I tell you," TJ ordered.

Grandpa Mal did as he was told, and TJ headed straight for the highest point of the rainbow. When they reached it they gently landed on the top of the arc. It was surprisingly firm underfoot but incredibly slippery. As they stood on the very top of the rainbow they surveyed the world beneath them: the hills, mountains, lochs and coastline in the distance. They were for all intents and purposes on top of the world!

They looked down at the brilliant red layer of rainbow on which they were standing. It was as smooth as glass and sparkled in the sunshine like a giant red ruby path. Through it they could see all the other layers of the rainbow colours. As TJ and Grandpa Mal looked at each other they understood immediately what the other was thinking. Their smiles grew bigger as they looked at the giant rainbow slide inviting them to embark upon the ride of their lives.

"Shall we, dear boy?" Grandpa Mal asked excitedly.

"Absolutely!" TJ confirmed.

They held hands as they carefully started to run down the red path. As they reached the point where the red path started to fall away beneath them, they sat down on what was in effect a slippery slide. They gathered more and more speed as the drop of the arc of the rainbow became more pronounced. The wind rushed violently again through their hair as they slid wildly and almost uncontrollably down the rainbow.

"Whee!" squealed Grandpa Mal. "A… ma… zing… dear… boy!" he shrieked as they plummeted down the slippery rainbow slide.

TJ looked across at Grandpa Mal as they slid in tandem. He had never seen such a smile or delight on his face before. How he wished he could see him this happy when he was awake. As they neared the end TJ was confident his Dreamguardian work was accomplished. It was time to attempt to exit the dream. He let go of Grandpa Mal's hand.

Knowing what was coming next, Grandpa Mal shouted across to TJ. "Do you remember how it is done dear boy?"

TJ nodded. He uttered "Grandpa Mal exit, Grandpa Mal exit, Grandpa Mal exit," under his breath, clinging on for dear life to the *Dreamswick* in his right hand.

Immediately the dream ended. TJ was back in his own sub-consciousness, now waiting for his own dreams to come. But he didn't get that far. After a short while he became aware that his body was shaking, and an alarm bell was ringing. As he slowly opened his eyes Grandpa Mal was stood over him, gently shaking his shoulder. "TJ, TJ, dear boy, wake up." He was smiling proudly and there was great excitement in his voice. TJ looked down. His robe and the *Dreamswick* were gone.

"You did it! You did it! Most fantastic my dear boy." Grandpa Mal beamed, silenced the alarm clock then turned his attention back to TJ. "A Flyer and the most amazing Extravaganza I do believe! Quite some achievement for your first proper outing and responsibility for gifting a dream." He chuckled. "There are certainly high hopes for you indeed dear boy."

TJ couldn't help but to grin from ear to ear. It turned out that he had gifted not one but *two* dreams after all, and an *Extravaganza* at that. Perhaps most importantly he made Grandpa Mal proud. What an amazing first experience as a Dreamguardian in training. He couldn't wait for the next time. So much fun!

In all the excitement, they had both missed something within Grandpa Mal's dream. A figure dressed in black hidden behind a large rock on the mountainside watching them intensely. Its fists were clenched with rage. Its face twisted with bitterness. Its evil eyes blazed with hatred. A Dreamstealer, watching and waiting...

*

Grandpa Mal looked over at the clock and turned back to TJ. "It is time for us to go dear boy," he said, "before sunrise rouses the rest of the house. But it has been the most amazing night and you have conducted yourself extremely well dear boy. I think we are already seeing the makings of a fine Dreamguardian. Your father would be so proud dear boy."

TJ smiled ruefully. Having shared such an intimate moment with Grandpa Mal seized his opportunity to ask a difficult question.

"Grandpa Mal" he said, "in the dream I stumbled into last night, I saw you with Dad and Uncle Bertie. You were in a wooden hut having breakfast. Although it was warm in the cabin, outside I could see snowy mountains and snow-dusted trees. Were you in Switzerland?"

Grandpa Mal's mood changed instantly. "I'm not sure I remember the precise details of the dream TJ. It might have been. I just remember seeing you there". He looked away evasively.

TJ recognised Grandpa Mal's reluctance to engage in conversation about a dream that involved Dad. Up to now this had been the normal way everyone had acted after Dad had died. But TJ desperately *needed* to know more about what had transpired. As they sat together in Grand Room TJ sensed the opportunity to broach the subject with Grandpa Mal for the first time. After all Grandpa Mal was opening up to him and sharing all about the Brethren.

"Were you dreaming about the last time you were there Grandpa Mal?" TJ asked. Grandpa Mal continued to look away and didn't answer. "Grandpa Mal, was the dream just before Dad had his accident?"

Grandpa Mal slowly turned back towards him. "TJ, now is not the time to be talking about this," he replied sternly and coldly. "Asking such questions serves little purpose other than to torment and upset us all. Much as we wish it wasn't the case, what is done is done. We cannot change what happened. So, we must continue to concentrate and focus on the things that we do have control over, dear boy. For they are also vitally important."

TJ felt stung by Grandpa Mal's reprimand. He wished he had obeyed the status quo instinct not to probe. However, he vowed then and there that one day he would find out exactly what happened. Only then would he come to some form of understanding of why it had to happen. He had yet to reach that point after all. But TJ remained adamant that even if he one day understood, he would never ever reach the point of acceptance.

It had been quite a night. It would take some time to fully comprehend the wonder and excitement of the revelation that he was a Dreamguardian and what could be accomplished as a result. He was still struggling to comprehend that he, TJ, was a member of the Brethren with all the honour and privileges that bestowed upon him. All that knowledge he would learn and all the encounters he would experience in the future. Not to mention all the time he would get to spend learning more about the being a Dreamguardian with his most favourite person left in the world.

But at the same time, he felt a mixture of emotions. He felt the huge weight of responsibility on his shoulders of being a Dreamguardian, protecting the safe passage of dreams. The thought of all the danger, risk and darkness he would now be exposed to threatened to overwhelm him. So too did the regret that with the exception of Grandpa Mal he would never get to fully share the wonderful secrets of the Brethren of the Dreamguardians with those he cared most about.

"Sorry Grandpa Mal," TJ said wearily. "It's been an incredible night, but I'm now really tired. Let's make our way back to the East Wing".

"Of course, dear boy," Grandpa Mal said sympathetically as they rose from the chairs. "That certainly is quite enough excitement for one night."

CHAPTER 14 – THE BLAME GAME

T he kitchen and breakfast room were abuzz with activity as bacon sizzled, cereals tumbled from giant boxes into smaller bowls, various fruits were chopped, an old-fashioned kettle boiled on the hob and a shiny toaster diligently performed its role.

Auntie Emma and Auntie Katherine expertly shepherded Lizzy Wizzy, Chatty and Benjy from the Chesterfield sofa to the table in the breakfast room. They then worked industriously together to bring the eclectic breakfast offering to the table.

"Where is that brother of yours Lizzy Wizzy?" Mum asked.

Lizzy Wizzy shrugged. She was hungry and not particularly bothered by TJ's absence. "I don't know" she replied, "probably still asleep. He can be such a lazy bones."

Mum rolled her eyes. Once upon time she would have yearned for TJ to sleep in for a bit longer. However, now that he had officially left primary school she feared they were embarking upon a move to the other extreme. "Oh well, he's the one missing out," Mum declared, "bacon sandwich anyone?"

Benjy's hand shot up in an instant. "Me please, me please Auntie Emma," he called out excitedly. Auntie Emma carefully laid the bacon on a bed of fresh fluffy white buttered bread. Benjy added a generous flood of tomato ketchup to the pool of melting butter and entombed the bacon with another slice of bread. Auntie Emma carefully cut the sandwich for Benjy and he jumped up and down excitedly in his chair. "Yummy yummy yummy" he said in his squeaky little voice. He grinned at the sight of his massive sandwich, revealing tiny teeth and a gap at the front where his first tooth had wobbled out last week. His face was still a little red from the beach visit, complementing his hair, while the exposure to the sun had made his freckles a bit more visible than normal.

CHAPTER 14 – THE BLAME GAME

"What do you say Benjy?" Auntie Katherine said as she sat down.

"Thank you Auntie Emma," he replied.

"You're welcome sweetheart," came the reply and Benjy beamed back at her. He loved Auntie Emma and the way she made him feel special and went out of her way to put him first, even though he was the youngest.

"Lovely fruit Auntie Emma. This peach is delicious, thank you," Chatty said, vying for some attention.

She bit into a peach slice that Auntie Emma had cut for her and the juice dribbled down her chin. "My, they're juicy aren't they Chatty?" Auntie Emma said smiling and Chatty nodded vigorously.

Chatty took another big slice of peach and made a loud slurping noise as she tried to extract all the juice before it departed down her chin. She and Auntie Emma smiled at each other. Auntie Katherine wasn't impressed.

"Chatty, that's enough, eat it properly," she scolded. Chatty looked forlornly at Auntie Emma who had turned her attention to Auntie Katherine.

"But Mummy, it's..." Chatty started to reply wiping her chin with her hand.

Katherine cut in very quickly. "No 'ifs or buts', eat it nicely. And use a napkin to wipe your chin young lady".

Chatty's eyes and head dropped and she looked sulkily down at the table. The fun and lively atmosphere around the table had evaporated pretty quickly.

"No sulking either, Charlotte," Katherine continued sharply. "Honestly, you're getting worse. Remember your manners and how to conduct yourself young lady. You're not at your fathers now. Is that how he lets you behave when you stay with him?" She made a tutting sound and shook her head.

Chatty immediately looked up and glared at her Mum.

"No!" she snapped back. "That's not fair. Leave Daddy alone. This has got nothing to do with him. Stop being so nasty about him all the time. Just because you don't like him anymore doesn't mean that we have to stop liking him too," she said defensively.

"That's enough Charlotte" Katherine said firmly. "You can be just as bad as him with all the arguing and the bad moods."

"Well you started it," Chatty said grumpily, pushing her bowl of fruit away.

"You're so horrible."

"Charlotte!" shouted Katherine loudly, making everyone around the table jump. "That's enough, or you can go to your room".

Chatty didn't even hesitate to think. She pushed her chair back noisily and got up from the table. "Fine, I'm going to my room," she said defiantly, though with the faint hint of a wobbly bottom lip.

"Sit back down young lady and finish your breakfast," came the stern yet contradictory reply.

Chatty ignored the demand and stormed out of the breakfast room.

It was quiet for a short while until an exasperated Katherine broke the silence. "Honestly, I don't know what's wrong with that girl," she said.

She was about to stand and follow Chatty, but Auntie Emma placed a hand on her arm. "Leave her for a while to calm down," she said soothingly. "Just give her some space. It's been a lot to deal with."

Katherine sighed heavily but remained seated. "I don't know what to do with her sometimes Emma. It's like she blames just me for, you know..."

"I'm sure she doesn't," Emma said sympathetically. "She knows it's not just your fault and that unfortunately these things can happen. Anyway, let's talk about it later," she added, motioning towards Benjy as she did so.

Auntie Emma turned and spoke directly to Benjy. "How's that beautiful bacon sandwich Benny-boy?" she asked in her cheeriest voice in an attempt to defuse the tension in the room. Benjy continued to stare down at his plate and didn't respond.

"Benjy, how's that piggy wiggy sandwich of yours? Is the piggy wiggy sandwich good?" She snorted a couple of times and made a squealing noise for good measure. It was a pretty poor impersonation of a pig and the whole thing would have offended any sensitive vegetarian for sure. But she didn't care as long as she got a smile or a laugh from Benjy.

He nodded. Auntie Emma made more squealing noises and then pushed her nose up, unattractively elongating her nostrils.

Benjy looked up and reluctantly started to giggle. So too did Lizzy Wizzy. "Mummy!" she exclaimed through her giggles, "that's disgusting!"

Placing her face towards Lizzy Wizzy's, Mum snorted again. "Oink oink, don't eat little piggy wiggy Lizzy Wizzy". It all looked rather strange but hilarious at the same time. Benjy and Lizzy Wizzy looked at each other and giggled infectiously. So much so that even Auntie Katherine caught the giggles.

As the atmosphere brightened, their laughter carried into the corridor outside where a grumpy Chatty stood listening with her arms folded tightly. She hadn't gone to her room. She expected Mum to come and find her. To make up like they always did when they argued about Daddy and why he no longer lived with them. But this time she hadn't followed and now they were laughing at her. She could feel herself getting angry; a flickering tightness in her chest that burned more intensely the more upset and angrier she got.

"At least Daddy doesn't shout at me or laugh at me like that," she said to herself angrily as a tear trickled down her face. "At least Daddy loves and cares about me. No wonder he left us if that's how she used to treat him..."

***

Despite the upset over breakfast, the rest of the morning passed by peacefully. When she returned to her bedroom after breakfast, Lizzy Wizzy found a rather upset Chatty lying on her bed. But over the course of the next few hours Lizzy Wizzy managed to cheer her up a little bit. They played together with the large dolls house in the corner of the room, stopping every now and then to dance to their favourite songs as they came on the radio.

A tired TJ had eventually surfaced, but only after Benjy had crept into his room and jumped on him. Given everything that had happened over the last couple of nights, Benjy's wakeup call had frightened the life out of TJ and shocked him awake quickly. TJ hoped that if any Dreamguardian was present in his dream, they had managed to escape in time.

TJ and Benjy spent most of the remainder of the morning outside in the hot sunshine. They ran around the vast grounds and kicked and threw a variety of balls of various sizes to each other. Undoubtedly the best pastime was a game of cricket they created. Three long sticks found underneath the oak tree formed the stumps, some smaller twigs the bails and a short fat broken branch from the oak was adopted as a bat.

Although some frostiness still remained between Chatty and Auntie Katherine, after lunch they all bundled into the cars again - some more enthusiastically than others - for another trip out. The clear blue sky and warm weather dictated another trip to the beach, although this time the two Aunties had planned to visit a different one.

As they turned off the main road, the number of cars and houses reduced, and the open fields of the countryside became dominant. They drove through a picturesque village, passing by the village green and duck pond on one side and an old welcoming inn on the other.

The convoy turned right and ahead of them a straight road stretched out for what looked like miles. As they travelled along, the unmistakable sight of the purple and green heathland returned. Every now and then a sign would appear warning of a bumpy road ahead. Each one was met with excitement rather than caution as the cars went up and over, along with the occupants' stomachs.

As they passed the ruins of an old monastery the road continued to narrow, and they slowed. Following the signs, they pulled up alongside each other in the beach car park, which was nothing more than an expanse of dusty land littered with pebbles as well as cars.

The summer heat hit them as they disembarked from the air-conditioned cars, but they were soon cooled again by the fresh sea air as they reached the top of the slope leading to the beach. The two Aunties gave them instructions not to wander far and sat down at a picnic table outside the café overlooking both the car park and beach.

Although the last beach they visited was sandy enough to dig, this particular one was predominantly stony. The children crunched their way over the stones and pebbles, then down a fairly steep pebble shelf as they made their way to the sea. The coastline stretched for miles in either direction. About two hundred yards to their right was a collection of fishing rods, their lines stretching out into the sea beyond the breakers. A couple of men were slumped in folding camping chairs, their body language suggesting it had been an unsuccessful fishing trip so far. Beyond them, some way off in the distance was the unmistakable sight of the nuclear reactor at Sizewell: a giant white golf ball permanently teed up on the coastline.

The children set about doing what they loved to do here. They picked up stones of various shapes and sizes and threw them as hard as they could. The competitions they would hold sometimes seemed endless: who could throw the furthest; who could skim a stone the most times; who could hit their own stone thrown up towards the sea with another of their stones; who could hit someone else's stone… And so, it went on.

When they had exhausted something as simple as throwing stones, they would turn their attention to avoiding the waves. If they all felt daring, they might even conveniently forget their instructions not to take off their shoes and socks and jump the waves. The final game would be to run and jump off the steep pebble shelf that marked the high tide. As they jumped off the shelf, they would contort their limbs, bodies and faces into different shapes. They would judge each other's efforts and award a score out of ten and then spend even longer questioning the consistency and equitability of their makeshift scoring system. At times their discussions moved beyond friendly banter, requiring some motherly intervention to restore peace and order.

As the activities were once again harmonious, Katherine and Emma sat at their table enjoying some peace and quiet in the sunshine with a pot of tea for two. Even though it was warm, a cup of tea would quench their thirst quite nicely. In any case it was still too early for them to indulge in a glass of something stronger, even though Katherine in particular felt she had already earned one today.

The two ladies sat with their sunglasses on and a slight breeze rustling their hair. Both were attractive ladies in their early forties, of similar above-average height and would often catch the eye of much younger men, which they found amusing. They both had long hair, although Emma's was light brown and Katherine's a more distinctive red. Although Katherine had been teased throughout the early years of education about her hair, she had grown to love its distinctiveness once she had left secondary school. As Benjy had inherited a similar colour, albeit his was more strawberry blonde than red, Katherine hoped he would be able to do the same one day. Children in particular, but not only them, could be so cruel sometimes.

The two ladies were so relaxed in each other's company that people often mistook them for sisters in spite of their different colour hair. They would reply kindly that was more or less the case as they were in fact sisters-in-law. Katherine's older brother Daniel had met Emma when they were both at the same University. It had been something of a strange affair. Even though it had taken them a while, somehow, they both knew deep down very early on they would get together. Emma could remember that Daniel had said to her he had seen it in a dream one night. They knew they wanted to get married, live in a large house in the countryside, have children and grow old together. Nearly all of their shared dreams had come true, apart from the last part of course. Now Emma was alone with just TJ and Lizzy Wizzy to invest all her love into.

Sat in the sunshine amongst the holidaymakers, she was now offering a sympathetic and listening ear to Katherine. "So how are you doing Katherine? I'm guessing things are a bit difficult?" Emma asked.

Katherine sighed heavily. "Yes, it's difficult, as you could see for yourself this morning. Chatty's not coping very well at all. She seems to blame me for the fact Bertie has left. You can see that Benjy misses his father too, but he's such a lovely little boy. He's still so young, innocent and full of fun. Nothing seems to bother him. Perhaps he doesn't fully understand. But as far as Chatty is concerned, her world has fallen apart. She was extremely close to Bertie, a proper Daddy's little girl. He doted on her too. At least he still loves one of the girls in our family…" She smiled weakly as she said it, but Emma could tell it still hurt.

"Well, I know the circumstances are different, but I do understand," Emma replied. Katherine immediately interrupted. "Oh, I'm sorry Emma, I don't mean to complain, to you of all people. After all, it's so much worse for you. At least Bertie is still around and sees the children from time to time. It breaks my heart that you, TJ and Lizzy will never, you know see..." She paused as she choked up and her sunglasses did a good job hiding the tears that were forming in her eyes.

Emma reached over the table and squeezed her hand. "I know Kat. He was such a special man. Such an amazing husband to me, father to TJ and Lizzy, son to Mal and of course brother to you." Katherine nodded as she sniffed back her tears.

"We miss him terribly. Every second of every day," Emma continued. "What I wouldn't give to see him again Kat. You know some people say they'd give anything for just one more day, or one more hour, or just one more touch from someone they've lost. But that wouldn't be enough for me. I'm selfish. I want him back for good. He had so much to live for Kat. He was so loved, wanted and needed by so many people, but especially us. All I know is that it shouldn't have been his time to go."

Emma paused to wipe her eyes underneath her large fashionable sunglasses. Although she found it hard and uncomfortable it was good to talk, especially to someone who knew Daniel as well as her, albeit in a different way. She continued shakily. "I guess in some way I'm angry with him Kat; angry he was careless enough to die on that mountain. Sometimes I'm angry he was there at all, although I never once stopped him from doing all the things he enjoyed. And as we know he did love to push the boundaries when he went skiing and live dangerously. Sometimes I'm just angry for no apparent reason!" She managed to let out a small, exasperated laugh. Katherine managed a smile and squeezed her hand back.

"I know Em. It's natural. I'm angry too Daniel's gone. I know brothers and sisters are not meant to get on, but we always did. I miss him so much too. I know things with Bertie had been going wrong for quite some time before the accident, but that might have been the thing that really broke it for us. I know it was a freak tragic accident, one of the dangers of skiing off-piste, but part of me still wants to blame Bertie somehow for Daniel's death."

She went quiet for a moment, as if wrestling whether to share her thoughts. Slowly, she continued. "I've never shared this with anyone else before Em, but sometimes in my darkest hours I wish it had been Bertie that had fallen off that mountain and not Daniel." She bowed and shook her head. "I know it's awful to think that, I really do. I'm not even sure if I really mean it or not. All I know is how far our relationship had deteriorated and of course how much I loved my older brother."

Emma nodded. "I know Kat. It stirs up so many emotions and plays so many cruel tricks on your heart and mind. I wouldn't wish some of those on my worst enemy."

As Emma finished her sentence she noticed Chatty stood at the end of the table out of the corner of her eye. She turned to speak to her. "Hello Chatty dear, we didn't see you there," she said a little flustered trying to cover up her and Katherine's rather emotional state. "Is everything ok?"

It was a somewhat redundant question as it was clear from Chatty's sullen face that everything was not 'ok'. Chatty replied grumpily to that effect, turned and stormed off back towards the beach.

Emma turned back to Katherine. "I'll go, don't worry," she said. "Sorry Kat, I didn't see her there, did you?" Katherine shook her head, as she hadn't seen her either before now. "She can't have been there long, surely?" Katherine asked, more in hope than expectation. "I hope not," Emma replied.

Emma quickly got up from the table and made her way onto the beach in pursuit of Chatty. She caught up with her just as Chatty plonked herself down on the pebble shelf, her legs resting on the stones that sloped down towards the sea. Chatty picked up a handful of stones and threw them into the empty space in front of her.

"What is it, Chatty dear?" she asked. "Has one of the others upset you?"

Chatty nodded her head. "The boys were being silly and wouldn't leave us alone," she said unhappily. "But it doesn't matter anymore".

"Well of course it matters sweetheart," Auntie Emma said softly as she sat down next to Chatty. She picked up a smooth round stone and rubbed it with her fingers. "I'll have a word with TJ. I'm pretty sure the boys will stop being silly then." She smiled, but Chatty didn't reciprocate.

"Is that it, or are you still upset about earlier today?" Auntie Emma probed, but Chatty just shrugged her shoulders. "I know it's tough for you," she continued, "but it's also tough on your Mum, and on your Dad too. You do know Chatty that just because they made the difficult decision not to be together anymore and for your Dad to move out, doesn't mean that either of them loves you any less."

Chatty looked across at her, but there was no break in her mood or expression. "It's nobody's fault sweetheart," Auntie Emma said softly, "not your parents and certainly not yours. Sadly, sometimes these things just happen." She put her arm around her and Chatty gently rested her head on Auntie

Emma's shoulder.

Chatty didn't say anything to Auntie Emma as they looked out to sea. They sat in silence watching TJ, Benjy and Lizzy Wizzy playing happily at the water's edge, oblivious to how Chatty was feeling as wave after wave rushed in and out. Although nothing more was spoken, Chatty had responded in her head to what Auntie Emma had just said. You're wrong Auntie Emma, Chatty thought to herself. It *is* her fault.

CHAPTER 15 – DARKNESS COMES CALLING

Despite multiple portions of café chips to keep them going, the beach succeeded in tiring out the children. TJ had been ordered to apologise for upsetting Chatty and the emergence from the car boot of some kites to fly on the beach had helped reunite the children. Lizzy Wizzy was pleased to welcome her playmate back into the fold, as it wasn't quite the same with just Benjy and TJ.

The kites had also managed to eke out another half hour for the two Aunties to continue catching up on their new lives without a man in the house. Even though the circumstances behind the absences were very different, the more they chatted the more they realised some of the practicalities and issues it generated were similar. It was good to talk and both Emma and Katherine had a lot to catch up on.

As they finally all made their way back home and into the Grand Hall, lazily casting off their shoes, they heard the unmistakable sound of loud classical music playing in the direction of the kitchen. It meant one thing: Grandpa Mal was around and cooking. The smell of supper hit them as they approached the kitchen.

"Grandpa Mal!" they all shouted over Boccherini's beautiful string quintet as they bundled into the room. Grandpa Mal spun round from tending the pots and pans on the hob and waved his wooden spoon in the air in time to the music to greet them, as if he were an overexcited conductor. His apron was fastened neatly, protecting his checked shirt and bright red trousers.

"Welcome home dear boys and girls!" he shouted over the music. "How was your day?" Lizzy Wizzy walked over to the CD player, turned the volume down and filled Grandpa Mal in on the main events and all the key activities on the beach.

"That all sounds like a lot of fun, dear girl," Grandpa Mal responded once

Lizzy Wizzy had finished. "I don't suppose you're hungry now with all those chips!" he laughed. They all shouted, each claiming simultaneously that they were "starving" and couldn't wait for Grandpa Mal to finish cooking. Supper was Grandpa Mal's infamous pasta dish, lovingly concocted with a special 'secret sauce' he promised to reveal to them one day.

As Grandpa Mal made the finishing touches to the sauce that bubbled furiously in the giant copper frying pan, Katherine drained a large saucepan of boiling salted water into the butler's sink, leaving a mountain of steaming tagliatelle in the colander. Emma opened the bottle of red wine Grandpa Mal had left to acclimatise on the kitchen worktop since fetching it up earlier from the cellar. She poured three large glasses for the adults and Grandpa Mal's homemade cloudy lemonade for the children.

Dinner was served, and they tucked in, laughing and joking about the events of the day. The recounting of one of Benjy's spectacular poses as he jumped off the pebble shelf at the beach had them roaring with laughter. Benjy then had them in stitches as he jumped down from the table and recreated the pose again, this time pulling an even sillier face as he did so.

"How funny, dear boy," Grandpa Mal said chuckling. The conversation continued to flow around the table in between their attempts to conquer the tagliatelle mountain range piled on their plates.

Against the background noise, Grandpa Mal leant over to TJ who was sat next to him and whispered to get his attention. TJ looked up from his plate. "What was that, Grandpa Mal?" he asked through a mouthful of food. "Shhh, not too loud!" Grandpa Mal replied quietly. "Tomorrow we're off on a little outing. Just you and me dear boy, so don't mention it to the others. Slip out the front quietly before the others have breakfast as we're being picked up at 8am sharp. Leave your mother to me as I have a good excuse up my sleeve. Just wear some long trousers, your walking boots and sound enthusiastic if your mother asks you any questions! All good, dear boy?"

"Yes fine," whispered TJ under his breath.

"One more thing, dear boy. Best you don't go 'wandering' tonight, if you understand what I mean?" Grandpa Mal winked at TJ.

Although TJ wanted to ask why not, he refrained and simply nodded his understanding. At the other end of the table, Chatty was watching suspiciously the surreptitious conversation between Grandpa Mal and TJ. Her mood began to darken again.

***

Chatty remained in a bad mood all evening and was finally sent to bed ahead of Lizzy Wizzy and TJ by her exasperated mother; sick and tired of all Chatty's grumpiness and answering back. Mindful that her protests had been ignored downstairs, Chatty slammed her bedroom door behind her as audible proof of her defiance. In doing so she woke Benjy who had gone up to bed earlier, frustrating Katherine even further when Benjy came back downstairs complaining he couldn't get back to sleep.

Chatty threw her shoes and clothes onto the bedroom floor and muttered under her breath how unfair everything was. Not only was Mum being horrible to her, *again*, but Grandpa Mal was definitely favouring TJ, *again*. Just like in her dream. And it wasn't *fair*.

She could feel herself getting hot and bothered as she put on her pyjamas and brushed her teeth. Reluctantly she jumped into bed, trying as hard as she could to break it as she did so, and switched off her light. She was too annoyed to read the stupid book that Mum said she had to finish over the holidays. So, she threw that on the floor too. Chatty tossed and turned for a while as a multitude of thoughts, scenarios and all annoying things in general ran through her mind.

Eventually her heart rate began to slow as she began to transition through the various sleep stages. Then after some time her REM sleep began.

*

Chatty fidgeted on the stool nervously as she looked at the piano keys beneath her fingers. The piano itself was a huge concert grand with a case that shone like a pristine black mirror. It reflected from every angle all the stage lights that shone on the piano and pianist. Without looking up from her position on the stage, Chatty could make out the reflection of a huge audience that waited expectantly for her to begin. The gentlemen were all wearing black tie dress and the ladies wore extravagant evening dresses.

Chatty herself was dressed in an elegant black dress with white tights and pretty black shoes as shiny as the piano. In any other situation she would have spent longer admiring her dress. But right now, it was impossible to concentrate on anything other than the ebony and ivory keys her fingers nervously hovered over.

She could feel the anxiety rise within her. "I can't remember the first notes," she said quietly to herself. "Then again, I don't even know what I'm meant to be playing." She heard someone in the audience cough and people shifting uncomfortably in their seats. Some impatient muttering started in the front row.

"What am I doing?" Chatty said again. Although she had passed her Grade 2 piano exam, she wasn't ready to perform in front of all these people at such a formal concert. She looked again at the reflection of her fingers in the shiny piano lid. Now it looked even more complicated, as if she had four hands and twenty fingers to control.

She took a deep breath and tried hard to remember one of her exam pieces. She decided quickly she would play the classical piece. That seemed appropriate for such an important concert. But then again, that was such a boring piece. Perhaps she should play the other one? That was a bit more lively and exciting.

"Get on with it," someone shouted some distance away from the back of the huge concert hall.

"Shhh," came the hissed reply from others in the audience, although Chatty sensed it wouldn't be long before they all started to revolt at the delay in the performance.

Caught in two minds, Chatty started to play what she thought was the best piece for the occasion.

Her fingers hit every wrong note and the dissonance was jarring. Chatty winced. So too did the audience. She could feel her cheeks get hotter and the sweat start to form on her brow.

She stopped, took another deep breath and tried again. This time she played different notes, but they were still very much the wrong ones. The sound they produced was awful. No matter how hard she tried, Chatty couldn't find the right notes to start the piece she wanted to play.

A loud and deep "boo" rang out from towards the back left of the hall. Another one resonated from the front right of the audience.

The tears started to well in Chatty's eyes. "No, no, please no," she said under her breath despairingly. "Why can't I play?"

She made one last attempt. It was even worse than the others. "If I keep playing, I'm sure it will come," she said to herself, now in something of a frustrated panic. So, she kept on playing. By now her fingers were uncontrollable and felt like they didn't belong to her. They hit every note she knew shouldn't be played and the beautiful piano filled the hall with the most ugly and terrible noise.

The audience erupted in a mixture of anger and pain. The booing spread across the vast hall and shouts tried to drown out the racket emanating from the piano. "Stop! Get off! Enough! Fraud!"

Chatty tried to stop but she couldn't. Her fingers were out of control, moving ferociously up and down the keyboard creating musical carnage. They bashed the keys to a crescendo until finally she managed to lift them off the keyboard and slam down the piano lid. It sounded like a shotgun firing in the room and silence quickly returned to the room.

Chatty turned red-faced to look at the audience. Her tears magnified their stares. After what seemed like eternity, Chatty got to her feet and moved away from the piano stool.

Then it happened. One by one the members of the audience started to laugh. It started as a trickle, then a ripple spread, and the wave grew, before a tidal wave of hysterical laughter came crashing over Chatty.

"What?" Chatty called out loudly to the audience. "Why are you laughing? What are you laughing at?" She looked desperately into the audience for some form of explanation, but all over the hall they were laughing uncontrollably, clutching their sides, knees as well as each other. Some were pointing at her.

Chatty turned her head to look behind her and saw the source of the hilarity. She had accidentally tucked the back of her black dress into her white tights. Her face hit an even deeper shade of red and her utter embarrassment was complete. She wanted the ground to swallow her up. Anything was better than bearing the brunt of the laughter of the audience.

Then she saw them. Sitting at the far end of the front row. Tears of laughter streaming down their faces and pointing at her unfortunate wardrobe malfunction: Mum, Benjy and TJ.

"How dare you," she cried as she turned and ran off the stage. The laughter rang loud in her ears and her anger raged ever stronger inside.

***

Lizzy Wizzy had enjoyed her bedtime cuddle with Mum as she was upset about Chatty. No matter how hard she had tried, Lizzy Wizzy had been unable to fully cheer Chatty up today and she felt upset for her best friend and surrogate sister. Mum loved these cuddles and had grown accustomed to them. Lizzy Wizzy was such a caring and sensitive girl and her emotions would bruise easily, even when others close to her were hurt.

As Mum held Lizzy Wizzy, she could picture the times Daniel would cuddle Lizzy in the same way. He would gently tell his special Lizzy Wizzy that she was beautiful on the inside as well as the outside. He made Lizzy Wizzy promise that she would look after her golden heart. Every day she saw how hard Lizzy Wizzy tried to keep the promise she had made to her beloved Daddy.

Lizzy Wizzy tucked down into bed and yawned. She picked up Blanket Bear, her bedtime companion from the day she was born. As she held her to her cheek, the soft material of Blankie's square body was soft and comforting. Lizzy Wizzy rubbed the tiny feet and hands that had been sewn on each corner of Blankie's body and kissed the small bear's head that had been made simply from a stripy pink material, without any attempt to add facial features. The pair of them had been through everything together. They knew each other's greatest secrets, dreams, disappointments and fears.

Lizzy Wizzy trusted Blankie implicitly to keep her safe during the night and didn't often let her down. But that was about to change.

*

Lizzy Wizzy was alone in a deserted fairground. It was dusk and an eerie mist rolled around the empty kiosks and rides. To her left, dodgem cars stood abandoned on their slippery roadway, while ahead of her the big wheel was stationary, its caged gondolas swaying in the breeze. The 'fun of the fair' had long departed. Lizzy Wizzy called out to see if anyone was there, but there was no reply. Out of the corner of her eye, something caught her attention.

Against the grey and bleakness of the scene, the carousel stood out. Beneath a glowing canopy of a thousand bulbs, brightly painted model horses of all different sizes and colours were mounted on twisted poles. Some valiantly pulled chariots with red velvet seats, while the largest looked as though they were dressed for war. As Lizzy Wizzy looked at the carousel, she was sure she saw one of the horses move. Then another, and another. When she heard the mesmerising sound of the carousel pipe music begin to play, she realised the carousel was starting. The horses began to slowly rise and fall as the carousel began to turn.

Lizzy Wizzy was drawn towards it, the music enticing her in. She stepped onto the carousel floor and walked up to one of the big stallions ready for battle on the inside ring of horses. Now that she was close up, it towered above her, its teeth bared and slightly frightening, even though it was inanimate.

From out of the shadows behind a row of horses, a gruff male voice spoke. Lizzy Wizzy jumped.

"No need to be afraid," the voice rasped. "Old Rasputin there's a gentle giant. He might look pretty fearsome, but he sure won't hurt you."

A mountain of a man, bald, with a huge dense beard stepped out from the shadows. He was dressed shabbily, with his vest revealing heavily tanned arms, complete with tattoos and bulging biceps. A money belt was loosely tied around his waist with a frayed piece of string.

Lizzy Wizzy cowered, but the man – seemingly accustomed to this reaction – tried to put her at ease.

"I'm not going to hurt you either." He tutted to himself. "Don't know why you little ones are always scared of me. Happens every time someone wants to have a ride," he said.

"Sorry," Lizzy Wizzy ventured cautiously, "it's just that you scared me, and to be honest you do look a little scary."

The man smiled at her truthful reply. "Yes, well I guess I do, but didn't your ma or pa tell you never to judge a book by its cover? There's a lot worse than me, even those much smaller than me too, you know." He gave her a broad smile, revealing more empty black spaces than there were teeth. Lizzy Wizzy dared think how each tooth had been lost.

"So, are you going to get on then?" the man asked gently. "Rasputin's been waiting for a rider all day. He'll be the envy of the others, especially little Princess over there," he said pointing to a beautifully painted white pony on the outer circle of the carousel. "She's normally the favourite for all the little girls. She can get quite jealous if the others get a rider and she doesn't. But I think Rasputin has taken a shine to you and I think you're strong and brave enough to take him into battle."

Lizzy Wizzy couldn't quite tell if the operator was joking or not. The horses were definitely not real, but he talked as if they were. Neither did she feel strong or brave at this moment. In fact, she wasn't sure what to do. Mum had always told her to be careful around strangers, though she did feel there was a kind heart underneath the rough exterior of the man in front of her.

"Look, as it's the last ride of the day, I'll even let you off the fare," the carousel operator said. He looked quickly over his shoulder. "But best not tell the boss if you see her, as she'll be after me. Not for the first time I should say either. She'll have me guts for garters." He held back his head and roared with laughter and Lizzy Wizzy felt like the whole earth shook.

He held a giant hand out and Lizzy Wizzy tentatively took it, as he helped her climb onto the back of Rasputin, still primed for war and frozen in battle.

"Remember to hold on tight little one, just in case Rasputin gets a little wild," the operator said, and he held back his head again and the laughter exploded again from within the big beard.

Lizzy Wizzy grabbed the twisted pole tightly and looked down to check her feet were on the metal bars replacing the stirrups. When she looked up again, the operator had gone.

The music got louder as the carousel started to turn quicker, and Rasputin rose up and down as he trotted. Lizzy Wizzy began to relax as the carousel picked up even more speed and Rasputin started to canter. She felt the breeze brush her face and ruffle her long blonde hair as the carousel continued to turn. She began to imagine she and Rasputin were riding into battle; fearless warriors for good in a war against all things bad in the world. Little did she know the enemy was already upon her.

The lights on the carousel suddenly flickered and the machine jolted. Lizzy Wizzy sensed something wasn't quite right and tensed. She felt a noticeable acceleration in the speed of the carousel. Rasputin's vertical movements gained momentum and before long turned into a gallop. Lizzy Wizzy gripped the pole so tight her knuckles started to turn white.

"Stop it, please!" she shouted, but there was no-one around to hear. The carousel operator had departed. "Please, I want to get off," Lizzy Wizzy begged, "I feel sick". Lizzy Wizzy got increasingly disorientated as the carousel turned faster and faster and Rasputin galloped up and down for his life. She tried closing her eyes, but it only made it worse.

A bright red glow appeared from the other side of the carousel and Lizzy Wizzy was sure she saw someone move in the shadows.

"Hey Mister, please stop the ride," she yelled, thinking it was the carousel operator. "I can't take much more of this."

Suddenly, the solid pole she was gripping turned into ribbon and she fell forward, putting her arms around Rasputin's neck to prevent her from hitting the ground.

He felt different and no longer wooden. Lizzy Wizzy's face felt the hair of his coat and mane as she buried her head into them. Just as she realised he was alive, he moved. Rasputin turned and shook his head, as if stretching from a long sleep, his teeth still bared and even more frightening now that he was alive. He neighed loudly and reared up on his hind legs with his forelegs off the ground. Lizzy Wizzy screamed as she clung on for dear life.

"Help! Help!" she cried. But still no-one came.

The carousel continued to gain speed and the mystical music got louder and louder. Terrified, Lizzy Wizzy started to sob as her head spun and Rasputin continued to rear up. The carousel started to creak and crack, threatening to fall apart if it sustained its pace for much longer.

"No, please... No... please stop," Lizzy Wizzy whimpered as she buried her face into Rasputin's neck, desperately trying not to fall off.

*

Lizzy Wizzy woke suddenly, her head buried deep in her pillow. She turned and sat up with a start. She took some deep breaths to try and calm down and turned on her bedside lamp. Her hair and pillow were wet, and her pyjamas drenched with sweat.

"What was that? Is there anyone there?" Lizzy Wizzy called out. She was still rather unsettled and very unsure now as to whether she was actually alone in the bedroom. Nobody answered but she remained on edge. After searching, she found Blankie on the floor. She regained a little warmth and some comfort from the familiar smell and softness as she pressed Blankie to the side of her face.

"It was so frightening," Lizzy Wizzy said to Blankie in a tearful vulnerable voice. "I don't know what happened, but it was scary."

Although she didn't know it, Lizzy Wizzy was absolutely right. Without doubt it was a Scarer.

***

As he looked down TJ saw he was dressed in shorts and a t-shirt. This gave him confidence he had heeded Grandpa Mal's warning and was experiencing his own dream rather than inadvertently straying into someone else's. He'd gone off to sleep very quickly and couldn't remember thinking about anything as he did so.

The grass was soft under his feet and TJ carefully avoided the rubble as he walked along. The sun had not long set and the light was beginning to fade fast. Despite the hour the atmosphere was extremely muggy and close. A storm was brewing that in all likelihood would clear the air and bring in with it a new front.

TJ found himself walking amongst the upstanding ruins and earthworks of what once must have been imposing buildings built from flint and stone. Every now and then he could see a medieval archway that had stood the test of time, unlike most of the rest of the structures. His surroundings looked familiar, but TJ wasn't quite sure from where.

Then he remembered. These were the crumbling walls of the monastery they had driven past on the way to the beach. He had tried hard not to look at it earlier as he didn't want to be reminded of the times they had visited before when Dad was alive. Dad had always found the 13th century Franciscan priory fascinating. On the first visit he espoused how much he loved the solitude and brutal honesty of the primitiveness of the surroundings. He said he could understand why the Franciscan monks would choose to live peaceful and contemplative lives up here close to the cliff's edge.

By contrast, TJ didn't like this place much now that Dad was no longer with them. It contained too many memories. On their second visit Dad had suddenly chanted like a monk at the top of his voice into the strong wind that was blowing in off the sea. Mum had told him off and said it was just as well they were the only ones around. Another time Mum had cuddled up into Dad as the sun was setting. She had whispered something in his ear and they kissed tenderly. Although TJ had felt embarrassed at the time, at this precise moment he would have given anything to see that particular memory recreated in real life again. Instead, right now TJ found the desolation and emptiness of the place unsettling and he was stuck in the middle of it for no apparent reason.

The ruin was situated within a vast expanse of grass. It was once enclosed within a flint wall, although time had since infiltrated the boundary wall in places. Nevertheless, the imposing gateways that served to keep intruders out and the Franciscan monks safe within the priory had remained largely intact. As dusk fell TJ's surroundings took on an even more eerie feeling. A sea mist started to blow in from the sea, over the cliffs and what little of the defences of the old medieval town that remained.

TJ approached the main section of the upstanding remains, part of a two-tiered cloister building that once formed the dining room of the monastery. He made his way towards the arched doorway that would take him behind the façade of the building into the earthworks and open expanse of what was once a large enclosed room. Over the cliffs he could see dark clouds forming and the sea mist was getting soupier; a sure sign a storm was coming. The mist started to swirl around and cling to the upstanding remains of the ruined priory.

As he walked round the building and through the archway, TJ got the unnerving feeling he was being watched. A shiver went down his spine. The light was fading fast and this was not the place he wanted to be, either in real life or in one of his dreams.

As TJ walked a figure appeared on top of the wall behind him. The figure wore a full-length black robe covered by a black monastic scapular, with a hood so large it made it impossible to see the head and face within it. From the left gaping sleeve of the robe a gloved black hand clenched a wooden staff. A demonic creature had been intricately carved at the top of it. By the way the staff was held it looked as if the creature was crouched atop the fist of its carrier. The carved creature's head was looking out over its shoulder as it crouched. It wore a menacingly sadistic grin on its human-like face, although its long-pointed ears and teeth confirmed the creature was far from human.

If anything, it looked like a sinister hooded ghostly monk was haunting the priory. But it wasn't. This was real and here for something else. It stood in silence watching TJ walk across the grass floor of the former dining hall. Then it moved, stealthily walking across the top of the wall of the ruin, all the time keeping close watch of the young boy's movement below.

TJ could sense something wasn't right and still had the feeling he was being watched and followed. He turned to look over his shoulder, but no one was there. When he turned his head back the hooded figure had jumped down from the wall and was stood blocking his way. It towered over him. The only face TJ could see was that of the carved mythical creature on the end of the staff. It grinned manically at him.

A high-pitched scream of genuine fear erupted from TJ at the figure that had appeared in front of him. It tried to echo around the ruins but was quickly devoured by the misty sea air. In that moment TJ wanted to wake but couldn't.

A deep growl emanated from deep within the hood. "*Silence,*" came the demand.

TJ was unable to escape, frozen by fear. He could feel the hairs on the back of his neck stand. "Who are you? What do you want?" TJ asked weakly.

The growled reply was aggressive. "I said *silence, boy.*" A black-gloved hand appeared from out of the gaped sleeve and a long index finger pointed at TJ.

"You will listen to *me, boy*. Tonight, *I* am in control of your destiny. There is nobody here to help you. But even if there was, they would be no match for *me*. For I am *strong,* and *they* are *weak...*" Once these words had been spat out a deep chilling laugh followed.

The laugh was accompanied by a twirling of the staff in the left hand. As it stopped, the carved creature ceased its somersaults and continued to stare and grin at TJ.

"Do you understand me *boy?*"

TJ failed to reply, making the figure angry. The question was shouted again in his face ferociously. "I said do you understand?"

TJ nodded, biting his bottom lip.

"Good. The old man has told you quite a few stories over the past few days, hasn't he? Revealing all the precious secrets of the *Brethren*... I was also informed you have that *filthy* gift too." The disdain was tangible.

"So, boy, did the old man tell you about *me* yet?" There was a pause. "Well?"

TJ shook his head from side to side. He whispered "no," as he looked down, petrified to even attempt to look into the blackness of the hood.

"*Speak up*, boy," came the venomous response. "I said did the old man *tell you* about *me* yet?"

"No," TJ said a bit louder as some defiance strangely began to stir deep within him.

A menacing laugh emerged momentarily. "I'm not surprised. Care to ask yourself why, boy?" The staff twirled again. "Because there is *no one* to challenge me. *No way* to defeat *me*." The staff continued to twirl violently causing the creature to spin and dance so close to TJ's face that he could feel the air from its movement. TJ flinched.

"There is nothing *they* can do to stop *me*, boy. Nothing *they* can do to stop *me* and my *army*." The figure leaned in and moved uncomfortably closer. TJ found some courage to look up and thought he could make out two blazing red eyes staring at him from within the hood.

The voice growled again in response to TJ's gaze. "If you persist in your *folly* with the old man *you* will *lose*. If you choose to continue as a Dreamguardian I will *hurt everyone* important to you. Underestimate me, or my power, at your *peril* boy. You will either *lose everyone important to you* or be *lost* yourself, *forever*..."

The rage and anger within the hooded figure were tangible and the carved creature continued to pull the same menacing grin at TJ.

"You and the *filthy Brethren* cannot win. You will *never* win. Rest assured you will remember all of this very clearly when you wake boy. Take it and the following message back to the old man, the old lady and all the other ineffectual and *feeble* Elders of the Dreamguardians."

The voice grew louder and angrier. "*I am gaining power and the Dreamstealers are rising.* We are gaining power with every night that passes. We are gaining power with every Dreamguardian we trap and cause to be *lost, forever*..."

The staff twirled vigorously again. "So... *sweet dreams, boy*," sneered the hooded figure. Immediately it turned and disappeared through the red sea mist that was now thick around the ruin.

TJ remained rooted to the spot, trying to take in everything that had just been spoken and threatened.

As he stood there anxiously, he felt powder grind between his teeth. The realisation slowly began to dawn on him. The powder in his mouth had been generated from one of his teeth. His heart began to thump as he processed what was happening. His teeth were disintegrating. He felt them crumble one by one in his mouth, just as the buildings around him had done so over the centuries. He began to cry and scream as the ground down powder from his teeth tumbled from his mouth.

In the distance the dark clouds rumbled, and a bolt of lightning streaked across the sky.

The storm had arrived.

CHAPTER 16 – A
SECLUDED COTTAGE

The two girls were very subdued when they finally made it downstairs for breakfast the next morning. Benjy by contrast was full of energy and life. So much so that he was told in no uncertain terms by Chatty to be quiet and leave her alone for the whole day. Lizzy Wizzy had withdrawn within herself and appeared very nervous and jumpy.

Katherine asked them if they had all slept well. Chatty and Lizzy Wizzy both said no without going into any details while Benjy's cheeky smile was a clear indication he had slept fine. Emma said she was sorry to hear that from the girls and could tell Benjy had slept well as he was full of beans again this morning.

As she pushed around the cereal in her bowl Chatty realised TJ was missing from the table again. "I can't believe TJ's still asleep. That's the second morning running he's missed breakfast," she said, trying to get TJ into some trouble with Auntie Emma. It was the least he deserved, Chatty thought.

"Not quite, Chatty dear," Auntie Emma replied. "TJ's gone out for the day with Grandpa Mal."

Chatty dropped her spoon in her bowl.

"What? The whole day, just the two of them?" Chatty said sounding annoyed.

"Yes dear," said Auntie Emma. "They'll be back later today. Not quite on their own, as they were picked up by Grandpa Mal's friend a short while ago. I've said it before and I'll say it again, I do love that car he drives."

Chatty couldn't have cared less about the stupid car. How dare TJ get to spend the day with Grandpa Mal all to himself.

"Well why couldn't I have gone?" Chatty asked grumpily. "I might have wanted to go."

Auntie Emma looked across at Katherine, who rolled her eyes in anticipation of another argument with Chatty.

Katherine started the explanation with some trepidation, fully expecting it to lead to yet another argument with her daughter. "Chatty darling," Katherine said, "they were going off to the nature reserve. They were going birdwatching and to observe the deer. Grandpa Mal wanted to take TJ before the stag shooting season starts. Darling, the last time we all went to the nature reserve TJ was the only one who had enjoyed it. The rest of you all complained how boring it was."

"No, I didn't, I enjoyed it," Chatty lied.

"Well I'm sorry young lady, but that's just not true. You did say it was boring. In fact, you said it was one of the most boring days of your life. You can pretend all you like but I remember it very clearly."

Chatty began to pull a face and was about to respond, but her mum continued.

"I remember it very clearly because Daddy thought you wouldn't enjoy it and blamed me for making us all go. He said it would have been better if he'd taken you and Benjy into town to do something else, and like normal we argued about it."

"You're making it up," Chatty said rudely. "I did enjoy it and so did Daddy." She knew that wasn't true and could remember the argument clearly, even though there had been so many. "If I'd have been *asked* then I would have gone," she said defiantly. "But now TJ has Grandpa Mal all to himself, *again*." She folded her arms like a spoilt child. "I wanted to go. It's not fair."

"That's enough of that young lady," Katherine said, "stop acting like a spoilt three-year old. You didn't enjoy it last time, it will be a long day and TJ after all is the eldest."

Chatty sat sulking in silence, her arms folded and her chin resting on her chest. She had looked forward for a long time to coming on holiday to the Old Girl and seeing Grandpa Mal and the others. A chance for some happy times she thought, to make up for all the miserable ones she had experienced recently.

But it wasn't proving to be a very happy time at all. In fact, it was getting worse each day. She scowled as she looked at Mum out of the top of her eyes.

It was all *her* fault. And *TJ's* as well. *It wasn't fair.*

***

A few miles from the Old Girl, TJ was enjoying himself for the first time that day. He was sat in the back of the most beautiful car he had ever seen, and they were effortlessly cruising down the country lanes. The noise from the powerful engine of the DB4 sounded like the purr of a ferociously elegant big cat but even so was only just audible over the stirring performance of Vivaldi's Gloria blaring from the car's modern entertainment system. The car's external bodywork was pristine and the internal leather immaculate; it even smelt expensive. The design of the DB4 was simply timeless and exquisite.

The day had started badly of course. TJ had been unable to go back to sleep after the encounter with the sinister hooded figure in his dream. The creature on the end of the staff threatened to torment him every time he closed his eyes. When he had gone down for breakfast Mum had offered to make him a crusty bacon roll, but he asked for porridge instead. This had confused Mum considerably, since he normally avoided porridge like the plague. TJ had said, quite truthfully, he couldn't face a crusty roll but ignored Mum's question as to whether it was because he had toothache, although it had made him flinch. Little did Mum know that the first thing TJ had done when he had woken up was feel and check all his teeth were there, first with his tongue and then his fingers just to be completely sure.

But the ride in the car and opportunity to spend more time with Grandpa Mal had allowed TJ to put the dream to the back of his mind for now. However, he would need to tell Grandpa Mal exactly what had happened at the monastic ruins once they were alone. After all, he wasn't quite sure how much Grandpa Mal's friend knew about the Brethren, if indeed he knew anything at all. Maybe he was just innocently giving Grandpa Mal a lift.

All TJ knew about Grandpa Mal's friend was that he owned the car and was a pretty good driver: fast but safe. So far, he hadn't spoken but TJ guessed from his appearance that he might be fifty-something. He was wearing an expensive looking tailored three-piece suit that matched the dark grey of the DB4, a dark grey woven silk tie and designer sunglasses. He wore fine leather driving gloves and sported a designer Swiss watch on his right wrist. His slicked back hair was now predominantly grey but used to be black. He didn't say much but TJ thought everything about him was stylish, expensive and cool.

Out of the window TJ noticed they were once again amongst the heathland. When he realised they were on the same bumpy straight road as yesterday he sincerely hoped they wouldn't be going anywhere near the monastery.

After about half a mile however, they turned right and headed deeper into the heath. The road wound its way gently through the open heathland on the edge of the forest before they made a sharp turn to the left. The resplendent purple heath was slowly replaced by the riotous greenery of ferns and trees. Quite quickly the forest thickened and before long the car was enclosed by densely packed trees as they moved slowly down a narrowing lane.

Overnight a storm had blown in and brought with it some well-needed precipitation. Although the rain had stopped just before daylight, the raindrops hung off the ferns like jewels. The temperature was much cooler than in recent days as a large blanket of grey clouds had done an effective job of smothering any morning sun.

The driver said something to Grandpa Mal who was sat in the front passenger seat which TJ didn't hear over the music and pointed to something ahead. The car slowed and then made a gentle left turn down a well-hidden track, taking them ever deeper into the forest. TJ looked behind him out of the back window. It was impossible amongst all the trees, ferns and undergrowth to see the lane they had just turned off. Wherever they were headed was certainly secluded.

The track was narrow but flat and easily navigable. The music was turned down and Grandpa Mal spoke for the first time since leaving the Old Girl. "Almost there, dear boy. You'll like this place, I'm sure."

"Where are we Grandpa Mal?" TJ asked.

"Somewhere deep in the nature reserve dear boy. There are very few people who know this place is here, which of course suits us rather well."

Ahead of them a clearing containing a small white cottage came into view. The property was surrounded by a white wooden picket fence and latched gate. Muntjac deer roamed around the clearing, as if keeping sentry. However, as the car approached the Muntjac quickly deserted their posts.

The cottage's paintwork was worse for wear and had clearly seen better days although its thatched roof was in better condition. They parked and carefully got out of the car. As TJ did so he noticed the unmistakable smell of a log fire and saw a wisp of smoke snaking from the chimney.

"The cottage and its inhabitant have been here for so long, it's been largely forgotten," Grandpa Mal said. "Come on, let's go in," he said opening the rickety gate. "Looks like the burner is already alight. No doubt the kettle is being boiled and I could do with a nice cup of tea, dear boy. Follow me."

They made their way not to the front door, but around the back. The garden was small but the borders down one side were packed full of pretty flowers, the grass had recently been cut and the edges were very neat. On the other side were some raised beds, hosting the unmistakable sight of developing sweetcorn, beetroot, onions, potatoes, carrots, radishes, lettuces and parsnips. A separate herb bed stood next to a greenhouse in the far corner. The latter was bursting with cucumbers and tomatoes.

The back door of the cottage was wide open although a multi-colour strip door blind was keeping unwanted insects out but also obstructing the view inside. Without knocking Grandpa Mal parted some of the plastic strips and entered the cottage into the kitchen. It was a small kitchen with just the bare essentials. There was a stainless-steel sink, small ancient looking cooker and a larder on the right. A small butcher's block on wheels was situated on the left where presumably food was prepared. A yellow-handled butter knife lay on a plate sat on the butcher's block amongst a pile crumbs. A small battered frying pan sat unevenly on the grid of the gas hob.

The cottage felt cold and caused TJ to shiver. His stomach also turned a bit as he breathed in a mixture of the mustiness of the old cottage, cooked kippers and a smoky log burner. As Grandpa Mal made his way through the kitchen he brushed past some metal wind chimes that were hung from the ceiling. The sudden sound took TJ by surprise and gave him even more goosebumps. Unsurprisingly he was still jumpy after last night. Behind TJ the driver closed the back door and TJ heard a key turn to lock it.

They entered the small sitting room, the sound of their footsteps accentuated by the bare wooden floorboards. The floor was very uneven, and the floorboards creaked wearily as they were disturbed. On the wall to the left a large log burner sat in the inglenook fireplace and was burning brightly. An old blackened kettle sat on top of it, waiting patiently to aggressively sound its whistle. Two old fashion wingback armchairs sat facing the fire. They were so large that TJ was unable to see from his particular vantage point by the door if anyone was sitting in them. In between them sat a side table upon which was a tray and a biscuit tin. On the tray stood four teacups each on a saucer, a large ceramic teapot and some teaspoons. None of the cups matched, while the saucers were also of different shapes, sizes and patterns.

Beyond the fireplace in the far corner a twisty staircase was hidden behind a closed door. Some of the daylight that had made its way through the forest was trickling in through the front windows, but it was dark in the other corner behind the solid wood front door. A rickety hat stand teetered next to the front door, threatening to collapse under the slightest weight onto any poor unsuspecting visitor.

In the corner diagonally opposite the front door was a large lampstand with an enormous flowery light shade decorated around the bottom edge with white tassels. It emitted a soft orangey glow, gently illuminating two old wooden chairs that stood with their backs against the wall next to the lamp. Although the chairs looked worn out, they looked inviting.

They all paused as they entered the room. As TJ took in his surroundings, he wondered who lived in the cottage and where they were currently. His curiosity was short-lived.

An old person's voice came from the direction of one of the armchairs facing the fireplace. "Welcome my dears, come and take a seat," came the invitation. TJ was caught by surprise and jumped at the welcome even though it had been perfectly polite. After all, he wasn't aware anyone was sitting there.

"Take the spare chair by the burner dear boy," encouraged Grandpa Mal. "We will sit over here," he said, motioning to the two wooden chairs for him and the driver, "after all, you are the guest of honour today."

The arm of a knitted jumper appeared at the side of the left armchair and beckoned them in. TJ obeyed and carefully made his way over, unsure as to who would be greeting him. As he approached, the chair's inhabitant spoke again. "That's it, help me up young man." The first thing TJ saw were the pink fluffy slippers, then the green crochet tights, a blue denim skirt and a thick grey knitted jumper. The owner of the eclectic mix of clothes was an old lady. Despite a full head of wavy grey hair, she looked to TJ as if she was at least a hundred years old.

Two hands were offered up. TJ took them and helped the old lady to her feet. She was as light as a feather, but then TJ realised that was because she was even smaller than his height of five feet. In fact, TJ guessed she was about the same height as Lizzy Wizzy as he could just about see over the top of her head.

"Thank you," the old lady said looking up at TJ. "You be the spitting image for sure. Quite the handsome chap, aren't you my boy?" Her strong West Country dialect meant the last two words were pronounced *moiy boiy*. TJ blushed and didn't quite know what to say. For a moment, he thought she looked very familiar to him in some way, but he couldn't quite put his finger on it.

"Bet you weren't expecting to see someone like me dear, was you?" she asked, making her way over to the log burner as she did so. Slipping on an old oven glove she took the kettle from the top of the burner and filled the teapot on the tray. After letting the pot brew for a short while she poured it into the four cups, spilling it liberally as she did so. "Oops, clumsy old me, *toide's owt*," she said, letting out a little cackle and giving TJ a friendly smile. He smiled and started to relax. She was a little eccentric to say the least, he thought, but very warm and friendly. But he still wasn't quite sure who she was or what they were here for.

After the tea had been somewhat clumsily poured, she handed a cup to Grandpa Mal, the driver and thrust one into TJ's hand. Although TJ didn't drink tea, he nonetheless took it politely. She did the same with the biscuit tin that contained homemade shortbread. This time TJ was more than happy to take one and was encouraged to take another by the old lady. He sat almost nervously on the edge of the seat, unsure as to what was about to come next.

The old lady perched on the edge of her chair too, drank her tea noisily and in one go. She placed her cup and saucer back on the table, let out a deep sigh, slumped back into her chair and closed her eyes. She remained quiet and motionless.

TJ looked nervously across at Grandpa Mal who smiled reassuringly at him. TJ put down his cup of tea quietly careful not to disturb the old lady and sat looking at her waiting for something to happen.

After an uncomfortable length of time, the old lady started to speak as she lay back with her eyes closed:

"Open the door,
Walk into the land,
Stand by the well,
Wish and count to 90,
Then the magic will begin...

You will feels yourself sinking,
You will see a cottage,
An old lady will be inside.
Tell her your fears and where you are going,
She will ask you for your dreams,
Give them to her.

Trust the red deer,
Who will take you to the river.
There could be a ferryman,
Offering to take you across the water,
But do not be fooled,
For the demon of the deep is no longer sleeping."

TJ felt uneasy and had no idea what the old lady was talking about. He went slightly cold, even as the heat from the log burner was tangible. As he felt himself start to shiver the old lady opened her eyes suddenly and quickly sat bolt upright, taking TJ by surprise yet again.

"Do you have a question for me dear?" she asked.

"Well," TJ said awkwardly, "I'm not sure I understood what you just said. I don't mean to be rude, but I'm not really sure what I'm doing here, or in fact just who you are..." His sentence trailed off. TJ was slightly embarrassed to have already said this much but knew he should stop before he was forced to admit that he also thought she was strangely peculiar.

"Well *me'ansum*," she replied with her country lilt, "I'm not quite sure myself what all that meant, but I think you understood some of it. I *'av* a feeling you'll understand more as time passes. As for what you be doing here, well your Grandpa Mal thought it best you understood a bit more about the origins of the Brethren." She smiled sweetly at him, as if it was something people spoke about all the time.

TJ looked across the room anxiously, first at the driver and then at Grandpa Mal. Had the old lady accidently given away a secret she wasn't meant to? The driver simply stared at TJ and gave nothing away whilst Grandpa Mal smiled, as if giving TJ the reassurance that this was a safe place and appropriate audience to discuss such matters.

Then the penny dropped, and TJ's mouth started to open in shock. "Are you *awright dear*?" the old lady asked, "you look a bit *betwaddled*." TJ looked at her even more curiously. "Oh, there goes me and my sayings," she continued, "I meant you look a little confused, you know, *betwaddled*.... perhaps I should have used *dawzled* instead seeing as we're around these parts..."

Over at the side of the room Grandpa Mal chuckled as he spoke. "You are priceless. I doubt TJ has ever met someone quite like you. Nor will he ever do so again in his life, of that I'm sure." TJ could tell there was no ridicule in what Grandpa Mal was saying and that he was being serious. He was right, Grandpa Mal had great respect and affection for the old lady. As for TJ himself, now that he knew who she was he was very pleased to have met her. He was even more excited about what he was about to learn from the old lady who he thought was bordering on crazy a few moments ago.

Grandpa Mal continued. "TJ, my dear boy, it is time to introduce you to someone very special. Someone, who for as long as I can remember, has fulfilled an important role within the Brethren with such passion, courage and skill. TJ, it is an honour and with great pleasure that I introduce you to the *Dreamorian*."

CHAPTER 17 – THE DREAMORIAN

A gasp slipped out of TJ's open mouth and his eyes widened further. He whispered, "the Dreamorian!" under his breath.

"Why thank you kind sir for that very grand introduction. He does like a bit of drama our Malachi, *don't he*? We'll get to everything *dreckly…* by that I mean at some point but let me tell you first about that Grandpa Mal of yours."

Grandpa Mal rolled his eyes, shook his head and looked down at his shoes in embarrassment as the Dreamorian continued. "As you know he *loikes* to be called Mal. Now that's short for Malachi, from the Hebrew meaning *'my messenger'* or *'my angel'*. I don't know how you are on your religious studies dear, but Malachi was a prophet in the Old Testament. Indeed, some claim the Book of Malachi foretold the coming of Christ the Messiah. So, we have one very important Malachi from thousands of years ago and another sat in my sitting room today."

"Yes, he's very special," TJ said, proud of his most favourite person left in the world.

"Now, I understand you had a very important question for your Grandpa Mal the other night in the Great Room," the Dreamorian said. "But as I understand it, he decided to leave it to me. *Roight?*"

TJ had suddenly been put on the spot and he was struggling to remember. After all, he had asked so many questions both to Grandpa Mal and to himself over the past couple of days. He began to feel a little silly that he couldn't remember. "I'm sure I did have an important question, but I don't remember what it was, sorry".

"Never mind dear," the old lady said reassuringly. "I was somewhat reliably informed by dear Malachi you were interested in the origins of the gift and the Dreamguardians, basically *'ow* it all started?"

TJ groaned as he remembered. "How could I have forgotten that?" he muttered, still feeling a bit stupid at his forgetfulness.

"Don't worry. I'm glad young Malachi left this to me. After all, this is my specialty. They don't call me the Dreamorian for nothing, you know." She winked at him before continuing. "Now, we need to go back in time. Not just a long time ago, but a *really* long time dear. Getting on for nearly 4,000 years ago to be a bit more precise, give or take a hundred years. And you thought I was old dear...!" She closed her eyes, sat back in her chair and cackled at her own little joke, but not in a sinister way. Her laugh made TJ giggle a little too.

She opened one eye. "Now, I'm about to start remembering, so best not interrupt. If you get bored of it all my dear, don't you just wander off and leave me at it. Just stop me and tell me you be bored. Otherwise I'll have wasted precious remembering time. Someone of my age doesn't have time to waste, especially when I still have some washing to hang out on the line." TJ couldn't work out if she was serious or still joking, but he nodded his agreement. He doubted he could ever get bored of listening to the old lady, not only because of her glorious West Country accent but because he was also never quite sure what was coming next.

"Make sure you're comfortable my dear. I'm sure you'll find it's all worth it as you discover the true origins of the Dreamguardians. Now let's go back almost four thousand years and start with Jacob, the father of the Israelites.

"Jacob was the son of Isaac, who *'imself* was the son of Abraham, who the good Lord covenanted would be the father of many nations. I think it's fair to say that Jacob *'ad* an interesting life. A life full of conflict dear. He fought with his twin brother, Esau, all his life. Even before he be born dear. In fact, Jacob's mother Rebekah had those twin boys jostling each other within her womb no less. Then young Jacob was born hanging on to his older brother Esau's heel. When they were older, Jacob even sold food to a starved Esau in exchange for his birthright. If you don't believe me on any of this, you can look it up in Genesis 25. It's all in there. You see, everything I tell you is God's honest truth dear.

"Now it didn't stop there either. Jacob even stole his older brother's blessing. You see old Isaac loved Esau more because he loved a bit of game to eat and Esau was a skilful *'unter.* But their mother Rebekah loved Jacob more. So, with her *'elp,* Jacob tricked his old father Isaac when he was old and his eyes weak into blessing *'im* rather than Esau. That's quite a story in Genesis 27. Jacob put on goatskins to trick old Jacob into thinking he was Esau to the touch as his older brother was really *'airy.* As a result, Isaac blessed Jacob. Said nations would serve Jacob and people bow down to him. He even said

Jacob would be the lord over his brothers and anyone who cursed him would be cursed *'imself*.

Our Jacob was an interesting character dear. In fact, he wasn't just *'appy* fighting his older twin Esau, Jacob even wrestled with God no less. All night too. Dear me. Wouldn't let him go until the Lord blessed him. And he did so *awright*. Even renamed him Israel because he struggled with both God and man and overcame. You must take some time to read that too dear. Genesis 32. Very entertaining I must say dear."

TJ made another mental note to himself that he needed to remember and read all these stories, but he felt he was already beginning to forget them all. He started to wonder where the Dreamorian was going with all these stories and how they were relevant.

"So, what's this all about then?" the Dreamorian continued, as if sensing the onset of TJ's confusion. "Well, I'm getting there *dreckly* dear. Needless to say, when Esau found out Jacob had stolen his blessing, he weren't best pleased. Held a grudge, surprise, surprise. Said *'e'd* kill Jacob. But Rebekah found out and warned Jacob. Sent him off to his Uncle's in a place called Harran to stay with him until Esau had calmed down. Well on his way to Harran, Jacob stopped for the night at a place he named Bethel. He took a stone for a pillow and lay down to sleep. Then he had a dream. This is *'ow* it's written dear in Genesis 28, word for word:

" *'He had a dream in which he saw a stairway resting on the earth, with its top reaching to heaven, and the angels of God were ascending and descending on it. There above it stood the Lord, and he said: "I am the Lord, the God of your father Abraham and the God of Isaac. I will give you and your descendants the land on which you are lying. Your descendants will be like the dust of the earth, and you will spread out to the west and to the east, to the north and to the south. All peoples on earth will be blessed through you and your offspring. I am with you and will watch over you wherever you go, and I will bring you back to this land. I will not leave you until I have done what I have promised you.'* "

As the Dreamorian paused, TJ's mind started racing. He recognised the description of Jacob's dream, but how? He'd never heard that particular story before. Then his heart started to race as he suddenly realised why the story was familiar. It was one of the prominent panels on the ceiling in the Great Room.

Before he could process anything further the Dreamorian spoke again.

"See how good at remembering I am dear. I don't need that dusty old Bible in the Inner Sanctum for all this. It's all up *'ere*," she said tapping the side of her head with a knobbly ancient finger, her eyes still firmly shut tight.

TJ's heart beat even faster at the mention of the Inner Sanctum. Not that he was surprised that she knew it existed. After all she seemed to know everything. But he was excited by yet another discovery. They were suddenly starting to come quite quickly. The revelation of the identity of one of the other two books in the Inner Sanctum alongside the Great Book.

"So that my dear, is the first documented evidence of the gift working through the bloodline. Not proper Dreamguardian 'stuff' at this stage, granted, 'cause it had yet to be fully developed back then. So, we must plod on. But we don't have to go far, just on a few more chapters in that big old Bible.

"Jacob went on to have twelve sons, he did. But we need only concentrate properly on his eleventh son, Joseph. You see back in those times dear, the 'usband he could 'av more than one woife, although to be fair Jacob did get tricked into marrying the first one by his father-in-law, no less. I guess some might say it serves him roight in a way, given what he did to Esau. But anyways, even though he was the eleventh son, Joseph was Jacob's first son with Rachel. Now Jacob really loved Rachel. I mean he'd even committed to work for fourteen years in return for Rachel's 'and in marriage. That's a long time to wait. Even older than you dear! And as he'd been born to Jacob in his old age, Jacob loved Joseph more than his other sons.

"You might already be familiar with our Joseph, dear, but I'm on a roll now, so give me 'ere a few more minutes." She was right in a way. TJ was vaguely familiar with Joseph in the book of Genesis. He remembered Lizzy Wizzy had watched some musical of that name on the television once. But he'd refused to watch it. He'd gone off and done something else instead, that at the time he thought was much more interesting. Right now, he wished he'd paid a bit more attention, so he would be one step ahead of the Dreamorian. But he hadn't, so he deepened his concentration.

The Dreamorian continued. "Now Joseph was a fine man if ever I saw one. Even that Bible say he was well-built and handsum. As Joseph was Jacob's favourite, all his brothers 'ated him. Couldn't even speak a kind word to 'im. Then to make matters worse, Joseph told them about a dream 'e'd 'ad and they 'ated him even more. Listen to this bit dear. Genesis 37 if I'm not mistaken:

" 'Joseph had a dream, and when he told it to his brothers, they hated him all the more. He said to them, "Listen to this dream I had: We were binding sheaves of grain out in the field when suddenly my sheaf rose and stood upright, while your sheaves gathered around mine and bowed down to it." His brothers said to him, "Do you intend to reign over us? Will you actually rule us?" And they hated him all the more because of his dream and what he had said. Then he had another *dream, and he told it to his brothers. "Listen," he said, "I had another dream, and this time the sun and moon and eleven stars were bowing down to me." '*

In a flash, in his mind's eye TJ was back in the Great Room. Up on the ceiling. The second panel. A young man asleep in a farmer's field; a wheat sheaf standing proudly as all the others around it were bowed down; above, the sun, moon and eleven stars were also bowing down. The sleeping young man was Joseph!

The Dreamorian continued. "So, don't be surprised when *I's* say *'is* brothers were *proper* jealous of him. Even the more so *'cause* Jacob had made a nice coat for him. A robe of many colours no less. Now it did its job that robe did. Not only did it make it clear to *everyone* that Joseph was the favourite, but it *also* sent those brothers of *'is* more than crazy. They *'ated* the poor lad so much they plotted to kill *'im* no less."

TJ was struggling to keep up. An ornate robe? Hang on a minute, he thought to himself, there was an ancient robe mounted in a glass frame in the Inner Sanctum. TJ had thought that night he could make out different colours on it too, as well as streaks of pale crimson smeared across parts of it too. He remembered it was tattered in places too.

"Thankfully one of *'is* brothers changed all of their minds. Took Joseph's coat from *'im* and ripped it. Sold poor Joseph for twenty shekels of silver to some merchants who came by in a caravan. Well I never dear.

"Those brothers, the bunch of *aapaths,* slaughtered some poor passing old goat then dipped our Joseph's lovely robe in the blood. Did a *roight proper job* of it they did. Then they took it back to poor old Jacob dear. *Ee* thought some ferocious animal *'ad* took our Joseph for its tea. Thought he were dead no less. Instead, Joseph *'ad* been taken to Egypt and sold to Potipher, the captain of the guard for Pharaoh.

TJ sat stunned. Surely not, he thought to himself. He'd have to check with Grandpa Mal or the Dreamorian once she'd finished. But it sounded like it. Surely not though! Was that ancient robe on the wall in the Inner Sanctum really Joseph's prized coat?

The Dreamorian interrupted TJ's thoughts as she continued her story. "Joseph did very well for Potipher because the dear Lord was with Joseph and gave *'im* success in everything he did. Potipher put him in charge of *'is* household and everything he owned. So, he was doing a good job was our Joseph.

"The next bit's a bit unsuitable for you to go into any detail dear. Potipher's *woife* found him quite *handsum* shall we say. Then accused him of all sorts and had poor Joseph thrown into prison when he said, 'no thank you madam'. Well I never dear, what an *'ussy* that woman was.

"But this is where it gets really interesting dear. You see Joseph was one of us dear, much like *'is* father was too. But he was a very *special* one of us. In prison, Joseph met Pharaoh's chief cupbearer and chief baker. They both *'ad* a dream the same night, each with its own meaning and were sad because they thought there was no one to interpret it.

"But Joseph did. And they came true. That's why he was a very special one. It was good news for the cupbearer but bad news for the baker dear. Look up Genesis 40 in more detail when you get back to the Inner Sanctum dear. Then Pharaoh had two dreams but no one to interpret them. But the cupbearer remembered Joseph was still in prison *'cause 'ed* forgotten to get *'im* out earlier. So, Joseph was got out and said to Pharaoh that God would give Pharaoh the answer to *'is* dreams. Then he did: seven years of plenty followed by seven years of famine.

"Old Pharaoh was so grateful that our Joseph was put in charge of the whole of Egypt. He stockpiled all of Egypt's food in their abundant years. So much grain that it was beyond measure. Then the famine came, just as Joseph had said, but in Egypt there was food. As the famine was so bad, they came from far and wide to buy grain from Joseph, both from within and beyond Egypt.

"Now of course Jacob sent his sons to Egypt to buy grain from Joseph, but they didn't recognise *'im*, even though he remembered them *awright*. They did indeed bow before *'im*, before he put them to the test. You see he made them bring his youngest brother Benjamin back to Egypt to see him, then hid a silver cup in his sack.

"When it was discovered, Joseph threatened to throw the young lad into prison. But after one of his older brothers offered to switch places with Benjamin, Joseph knew his brothers were sorry *awright*. So, he revealed himself to his brothers and they were all reunited, including Joseph with Jacob. It's an important and touching story for sure dear, but that's not all we need to explain the Brethren."

TJ shuffled a little impatiently in his chair. He didn't mean to, but he was anxious to fully understand everything. Why had the Dreamorian spent so much time telling the story of Joseph being reunited with his family if that wasn't the full explanation? He secretly wished she would hurry up.

"*Ullonaminit…*" the Dreamorian said suddenly, still with her eyes closed. "I means, holds on just a moment dear. *I's* gets the feeling you be getting a bit impatient my dear. Don't worry my dear, we be getting there soon enough."

TJ blushed. She really did know everything that was going on, both around her and within her head.

"Now we need to go back to the story before famine came. You see Pharaoh was so grateful to Joseph for his dream interpretation 'e gave him Asenath daughter of Potiphera, priest of On, to be 'is woife. Then before famine came, Joseph and Asenath had a son and named him Ephraim. It is through dear Ephraim that the one true bloodline runs. And it is Ephraim that explains the existence of the Dreamguardians and origins of the Brethren."

With that, the Dreamorian fell silent...

TJ sat waiting. He looked at the Dreamorian, expecting something to happen, then shot a worried glance over to Grandpa Mal. He held his hands up and mouthed, "wait, dear boy".

The Dreamorian sat motionless, still slouched back in the large armchair. Not even her green crocheted tights or pink fluffy slippers, already struggling to touch the floor, moved.

TJ took the opportunity to think. Surely the Dreamorian wasn't finished already? He'd made some exciting discoveries, for sure. For instance, he had now discovered that the gift was first recorded in the Old Testament, with Jacob's dream in the book of Genesis. Jacob's beloved son Joseph was a 'special one' according to the Dreamorian, but the existence, origins and bloodline of the Brethren of the Dreamguardians was established through Ephraim. Wait, TJ thought to himself, of course this can't be it. What about the Dreamstealers? Who or what are they and where did they come from?

The Dreamorian sat bolt upright again. Her sudden movement made TJ jump. She turned her head in TJ's direction and opened a beady right eye.

"Why you be thinking about *them*?" she asked him both sharply and accusingly, sounding a little upset as well as cross. "You be thinking about them just now, ain't you?" TJ nodded nervously. The Dreamorian sighed. "Why do we always end up having to talk about them?" she muttered with an air of resignation. Slowly she sat back in her chair and shuffled about to get comfortable. Her right eye closed again so it matched her left.

"So dear, we've come to the bit we can avoid no longer," the Dreamorian continued, her country accent drawing out the last word. "The reason for all this conflict and 'eartache."

Still with her eyes closed she summoned Grandpa Mal. "'Ere, Mal my lovely, give the young man my special book so he can follow. It's important he understands what I's about to tell."

Grandpa Mal obliged. He rose steadily from his chair and walked over to the inglenook. Ducking under the huge wooden lintel he carefully moved into the fireplace, careful not to touch the burner. From within the fireplace TJ heard some bricks being moved. When he emerged, he was carrying a small thin black book, its leather cover still in good condition. Grandpa Mal gave it a little shake and the small particles of brick dust rained down like fine confetti onto the hearth. He proceeded to give the book to TJ.

"So dear," said the Dreamorian, "here's my special little book for you to follow. Just remember, it's not the version you can read today. This is the *original* account of Genesis, before we managed to remove all the parts that would have revealed all our secrets to the world."

She took a deep breath. "The story *I's* about to tells you, is a mixture of many things. We can certainly celebrate the anointing of the bloodline through which the gift can be passed through the generations. But at the same time, we can but mourn for the darkness and bitterness that resulted from this very *'appening.*" She paused as if doing just that, before continuing.

"So, my dear, this is the true story of *'ow* and *why* the Dreamguardians and the Brethren came into being. But best not forget that just as much as it does that, it also confirms the foundation of our greatest enemy and source of danger." She shook her head from side to side slowly. "Brace yourself dear for the true story behind the establishment of the *Terror of the Dreamstealers...*"

CHAPTER 18 – 'THE BEGINNING'

H e shivered as the Dreamorian uttered those four words.

TJ knew mention of the Dreamstealers had to come, since the very purpose of a Dreamguardian and establishment of the Brethren was to protect dreams from 'them'. But he still didn't like hearing the name or even having to think about them, especially after his intense encounter with one just a few hours ago. Furthermore, while the mere mention of the Dreamstealers was bad enough, the Dreamorian's reference to the word 'terror' escalated its threat and menace. It suggested the antithesis of the Brethren; a large, structured and organised body of darkness that he hadn't fully comprehended, or even cared to contemplate, up until now.

The Dreamorian interrupted his thoughts, which was just as well since they were threatening to overwhelm him. "I must apologise to you dear because I didn't tell you all the story just then, which was wrong of me. But since you're a clever young chap, I'm guessing you sensed that and that's why you thought *'bout* 'them'."

TJ seized the opportunity and dared to speak for what seemed like the first time in ages. His mouth was dry, and his voice cracked at the start of his sentence, but he coughed it away.

"Sorry to interrupt," he said, "but am I right in thinking that the Dreamstealers are in some way connected to the way Jacob treated his brother?"

The Dreamorian raised her eyebrows, pulled the sides of her mouth down in a somewhat thoughtful pose and bobbed her head from side to side as if contemplating whether he was right or not.

"Nice try dear," the Dreamorian replied kindly, "but no. In actual fact, Esau found it in his *'eart* to forgive his brother Jacob. When eventually they met again, Esau threw his arms around Jacob's neck. Not to strangle him though, but to kiss him. Even though Jacob thought he needed a peace offering and gave *'im* a load of goats, ewes, rams, camels, cows, bulls, donkeys, you name it, Esau didn't care *'bout* all that. He'd already *forgave* him. In fact, when the sad time came, Jacob and Esau, the pair of 'em, together, buried their father Isaac when he died at the ripe old age of a hundred and eighty years. And you thought *I's* old dear!"

She cackled another laugh, but Isaac's age and the Dreamorian's quip concerning it was completely lost on TJ. He felt a bit crestfallen as he thought he'd been one step ahead of her. The Dreamorian wasn't in the slightest bit concerned about either the interruption or the wrong guess and she carried on regardless.

"When I said that Joseph and Asenath had a son, Ephraim, that was quite the truth *awright*. But what I didn't mention was that he was the youngest of two sons. You see, Joseph and Asenath already *'ad* another son. An older brother to Ephraim." The Dreamorian paused as if she was deep in thought. "Look it up in my special book dear. It is the only original text translation in existence. The original manuscript is safely stored within the Inner Sanctum of course, since the two must never be kept together. Just in case. I forget the exact page number but look up chapter 41 in the original text of the very first book of Genesis that you are *'olding* there. Look and read what it says to me dear in verses 50 to 52."

With shaking hands, TJ held up the thin old book. It was not much bigger than the size of his hand. Its pages had been gilded with gold leaf which still gave it the look of an expensive item. But TJ guessed its real value lay in its contents.

He delicately opened the book to its title page and read the small neatly printed text carefully:

To the most high and mighty
DREAMGUARDIANS
By the grace of the Gift

The one true account
Of the origins of the Brethren

Translated out of the original tongue

May grace, mercy and peace
from the Brethren
and the all-powerful protection

of the Dreamswick
be upon the

Defenders of the
safe passage of dreams

Amen

TJ's pupils dilated as he digested what was within this book, although even then he had yet to fully appreciate its history and significance.

With trembling fingers, he carefully turned the page.

On the page were two columns of small typed text and either side of those a small margin that contained notes and references. The title that lay across the top of the page read:

THE FIRST BOOK OF MOSES

CALLED

GENESIS

TJ read on. The start of it was exactly as he'd remembered it from his Sunday School days:

" 'CHAPTER 1

IN the beginning God created the heavens and the earth.' "

Thereafter, it looked to TJ to be no different to any other account of Genesis in any ordinary Bible he'd ever seen. He continued carefully turning the pages and felt some panic start to rise as he fumbled to find the precise location the old lady had requested.

"Don't you *frettle* dear, no need to rush," the Dreamorian said reassuringly, her eyes still shut but acutely aware of everything that was going on around her.

TJ turned page after page, before he arrived at Chapter 41. He scanned down the page and, with as steady a voice as he could manage, he read aloud carefully the small font:

" '*50 And to Joseph were born two sons before the years of famine came, whom Asenath, the daughter of Potiphera priest of On, bore to him. 51 Joseph called the name of the firstborn Manasseh:[II] "For God has made me forget all my toil and all my father's house." 52 And the name of the second he called Ephraim:[II] "For God has caused me to be fruitful in the land of my affliction.' "*

The Dreamorian helped him with the names as he struggled with them but praised him nonetheless for his efforts.

"So, our Joseph had two fine boys, Manasseh and Ephraim. You notice those reference marks dear? What does it say in the margin of Chapter 41 next to Manasseh?" the Dreamorian asked. TJ looked carefully and responded.

" '[II] That is, Forgetting' "

"That's right, *forgetting*. Now what does it say in the margin next to Ephraim, dear?" she asked.

" '[II] That is, Fruitful' "

"Very good, yes, fruitful. Now, *'olds* those thoughts dear. We be moving on."

With that, she shuffled in her chair again and her pink slippers danced on the end of her feet as she gave her legs a bit of a shake. "Me circulation be playing me up again," she said, "but I can't complain at my age. After all, I'll be a long-time dead." She cackled a laugh again which TJ barely noticed as he tried to put together all the pieces of the puzzle that were slowly being laid out before him.

"*Awright*, the time has come young man to finish our story," the Dreamorian said, firmly grabbing TJ's attention. "After Jacob had reached the ripe old age of one hundred and forty-seven, the time drew near for him to die. Joseph was called to see *'im* and he took his two sons with him, Manasseh and Ephraim. As he sat up in his bed, Jacob made them both heirs of the house of Israel, as if they were his own sons. Then it *'appened*. Read it for me dear as it's quite long. But read it carefully and understand its significance. So, Chapter 48, from verse 8 onwards my dear. TJ began reading again:

" '8 Then Israel saw Joseph's sons, and said, "Who are these?"

9 And Joseph said to his father, "They are my sons, whom God has given me in this place." And he said, "Please bring them to me, and I will bless them."

10 Now the eyes of Israel were dim with age, so that he could not see. Then Joseph brought them near him, and he kissed them and embraced them. 11 And Israel said to Joseph, "I had not thought to see your face; but in fact, God has also shown me your offspring!"

12 So Joseph brought them from beside his knees, and he bowed down with his face to the earth. 13 And Joseph took them both, Ephraim with his right hand toward Israel's left hand, and Manasseh with his left hand toward Israel's right hand, and brought them near him.

14 Then Israel stretched out his right hand and laid it on Ephraim's head, who was the younger, and his left hand on Manasseh's head, guiding his hands knowingly, for Manasseh was the firstborn. 15 And he blessed Joseph, and said:

"God, before whom my fathers Abraham and Isaac walked,
The God who has fed me all my life long to this day,

16 The Angel who has redeemed me from all evil,
Bless the lads;
Let my name be named upon them,
And the name of my fathers Abraham and Isaac;
And let them grow into a multitude in the midst of the earth.' "

Suddenly, the Dreamorian opened both her eyes and sat bolt upright. She stared intensely at TJ, slightly unnerving him. "This is it," she said, "read it slowly and understand it fully."

TJ nodded, composed himself and continued reading:

" ' 17 Now when Joseph saw that his father laid his right hand on the head of Ephraim, it displeased him; so he took hold of his father's hand to remove it from Ephraim's head to Manasseh's head. 18 And Joseph said to his father, "Not so, my father, for this one is the firstborn; put your right hand on his head."

19 But his father refused and said, "I know, my son, I know. He also shall become a people, and he also shall be great; but truly his younger brother shall be greater than he, and his descendants shall become a multitude of nations."

20 So he blessed them that day, saying, "By you Israel will bless, saying, 'May God make you as Ephraim and as Manasseh!'" And thus he set Ephraim before Manasseh.

21 Then Israel said to Joseph, "Behold, I am dying, but God will be with you and bring you back to the land of your fathers. 22 Moreover I have given to you one portion above your brothers, which I took from the hand of the Amorite with my sword and my bow.' "

"Stop there," the Dreamorian demanded. TJ did as he was told and looked wide-eyed over at her and then to Grandpa Mal who looked quite serious. TJ could feel his hands, upon which the book rested, start to shake. The Dreamorian continued to stare at him before she asked him if he'd understood what he'd just read.

TJ spoke quietly and deliberately, careful not to make any mistakes as he shared his understanding with the Dreamorian. "So even though Jacob, or Israel as he had been renamed by then, blessed them both, he chose to lay his right hand on Ephraim, even though Manasseh was the firstborn. In doing so he set Ephraim, the younger brother, before his older brother Manasseh. And he declared that Ephraim would be greater than Manasseh." He blew out his cheeks. "That must have been hard for Manasseh to accept."

"Right you are, dear," replied the Dreamorian. "Now, stay switched on dear. If you were to read any other Bible in all the world, no matter what language, the next you 'ear 'bout Ephraim and Manasseh is at the very end of Chapter 50, where the book of Genesis as the world knows it ends. All it says is that Joseph lived one hundred and ten years and that he saw Ephraim's children through to the third generation and also the children of Machir, who was the son of Manasseh. Notice my dear that none of Ephraim's children are named. This was deliberately done of course, to make it harder for 'them' to trace the genealogy.

"Now, what you 'av there in front of you in my book is the original text in Genesis of what 'appened after Israel's blessing of Ephraim over Manasseh. What *really 'appened*. What you 'av there in front of you is the text the Brethren successfully removed from the version of Genesis everyone knows today.

"You see my dear, the original book of Genesis didn't have Chapter 48 stopping at verse 22. There was much more. Furthermore, the original book of Genesis didn't just 'av 50 Chapters like it does now, but it had 52. The two at the end had to go missing of course to protect the Brethren. As a result, six verses, as simple as they could be, were added to the end of Chapter 50 just to finish it off. So, you see my dear the original Chapters 51 and 52 can only be found in one of two places. That book there that you have in your 'ands and the original language version within the Inner Sanctum."

The Dreamorian smiled. "It would all be quite exciting, apart from the seriousness of why the end of Chapter 48 and those two Chapters had to be removed. Take another look at Chapter 48 dear and read what really happened after verse 22. As you do so, enjoy the knowledge and privilege that you be one of very few people throughout 'istory to have read what really 'appened."

TJ's hands shook even more, and he felt the blood pulsating in his temples. It all seemed quite extraordinary. He felt both the weight and excitement at the prospect of reading something so few had done so before. TJ took a deep breath and read the verses that as far as the rest of the world was concerned didn't exist:

23 As Israel weakened and lay back down in his bed, Joseph and his sons departed. 24 But a great divide had opened between Ephraim and Manasseh, and the firstborn protested vigorously as he left.

25 "He has stolen my portion," Manasseh argued, but Joseph declined to listen.

26 Now to each son the gift had been passed from Joseph, just as it had to him from Jacob before.

27 That night, Manasseh raged as he lay his head down to sleep, 28 vowing to avenge the blessing he believed stolen from him by his younger brother.

29 As Manasseh's heart was twisted by bitterness and mind consumed with vengeful thoughts, the gift came. 30 Then he was within a dream, and behold, a stairway was set up on the earth, and its top reached to heaven; and there the angels of God were ascending and descending on it.

31 At the bottom stood Jacob, who spoke to Joseph and Ephraim, saying "this is the stairway that I saw toward Harran, at the place I named Bethel.

32 The Lord stood above it and said to me: 'The land on which you lie I will give to you and your descendants. 33 Also your descendants shall be as the dust of the earth; you shall spread abroad to the west and the east, to the north and the south; and in you and in your seed all the families of the earth shall be blessed.' 34 This is none other than the gate of heaven and from where the gift comes."

35 Then Jacob issued a warning to Ephraim and said to him: "You must beware, for Manasseh and his offspring will come to corrupt and destroy the gift. 36 They will seek to take captives and overturn the blessing bestowed upon you and your descendants that you all shall be greater than Manasseh and his lineage."

37 As Jacob spoke a new stairway appeared, and its bottom reached down into hell; and there, angels of darkness were ascending and descending on it. 38 They carried cages of trapped figures of light down the steps, tormenting, taunting, clawing and gnashing their teeth at the captured figures as they went.

39 Jacob was disturbed as he slept. "What is this? Who is there?" he cried out in his dream, but Manasseh did not answer from the shadows. 40 When Jacob awoke from his sleep he remembered nothing.

41 From that day on, Manasseh refused to accept the loss of the firstborn blessing. 42 As time passed it caused his heart to wither; his good fruit shriveled and died just as the grapes in winter.

43 Now Ephraim embraced his blessing daily and was continually renewed. 44 And he became greater with the passing of each day.

45 Just as Ephraim had been named, great fruitfulness through the gift was destined and strengthened by his blessing. 46 But Manasseh, considering both himself and the earth cursed, took it upon himself to corrupt the gift.

47 So it was that just as Ephraim pressed into his righteous inheritance, Manasseh embraced jealousy and bitterness and mourned the loss of his. 48 Consumed by a pursuit of vengeance, Manasseh made an unholy covenant with the Serpent. 49 He and his descendants would never serve his younger brother and his undeserving bloodline, 50 nor the Lord from whom the gift was bestowed.

51 Manasseh vowed he would rise from beneath his younger brother and rule over him, even if it meant the destruction of his brother's line.

52 Manasseh covenanted with the Serpent he would not rest until the goodness from the fruit of the gift had rotted, 53 or the gift itself was forgotten, just as he had been named.

54 From this moment a great darkness came, which the light would have to overcome. 55 The gift, bestowed from on high, had split and its purity gone.

56 Now two houses were birthed and carefully nurtured down divergent paths. One would defend its rightful inheritance and seek to protect the purity of the gift. The second would grow darker in its obsession to corrupt, steal or destroy the other. And with it the gift.

57 A great darkness had descended upon the earth and the great battle had begun.

The hairs on the back of TJ's neck and arms were still raised and he started to tremble at what he had just read, despite the safety and warmth within the room. Sensing his discomfort, the Dreamorian levered herself up from her chair and clumsily poured another cup of tea for her and TJ.

"Don't know about you, but I'm *chacking* for another cuppa after all that dear!" she exclaimed cheerily, as if nothing had happened. As she shakily handed TJ his cup and saucer, she took the book from him and placed it on the table. "You know I think that's enough for now dear," she said. TJ wasn't sure if he felt disappointed or relieved. He felt he had looked straight into the eyes of Manasseh across history and it unsettled him more than he cared to admit.

The Dreamorian continued. "I think you've got the idea where all that was *goin'*. I *'av* to be honest and say that the two missing Chapters get quite dark and oppressive at times. I don't think it's good for someone so young and inexperienced to be exposed to that, not without having your proper instruction from *'im* over there." For some reason she nodded in the direction of the Driver. "So *I's* think it's best if *we's* leave it there for another time dear."

Although uneasy about what was yet to come, TJ felt like protesting and asking the Dreamorian to carry on. After all, he was eleven years old and not completely afraid. However, out of the corner of his eye he noticed the Driver staring at him and immediately thought better of arguing with the Dreamorian.

Instead, Grandpa Mal intervened. "So, there you have it dear boy," he said from the edge of the room. "And straight from the Dreamorian herself no less. Thank you my dear," he said to the old lady who smiled back at Mal.

"No matter how many times I hear about the beginning," Grandpa Mal continued, "I still have so many conflicting emotions. Gratitude and thanksgiving of course for the beauty of the gift bestowed upon us through Ephraim and his descendants, of which we can count ourselves. We can be thankful that we have the weight of history and destiny on our side, dear boy, as we seek to live out our calling that originated with Ephraim. After all, we should never forget that his name in Hebrew meant *double fruitfulness*.

"But at the same time there is such intense sadness and sorrow for Manasseh's bitterness, which persists and seems to intensify with each passing generation. It should come as no surprise that since the gift split with Manasseh, whose name in Hebrew meant *causing to forget*, he and his bloodline have never relented in their attempts to destroy the gift as it was first given. Manasseh passed down his bitterness and the corrupted gift to his son Machir, and so it continued. As the Dreamstealers gained proficiency in corrupting and perverting the gift, the *Terror of the Dreamstealers* was established to ensure its reach extended and was manifest through the generations.

"It was this threat and corruption of the pure gift that caused the Brethren to rise to defend the safe passage of dreams. Thanks to the righteous power of the established Brethren, the Dreamguardians have, so far, been able to remain greater than the Dreamstealers. But I use 'so far', deliberately dear boy. As I have said to you before, it is getting harder and the current threat is quite honestly the greatest the Brethren have known for many generations."

Grandpa Mal shook his head slowly.

"So, consider yourself enlightened my dear boy. The story of the younger brother Ephraim, who became greater than his older brother Manasseh. The wonder of how and why the first Dreamguardian, Ephraim, ruled over the first Dreamstealer, Manasseh. We still owe our gratitude to our founder of the house of the *Brethren of the Dreamguardians*, that still rules to this day over the house of the *Terror of the Dreamstealers*."

TJ saw a tear roll down Grandpa Mal's cheek as he finished. But the moment was broken by the sound of a strong and commanding French accent.

"*Oui Monsieur*, we rule for now," the Driver said as he stood, pulling his leather driving gloves back on. "But we must make sure this continues. My apologies *Madame* Dreamorian, but it is time for the talking to stop and for the action to start, you know?"

The Driver looked questioningly at Grandpa Mal who nodded, and then sternly at TJ. "*D'accord*," he continued, "it is now time for my turn with *le petit garçon*." As he moved towards the Dreamorian his face surprisingly softened and he smiled gently as he reached her chair. "*Merci beaucoup madame, enchanté*," the Driver said, bending down to kiss her gently on both cheeks.

"Such a charmer when you want to be my dear. You should try it more often," the Dreamorian replied, quickly followed by a bout of cackled laughter. The Driver held out his hands and helped the old lady up out of her chair.

The smile disappeared quickly from his face as he turned towards TJ. "*Allez!*" came the order, but TJ failed to understand its meaning and significance. "But...," TJ spluttered, "...I need to tell the Dreamorian about..."

"*Non!* No more talking! *Allez!*" came the sharp reply. "We go. Now!"

Reluctantly, TJ stood, but he didn't want to leave without learning more from the Dreamorian. He guessed all the secrets of the Brethren over the centuries, or even millennia, were all safely tucked away inside her head, ready to be unlocked by a cup of tea and a friendly chat by the fireside.

TJ looked despairingly across at Grandpa Mal who remained seated. "Grandpa Mal?" TJ asked hopefully, "I have something I need to ask the Dreamorian." Turning to the Driver TJ plucked up the courage to ask him a question directly. "Please *Monsieur*, may I ask one question of the Dreamorian before we leave?"

The Driver threw up his hands, muttered something under his breath and turned to Grandpa Mal as if to ask him to decide.

"I know you are keen to commence," said Grandpa Mal to the Driver, "but we have time to hear young TJ's question to the Dreamorian. This seems only fair since we have made a special effort to come and allow TJ to understand more about the Brethren."

The Driver thought better of protesting and simply shrugged his shoulders. "*Mais oui, Monsieur*," he said in resignation. "I guess we stay a little longer." He bowed to the Dreamorian as if to apologise to her and then shot a glance at TJ, before he made his way back to his chair. TJ was sure it was a scowl. He felt bad that he had upset the Driver and hoped it wouldn't cause any problems in the future.

"So, what it is you want to ask me then dear?" the Dreamorian asked TJ. "What was it that you didn't understand just now?"

TJ took a deep breath and steadied himself. "Well, I don't think I misunderstood anything just now, so I would say it's a related question really. You see, I had a dream last night. I'm not sure if it was a Scarer, more like a Nightfright or even a Horror maybe. All I know is that there was someone or *something* in it that was frightening, that was bad…" He paused. "Something that was evil."

The room was silent as the Dreamorian, Grandpa Mal and the Driver stared intensely at TJ, hanging on his every word.

TJ continued. "Whatever it was, it spoke to me. It asked me whether I had been told about it yet. Then it said I needed to give you a message. It said deliver a message to the old man, to the old lady - which I now know means you - and the other Elders of the Brethren."

The Dreamorian slowly covered her mouth with her feeble hand and it started to shake. "Oh, dear me, no," she said shakily.

"What was the message, TJ?" Grandpa Mal asked quickly with such urgency and panic in his voice that it began to frighten TJ.

As TJ closed his eyes to remember, the vision of the dream was there, so he opened them again. "Whatever this thing was, it said there was no one to challenge it, or defeat it. It ordered me to tell you there is nothing the Brethren can do to stop it and its army. It said it was gaining power and the Dreamstealers are rising. Grandpa Mal, it said we will never win."

"What did this *thing* look like TJ?" Grandpa Mal asked immediately. "Think carefully, this is very important".

However, TJ didn't have to think very long. It was firmly etched in his memory.

"It towered over me Grandpa Mal and was dressed in a black robe with what looked like a cape at its front and back. I couldn't see its face as it was wearing a hood, but I thought I saw two blazing red eyes from deep within it."

Slowly but surely the Dreamorian began to make a noise. It started quietly. A small moan before it started to get louder and turned into a wail.

The Driver fired a question at TJ over the wailing noise building from the Dreamorian. "Anything else *petit garçon*? Was it carrying anything? Think!

This is *très, très importante.*"

TJ could sense the agitation. "Yes, it was carrying a staff with a demonic creature carved at one end. It was crouched down and had long-pointed ears and teeth. It almost looked alive and seemed to dance menacingly when the staff was twirled."

"*Mon dieu. Non!*" exclaimed the Driver.

The Dreamorian's wail turned into a blood curdling scream. Without warning she collapsed back in her chair, motionless.

CHAPTER 19 – PROPHECIES

G randpa Mal jumped up from his chair as quickly as his aged body allowed to tend to the Dreamorian. He bent over her to see if she was still breathing and felt for a pulse on her left wrist.

"Grandpa Mal, is she dead?" TJ asked nervously, rooted to the spot. He'd never seen a dead person before and didn't want this to be his first. Especially as it would have been the shock of his revelation that had caused it.

"No, she's alive, dear boy, she's breathing," Grandpa Mal replied.

"No thanks to you, *petit garçon*," the Driver said as he left the room to make his way into the kitchen. He returned a few moments later with a glass of water for the Dreamorian.

"That's enough," said Grandpa Mal. "It's not young TJ's fault. I think she must have just fainted from the fright." The Driver returned to his seat, sat down and folded his arms. His time would come.

TJ heaved a sigh of relief, firstly that he hadn't unwittingly frightened the Dreamorian to death and secondly that Grandpa Mal wasn't blaming him.

"However," Grandpa Mal continued, "we will come back to what you were saying TJ very shortly, once we have the Dreamorian back with us. Needless to say, it is very important. In fact, I'm surprised you didn't say something sooner dear boy."

TJ felt stung by Grandpa Mal's comment and he offered a sheepish apology.

At that moment, the Dreamorian's eyelids flickered and she opened them up.

"Well, I never," she said. "What's all gone on 'ere? What be the matter Malachi?"

Grandpa Mal broke into a smile that spoke of relief rather than happiness. "Nothing my dear, we just lost you for a few moments. Do you remember?"

The Dreamorian looked a bit puzzled and thought for a moment, before her face turned unusually serious. "Ah yes, *I's* remembered now. The poor dear and his dream."

"I think I'd better sit down again," Grandpa Mal said as he picked up his chair and positioned it to the side of the burner just in front of the Dreamorian's. He wanted to give her support as well as keep an eye on her, just in case it all got too much for her again.

"I'm sorry," TJ said, suddenly bursting into tears, "I didn't mean to do that to you, I just wanted to tell you about the dream. It was horrible." After he had composed himself, he then filled them in on the end of the dream with his crumbling teeth and how it was all so real that the first thing he did when he woke this morning was to check all his teeth were still there.

"There, there *me'ansum*, no need to cry. I'm a tough *ol'* bird. I was just a bit shocked that's all. But it'll take a lot more than *'im* to finish me off."

She cackled a laugh again and TJ immediately felt a bit better. More than that he felt his inquisitive nature stir again. "I take it then that you know who or what that thing in my dream was?" TJ asked.

The Dreamorian looked across at Grandpa Mal and he nodded.

"Yes dear," she said. "We have feared this moment for a very, very long time. I know who that was in your dream. It was *Dominus Tenebris*…" She stopped, as if the pain of saying the name was too much to bear.

Grandpa Mal continued. "*Dominus Tenebris* is a Latin name, dear boy, for Master of Darkness. It would seem my dear boy that you may have had the misfortune to come face to face with none other than the Head of the Terror of the Dreamstealers."

The Dreamorian quickly took back the initiative from Grandpa Mal. "The missing chapters of Genesis we spoke *'bout* a few moments ago speak of such a person. After all, I did say *theys* gets a bit dark, didn't I?"

She picked up her leather book from the table and flicked through towards the back. "*'eres* we go," she said, "some extracts from Genesis 51. Remember, these *'av* been seen by only an *'andful* of people over the past four thousand years. I'll start at verse 12:

" '*12 Manasseh said to Machir, "Behold, I am dying, but the Serpent will be with you and guide you back to the rightful inheritance of your father. 13 Manasseh called all his sons and said, "Gather together, that I may tell you what shall befall in the generations to come. Listen and hear, you sons of Manasseh, sons of the stolen birthright.*

14 "You will covenant, just as I with the Serpent at the beginning, to rise from beneath my younger brother's line. 15 Through my children, and your children's children, we shall become ever more powerful. 16 The guardians of the unrighteous pure gift will be captured and destroyed, 17 and our corrupted gift shall reign over all creatures.

18 "Hear me, my children, and your gloriously wicked offspring. 19 There shall come a time when One of our line shall come in such power, that even the carriers of the corrupted gift shall live in fear and shield their eyes.

20 "The line of the filthy Brethren shall quake with fear at its coming. 21 The One will hasten the rot, decay and death of the fruit of Ephraim and his unrighteous line. It shall come and rule, with its carved staff of evil striking fear, distress and darkness into the hearts and minds of mere men.

22 "As The One is victorious, the guardians will be no more." 23 The children listened and promised it would be. 24 With his final dying breath, Manasseh said, "The righteous line of Manasseh will prevail, and the line of the unrighteous will be lost forever.

25 Dominus Tenebris, the Master of Darkness, will come."' "

The Dreamorian stopped and looked up at TJ. "That's not the way it should be, is it dear?" she said to him. "We can't have that *'appening* can we?" TJ shook his head in agreement.

The Driver could contain himself no more. He exploded into a volley of French which TJ had no chance of understanding. As he calmed down, he reverted to English. "This cannot happen, and will not happen, not as long as I live and breathe," he said defiantly. "They will *jamais, never,* be victorious over me nor the Brethren. *Jamais...*"

"Indeed, indeed," Grandpa Mal said interrupting. "But we cannot, and must not, be complacent my dear fellow, for the threat is real. After all, we have ourselves observed the deepening darkness for some time within the Eldership. We must keep calm heads, even as the pressure builds, and the darkness deepens. These are dangerous times and we must tread carefully. After what young TJ has just described and all the warnings of our ancestors through the centuries, the signs are that *Dominus Tenebris,* our worst enemy, has finally come."

The silence in the room hung heavily and oppressively. It felt to TJ as if all the life and goodness had just been sucked out of the room. A log in the burner suddenly cracked loudly, like the explosion of a small incendiary device. TJ and the Dreamorian jumped.

"But how do you know it is *Dominus Tenebris*?" TJ asked, hoping that either he had been wrong or that Grandpa Mal was mistaken in his identification of the figure that had spoken to him in his dream last night.

"Well, my dear boy, the figure you described, dressed in a hooded black robe is very much a Dreamstealer. However, the monastic scapular – the length of cloth hung both front and back from the shoulders – is one tell-tale sign of someone very important in the hierarchy of the *Terror*.

"The second is the staff, with the carved demonic creature sitting on top of it. Any ordinary Dreamstealer would carry a plain staff, which is far inferior to most *Dreamswicks*, although ultimately the power of the *Dreamswick* depends on the quality of the Dreamguardian wielding it. However, you have heard in that passage just now of one of the tell-tale signs of the coming of *Dominus Tenebris*.

"Can you read that section again, please, my dear Dreamorian?" Grandpa Mal asked. "What Manasseh says to his family on his deathbed".

The Dreamorian pointed at the page with her finger and read aloud:

" *19 "There shall come a time when One of our line shall come in such power, that even the carriers of the corrupted gift shall live in fear and shield their eyes. 20 The line of the filthy Brethren shall quake with fear at its coming. 21 The One will hasten the rot, decay and death of the fruit of Ephraim and his unrighteous line. It shall come and rule, with its carved staff of evil striking fear, distress and darkness into the hearts and minds of mere men.*

22 "As The One is victorious, the guardians will be no more." "

"I believe you have seen the very staff that is mentioned there, dear boy," Grandpa Mal said to TJ, who couldn't help but gulp in reply.

"At some point in history the creature carved upon it was believed to be an *Alp*, a supernatural Elf-type being that in German folklore was said to control dreams and create horrible nightmares. Hence the German word *Alptraum,* or '*elf dream*', that means 'nightmare'. You see the Dreamstealer movement was very prominent in Europe around the turn of the 19th century and gained quite a bit of ground then. The next time we are in the Great Room, I may show you a book that contains the painting '*Nachtmahr*" by the Swiss painter Johann Heinrich Füssli. That depicts an Alp sitting on the chest of a sleeping lady." He paused before continuing. "Hmm, but then again, I'm not sure whether I should expose you to that, as it is potentially quite disturbing for someone so young."

Before TJ could assure him that he would be fine to view the painting, as he was made of quite stern stuff after all, Grandpa Mal continued.

"But as well as the staff, the other clue lies in the fact that the Dreamstealer spoke to you. Ordinarily, a Dreamstealer will never directly engage or speak to a dreamer, since their power lies in the shadows. Such is our power and reach that the Brethren would soon learn of such direct interference in a dream and a Dreamguardian be deployed quickly to expel the Dreamstealer.

"However, while the aggression and arrogance of *Dominus Tenebris* – fuelled by what Manasseh prophesied on his deathbed – is a strength, it is also a weakness.

"We need to be on our guard though, dear boy. The Book clearly documents there will come a time when the most powerful Dreamstealer ever known will rise up to challenge and potentially overcome the Dreamguardians and destroy the Brethren."

TJ was indignant. "No!" he challenged. "How can that be? After all, we are Dreamguardians from the true line of Ephraim. How can the positive power of the gift be overcome by darkness and evil?"

Grandpa Mal admired his loyalty and spirit. The more time he spent with him he realised TJ was so much like his father.

He replied respectfully to TJ. "We cannot take anything for granted. The Book is very clear that *Dominus Tenebris* has the power to do such things. At various points in history, many false prophets have asserted the claim to be *Dominus Tenebris*, but fallen well short. But I agree with you dear boy. I believe wholeheartedly that while Manasseh was right that someone would come from his line that would be all powerful, he was very wrong in his assertion that *Dominus Tenebris* would be victorious."

By the time he was finished Grandpa Mal's hand was curled up in a fist, his knuckles white from squeezing his fingers together so tightly.

"*Exactement! Bravo!*" the Driver called out. "*They* are wrong. *They* are the *filthy* ones! And *we* will be victorious!"

"Yes, right you are dear," said the Dreamorian to the Driver, "prophesies do need to be treated with caution, but we should not forget that in this instance they are not one-sided." Turning back to TJ, she smiled. "You see, my dear, Manasseh's prophecy was not the only one. There is one for our bloodline, and it's quite something."

Grandpa Mal stood and walked over to TJ. He placed his hands on his shoulders and looked him direct in the eyes. "For sure, we shouldn't underestimate the enemy and need to be on our guard. But wait until you hear this my dear boy. It is the reason why we can have such hope and faith that when all is said and done, the Brethren will emerge victorious and *Dominus Tenebris* and the *Terror of the Dreamstealers* will be defeated.

"Dear Dreamorian," Grandpa Mal continued turning to the old lady, "it is time. Time to reveal to our young guest the most glorious passage ever to have been recorded in the one and true version of Genesis. The reason we have hope and confidence that the Dreamguardians will triumph over the Dreamstealers. My dear boy, read and be inspired."

With that, the Dreamorian handed the book to TJ and he began to read Chapter 52 of the original and true Book of Genesis:

52 Ephraim and the Brethren

1 Ephraim survived his older brother and lived a hundred and thirty years.

2 Since the time he was set before Manasseh, great fruitfulness came through the gift strengthened by Israel's blessing.

3 But the covenant Manasseh forged with the Serpent was strong and the corrupted gift of his own line began to reign over all creatures.

4 Then his father Joseph appeared to Ephraim within a dream, and behold, a stairway was set up on the earth, and its top reached to heaven; and there the angels of God were ascending and descending on it.

5 At the bottom stood Joseph, who spoke to Ephraim, saying "this is the stairway that my father Jacob saw toward Harran, at the place he named Bethel.

6 This is none other than the gate of heaven and from where the gift comes."

7 Then Joseph issued a warning to Ephraim and said to him: "You must beware, for Manasseh and his offspring will come to corrupt the gift and destroy you and your bloodline.

8 They will seek to take captives and overturn the blessing bestowed upon you and your descendants."

9 As Joseph spoke a new stairway appeared, and its bottom reached down into hell; and there, angels of darkness were ascending and descending on it.

10 They carried cages of trapped figures of light down the steps, tormenting, taunting, clawing and gnashing their teeth at the captured figures as they went.

11 And so it was that the gift would collide; the pure righteous gift of Ephraim's line with that of the corrupted gift of Manasseh's.

12 Then one night, Ephraim received a powerful vision. 13 Before him stood Joseph and Jacob, his grandfather, as if both were still alive to touch.

14 Jacob held a strange object in his right hand and placed it in Ephraim's same hand. 15 It was a wooden staff with a misshapen hoop at one end, across which an intricate web was woven in strips of fine leather.

16 Jacob said, "Take this, my favoured son whom I blessed over all others. 17 Your brother, considering both himself and the earth cursed, has corrupted the gift and begun to reign over all creatures.

18 "You shall take this Dreamswick to protect yourself and fight the corrupters of the gift and stealers of dreams through Manasseh's line."

19 Then Joseph took off and handed him the ornate robe and coat of many colours he was wearing. 20 Joseph said, "Take this, my favoured son who was blessed over all others.

21 You will raise up a Brethren of blessed brothers to protect the gift. 22 Each of you will wear this special coat to identify you as a chosen people, the protectors of the one pure gift and the defenders of the safe passage of dreams."

23 Empowered by his dream, Ephraim fought hard for the purity of the gift and rose up a Brethren of Guardians of Dreams.

24 But despite the power of the Dreamswick, the Terror of the Stealer of Dreams intensified.

25 Many Guardians became trapped and lost for eternity in a place worse than Hades.

26 As the end of his life drew near, Ephraim grew weaker in body, but not in his gifting. 27 One night, as he slept, he had a vision. 28 A person sent to bear witness of The Dreamologist, that would give light and hope to the Brethren.

29 It said, "I am the voice of one calling out to Ephraim's line: Do not fear, hold on for The Dreamologist will come. 30 The Dreamologist full of light will come with the power to defeat the Stealer of Dreams and overturn the Terror and its corruption.

31 The Dreamologist will come with the ability to acquire, retrieve and interpret dreams like no other.

32 And The Dreamologist will come with the authority and power to rescue a Guardian lost in a dream.

33 Mark my words, for even the corrupted gift can be made straight and pure again, and the great struggle come to an end for good."

34 Upon waking, the vision sustained Ephraim for a few days longer and strengthened the Brethren through its toils and struggles.

35 And Ephraim called his sons and said, "Gather together, that I may tell you what shall befall you and your descendants in the years to come."

36 With that he spoke of his vision of The Dreamologist to his children and made them covenant they would tell their children and their children's children.

37 When Ephraim had finished sharing about the great hope and promise of the coming of the Dreamologist, he drew his feet up into bed and breathed his last.

38 Although the first Guardian of Dreams was no more, his legacy lived on, emboldened by the promise of what was to come.

39 May grace, mercy and peace, the all-powerful protection of the Dreamswick and the promise of the coming of The Dreamologist be upon the Brethren of the Guardian of Dreams, 40 the brave and righteous defenders of the safe passage of dreams. Amen.

TJ sat in silence after he had finished reading the chapter, absorbing everything he had just read and trying to process it as efficiently as possible. But it was difficult. Some of it just didn't make sense to him.

"So, who is the Dreamologist then, and when will he or she come?" he asked. The silence was deafening as no answer was forthcoming. Finally, Grandpa Mal chose to answer. "Unfortunately, dear boy, neither this true account of Genesis nor the Great Book in the Inner Sanctum provides us with the answer to your questions. Believe me when I tell you that many have asked those very same questions before."

"'*Ee's* quite *roight*," added the Dreamorian. "There is *nothin'* documented '*bout* that. If truth be told, not so long ago the Eldership had high '*opes* that the prophecy may have been on the way to being fulfilled, through one of the finest, bravest and most exceptional Dreamguardians ever to have graced the Brethren." Her eyes lit up in admiration as she spoke, but then her demeanour changed in an instant. "But tragically and quite unexpectedly, this one was lost. Ambushed by... well, they *was* lost, let's leave it at that shall we."

TJ was shocked by what the Dreamorian had just said and she certainly looked crushed having told the story. "So, what you're saying is The Dreamologist may have already come, but been defeated?" TJ asked almost rhetorically. "Surely not," he continued.

"We just don't know dear," the Dreamorian said, taking TJ by surprise. Up to now he thought she knew everything. He probed further.

"So according to this book here, The Dreamologist can rescue a Dreamguardian lost in a dream? Is that true? I mean, this is the first time I've heard this might be possible. Has it been done before?"

Grandpa Mal shifted uncomfortably in his chair. "We believe it to be true, dear boy. But I'm afraid it has never been done before." Grandpa Mal slowly shook his head. "Sadly, over the course of nearly four thousand years there has never been a recorded case where a lost Dreamguardian has been saved from wherever it is that they languish." He now hung his head as he spoke.

"I'm sorry I didn't mention this to you before my dear boy. At that stage I wasn't sure we would reveal this level of detail to you. At the time, I just wanted to make sure you understood the serious risks a Dreamguardian undertakes, without you thinking there was an automatic back-up plan. I am sorry for not being completely honest with you, dear boy. Please forgive me."

TJ accepted Grandpa Mal's apology but was struggling with the answers that had been given to his questions just now. He felt bad to think negatively, but TJ was not being convinced by the veracity of the prophecy of The Dreamologist.

The Dreamorian sensed his doubt. "My dear, we cannot prove anything to you or anyone else for that matter. But the mere fact that this book talks about The Dreamologist, with the ability, authority and power to do all those things it says, explains the *'ope* and confidence that we *'av* dear. But you're *roight*. It's true that we just don't know. We do *'ope* the prophecy is true. In fact, we *'av* **faith** that it's true dear. That's all, but sometimes that's all you need dear."

TJ admired the Dreamorian's sentiments, but at this precise moment he wasn't convinced at all. And that made him even sadder. After all, how could anyone be sure that The Dreamologist wasn't anything other than a dying man's hallucinations? Or that if the prophecy was indeed true, The Dreamologist had already come but been beaten by a more powerful being and lost forever. After all, the prophecy didn't say that The Dreamologist **would** defeat the Dreamstealers, or **would** retrieve and interpret dreams like no other, or **would** rescue a lost Dreamguardian. All it said was that The Dreamologist would possess the power and authority to do all those things, without saying explicitly that it would achieve them.

To make matters worse, TJ now knew he had come face to face with *Dominus Tenebris*, who was certainly real. Perhaps the Elders were right all along:

the threat the Brethren faced **was** the greatest it had ever been. Darkness was rising, *Dominus Tenebris* had come, and despite some promises in a dusty old book there wasn't anything anyone could do about it.

CHAPTER 20 – SURPRISE!

Back at the Old Girl, the rest of the children had opted to stay indoors for the morning. The cooler temperature outside had infiltrated the rooms inside, so Chatty, Lizzy Wizzy and Benjy were curled up in the family lounge watching a film. Even though it was meant to be the height of summer, an open fire worked hard to heat the room, such were the joys of a vast old house.

Chatty and Lizzy Wizzy lay sprawled out together on a large sofa, a fluffy blanket covering their legs and matching unicorn slippers. Benjy had a large snuggler armchair all to himself. He looked like a small King slouched lazily on a rather large throne as he enjoyed the entertainment before him.

Benjy wasn't bothered that TJ had gone off with Grandpa Mal and was rather content to be relaxing with a throne all to himself. Chatty, however, had continued to protest and was still sulking. She had even managed to influence Lizzy Wizzy into also feeling a little aggrieved. But this was more out of sympathy for Chatty as even Lizzy Wizzy wasn't too concerned to miss walking around the Nature Reserve for the whole day.

As the film was nearing the end, Katherine entered the room. As the children were engrossed in the film, they hadn't noticed her arrival. Katherine seized the remote control and hit the pause button. The protests were immediate and escalated from Chatty as she realised it was her Mum that had stopped the fun. As usual.

"Thanks, we were watching that" Chatty moaned. "What did you do that for?" she asked grumpily.

"Excuse me, young lady, there's no need to be so rude," Katherine responded. "After all, I have a surprise for you and Benjy. And you too Lizzy Wizzy, I suppose."

Benjy and Lizzy Wizzy's ears pricked up as soon as the word 'surprise' was mentioned and they immediately forgot about the film, now frozen in time and only of secondary importance.

"Yeah right," Chatty grumbled, unwilling to be even a little bit excited by what the surprise might be. "I bet it's boring and nowhere as good as the one TJ's got with Grandpa Mal."

"Oh Chatty, do be quiet," came the exasperated reply. "I've just about had enough of you and your rotten attitude."

Good, thought Chatty. At the end of the day she didn't care.

Mum continued. Although she was trying to sound enthusiastic about what she was about to say, she knew she would struggle to convince anyone. Deep down she was furious.

"It's all very unexpected, but you have a special visitor Chatty and Benjy. Someone is here to see you."

Immediately, Chatty's attention was grabbed. In an instant, she knew who she wanted it to be. "Who is it?" she asked inquisitively. Instantaneously her mood changed. "Is it who I think it is?" she asked excitedly.

Katherine noticed the change in Chatty and felt compromised. She was pleased that her daughter was happy and excited for once. In fact, the first time in a long while. But at the same time, she was disappointed that she was no longer able to make her daughter this happy herself. She put on a brave face.

"Well, I don't know who you think it is," Mum replied, knowing full well who Chatty hoped the guest would be. Benjy smiled and looked at Chatty. He hoped it was who he was thinking about too.

"Come on, they're waiting in the Grand Hall," Mum confirmed. Chatty and Benjy looked at each other and grinned. Then without warning they jumped out of their seats and raced each other to the door. They giggled and shouted as they went flying down the long corridor. As they burst into the Grand Hall they stopped their movement and noise immediately.

There was no-one there. Then just as they were about to erupt with indignation and protest, a man jumped out from behind one of the pillars on the other side of the room by the front door.

"Surprise!" he exclaimed.

"Daddy!" screamed Chatty and Benjy in unison and their noisy race was off again. This time the finish line and prize for the winner was clear. The first cuddle with their Dad for quite some time.

Chatty, helped on by her longer legs, was the winner and ploughed into her

Dad's welcoming arms, almost knocking him over. Benjy followed suit and the two children buried their faces into him as he embraced them both, squeezing them tightly and kissing the tops of their heads.

"Hello, you two," Dad said cheerfully, "long time no see. I've missed you both, very much."

The muffled replies from within his embrace confirmed both Chatty and Benjy had missed him too. They squeezed him as tightly as they could, as if they would never let him go.

"Come on, let me take a good look at you both," Dad said, prising them away. He bent down on one knee to see how much they had grown and changed since the last time he saw them.

"Benny boy, wow, look how much you've grown since I last saw you," he said, patting him on the top of the head. "You're nearly as tall as me already! Looks like you've been getting lots of fresh air and sunshine by the look of it too," he added, smiling at the explosion of freckles that had detonated across Benjy's cheeks and a face that was still a little red from sunburn. "Been on the beach the past few days by any chance?" he asked. Benjy nodded vigorously and grinned from ear to ear.

"And just look at you my darling," Dad said turning to Chatty, "don't you look so pretty and grown up. Where did my little princess go?" Chatty smiled sweetly. "Thank you, Daddy," she replied gently and as grown up as she could manage. "Yes, I'm getting older, but I'll always be your little princess."

Dad smiled. "Of course," he said gently, "you'll always be my little princess, and the most beautiful one in the kingdom."

With that, Chatty put her arms back around him and gave him the hardest squeeze she could manage.

"I've missed you so much Daddy," she whispered in his ear. "I'm so glad you're here," she added, and found some more strength from somewhere to squeeze him even tighter.

"Hello Uncle Bertie," came the cheerful greeting from Lizzy Wizzy who had made her way to the Grand Hall at a much slower pace than her excited cousins. "Ah Lizzy Wizzy," Uncle Bertie said, ending his cuddle with Chatty. "Good to see you, young lady. How are you doing?".

Lizzy replied she was fine and gave Uncle Bertie a quick hug and kiss on the cheek. She smiled at Chatty who beamed back. Lizzy Wizzy was pleased to see how happy Chatty was to see her Dad.

"Where's that brother of yours, then Lizzy Wizzy?" Bertie asked, looking around to see if he could see TJ.

"He's not here. He's off with Grandpa Mal," she replied. "Think they went to the Nature Reserve to spot the red deer."

"Oh, that's a shame to miss both TJ as well as Mal," Uncle Bertie replied, "but that sounds like lots of fun for them both. Just the right time of year to see the spotted calves of the hinds. You'll have to make sure that you give that brother and Grandpa of yours my apologies for missing them. Give them my best regards too. Hopefully I'll catch up with them again at another time."

Lizzy Wizzy promised she would pass the message on, and Uncle Bertie thanked her for her promise. "Is your mother here too?" he asked Lizzy Wizzy, "I'd like to say a quick hello to her too if she's around?" Lizzy Wizzy confirmed she was.

"Go on you two," he said to Lizzy Wizzy and Benjy, "let's see who's the quickest out of the pair of you". Challenge accepted, the pair of them ran off in the direction of the kitchen to try and find Emma.

Chatty didn't waste much time to air her grievances. "Daddy, I'm so glad you're here. It's just horrible. All Mum does is moan and be nasty to me. You know what she's like. Now she's the same with me as she was with you. All the time."

Dad raised his eyebrows and looked sympathetically at Chatty. "I'm sorry to hear that. Your Mum can't be that bad, surely?" he said, although he could remember clearly just how bad things had got between him and Katherine.

"You know she loves you very much," he said reassuringly to Chatty. "We both do of course. And you do know that even though your Mum and I are not together anymore, it's not your fault. I know for a fact that I don't love you any less. In fact, I love you even more. After all, they do say absence makes the heart grow fonder."

He smiled and Chatty responded with a forced pained smile. She would have rather he agreed than tried to make excuses for Mum. She turned her attention to the other issue bothering her. "It's not just Mum. All Grandpa Mal does these days is spend time with TJ or stick up for him. It's just not fair."

Bertie deliberately pulled a sad face to try and make Chatty smile. "Oh dear. What makes you say that? Your Grandpa Mal thinks the world about all of you children. Knowing Mal like I do, I'd be surprised if he favoured one of you over another, princess."

"Well, he does now," Chatty said grumpily, "in real life and even in my dreams." She was struggling to forget her dream at the boating pond. "I mean this morning Grandpa Mal and TJ disappeared with no warning or invitation to anyone else, and they've been whispering to each other when they don't think anyone else is looking. But I'm watching and they're up to something. I don't know what it is, but whatever it is, I'll find out. They're acting strangely and leaving the rest of us out. It's just not fair."

Bertie pulled another face to try and appease Chatty, but it didn't have much success. "I'm sorry, princess," he said, inviting her into another cuddle. It had been a long time since he'd seen her, and he'd missed cuddles with his special girl. "There, there, never mind. I'm sure it's nothing. It does seem rather out of character for your Grandpa Mal."

The days and months of frustration were too much for Chatty and she began to cry as she fell into her Dad's embrace. "I really miss you, Daddy," she sobbed, quietly at first but then almost uncontrollably as Bertie squeezed her tighter.

"I wish I could be with you, Daddy," she said through her tears.

"I know princess, I know," Bertie replied. "It'll all work out," he said reassuringly, "I promise."

*

For the sake of the children, Katherine tried to suppress her anger at Bertie for turning up unexpectedly and invited him into the kitchen for a drink. Emma joined her for some moral support as they all sat at the kitchen table with a cup of coffee, cookies and soft drinks for the children. At times the atmosphere was tense and there was a very awkward moment as Bertie asked Emma how she was coping on her own with the children.

Katherine felt like strangling Bertie for being insensitive and mentioning Daniel, even if he had done so indirectly. But Emma didn't seem to flinch at his question and thanked him for his concern. She replied with her standard answer that although it was hard, and they missed him, they were getting there. Thankfully Lizzy Wizzy was preoccupied with Chatty and Benjy at the other end of the table, so the subject was navigated without any external upset.

"So, when are Mal and TJ due back?" Bertie asked the ladies. "Will I get to see them?"

Katherine jumped in quickly. "I don't think so, sadly. I think Dad was planning to stay out quite late with TJ. There's something quite magical about dusk falling on the Nature Reserve, especially at this time of the year."

Chatty's ears perked up. "But Daddy, you can stay until then can't you," she said, more as a demand than a question. "Then you can say hello to Grandpa Mal and TJ yourself."

Bertie looked across quickly at Katherine and then back to Chatty. "Well, I'm not sure about that darling. I don't want to overstay my welcome."

"No, I'm afraid Daddy can't stay until then Chatty. He's welcome to stay a little longer to spend some time with you and Benjy, but we've already made plans to go out this afternoon."

Chatty wasn't impressed. This was the first time she'd heard that anything was planned for today. She didn't believe her and wanted to spend more time with Daddy. It felt like a long time since she'd done that.

"Surely Daddy can come with us this afternoon, wherever it is we're going? Actually, where *are* we going this afternoon? It's the first time anyone's mentioned it all day."

Katherine could feel her face redden through a mixture of embarrassment at her flimsy excuses and rising anger at Chatty's defiance. The last thing she wanted to do was spend any more time than she needed to with Bertie, especially as he'd had the audacity to turn up uninvited.

"I told you, we've already arranged something. In any case, Daddy has a long drive ahead of him in order to get back home. I'm sure he doesn't want to hang around here too long. You'll want to be off well before the rush hour kicks in won't you Bertie?"

Bertie answered quickly. "No, it's fine, I wasn't planning on being back until late tonight, so I can always leave after the rush hour."

"See, there you go," Chatty said, "Daddy can stay as long as he likes".

Katherine wasn't impressed. "I don't think you heard me correctly, Charlotte," she said, her anger beginning to rise. "I said we had made plans for this afternoon. Of course, it's a lovely surprise that your father just chose to drop in and grace us with his presence. But unfortunately, I didn't know he was coming, he didn't tell me he was coming, and we have alternative plans that sadly don't involve him."

Katherine turned to Bertie. "I'm sorry Bertie, it's been nice to catch up, but you'll have to come back another day when it's more convenient and we know to expect you." She was beginning to feel quite irritated at what Bertie was doing.

Bertie chose his words carefully. "Well I don't really know when I'll be able to come up here again, especially if you're planning on being here for nearly all of the summer holidays. I'm sorry for the lack of warning about today, but it was all a bit last minute at work. So, I thought I would take the opportunity to come up here and it would be a lovely surprise to dash up to see you and the children. But obviously if you have something more important to do this afternoon then..." He trailed off and shrugged his shoulders.

"Well I want you to stay Daddy," Chatty said loudly. On the other side of the table, Benjy didn't know what to say or who to look at, so he looked at his feet. Another argument. He'd seen and heard it all before.

"Charlotte, that's enough!" Katherine said loudly. "I've made my decision and that's final."

"But that's not fair!" Chatty shouted back. "*Don't* listen to her Daddy. *I* want you to stay. *I* want to spend the afternoon with *you*. Not with *her*, but with *you*."

Bertie spoke calmly and softly to appeal to Chatty. "I know princess, I can't think of anything I'd like more than to spend the afternoon with both you and Benny-boy. But apparently your mother has something more important for you to do. I don't know what it is, but we must respect that. I'll just have to see you another time, whenever that might be of course."

Slowly, Bertie got up from the table. "Perhaps this wasn't such a good idea, after all," he said sadly. "I think it's best if I go."

"No!" Chatty cried immediately. "That's not fair. I want to be with *you* Daddy. Not *her*, but *you*. Take me back with you. I don't want to be here anymore."

Katherine got to her feet, gave Bertie a steely stare and made sure he would understand very clearly what she was about to say. "Yes, it's about time you left," she ordered harshly. "You weren't invited. You've already been told and warned about this, but as usual you never listen. Now go, you're not welcome, especially here. Do you understand?"

With that, Bertie took his jacket from the back of his chair and put it on. "Yes, that's clear," he said softly. "I'm sorry you feel this way Katherine. I only wanted to stop by and see you, Chatty and Benjy. And the rest of the family of course."

He walked over to Benjy and gave him a kiss on the top of his head and did the same to Chatty.

"No Daddy, don't go," cried Chatty, her tears now evident. "Please stay."

"I'm sorry, princess," he whispered in her ear. "I love you, always. But your mother says I must go. See you soon."

He gave her another kiss on the forehead. Then without saying anything further he left the room. Around the table, no-one spoke. The only audible sounds were Chatty's sobs and Benjy's sniffs as he tried to hold back his own tears. Then in the distance they heard the wooden front door slamming, echoing and reverberating down the corridors.

Chatty was the first to say something.

Glaring at her Mum, she started it as a whisper. Then it got louder and louder until she was screaming at her.

"*I hate you, I hate you, I hate you, I HATE YOU!*"

CHAPTER 21 – THE CEREBRUM

After they had said their goodbyes to the Dreamorian, the two men and TJ left the cottage and made their way to the DB4. As they did, Grandpa Mal put a hand on TJ's shoulder and patted it reassuringly. TJ hoped that wherever they were going he would have the chance to spend some more time with the Dreamorian at some stage. She was a fascinating person. As it was, TJ now appeared to be very much to be in the hands of the Driver and he had no idea what was about to happen.

As he squeezed into the back of the car, the engine roared back to life. The choral excellence of Vivaldi's Gloria filled the car again as the Driver turned the music back up.

"*Petit garçon,*" the Driver shouted loudly to TJ in the back of the car. "Seatbelt, *s'il vous plaît. Maintenant! Rapidement!* We have much to do. It is time for you to get active and be put through your paces, especially if you have already come face to face with *Dominus Tenebris*. The *Dreamswick* waits for no man, or *petit garçon* I should say for that matter."

With that, the Driver carefully maneuvered the DB4 to face the track and depressed his right foot on the pedal. In the rear, TJ was suddenly pinned back in the expensive leather seats as the engine revved loudly and the car shot back up into the forest. From the front door the Dreamorian cackled with laughter. "Go on *me'ansum*, give it some welly!" she shouted excitedly, waving as the car quickly disappeared from sight.

TJ felt exhilarated at the sudden acceleration and speed. But he was also very apprehensive about what would come next. All he knew was that wherever the DB4 was headed next, it was in a hurry. A*llez* indeed!

Settling down into the back seat amongst all the noise, TJ tried to gather his thoughts. After all, the Dreamorian had told him so much. Just before he had left, the Dreamorian had spoken to him the following words, which now went around in his head:

"You must promise me my dear, at all times, that you be strong and keep the faith. Never, ever, be tempted to stray from the path of loight that has been given you by virtue of Ephraim's line, or use the gift for anything other than the purposes it was intended for. The consequences are too awful to consider. Be bold and courageous my dear, just as those fine people who 'av gone before you 'av done. Just as the original book of Genesis promises, we shall be victorious."

TJ had promised the Dreamorian with all his heart that he would be bold and courageous. He would fight with all his strength to defend the safe passage of dreams. But he was still struggling to find the faith that the Brethren would have the victory over the Dreamstealers, especially now that *Dominus Tenebris* had come.

After a while he looked out of the window and saw the hedgerows and fields flashing past as the car sped down the country lanes. The Aston Martin effortlessly conquered any winding corners that presented themselves. The choral music with its baroque instrumentation played on, and TJ began to enjoy the ride as his senses began to be stirred by his surroundings, both inside and outside of the car.

The landscape became ever more remote as they made their way down narrowing roads and lanes. The Driver had eased up on the speed but knew precisely where they were headed. Although it was still much cooler outside than in recent days, the grey cloud was finally thinning and TJ could see the coastline in the distance.

After a few more minutes, the lane took them up to a stone church. Its tower remained intact but the rest of it was in ruins. In the distance ahead, the road had been eroded away and ended abruptly, offering any unsuspecting driver a quick route over the cliff edge onto the beach below. Just after the church they turned left, down a track that led parallel with the sandstone cliffs. It was flanked either side by hedgerows and was barely visible from the road they had just turned off.

TJ leant across and looked out of the front windscreen to see where they were going. He saw the track snaked ahead of them up an incline. They were headed for the brow of the hill about a quarter of a mile ahead. To TJ's right he could see the uninviting and bleak expanse of the North Sea that would ultimately end up due east on the shores of The Netherlands over one hundred miles away.

The car gained speed again as it accelerated and easily climbed up the track ahead. As they came over the brow of the hill, TJ saw it and gasped. In a giant man-made hollow, a little way beneath them was a huge, sleek ultramodern villa, constructed almost entirely of steel, glass and white rendered concrete. Its beauty lay in its design, as well as its seclusion amongst the wild coastline. Although it had been hunkered down and was hidden from view on the north, south and west by the hillside, it held a commanding view looking east over the cliffs, out to sea.

The angles of the villa were sharp, as if it had been designed by an extremely imaginative and sophisticated child placing building blocks of various sizes next to, and on top of each other. The one exception to the building's angular appearance was a glass dome that protruded from the top of the main roof expanse, giving it the appearance of a strange mix of designer lighthouse and observatory. The villa was huge and looked immensely stylish and expensive. TJ knew that could only mean one thing: it must belong to the Driver.

As they approached, the Driver pressed a button on the dashboard of the car and some gates at the end of the track leading to the villa slid open. The Driver sped in and headed straight for the rear of the building where a garage door was opening. It was all timed to perfection and the car made its way without stopping into an underground garage beneath the house.

The garage was heavily lit and housed a collection of the most impeccable vintage and modern sports cars. Although TJ didn't know that much about cars, he recognised a Ferrari, a Porsche and a Bugatti, as well as others he didn't know but still thought were incredibly beautiful. The Driver parked the car in an empty space next to a glass lift and turned off the engine. Peace returned to the car.

The Driver looked round to address TJ. "*Bienvenue,*" he said. "Welcome to my *maison*... my humble abode." TJ looked at him incredulously. There was nothing humble about this place, he thought to himself! They got out of the car and headed into the lift. As the doors closed and they started to go up, what looked like one of the world's most expensive garages disappeared. The view of the cars was replaced by the excavated stone walls of the lift shaft that were visible through the glass walls of the elevator.

The lift reached the ground floor and the doors opened. They stepped out into a giant room facing the coast. The entire wall opposite them was made up entirely of huge glass panels, giving them an uninterrupted view and living landscape of the panorama before them. The grasses on the cliff blew in the stiff breeze and beyond them out to sea the waves swelled and rolled. The grey clouds streaked across the sky and patches of bright blue tried hard to break through. Despite the wind and motion outside, it was silent and calm on the inside.

The room itself was open plan, but minimalist and sleek. The floor tiles were polished and slippery, reflecting the light streaming in from the floor to ceiling window panels. At the far end of the room, which to TJ seemed almost a mile away, was an open-plan kitchen. The units were white and shiny, and polished marble worktops helped reflect yet more light into the room. Stylish stools were dotted around a polished concrete island unit.

In the middle section of the room, huge grey leather seats demarcated the lounge area. They were positioned around an expensive looking rug and a bespoke item of furniture that almost looked like a sculpture, but TJ guessed was an elaborate coffee table. In the far-right corner of the room some steps led down to a sunken area. A large interior stove hung down from the ceiling like a giant black exclamation mark. Near the stove were a couple of antique brown leather armchairs and a floor lamp with a giant brass dome that curved overhead. TJ thought it looked like the perfect place to read a book and watch the changing of the seasons roll past.

Immediately to his left, TJ noticed a glass staircase with stainless steel rails, and beyond that a corridor leading to another part of the house. Underneath the staircase he saw a Japanese Samurai warrior's suit of armour and sword displayed in a large glass cabinet, carefully lit from above by spotlights. Down the corridor he could see a number of large oriental vases displayed upon pedestals, also carefully lit so as to show off their design, age and decoration.

"I see you are taking everything in carefully my dear boy," Grandpa Mal commented. "Quite right too, as this is indeed a fantastic place. No expense spared, as I'm sure you can see." He smiled at TJ, who reciprocated.

"You can say that again," TJ replied somewhat awestruck by the size and grandeur of the place, "this is incredible."

"*Merci, petit garçon*," the Driver said from behind TJ, making him jump. He was so taken by his surroundings and the stunning view of the coastline in front of him that he'd forgotten the Driver was there and whose house he was in.

"This is what you can achieve when you work hard *petit garcon*. I must admit I have been very fortunate in what I have achieved. It is a great privilege that I have been able to commission houses like this, designed and built in some of the most beautiful parts of the world."

TJ could hardly believe what he was hearing. Not only was this place spectacular, but it sounded like there were others, presumably just like this, in other countries.

"Each one," the Driver continued, "provides me with an opportunity to escape, to think, to contemplate, to plan, and to prepare. Then there are some truly special places, like this one, which also give me the opportunity to observe, train and instruct."

"My dear boy," Grandpa Mal interrupted, "although our time here is essential for your training, you are in for a very special treat. What you are about to encounter here is beyond anything anyone has ever seen before in the world outside the Brethren. At the extreme frontiers of technology, science and medical research, dear boy."

The Driver smiled as Grandpa Mal talked. He liked being associated with the best of everything, especially after he had invested millions of his own Swiss francs into these projects.

Then he spoke. "*Merci beaucoup* Malachi, you are most kind. Indeed, there is nothing as sophisticated as this on the planet, and it is all thanks to the investment, dedication and skill of our people. Would you like to explain over coffee?"

Grandpa Mal nodded. "Yes please, thank you my dear fellow. I will give TJ a brief introduction but will leave the intricate details to you."

"*Mais oui, très bon*" the Driver said as he made his way into the vast room and over in the direction of the kitchen.

Grandpa Mal and TJ followed. They each perched precariously on one of the designer stools by the island unit as the Driver fetched three exquisitely designed white espresso cups from a cupboard and placed one underneath an enormously complicated looking coffee machine by a cavernous stainless-steel sink. He pressed some buttons and after some gentle whirring, dark liquid gold oozed out from some of the finest coffee beans money could buy. A strong and delicious aroma filled the kitchen, although TJ knew he hated the taste of coffee.

Grandpa Mal turned to TJ. "My dear boy," he started, "I realise a formal introduction is long overdue. Up to now I've deliberately tried to keep it as simple as possible for you, rather than overload you from the start. But now is the perfect time for you to spend time with, and learn from, another of the Elders of the Brethren."

TJ felt a little silly at his own stupidity, since for most of the day he thought The Driver was simply a chauffeur. Now he had confirmation he was someone important in the Brethren.

"*Merci beaucoup*. It is *très bon,* very good, to finally have the chance to talk to you properly *petit garçon*."

He carefully placed the first tiny cup of espresso in front of TJ and proceeded to prepare another two for Grandpa Mal and himself.

"Thank you, likewise," TJ replied respectfully. He sipped the espresso and it tasted even more bitter than he remembered. He resisted the urge to stick his tongue out and exclaim "urgh". Instead, he persisted in sipping the drink. Perhaps drinking the espresso would help win him back some favour and respect from someone clearly important in the Brethren.

"*Très bon*, the coffee will sharpen you up *petit garçon*. My name is Christophé," he continued, "but you shall address me as *Sensei*. You need to understand well that it means 'teacher', from the literal translation of 'one who comes before'. I have travelled extensively throughout Japan and the rest of Asia during my life and learnt myself from the best. So, believe me when I say I am one who comes before. As he spoke, he handed Grandpa Mal his espresso and knocked back his own in one gulp.

"We have brought you here, not only to one of my homes, but to the *quartier général* – the headquarters – of one of the most important sections of the Brethren. At one point in time, when my great, great grandfather was *Sensei*, it was called *L'Ecole des Armes - The School of Weapons* – but now it is referred simply as *The Armoury*."

TJ forgot quickly about the bitter taste of coffee in his mouth and homed in on mention of *The Armoury*. He remembered the room of the same name very clearly. The room he had gone through before entering Grandpa Mal's dream. The room Grandpa Mal subsequently told him that every Dreamguardian *should* pass through before they enter a dream to put on their robe of light and pick up their *Dreamswick*.

"Formally within the Brethren I am known as the Master of the Armoury, but as I just mentioned, you *petit garçon* will address me as *Sensei. D'accord?*"

"*Oui, Sensei*," TJ responded, again trying to show respect.

"*Très bon, petit garçon*, very good," came the reply. "Now, drink your coffee, we have work to do."

TJ took the plunge and swallowed the rest of his bitter espresso. It made his eyes squint and *Sensei* smile. "Already you are learning the importance of obedience and respect," he said to TJ. "This is very pleasing *petit garçon*. Now, *allez!*"

With that he marched quickly back across the vast room towards the staircase. TJ and Grandpa Mal dismounted carefully from the stools and followed him. "Now remember dear boy," Grandpa Mal said as they went, "you must listen very carefully and do *exactly* as *Sensei* says."

"Of course, Grandpa Mal," TJ replied. Having just pleased *Sensei* by drinking coffee that he thought tasted disgusting, TJ had no desire to undo all his good work.

As they reached the top of the stairs, they entered a long dark narrow corridor that stretched out into the distance to both their left and right. *Sensei* turned left and walked down the corridor, his motion turning spotlights in the ceiling above him on as he went. As he reached the first doorway he came to, *Sensei* carefully placed his eye in front of an electronic pad to the side of the door. His eye lit up with blue lasers that danced across and scanned his eyeball. Without touching anything, the door slid open.

TJ could not believe his eyes as he entered the room. Although they were directly above the vast room flooded with light from the panoramic view below, all the windows in this particular room had been obscured by metal shutters that were tightly closed. As a result, the room was dark, save for the lights that glowed from bank upon bank of large computer flatscreens in the middle of the room. They were positioned around a large arched control desk that TJ thought wouldn't have looked out of place on the bridge of an elaborate spaceship. Somewhere, something appeared to be processing information very quickly, such was the flash of images coming from the screens and from buttons of various colours on the control desk. There was one huge black leather chair behind the desk, which *Sensei* headed for straight away.

Beyond all the computer screens, a 3D hologram globe hovered in the air. TJ had no idea where it was projected from and it was unlike anything he'd ever seen. The globe glowed various shades of blue, and small dots of light were flashing all over the globe.

"Wow!" exclaimed TJ, "this is so cool."

Sensei leant over an ergonomic keyboard and began tapping away. "This, *petit garçon*," he started to explain as he typed, "is the most sophisticated technology you will ever see in your life, driven by the most advanced computers and powerful processors the world has ever known."

"It's incredible," TJ enthused as the globe began to spin and move around in multidimensional space. *Sensei* walked behind the control desk and waved his hands in front of the image. As he did so, the globe grew bigger.

"Come, take a closer look," he called over to TJ, who was quick to obey.

Sensei brought the back of his left hand towards his own face, magnifying certain areas of the globe and grabbed pieces of textual information with his right hand. When he was done with the information, he swiped it away quickly with a casual flick of the fingers of his right hand.

To TJ it was information overload. "What is all this for?" he murmured, almost to himself.

"This is a map representing Dreamguardian activity, *petit garçon*. All these pinpoints of light you see on the globe represent a Dreamguardian engaged in the finest and purist activity a human could ever aspire to: protecting the safe passage of dreams."

TJ could hardly believe it. Of all the things he had been told and seen, this was up there in terms of the most staggering.

"So, from this you can track each and every Dreamguardian engaged in a dream?" TJ asked, his curiosity well and truly aroused.

"*Oui.* Essentially, the technology is an infinitely more advanced form, *naturellement*, of Electroencephalography – often called EEG for short - that in the twentieth century was used to measure brain waves during sleep. Of course, it is far too complex for someone as young as you to understand, *petit garçon*."

"Please, *Sensei*, could you explain it a little more?" TJ begged. "I'd like to know and understand. I think this is fascinating."

Sensei sighed and muttered something inaudible under his breath in French. Then he spoke directly to TJ. "If you insist," he conceded and selected a few holographic buttons to the side of the globe with his left hand. Up came a three-dimensional diagram of a human brain and another of a Dreamguardian robe, both of which were able to spin and rotate in all directions.

"Do you remember those robes that were hung up in The Armoury that you passed through the other night, just before you entered your Grandpa Mal's dream?"

"Of course," TJ replied.

"*Très bon*. Well you must remember then that lines were embroidered into each robe with what looks like gold and purple thread. But this is no ordinary thread. It is a specially designed material by our people that detects neuronal activity such as brain waves. Indeed, it is so super sensitive and advanced that it is able to pick up the synchronised electrical pulses taking place across the circuits of the reticular activating system running through the thalamus from the brain stem to the cortex."

As he spoke the complicated names, the parts of the brain that they referred to were lit up on the screen, and a description appeared next to it for TJ to read. It was bordering on sensory overload for TJ and *Sensei* was enjoying showcasing the result of decades of intense research, development and investment.

"We have been able to scientifically identify and establish the difference between the neural activity of a Dreamguardian compared to an ordinary dreamer. In some respects, it is not so difficult, considering the electrical pulses are so much stronger and more advanced in a Dreamguardian. *Naturellement,* since we are superior beings after all. As a result, the threads in the robe detect this superior neuronal activity. In turn, this triggers a complex process, resulting in the location of an active Dreamguardian being sent to *The Cerebrum,* the name of the supercomputer which powers everything you see before you now."

TJ was stunned. He didn't like to admit it, but *Sensei* was right. He hadn't understood much, apart from the fact that somehow the robe was acting something like a tracking device.

Grandpa Mal could sense TJ's struggle to take it all in.

"Let's stop for a minute," Grandpa Mal interjected, "as you need to be careful in your understanding, dear boy. There is one very important distinction that must be made and remembered. The globe tracker you see before you, courtesy of the majestic supercomputer *The Cerebrum,* tells you only the physical location of an active Dreamguardian. That is, a Dreamguardian engaged within a dream somewhere. However as yet, and quite frustratingly I must say, dear boy, we still remain very much in the dark in terms of ascertaining *where* an active Dreamguardian actually goes once they are in someone's dream somewhere.

"For this, we remain at the developmental stage. We can track a Dreamguardian as far as The Armoury in their own dream before they enter someone else's, but, as yet, no further. Although there is some frustration with this, dear boy, we should be careful and note there is no criticism of anyone. We know that all working streams of the Brethren, those that combine the finest minds in medical science, research, technology and even The Armoury, continue to work collaboratively on this night and day, even as we speak."

TJ could see *Sensei* bristle. He could tell he didn't like failure or countenance mediocrity, and that he took the failure to physically track a Dreamguardian into another person's dream somewhat personally. As TJ thought he had noticed something peculiar, he changed the subject.

"It's all amazing but I have a question. I notice that most of the light intensity on the globe is concentrated far beyond the European continent and extends into Asia and the Americas in particular. Why is that? After all, most of the important Brethren activity seems to be centred here in the UK?"

Sensei rolled his eyes. "*Zut alors!*" he exclaimed. "What do they teach you in school these days, *petit garçon*?" It was a rhetorical question of course. "Most of the lights are elsewhere because it is night-time there my dear boy. And when it is night-time, people dream and the Dreamguardians go into action. *Mon dieu*, give me strength."

TJ felt rather stupid. Of course! Why hadn't he thought of that before he asked the question? But then he noticed something. "In that case, why is there light in the European time zone, where it's definitely not night."

Sensing *Sensei's* irritation, Grandpa Mal quickly answered. "There will always be some Dreamguardian activity even though a country is experiencing daylight. Don't forget that people's sleep habits and lifestyles can be quite different, dear boy."

"Of course," said TJ, still staring at something odd. "But what about some of these areas," he said pointing to a dense area of light that looked to be about one hundred miles to the south west of where they were presently. "This area of light density looks like it's somewhere in London. There can't be that much Dreamguardian activity at this time of day surely? Perhaps *The Cerebrum* is not working properly, *Sensei*," TJ said tongue in cheek.

The joke, however, was not taken well. *Sensei* shot a burning look over at Grandpa Mal and TJ felt bad for saying it almost immediately. *Sensei* clearly took great pride in everything he did and scolded TJ quickly.

"There is nothing wrong with *The Cerebrum*, and don't be so insolent. It just goes to show you are still deserving of the name *petit garçon*."

"I think it was a joke on young TJ's part," Grandpa Mal interjected, trying to act as peacemaker. "I don't think any harm was meant, was it dear boy?"

TJ shook his head from side to side. "No, sorry *Sensei*. It was a silly thing to say, to try and be funny."

Sensei nodded his head in the briefest of acknowledgements of TJ's apology and quickly swiped his hands. The globe showing all active Dreamguardians disappeared and he turned back to face TJ.

"Well, that's enough of that then," he said rather nonchalantly, as if to punish TJ's lack of respect. "If anything, that was only of secondary importance."

TJ wondered what he meant. How could all that be of secondary importance and, if it was, what could possibly top it?

Sensei walked towards, but right past TJ. As he disappeared into the darkness, he called "lights quarter up, spots on" and one end of the room was dimly illuminated, with bright spotlights illuminating two items of furniture.

Within the glare of the spotlights stood two leather reclining chairs, surrounded by various machines, computers and wires. TJ thought they looked suspiciously like dentist chairs, or more appropriately like very well designed and expensive chairs that lived in the practice of a very wealthy dental surgeon. Resting above the head end of each chair was an iron Samurai helmet, a *Kabuto*, unmistakably adorned with a front crest of golden horns. A black ceramic visor to cover the wearer's entire face was hinged upon the visor of the original helmet. Countless cables and wires protruded from the *hachimanza*, the small opening in the top. Leather straps hung down from various points along each side of the chair.

"We have wasted too much time already," *Sensei* said, now sounding rather irritated. "This is the real reason we are here *petit garçon*."

"But… but what are we doing?" stumbled TJ, feeling unsure about what was going to happen.

Sensei had the upper hand and was now pulling no punches. "This is also the product of millions of Swiss francs of research and what the finest minds in modern medicine, neuroscience, psychology, computer engineering and The Armoury can achieve."

He stood next to one of the chairs and beckoned TJ over to join him. "Now you will learn how to hunt down a Dreamstealer and how to use a *Dreamswick* and its power to expel that filthy creature from a dream. All with the help of this."

He gently patted the *Kabuto* and then the chair.

TJ was now extremely nervous. "What… What is this?" he asked with great trepidation.

"This is the *Dreamswick Simulator, petit garçon*," *Sensei* replied. "It is able to simulate a dream quickly, even when you are awake, allowing the student to experience and act as if they were inside a real dream."

As TJ reached the chair he was almost shaking. He waited for Grandpa Mal to intervene, but no such intervention came.

Sensei continued. He was quite enjoying himself now. "The *Dreamswick*

Simulator allows us to recreate pseudo-confrontations and battles with a Dreamstealer. Some are based on real-life experiences as relayed by brave Dreamguardians through the ages, while others are randomly generated by *The Cerebrum*.

"The *Dreamswick Simulator* is very advanced and utilises all the latest developments in artificial intelligence and machine learning too. That is a clever way of saying that the Simulator itself is able to fully control and calibrate the difficulty level accordingly to the abilities of the Dreamguardian in training.

"I will be with you at all times to instruct you in the power of the *Dreamswick*. You listen to me and me alone. This is extremely important. In your handling of the *Dreamswick* in action, you will find elements of different disciplines, such as ancient martial arts, as well as *l'escrime*, or fencing as you call it in your tongue."

With that, *Sensei* picked up some of the leather straps and invited TJ to jump on to the chair they were attached to.

"It is time to get you strapped in *petit garçon*. Your *Dreamswick* training starts now."

CHAPTER 22 – THE SIMULATOR

The chair was slightly reclined as TJ climbed on. Sensei tightly strapped the young boy's ankles and wrists individually to it, making TJ wince. Longer straps were fastened across TJ's upper chest, waist, thighs and just below his knees.

"This is to make sure you do not move during the simulation," *Sensei* said, "just as in a dream your voluntary muscles are paralysed."

TJ remembered Grandpa Mal telling him in the Great Room about the paralysis that occurs naturally in a dream to protect the dreamer. He attempted to move now but was unable to. In fact, it hurt. "Ow!" TJ complained as the straps pinched the skin on his wrists.

"Keep still then," *Sensei* said sternly, "otherwise it will hurt even more. A Dreamguardian must be fearless, show bravery and demonstrate courage. Clearly you have much to learn *petit garçon.*"

"Sorry," TJ said sheepishly, trying to keep as still as possible. But he was feeling very uncomfortable and increasingly nervous about what was to happen.

Sensei pressed a button on a machine close by and the chair slowly moved into a more reclined position, about forty degrees short of horizontal. He then reached above TJ's head and picked up the Samurai helmet. As it was lifted off its stand, it started to beep. The computers and machines surrounding the chairs came to life. Blue and white lights around the dome part of the helmet, the *hachi*, started to blink. Flashing lights ran up and down the cables leading to the computers from the *hachimanza* in the top of the helmet.

As the iron Samurai helmet rested on TJ's head, he was staggered at how heavy it was. But he daren't complain. "Are you ready?" *Sensei* asked, although TJ knew he would not accept anything other than *"oui Sensei"* in reply. He was right, as before TJ could even answer, *Sensei* turned to another of the machines and pressed another button. Slowly the black ceramic visor started to move. It slid over the visor of the original helmet and kept moving down until it completely covered his face. It pressed in within a whisker of his nose before something clicked into place and everything went dark. TJ now felt very claustrophobic and was even more anxious than before.

"How are you doing, dear boy," came a familiar voice from close to the chair. It helped ease some of TJ's anxiety and gave him an opportunity to showcase some fake resilience.

"I'm fine Grandpa Mal, I can't wait," TJ lied.

"Non," said *Sensei*, "this is not the truth. Now I tell you that all your vital statistics are being constantly monitored and recorded by *The Cerebrum*. They already confirm you are showing signs of anxiety. According to these parameters, you are far from being 'fine' as you suggest. It is very important you always tell the truth, *petit garçon*. To become a true Dreamguardian demands a pure heart and exemplary character."

TJ muttered another sheepish "sorry" and *Sensei* said no more. He fiddled with a few more switches and buttons on the machines and then sat down on his own chair. He did all the straps he could do on his own and then asked Grandpa Mal to help him with the final ones for his hands and chest.

"Are they tight enough, dear fellow?" Grandpa Mal asked him after he had fastened all the remaining straps and *Sensei* nodded. Then, straining, Grandpa Mal lifted the iron Samurai helmet onto *Sensei's* head. It too burst into life and a multitude of lights on the various machines and computers flashed ferociously. Grandpa Mal found the right button and the black ceramic visor slid into place, completely covering *Sensei's* face.

"Petit garçon, are you ready?" *Sensei* called out to TJ.

"Oui Sensei," came as confident a reply as TJ could manage.

"D'accord. En garde! Prêts? Allez!"

*

Suddenly the darkness disappeared, and the inside of TJ's black ceramic visor came to life. TJ was in a small room painted white. The room was completely bare, save for a green 'Exit' sign that hung over a door off to his right. Everything seemed so real, although he guessed it wasn't. TJ looked down and could see he was standing. His arms and legs were not strapped to anything, and he was able to move them freely. He felt for a Samurai helmet but was not wearing one. He just felt his hair and then all the usual features on his face. He saw he was dressed all in white, with jersey long-johns and a long-sleeved top, but was barefoot.

As he turned to his left, *Sensei* was standing next to him, dressed the same. TJ wondered if they could communicate.

"*Sensei*, can you hear me?" TJ asked cautiously.

"Of course I can hear you," came the reply. "We can do everything here. This is extremely advanced technology, as I have been trying to explain."

"Where are we?" TJ asked.

"We are already well advanced in a sleep stage cycle. The technology is able to simulate advanced Stage four *Delta Sleep* and will soon move us on into simulated REM activity. This is a very sophisticated process. Essentially the Simulator is controlled by *The Cerebrum* supercomputer and has already been able to influence and take over some of the neurological and physio-logical workings of your brain and, hence, your body. This is how it is able to simulate a dream quickly. While *The Cerebrum* will present us with what-ever dream situation it chooses, it does not have any control over your own thoughts and actions. You remain completely responsible for those."

"So, I am dreaming," TJ responded, unsure whether it was a question or statement.

"Well, sort of," came the reply. "*The Cerebrum* is responsible for your dream, but you are responsible for your own actions within it. We must progress through The Armoury to be properly equipped. Come."

Sensei walked past him, over to the door beneath the 'Exit' sign. He opened it, went through and TJ followed.

Although it was quite dark, the next room was instantly recognisable. Rows of hanging robes stretched out into the blackness ahead. Beside each robe the wooden staff of a *Dreamswick* stuck out from a wicker basket.

Sensei marched up to a hanging robe and quickly put it on. He picked up the accompanying *Dreamswick* and held it in his right hand. He pumped his right arm and started to turn the *Dreamswick* clockwise then anti-clockwise as if testing its robustness.

TJ put his own robe on and admired the embroidered stripes in the fine soft cotton robe, this time from a completely different perspective. It was such fantastic technology, he thought. He grabbed his *Dreamswick* with his left hand and admired the beautiful simplicity of that misshaped hoop and the intricate fine leather web that had been woven across it.

"Non!" *Sensei* said aggressively, "*à droite, pas à gauche!* Right, not left! That is *très important.* Ephraim was blessed with Jacob's right hand. The left hand is for Manasseh and those filthy Dreamstealers."

TJ switched hands quickly and apologised profusely. He vaguely remembered Grandpa Mal's instruction to hold the *Dreamswick* in his right hand for it to be effective. Now he understood the significance and kicked himself for not remembering.

"Never again *petit garçon*," *Sensei* warned and beckoned for TJ to follow him again as he strode to the far end of the long room. *Sensei* found the smooth brass doorknob without any trouble, pushed the door open and light flooded into The Armoury. It illuminated the robes behind them. They looked like soldiers on parade, reporting for duty. *Sensei* walked through into the light and TJ followed closely.

*

They were standing outside on a covered wooden veranda, around the edge of a dry gravel courtyard garden protected from the outside by a huge wooden gate. They were at the heart of a 13th century Japanese Zen Buddhist temple. In the distance, TJ could see acer trees and the delicate pink of cherry trees in full blossom. The unmistakable impressive roofs of other nearby temples and shrines were just about visible in the distance, dotted amongst the surrounding hillside.

They turned and entered a small room via an opening created by wooden sliding doors. TJ noticed the difference as he stepped off the wooden floor onto a softer, but still firm, tatami mat made from rice straw and woven soft rush grass. Around the internal walls were screens, with elaborate black, red and white ink paintings of dragons rampaging across them. Across the ceiling two dragons looked menacingly at each other, although they were simply smaller copies of the *Sōryūzu* Twin Dragons that dominated the enormous ceiling of the main wooden hall in the next room.

"Stand there," *Sensei* said to TJ, facing him in the direction of the main hall. *Sensei* stood opposite him, looking out towards the dry garden. "This is your *Dreamswick* training, which is paramount. We will learn the basic moves together here, before the Simulator, courtesy of *The Cerebrum*, puts your newfound skills to the test. Listen and learn *petit garçon*."

TJ nodded. He was beginning to get excited. *The Cerebrum* had provided them with surroundings that made him feel as if he was an authentic martial arts student.

"To warm up, let us adopt the starting position. Feet together," *Sensei* instructed. He carefully adopted a stance where his right leg faced TJ, and his left leg was at right angles to it, forming a reverse L-shape. Leaving his left leg firmly anchored, he took a small step forward with his right foot.

TJ thought it looked a little odd, but suppressed any desire to smile, laugh or look anything other than deadly serious. After all, *Sensei* demanded nothing less. In any case, TJ thought he'd seen a stance similar to it when watching Olympic fencing once on the television.

His thoughts were interrupted by *Sensei*. "This is the most secure and balanced foundation for *Dreamswick* work *petit garçon*. It is no surprise that some Dreamguardians in history became great fencing masters. They copied the stance and adapted it for their sport. But this is not sport, this is serious." He bounced his upper body up and down on his thighs as if to emphasise the strength and solidity of the stance.

"*Petit garçon*, the starting position. Try."

TJ did as he was instructed and carefully placed his feet together at right angles and then took a step forward with his right foot. *Sensei* came over and moved his feet slightly. He straightened TJ's back and lifted his chin up, manipulating him into the correct position. It was all about channelling and commanding authority, he informed TJ.

"Good, we move on," *Sensei* confirmed. "Now, before a Dreamstealer is defeated, the webbed hoop of the *Dreamswick* must face up and towards the enemy," *Sensei* explained, "ready to expel the filthy creature from a dream. Once this has been done, only then should you lower the hoop as a sign of your victory and control over the dream.

"As Malachi has already instructed you, the *Dreamswick* allows you to gift a dream. To do this, you must hold it in your right hand with the hoop facing the ground. The *Dreamswick* must be as close to vertical as possible, as a sign of the uprightness and virtue of the Dreamguardian. Then all that remains is to concentrate on a dream from the Great Book. Remember, the straighter the *Dreamswick*, the more successful the gifting will be."

Sensei told TJ to hold out his right arm holding the *Dreamswick* and adjusted his grip and its position on the staff after he had done so. "In the middle of the *Dreamswick*, here," he instructed, and TJ did as he was commanded. As he completed the move, twisting his arm and rolling his wrist over to the left so that the hoop faced vertically down, *Sensei* again moved TJ's arm and the *Dreamswick* into exactly the correct position. TJ winced but Sensei either didn't notice or didn't care.

"*Très bon, petit garçon,* good. Remember, this is the position to gift a dream." Even though the *Dreamswick* was light, TJ's arm started to ache from being outstretched and twisted down.

After admiring the position from all angles, *Sensei* announced it was time to move on. TJ was relieved to relax his arm, but his relief was short-lived.

Sensei positioned himself next to TJ and took two large sidesteps to put some space between them. He demanded they both adopt the starting position.

"This part is also critical," he continued. "Next is how to use the *Dreamswick* to attack and defeat a Dreamstealer. I will demonstrate slowly to start. Watch carefully."

With that, *Sensei* held out his arm and adeptly spun the *Dreamswick* slowly in his right hand. The *Dreamswick* went from one side of his body to the other in a figure of eight motion. As he did it he called through the motions of his wrist. "Right hand over, and down, then back the other way. Keep the motion in the bottom of the elbow and the wrist, and keep your left elbow tucked in. Draw a sideways figure of eight with your thumb." He made it look easy, as the *Dreamswick* spun effortlessly in his right hand and moved from one side of his body to the other.

After a short while effortlessly spinning the *Dreamswick* he stopped and turned to TJ. "There are variations of this, such as an underarm spin. Over time you will learn these, but for now, this is the fundamental attacking move to expel a Dreamstealer. If you must, it is possible to use two-hands, but your right hand *must* be the dominant one of course and remain above the left on the *Dreamswick*."

TJ took a deep breath then started to spin the *Dreamswick*. But he had little coordination or success. His first attempt ended as he dropped the *Dreamswick*, then on his second he accidentally hit himself painfully on his leg. He winced and began to get frustrated.

"Don't worry, this is normal for a beginner," *Sensei* said, almost reassuringly for a change. "Practice, *petit garçon*."

Together they spent a long time working on TJ's technique and mastering the motion of spinning the *Dreamswick* in his right hand, from one side of his body to the other. It was slow and painful at first, before he finally got a little bit faster.

"*Excellent!* Getting better, *petit garçon*," came some unusual encouragement from *Sensei*.

"*Merci*," called TJ as he continued to concentrate and work hard on the spin.

"Now, I am sure you are wondering how this expels a Dreamstealer," *Sensei* correctly guessed. TJ nodded, still focused on his spins.

"Well this is how. It is unusual to physically engage in hand-to-hand combat with a Dreamstealer as they prefer the shadows. Unless of course, they are a very confident and powerful Dreamstealer. But the beauty of the *Dreamswick* is that a good Dreamguardian can generate sufficient power for it to expel a Dreamstealer over quite some distance. Stop your practice and stand well back to the side, *petit garçon*," he said, motioning TJ to the side of the room. TJ obeyed and was glad to give his arm and wrist a rest.

Facing the open door through which they entered the training room, *Sensei* adopted the starting position. Slowly he began to spin the *Dreamswick* in his right hand, the motion and momentum beginning to build. TJ gasped as the speed increased and the *Dreamswick* became something of a blur and began to look as if there was more than one.

Then TJ saw it. An orb of what looked like white energy began to build in both size and intensity in the centre of the *Dreamswick*, where his right hand gripped the staff. When it had reached a certain critical mass, about the size of a cannonball, the energy orb glowed. It got more intense the faster *Sensei* spun the *Dreamswick*. TJ could see the sweat build up on *Sensei's* forehead as he rocked his body gently from side to side, helping the *Dreamswick* gain even more speed.

As he reached an incredible spinning speed, it happened. *Sensei* suddenly rocked back on his left leg, then threw all his weight forward onto his right foot. As he did so he also thrust the hooped end of the *Dreamswick* forward and let out a shout of aggression, almost like a war-cry. The intense white energy orb was expelled from the end of the *Dreamswick*. It shot first out of the *Dreamswick,* and then out of the room with an incredible force, the likes of which TJ had never seen before. It rocketed about fifty yards in total, before it exploded in a flash of light against a wall in the courtyard outside.

Everything went silent and TJ stared in disbelief.

Breathing heavily, *Sensei* turned to TJ, his eyes glaring and the veins on his neck raised up because of all the exertion. "There you have it, *petit garçon*, the power of the *Dreamswick*. When it is spun sufficiently by the dominance of the right hand, it generates a force that can be used to repel, that is drive or force away, the Dreamstealer. A Dreamstealer will exit a dream very quickly if it either sees one of those coming or it is hit by one."

Without warning, he strode forcefully over to TJ and bent down to look him in the eyes. "Never, ever," he started, jabbing his left index finger at him as he spoke those words, "allow yourself to be separated from your *Dreamswick*. If a Dreamstealer gets hold of it, they will spin it in their right hand at the same time as their own staff in their left hand. Once they do this, it creates a negative force so powerful it will incapacitate a Dreamguardian. Do you know what that means *petit garçon*?"

TJ thought Grandpa Mal had said something similar to this before, but he couldn't remember for sure. He shook his head to that effect quickly.

"If you are incapacitated then you will be deprived of all your strength and power," *Sensei* continued. "Unable to move. There is a name for it: *Transfixation*. Unless you can somehow recover, which is almost unheard of, it will most likely lead to the unbearable consequence of being lost forever inside a dream when the dreamer awakes. *Ce serait horrible.*"

TJ couldn't bear to think about that, even more so after reading with the Dreamorian all the secret Genesis passages about stairways leading down into hell. *Horrible* indeed!

"Now it is your turn. Simulator, generate a target."

When TJ looked back to his left an archery target stood in front of the open doorway *Sensei* had just fired the *Dreamswick's* energy orb out of.

"*Bon chance, petit garçon,*" *Sensei* said and invited TJ forward.

TJ moved to the centre of the room and took a few deep breathes to calm his nerves. He adopted the starting position and slowly began to spin the *Dreamswick* gripped in his right hand. After a few false starts he managed to gain some momentum.

The longer and faster he went, the more he got into a rhythm that began to beat faster. Although he was nowhere near as proficient as *Sensei*, the Dreamswick began to hum and whoosh as it cut through the air in front of his nose, sweeping from one side of his body to the other.

Suddenly, a small orb of white energy appeared in the centre of his *Dreamswick*, where his right hand gripped the staff tightly. "Good, faster," encouraged Sensei. TJ tried to spin his *Dreamswick* faster, but found he was already at maximum velocity. The energy orb remained no bigger than a ping-pong ball.

As he was tiring, TJ thought it was time to mimic *Sensei's* movements. He rocked back on his left leg and thrust his right leg and *Dreamswick* forward. He let off a shout and the white energy orb sputtered out from the *Dreamswick* with little speed towards the target. It just about made the short distance and hit the target softly on the outermost ring.

TJ sighed and was despondent at his effort. He thought it had been clearly inadequate and was also tired from the exertion. He braced himself for Sensei's reprimand, but it didn't come.

Instead, clapping filled the room. "*Bravo, bravo! Excellent petit garçon, excellent. Très bon, très bon,*" exclaimed *Sensei.* TJ had also done the unthinkable and managed to elicit a little smile from *Sensei* too.

"But... But that wasn't very good," a somewhat perplexed TJ said.

"*Non*, you don't understand *petit garçon.* For a beginner that was very good. For sure, we have a long way to go, but a very good first attempt. It is certainly good enough for us to progress to the next stage. In any case, do not forget that *The Cerebrum* will calibrate the Simulator accordingly for what is ahead of us."

TJ smiled and breathed a huge sigh of relief. Perhaps *Sensei* wasn't so bad after all. In any case, TJ was confident he had tried his hardest and done his best, and that had, at last, been recognised by someone who up to now had been *very* difficult to please.

"*Merci beaucoup, Sensei,*" TJ said happily. He was finally beginning to enjoy his training within the *Dreamswick* Simulator.

Just as TJ was feeling more comfortable, *Sensei* announced the next stage: defensive work.

"Although it is unusual for a Dreamstealer to have sufficient power and skills to overcome a Dreamguardian, it cannot be ruled out, especially if you have the misfortune to encounter a very powerful Dreamstealer." TJ and *Sensei* looked at each other carefully. They both knew who *Sensei* was talking about but neither wanted to speak its name.

"A Dreamstealer is able to attack in exactly the same way, except the spinning of their *inferior* staffs is performed in the left hand, in honour of Manasseh. Of course, a *Dreamswick* **should** be more powerful because it is in the hands of the righteous, but sadly this has not always proved to be the case. Therefore, we need to work on your defensive *Dreamswick* handling."

He stood next to TJ with his feet a shoulders width apart. Taking the *Dreamswick* in his right hand, he extended his arm out in front of him with his palm face down. He talked through the procedure as he demonstrated it slowly. He placed his left hand with his palm facing up over the wrist of his right hand. Then he rotated the *Dreamswick* clockwise, avoiding his left hand on the first rotation, but on the second he rolled the *Dreamswick* into his left hand.

"Now face the palm of your right hand down, spin the *Dreamswick* round again but avoid that right hand on the first spin. Then on the second spin place the *Dreamswick* back into the right hand. Then put the palm of your left-hand face up again, ready to repeat the whole procedure."

He continued to repeat the movement, talking TJ through it as he went. "Don't separate your wrists. Spin, skip, catch, palm down, skip, catch, palm up, skip, catch, down, skip, catch, up…" He repeated "skip, catch, down, skip, catch, up" faster and faster, as the *Dreamswick* rotated at ever increasing speed until it was spinning so fast that TJ thought it resembled a turbine propeller. It was spinning round so quickly it almost took on the appearance of a solid *Dreamswick* shield in front of his body.

"Simulator, fire!" yelled *Sensei*, taking TJ by surprise. A flaming red energy orb streaked into the room from the courtyard outside. *Sensei* didn't flinch even as it headed straight for his head. He kept spinning his *Dreamswick* at breath-taking speed and moved his arms up to cover his face with the *Dreamswick* shield he had created. The incoming missile hit the spinning *Dreamswick* and shot off into one of the internal screens. It hit one of the dragons in the face, turning it into a fire breathing creature for a short moment.

Sensei finished his defensive lesson off with some elaborate and advanced moves that he had no intention of teaching TJ today. He spun the *Dreamswick* above his head, behind his back, made some thrusts as if he was engaged in hand-to-hand combat, then finished with the *Dreamswick* vertical in his hands in front of his face, the webbed hoop still facing up. Symbolically his right hand finished above his left.

TJ had been taken completely by surprise and had dived for cover as soon as he saw the red energy orb come towards them like a heat-seeking missile. "What was that?" he shouted from the tatami mat, once *Sensei* had finished his moves.

Looking down at TJ, *Sensei* bowed deeply and reverently. He then broke into a huge smile and, offering out his left arm, reached down and helped TJ back up to his feet.

"That my young friend is how to fend off those filthy Dreamstealers, should one be stupid enough to launch an attack. Let me help you with your *Dreamswick* handling on this one. It is tricky, but as you've just seen, good fun once mastered."

TJ picked up his *Dreamswick* and *Sensei* stood opposite him in very close proximity. TJ followed *Sensei's* instructions as he held out his right hand with his palm down, then placed his left hand over the top of it with his palm facing up. He proceeded to spin the *Dreamswick* alternating his hands. The contemporaneous spinning and instruction continued as TJ worked hard to perfect the two-handed spin.

As TJ got into a good rhythm, *Sensei* stood back and to the side. He applauded TJ. "*Bravo*, my young friend, *c'est beau, c'est beau.* Now are you ready?" he asked.

Before he could answer, *Sensei* decided he was. "Simulator, fire!" he yelled, and another flaming red energy orb streaked into the room from outside. TJ screamed and closed his eyes as it came straight at him. He kept spinning the *Dreamswick* as quickly as he could. As it was about to hit him, the *Dreamswick* connected with the energy orb. It deflected at great pace just over *Sensei's* head, causing him to take drastic evasive action to avoid being hit. It powered into another of the paintings on the wall, creating another fire breathing dragon. The force of the hit on his *Dreamswick* took TJ by surprise and he staggered backwards.

"*Bravo*, my young friend, *bravo*," *Sensei* cried excitedly, picking himself up off the mat, applauding TJ's achievement as he did so. "You did it. *Magnifique!*" He slapped TJ on the back and ruffled his hair. "*Bravo!*"

A big grin appeared on TJ's shocked face, which then evolved into a wide smile. Then the laughter came, nervously at first at the shock of everything. Then a proper laugh erupted from him at what had just happened. *Sensei* reciprocated with a rich deep laugh, as they enjoyed the moment together: teacher and student in perfect harmony.

*

After they had stopped laughing, they debriefed on what had just happened and *Sensei* refined some of TJ's technique. He complimented TJ on his application so far before announcing they were ready to move onto the next phase of *Dreamswick* training.

"The next stage is practicing how to hunt a Dreamstealer and expel them from a dream, putting what you have just learnt into practice. I will now hand over to *The Cerebrum* which will be in full control of the Simulator in the next phase. It will present you with a dream situation previously experienced by another Dreamguardian, or will randomly generate a dream situation, as it wishes. It is very clever. As I said earlier, *The Cerebrum* is guided by the most advanced artificial intelligence and machine learning technology and will carefully select and calibrate this training encounter. *D'accord?*"

"*Oui, Sensei*," TJ replied confidently. With all the *Dreamswick* skills he had just been taught and been able to demonstrate, he was ready to be put through his paces.

"Let's go Dreamstealer hunting *Sensei*," he said excitedly.

CHAPTER 23 – THE HUNT

As soon as Sensei uttered the words, "Simulator, next stage, *commencer*," the Japanese temple training room disappeared. The backdrop was instantly replaced, and TJ and Sensei now stood on the ramparts of a relatively narrow wall. The grey bricks beneath their feet were very old and well worn. They felt slightly slippery too, even though they both remained barefoot.

The humidity was high, almost oppressive, and a thick fog limited their visibility. Had it been a clear day, they would have been able to admire the spectacular view of the Chinese valley from their vantage point. This would have included a large section of the Mutianyu section of the Great Wall upon which they now stood, snaking out ahead of them as it climbed and slithered over the mountainous terrain and across the landscape.

As it was, they could just about make out a Watchtower about one hundred yards ahead of them, up a relatively steep climb. The battlements lining this particular section of wall were so tall that TJ struggled to see over them. However, through the gaps he was able to ascertain they were quite high up and well above the canopy of the surrounding trees and dense woodland.

The fog gave the location an eerie feeling and TJ found it difficult to breathe given the humidity and altitude they were at.

"Where are we, *Sensei?*" he asked cautiously, gripping his *Dreamswick* tightly in his right hand. He'd been here less than a minute and already had a bad feeling about this place. He'd had this same feeling once before, within his own dream last night, and that gave him a sense of foreboding.

"The Great Wall of China I believe," *Sensei* replied, oblivious to TJ's concern. "I have visited here a few times in my lifetime, as well as within dreams, so I am not completely surprised by the location *The Cerebrum* has chosen. There are many places for filthy Dreamstealers to hide, but together we will find them. I must say this simulation of the Great Wall is *très* realistic. This is exactly how I remember it from when I was physically here last. Then, like now, the fog was thick, which was most unfortunate. Spoils the view, *naturellement.* But, believe me when I say that on a clear day the view is simply *magnifique*."

"I'll take your word for it," said TJ, slight disappointed not to be able to see the full view, even if it would have been generated by a supercomputer.

"Now, let's talk strategy," *Sensei* said as he surveyed their surroundings, at least as far as the fog allowed them to see. "A typical Dreamstealer will remain hidden in the shadows, for as long as they can get away with in the hope you will not find them and disappear, leaving them to torment the dreamer at will. Your job is to hunt them down, find them and expel them.

"In fact, a Dreamstealer will try to do one of the following to you: stay hidden until you choose to exit and then corrupt the dreamer; trap you by waking the dreamer suddenly with a severe dream before you can intervene; or fight you and incapacitate you."

"So how do I hunt one down, *Sensei*?" TJ asked.

"Experience, and your gut. That is the honest answer," came the reply.

"My gut?"

"How do you say that better in English? Your instinct, yes, *instinct*, that's it. And I think yours is good *mon amie*."

The change in *Sensei's* tone and language was not lost on TJ. *Petit garçon* had now been replaced by *mon amie*. Progress indeed, and well-earned of course. But now was not the time for TJ to rest on his laurels.

"You must always look for the shadows and the hidden parts of the dream environment you are within," *Sensei* continued. "Think of 'them' as snakes hiding under a rock. The other thing to watch for is the process by which a Dreamstealer corrupts and influences a dream for their dark purposes. It is achieved like this. Simulator, generate a Dreamstealer."

From out of the fog a Dreamstealer walked towards them. It was dressed in a hooded black robe with its face hidden. A simple wooden staff was held in its left hand. TJ was relieved to see there was no carved creature at the top of the staff or monastic scapular worn from the shoulders. This meant it wasn't *Dominus Tenebris*.

The Dreamstealer stopped, then adopted its starting position. Its left leg was out in front of its right and was the mirror of the starting position TJ had learnt at the beginning of his training. The Dreamstealer held its staff with two hands, its left resting above the right and began to spin it from side to side, moving its hands together up and down in a scooping motion.

"It is the same spin I taught you, but we Dreamguardians perform it purely with our right hand," *Sensei* whispered in TJ's ear. "The Dreamstealer uses its dominant left hand which corrupts the purity generated from the right."

As the Dreamstealer's hands moved quickly just in front of its face a red energy orb appeared and began to grow and glow.

"These are the giveaway signs," *Sensei* whispered again. "Firstly, the sound of the staff as it cuts quickly through the air. Tune in to this carefully and it can be picked up from a great distance. Secondly, the red glow of an orb can alert you to a Dreamstealer's presence, especially, but not only, if the dream environment is dark. This is a sure sign that a Dreamstealer is about to discharge its staff, which it will do either at you or into the sky as a sign that a corrupted dream has been bestowed upon a poor unsuspecting dreamer."

At this moment, the Dreamstealer stopped spinning its staff and held it aloft high above its head in just its left hand. The red orb of energy streaked through the staff out into the sky, as if it were a lightning bolt of blood. The small explosion of red from the end of the staff was both audible and visible.

"So, you must listen and observe at all times when you are hunting," *Sensei* advised TJ. "Of course, if the Dreamstealer was aiming at you, a red energy orb would be heading for you, *rapidement*. But if the orb is fired in the air then the filthy deed has been done and a dream is well on its way to being corrupted. Maybe it would have been an Embarraser, or a Stresser, or Scarer, or Forgetter, or Twister, or Deceiver, or Multiplier, or Convincer, or Tamperer, or a Nightfright, Horror or Stealer. So many wretched dreams from those filthy Dreamstealers."

Sensei stared hard at the Dreamstealer that the Simulator had since frozen, with its staff raised high above its head in its left hand discharging red lightning. It reminded him yet again how much he hated the enemy, and how he would do *anything* to overcome them.

"*Mon amie*, if you see the red glow or hear that type of explosion within a dream, you must be quick. Quick to hunt down the Dreamstealer. Quick to expel it. And quick to then overturn the corrupted dream with one of your own.

"If, for whatever reason, you cannot expel the Dreamstealer quick enough after that has happened, then you must escape from the dream. Again, quickly, before you are caught within it and lost forever. The corrupted dream that the Dreamstealer has just caused may wake the dreamer quickly and we cannot take any chances. Sadly, it has happened many times before. *Understand?*"

"*Oui, Sensei*," TJ confirmed, "I understand."

"So, handling the *Dreamswick* with care and proficiency is *très important*. Very important. And in all areas too, be it as part of defence, attack or gifting a dream."

He paused, as if he was contemplating what to do next.

"*Oui*, I think it is time to put all your newfound knowledge into practice. However, this time the Dreamstealer will not be so compliant."

He turned to TJ and bowed. TJ did the same back.

"*D'accord. En garde! Prêts? Allez!*"

The Dreamstealer in front of them instantly disappeared.

"Where did it go?" TJ asked, somewhat confused.

"*The Cerebrum* has reset the Simulator. Proper Dreamstealer hunting starts now *mon amie!*"

Sensei sounded quite excited by the prospect.

TJ scanned the area carefully all around him. Visibility had not improved much and the furthest he could see was still the Watchtower up ahead.

"What are you thinking *mon amie*?" *Sensei* asked in a whisper.

"If a Dreamstealer is here, I'm thinking about where it may be hiding," whispered TJ back as he cautiously made his way up the relatively steep incline ahead.

"Good, good. Where do you think it might be hiding? What does your gut say?"

"The Watchtower. Maybe in the shadows," TJ replied quietly.

"*Oui*, this is good, carry on," *Sensei* confirmed.

They carried on stalking towards the Watchtower, glancing out of each battlement on either side whenever they went past one just to make sure there were no surprises anywhere. The Watchtower was square and wider than the Wall itself. Its two stories meant it protruded high above the Wall. Ramparts all around the top of the tower made it look like a miniature castle rising from the Wall and it offered the perfect location for a lookout position and place to fire at approaching invaders.

Historically the Watchtowers had played an important part in defending the Wall. At militarily critical points they were close together, yet some distance apart at other points. As TJ could not see another one nearby, he guessed this once was considered a safer part of the Wall. If only that were true now, he thought.

Up ahead was a very narrow single door leading from the Wall into the Watchtower. This had been deliberately designed so as to slow down marauding enemies by forcing them to enter in single file. At his current pace, TJ was anything but marauding, but he was very much the enemy as far as any Dreamstealers were concerned.

As they came within fifty yards of the building, TJ suddenly saw it. Crouched up on the ramparts, looking in a different direction from one of the battlements. A Dreamstealer. It hadn't seen them, yet. TJ stopped and immediately adopted his starting position. He began to spin his *Dreamswick* just as *Sensei* had taught him a short while ago. The *Dreamswick* began to turn, slowly at first before picking up momentum.

As TJ reached a good speed the white orb of light appeared around his right hand where it gripped and turned the *Dreamswick*. It grew bigger and surpassed the size TJ had managed to generate before. Although it never reached the cannonball size that *Sensei* produced, it nonetheless started to glow intensely.

His heart pounding, TJ rocked back and then forwards, thrusting the webbed hooped end of his *Dreamswick* towards the Dreamstealer. He let out a more convincing shout of aggression as the orb of light streaked up towards the roof of the Watchtower. TJ's shout startled the Dreamstealer and it stood and turned towards them. The ball of energy hit it square in the chest, producing a blinding flash of brilliant white light. Then it, and the Dreamstealer, was gone.

"*Bravo!* Good shot!" screamed *Sensei* as he pumped his left fist in victory. "First time as well! *Bravo!*"

TJ was a bit taken aback at what he had just done but was also elated. Not only had he spun the *Dreamswick* correctly, but he'd also managed to fire a light orb, **and** hit and expel a Dreamstealer. He had done it! They both looked at each other and *Sensei* began to chuckle. "*Très bon mon amie.* Well done. That was very impressive for a beginner."

TJ smiled too at both the compliment and his achievement. Then, out of the corner of his eye, he saw something move. A shadowy figure moved across the narrow doorway into the Watchtower.

The smile disappeared from TJ's face quickly. "*Sensei*, there's something there," he said nervously. *Sensei's* laugh evaporated.

"Where?" he asked quickly.

"Just inside the doorway," TJ replied, "it must be another one."

Sensei looked a little surprised, as if he wasn't expecting another one, which concerned TJ a little.

"Are you sure *mon amie*?"

"*Oui*, positive," TJ confirmed.

TJ had a funny feeling in his stomach, as if something bad might be about to happen. As a precaution, he solidly positioned his feet a shoulders width apart and extended his right arm out holding the *Dreamswick*. With his right palm facing down and left hand facing up over his right wrist he began rotating the *Dreamswick* clockwise. On the second rotation, he rolled it into his left hand and repeated the process, gaining speed each time the *Dreamswick* changed hands.

As the adrenaline pumped through his veins, TJ found the *Dreamswick* spinning faster and faster. Not quite the turbine propeller speed that *Sensei* demonstrated, but much quicker than TJ managed before.

A red glow appeared from within the darkness of the Watchtower doorway. Its intensity built very quickly, and a flaming red energy orb suddenly streaked towards them like a heat seeking missile. TJ closed his eyes, span the *Dreamswick* as fast as he could and hoped for the best. A missed spin now would be disastrous. The red orb hit the spinning *Dreamswick* and deflected into one of the battlements where it exploded.

Sensei looked shocked and struggled to speak. When he did, he congratulated TJ on his successful defensive manoeuvre, but looked increasingly confused.

"What's up *Sensei*?" TJ asked, "is there a problem?"

There was a long pause. "*Non, mon amie*," Sensei finally said, failing to reassure TJ.

"What's the matter?" TJ asked.

"It's… it's just unusual for *The Cerebrum* to give a beginner more than one Dreamstealer in a session, especially one that attacks. But clearly it must think you are up to the job, so nothing to worry about, I guess. *Très bon mon amie."*

TJ's concerns dissipated, and he felt good. He had managed to surprise *Sensei* after all. He must be doing something right he thought to impress not only *Sensei*, but also *The Cerebrum*.

With a more confident stride, TJ marched up to the narrow door leading to the Watchtower. He listened carefully as he approached, straining to hear whether there was anything moving around in the darkness inside, including a Dreamstealer staff.

They made their way cautiously inside, where the stonework was thick and the atmosphere cooler and damp. It was very dark in the places untouched by the occasional arch window that looked out over the foggy valley below. Ahead of him, TJ could make out low height arches that seemed to lead to different areas of the tower, offering numerous places to hide. Centuries ago this floor would have housed soldiers, weapons and provisions. Now it might house a filthy Dreamstealer.

There was complete silence as they moved cautiously down the corridor, further into the Watchtower. The mixture of dark, light and shadows made the place creepy and TJ didn't like it one bit. He carefully rounded an opening in the corridor only to find another short corridor, with three archways promising to lead somewhere else. It was beginning to feel like a sinister stone maze. TJ poked his head round the first archway and peered inside into a small room. He quickly scanned the shadows, but there was nothing there. He did the same to the second archway, with the same result. The last one led to another short corridor with more archway openings that TJ thought must lead to some more rooms.

The first, however, led to another corridor that ran behind the two smalls room he had just observed. The next archway was guarded by a closed wooden door. TJ pushed on it, but it didn't move. He carried on down the corridor to the last archway. It too had a door, but it was slightly ajar. TJ turned back to tell *Sensei*, but he wasn't there.

"Sensei," TJ whispered as loud as he dared. But there was no reply. He tried again, with a little more urgency in his voice, *"Sensei!"* He waited, but there was nothing.

TJ was caught in two minds; whether to turn back or keep going. After some thought weighing the pros and cons, his inquisitiveness took over and he carefully pushed the door open. It creaked loudly, and TJ winced at the noise that would surely give him away should anything be lurking in the shadows within.

The room was completely dark, and he entered it stealthily with his *Dreams-*

wick poised, not sure what he would find the further he got in. As his eyes tried to adjust to the darkness, they detected some soft light from what looked like yet another corridor leading from the far-right corner of the room. As he made his way over, TJ was suddenly aware of something strange. The cold stone floor beneath his feet was now soft, like a carpet of grass.

Confused, he continued towards the soft light. As he reached the corner of the room, he realised it was another passageway, and up ahead he thought he could see open sky. He was relieved that he had successfully made it through a Watchtower that was far too eerie and claustrophobic for his liking.

As he exited the Watchtower via the passageway, he realised almost everything had changed. The atmosphere was still oppressive but was much cooler than before. It was now dusk and what daylight was left was fading fast. The most disconcerting discovery was that he was no longer walking on the Great Wall. It had completely disappeared, and he was surrounded by a vast expanse of grass. It looked uncomfortably familiar.

The one constant was the fog and TJ peered through the soupy haze trying to obtain his bearings. He thought he saw something familiar in the distance but immediately hoped he was mistaken. He began to walk towards it, clutching his *Dreamswick* ever tighter in his right hand as he went. After a few steps, he stumbled on some earthworks, hurting his foot. He muttered crossly under his breath. Simulator or not, this was no longer enjoyable.

His worst fear was confirmed. He had indeed seen a medieval archway up ahead, built from flint and stone. The further he walked, the more he saw until he reached the two -tiered cloister building that once formed the dining room of the monastery. His heart raced, and he felt disturbed. It was the ruins of the thirteenth century Franciscan priory. The place where, just last night, he had encountered *Dominus Tenebris*.

He shivered at the thought. Or maybe it was from the cooler temperature, as the sea breeze from beyond the monastery began to pick up, swirling the fog as it arrived. It clung to the upstanding remains of the ruined priory, just as TJ had seen it do once before.

The same feeling came over him. A feeling of being watched. He stopped and carefully looked all around him but couldn't see anything. He took some deep breaths, trying to compose himself. But he couldn't. He was fearful and had started to shiver harder. Not even the feeling of soft grass on his bare feet could soothe him.

Then he saw something, standing on top of the wall. A figure dressed in a full-length black robe. Its black monastic scapular blowing in the breeze.

A wooden staff tightly clenched in a gloved left-hand. A demonic creature crouched at the end of the staff, grinning sadistically at TJ.

Dominus Tenebris.

TJ was frozen by fear. His mind started to race. What was happening? It all looked and felt very real. Was he still in the Simulator, or had he gone back into his own dream, or had he strayed into someone else's somehow? But this was no time to lose focus or become a slave to fear. He quickly regained his faculties and adopted the starting position and began spinning his *Dreamswick.*

Dominus Tenebris growled a deep and sinister laugh from the top of the wall and shouted down fiercely to TJ.

"You really think you can defeat *me* with that *thing, boy?*"

The *Dreamswick* thudded into TJ's right knee as he was unable to fully concentrate on what he was doing.

"I see you failed to listen," *Dominus Tenebris* growled again. "Instead you have chosen to persist in your *folly* with the *old man.* To listen to the decrepit and senile *Dreamorian.* And now you are being taught by an ineffectual *Sensei.*"

Dominus Tenebris laughed again as TJ tried to generate some speed spinning his *Dreamswick.*

"*I* am the *strong* one," *Dominus Tenebris* continued, "and you and the Brethren - the unrighteous line of Ephraim - are *weak. I* am in control of your destiny, *boy.*"

By now TJ had started to gain some speed with his *Dreamswick* and he tried hard to muster some defiance.

"You will never win," TJ shouted back as he spun his *Dreamswick* from side to side of his body with his right hand.

From deep within the hood, *Dominus Tenebris* laughed again; a sarcastic yet still sinister laugh.

"You are *so* wrong *boy.* And you know you are. I have already warned you once. You will lose everyone important to you. Then *you* will be *lost* yourself, *forever...*"

"No!" shouted TJ defiantly as he saw a white orb of light emerge around his right hand and grow larger than he had managed before. He spun faster, and the orb glowed bright white, lighting up TJ's face and the surrounding area.

"Foolish *boy*," *Dominus Tenebris* laughed, the staff spinning in front of the hood at a speed TJ had never seen before.

TJ rocked back then thrust his *Dreamswick* forward as he slammed his right foot down in front of him onto the grass. The orb of light powered out from his *Dreamswick* at some pace, much stronger and more powerful than he had managed before.

As it reached *Dominus Tenebris*, a blinding flash of bright white light erupted. TJ shielded his eyes. When he looked again, nothing remained, apart from silence and the swirling fog.

TJ stood rooted to the spot, every muscle in his body tensed to within a whisker of snapping. Then he started quivering, unable and unwilling to believe what had just happened. Had he done it? Had he, TJ the beginner, managed to expel *Dominus Tenebris*? Was this significant, even if it was within the Simulator, assuming he was indeed still in the Simulator?

Slowly he gathered himself up from his attacking position and tried to compose himself again.

It was so quick he didn't even see or hear it coming. From the base of the wall it had just been stood on, *Dominus Tenebris* had discharged the demonic staff with such speed and venom that the red orb of energy was glowing the darkest red imaginable. An orb seemingly filled with the deepest crimson of blood.

TJ saw it too late and was unable to evade the incoming orb. As he tried to dive for cover, it hit his *Dreamswick*, catapulting it out of his hand some distance away. It landed softly in the grass, steaming. As TJ lay sprawled on the grass, his hand stung from the force of the strike. He was now at his most vulnerable.

Before he could react, *Dominus Tenebris* had moved again. The speed was terrifying. As TJ picked himself up from the grass, *Dominus Tenebris* was about twenty paces away from him. From the left hand, the demonic creature grinned manically as it spun. In *Dominus Tenebris'* right hand, TJ's *Dreamswick* spun powerfully.

In each hand, an orb appeared. One dark red and the other bright white, the perfect representation of corruption and purity. As they grew bigger and more powerful, lightning suddenly streaked between the two. They clashed in front of *Dominus Tenebris'* body, each orb seeming to both fight yet absorb the power of the other, as if part of some frightening, yet powerful, paradox.

TJ stood rooted to the spot, unable to take his eyes off what was happening before them.

The new orb created by the simultaneous spinning of *Dominus Tenebris'* demonic staff and TJ's *Dreamswick* sparked and crackled violently, as small lightning bolts spat out of it. Then, without warning, it shot towards TJ with unnatural speed.

It hit him square in the chest and threw him back some distance. As TJ lay on his back on the soft grass, he tried to get up. But he couldn't move. He was paralysed. His brain told him to move his arms and legs. *Quickly! Get up! Danger! Move!*

But he couldn't. He could hear the deep growled laugh get louder as *Dominus Tenebris* approached. The menacing figure stood threateningly over TJ's motionless body on the grass, but TJ's brain was anything but inactive. It was fighting, desperately telling his body to move, to get up and get away from *Dominus Tenebris*.

*

Grandpa Mal had taken a seat just off to the side of the two reclined chairs, upon which *Sensei* and TJ were strapped in under the Samurai helmets. They had been there some time, their bodies straining the straps every now and then as presumably they were undertaking some activity within whatever simulated dream *The Cerebrum* had put them in.

Suddenly TJ's chair jerked violently as his body tried to escape its restraints. It frightened Grandpa Mal and he jumped out of his chair. "TJ!" he cried, "are you ok?" But he knew it was useless. He couldn't hear him.

All he could do was watch as TJ's little body fought against the straps, almost as if he was having a seizure. But the straps did their job, and nothing moved.

*

Dominus Tenebris towered over TJ, who lay on the grass, unable to move. As TJ looked up, all he could see was the dark robe stood over him. He was terrified. He tried to move but couldn't. The demonic staff was slammed down, right next to his head with such force, that it dug into the grass. Only TJ's eyes flinched on the outside, as the rest of him was unable to. Inside he was petrified.

A black boot was placed under TJ's leg and gave him a nudge. TJ could feel it, but even though he tried to strain his body he was unable to respond by moving. The boot did it again, this time a bit stronger and TJ rolled lifelessly over onto his front, his face now buried in the soft grass. He could feel the dew that had begun to settle on his tongue. *Dominus Tenebris* gave another kick of the boot and TJ rolled onto his back again. Now he was staring into the abyss of a black hood, save for two red eyes that bored into TJ.

As *Dominus Tenebris* hunched over TJ, another laugh emanated from within the hood.

"Foolish *boy,* to think you are a match for me. You fail to listen at your peril, boy. Unable to move are we, boy? This is the power of *Transfixation.* The horrifically beautiful combination of the staff of evil with that ridiculous, yet powerful, *Dreamswick.* It is the only useful thing that will ever come of the *Dreamswick.*"

TJ tried to close his eyes, but even that was impossible.

"I think you know what will happen next *boy*, after *Transfixation.* I will corrupt a dream so severely that the dreamer will wake and you, unable to respond, will be lost. Forever. Quite right too, you filthy *Dreamguardian.*"

Dominus Tenebris sneered, then laughed again. TJ feared the worst.

"Remember *boy*, as you seem to have a short memory. *I* am gaining power and the Dreamstealers are rising. I have told you before, we are gaining power with every Dreamguardian we cause to be *lost, forever… just like I am at liberty to do to you now.*"

TJ braced himself for what was about to happen. The questions went screaming round in his mind. What was about to happen? Would it work? Would it hurt? Where would he go? He wanted to cry, but the *Transfixation* was so complete he couldn't even manage that.

"On this occasion, I will leave you with a choice," *Dominus Tenebris* said. "You can choose to join me and the Terror of the Dreamstealers, before it's too late. Or you can be left with a memory, *boy*, that will torment you for the rest of your life. The memory of the day you came face to face with *Dominus Tenebris* and experienced *Transfixation.* You will then understand what can, and will happen in the future, to those that you love who choose this foolish path. And then when I am done with them, I will come back for you also."

Dominus Tenebris bent even closer to TJ's face. All TJ could see was the small red eyes. He felt as if he was looking into the depths of hell.

"So… *sweet dreams, boy,*" he sneered.

TJ's *Dreamswick* was thrown down onto the grass next to his body and the evil staff was spun vigorously just above TJ's face. Then it, and its owner, was gone.

TJ lay there for some while, unable to move. He vehemently hoped that *Dominus Tenebris* would not return. He could think of no fate worse than being trapped in a dream in this way. He began to wonder how he would ever recover from this experience.

Suddenly a concerned voice rang out a short way away, *"Mon amie, mon amie, are you ok?"*

Although he was unable to physically respond, TJ felt a relief unlike anything he'd ever experienced before.

Sensei ran over to TJ's lifeless body and fell to his knees. *"Mon dieu, what has happened?"* He was relieved to see TJ was alive through a small flicker in his eyes.

"I am sorry mon amie," he whispered to TJ, *"I just don't understand how this happened"*.

Then, as he knelt next to TJ, *Sensei* called out loudly, "Simulator, **terminer... fini.**"

*

The lights and buttons on the helmets and surrounding machinery died instantly and Grandpa Mal knew what to do. With his hands shaking he quickly took off *Sensei's* helmet and undid the straps on his right hand.

"Christophé," Grandpa Mal shouted anxiously, "what happened?"

Christophé shook his head as he undid the rest of his straps himself and Grandpa Mal took the helmet from TJ's head and began unbuckling his straps.

"I'm not sure Malachi. In all my years as *Sensei* and Master of the Armoury, I have never experienced anything like that before," Christophé replied. "He just disappeared. How is he? I presume he is alive?" He looked quickly over at the computer for confirmation of TJ's vital statistics.

Grandpa Mal was furious. "I very much hope he is alive, otherwise you and this machine have a lot to answer for." He bent over TJ to check he was breathing and was relieved to discover he was. He gently patted TJ's face and called his name, trying to rouse him from wherever he currently was.

After a few minutes, TJ began to stir. He opened his eyes, which were still full of fear, and rubbed them with trembling hands.

Grandpa Mal's relief was enormous. He patted TJ's head and reassured him he would be fine.

"I'm sorry, *Sensei*. I'm sorry, Grandpa Mal," TJ said weakly. "I tried my hardest, but it was no match for me."

Grandpa Mal and *Sensei* looked at each nervously. "What do you mean TJ?" Grandpa Mal asked urgently.

"*Dominus Tenebris* overpowered me and took my *Dreamswick*. Then used it against me and subjected me to *Transfixation*." TJ went silent as it all began to replay in his head again. It would take him quite some time to recover and forget about this, he thought.

"*Dominus Tenebris* said I had a choice. Join the Dreamstealers or know what it will be like to lose people I love in that way. Then *Dominus Tenebris* said it would come for me." A large tear rolled down TJ's cheek.

"It's ok, dear boy. You're safe now," Grandpa Mal said gently, as TJ closed his eyes to stop any more tears from escaping.

Grandpa Mal turned angrily to *Sensei*. "He wasn't ready for that Christophé, he's only a boy, a beginner," he shouted.

"I'm sorry," Christophé replied, "but it had nothing to do with me."

Grandpa Mal looked at him accusingly.

"*The Cerebrum* was in full control. But the difficulty level it chose was clearly way too advanced for a beginner like the *petit garçon*," Christophé said defensively.

"Well, quite," Grandpa Mal snapped back, "but how and why did *The Cerebrum* simulate *Dominus Tenebris*? How does it even know what *Dominus Tenebris* looks like, and how the creature thinks or acts?"

"*Je ne sais pas*," said a chastened Christophé. "I don't know the answers to your questions."

"What could have happened?"

"Honestly, I just don't know, Malachi, *Je ne comprends pas*... I just don't understand."

"There must be a problem with *The Cerebrum*," Grandpa Mal said, feeling his anger rise again.

"Perhaps... I don't know," Christophé replied, struggling to make sense of everything that had just happened. "It is the most sophisticated and secure technology. It should be impossible for it to malfunction. Maybe it has been compromised somehow, but then, *non*, the servers are completely secure. Unless…"

"Unless what?" asked Grandpa Mal anxiously.

"Unless it has been *sabotaged* by someone from *within* the Brethren," Christophé said nervously.

"Is that possible?"

Christophé thought long and hard before replying. "Well, it would be very hard to do. But is it *possible*?" he posed Grandpa Mal's question to himself. "*Oui, Monsieur*, I guess it is *possible*. Extremely difficult, but not *impossible*."

"The Armoury and all your relevant partners must investigate this thoroughly Christophé, this is very important."

"*Oui, Monsieur*," came the serious reply.

TJ opened his eyes slowly again and sat up in the chair.

"Take it easy, dear boy," Grandpa Mal said, concerned for the wellbeing of his precious Grandson.

"Don't worry, I think I'm ok Grandpa Mal," TJ said as he swung his legs from the chair and stood up. But as he looked at Grandpa Mal his eyes rolled, and his legs gave way beneath him. He collapsed to the floor with a thud.

"TJ!" cried Grandpa Mal, bending over him. "Wake up," he said, tapping the side of his cheek gently with his old bony fingers. "Oh dear, wake up, dear boy."

There was no response.

Grandpa Mal looked over at Christophé with great concern.

"What have you and your computer done to him?" he cried.

CHAPTER 24 – A CALL TO ARMS

The rest of the day had gone from bad to worse. Chatty had refused to come down from her room and the afternoon event was cancelled, if indeed one had ever been planned as far as Chatty was concerned.

Lizzy Wizzy had played various board games with Benjy to try and keep him entertained and his mind off what was yet another big argument between his Mummy and Chatty. As for Benjy himself, he wished things would go back to how they used to be before everyone just got angry with each other.

The altercation between Chatty and Katherine had reminded Emma of how precious her time with Lizzy Wizzy was. So, Emma made a special effort to bake cupcakes with Lizzy Wizzy in the afternoon. As well as being good fun, she thought it would also give her some happy memories to remember just in case her daughter also ended up grumpy and moody when she was older.

Baking was one of Lizzy Wizzy's favourite things to do as well. Not only did she get to spend time with Mummy, but she loved putting on an apron, mixing all the ingredients in the bowl, smelling their creations being baked and then squeezing glorious butter icing out onto the cupcakes. Clearing up was less fun of course, except the part where she got to lick the wooden spoon.

Teatime was a quiet affair as Chatty, Grandpa Mal and TJ remained absent. No matter how hard the remaining four tried to pretend this morning hadn't happened, it had.

Lizzy Wizzy was glad when the day eventually fizzled out, but she was determined to spend some time with Chatty. She could at least try and cheer her up, even if it was only a little bit.

After she had put on her pink gingham pyjamas, dressing gown and said goodnight to Mummy and Auntie Katherine who were enjoying a glass of wine in the living room, Lizzy Wizzy wandered down the corridor. She knocked gently on Chatty's bedroom door. It had been slammed shut some hours ago and, so far, Chatty had refused to open it for anyone, not even to her Mum when she demanded Chatty come downstairs for tea.

If anyone else had asked her, Chatty probably would have gone down for tea as she was really hungry. But as it was her Mum, Chatty was quite content to be adamant she didn't want anything to eat. Her stomach was now paying the price for her stubbornness.

There was no answer. Lizzy Wizzy could hear music playing faintly from within the room and as a light was shining under the door, she guessed Chatty was still awake. Just sulking still.

"Chatty," Lizzy Wizzy called through the door, "it's me, Lizzy Wizzy. Please may I come in?"

Still no reply.

"Chatty!" Lizzy Wizzy called with a bit more urgency, "let me in!"

She paused. Then, after looking over her shoulders down both sides of the corridor to make sure nobody was watching or listening, she continued.

"I've got something for you Chatty, quick, let me in."

An ancient old iron key rattled in the lock and the door opened sufficiently to let Lizzy Wizzy in. It was slammed closed quickly behind her, just in case any intruders tried to barge in.

The room was a mess of half-read magazines, colouring books, stencils and pencils and cuddly toys that had been unceremoniously evicted from the bed. Chatty's eyes were red from crying and her brown bobbed hair was all messy from where she'd buried her head into her pillow more than once this afternoon. Even though it was getting late in the day she was still dressed; another act of unseen defiance.

"What is it? What do you want?" Chatty said miserably sitting back down on her bed, even though deep down she was very pleased to see Lizzy Wizzy.

"I've been worried about you, are you alright Chatty?" Lizzy Wizzy asked.

"What do you think?" Chatty replied somewhat harshly, then immediately regretted her tone. She knew Lizzy Wizzy was sensitive and had a genuine caring side, which was one of the things she admired about her younger cousin.

"Don't be like that Chatty," Lizzy Wizzy said, choosing to not take her bad mood to heart. After all, Chatty wasn't upset and angry at her. "What do I think?" she continued. "Well, I think that you're feeling miserable and that you're also pretty hungry".

Chatty sniffed, cuffed her nose with her sleeve, and nodded vigorously.

"Thought so. Which is why I brought you these," Lizzy Wizzy said smiling, as she dug deep into both square pockets of her dressing gown and pulled out handfuls of cookies.

Chatty's sullen face lit up in an instant, as if Lizzy Wizzy had flicked a switch to her smile.

"Cookies! My favourite," came the excited response as Chatty reached up and took them from Lizzy Wizzy's outstretched hands. She immediately stuffed one into her mouth.

"Thank you, Lizzy Wizzy," she just about managed to say through a mouthful of cookies.

"You're welcome, I'm happy it's made you smile".

Chatty pulled a massive grin, her mouth still closed and full of cookie. It made Lizzy Wizzy giggle.

As she giggled, so too did Chatty. Her eyes became like saucers and her hand covered her mouth as she tried to suppress her laughter and prevent the cookie from shooting out.

Once she managed to finish her mouthful, their giggling erupted into full-scale belly laughs and they both rolled about clutching their sides.

After the frivolity had calmed, they sat on the bed and finished off the rest of the cookies. The crumbs in the bed and chocolate chips smeared around their lips were testament to how much they enjoyed the treat.

Chatty was glad Lizzy Wizzy had sneaked the cookies upstairs. Not only had it taken the edge off her rumbling tummy, but it had cheered up what had been a pretty miserable day as far as she was concerned.

As they lay sprawled out at opposite ends of the bed, listening to some music, Chatty tickled Lizzy Wizzy's foot when she wasn't looking.

Lizzy Wizzy jumped. "Oi! Pack it in," she laughed, moving her feet out of the way pretty quickly.

"You know what Lizzy Wizzy?"

"Nope, what?"

"Teapot!" joked Chatty.

Lizzy Wizzy rolled her eyes and laughed again.

"You're so funny, not!" she joked back at Chatty.

"You know what Lizzy Wizzy?"

"Not again! Nope, what?"

This time Chatty was not joking.

"You're my best friend. Like the sister I never had."

Lizzy Wizzy smiled and felt warm inside.

"I agree," she replied. "You're my special big sister."

Chatty smiled. "Better than a smelly brother any day," she declared. They both looked at each other, pulled funny faces and burst into laughter again.

*

The two girls enjoyed each other's company for a little while longer, before Lizzy Wizzy could feel tiredness creeping in.

"I'm tired big sis'," she yawned, "I need to go to sleep."

"Really? I'm not tired," Chatty replied, "I want to stay up later."

"I'd like to, because I don't want to have another scary dream. But I can't, I'm too tired."

Chatty knew Lizzy Wizzy well enough to know that once she was tired and had reached the point of no return, she would be asleep within a matter of minutes.

"Did you have a scary dream then?" Chatty asked.

"Yes," came a sombre reply. "It was horrible."

"What was it about then?"

Lizzy Wizzy paused. "I'd rather not talk about it. I'd just like to forget about it."

"Sure," said Chatty. She could see how upset just mentioning it had made Lizzy Wizzy, so she decided not to pursue the issue.

Lizzy Wizzy closed her eyes and let off another massive yawn. "I'm off to bed," she confirmed, her eyes barely open and feet fumbling around the floor for her slippers.

Once she found them, she gave Chatty a weary hug and made her way to the door as if in a zombie trance.

"Goodnight, little sis'" Chatty called out.

"Goodnight, big sis'," Lizzy Wizzy responded, blowing her a kiss through sleepy eyes. "Best friends forever."

"Best friends forever," Chatty agreed. "Sleep tight and don't let the bed bugs bite."

Lizzy Wizzy ignored the last comment. She hoped nothing would disturb her tonight as she needed a good night's sleep for once. She crept out of Chatty's room and made her way down the corridor to her own bedroom. Before she went in, she looked further down the corridor towards TJ's room. There was no sign he was back yet. His bedroom door was open, and the room was in darkness.

She hoped that TJ would have had a good day with Grandpa Mal. It couldn't have been any worse than their day, she thought. At least he had missed the surprise visit from Uncle Bertie that had turned sour and led to yet another huge argument between Chatty and Auntie Katherine.

She fell into bed. At least the day had ended slightly better, Lizzy Wizzy thought. She'd spent some time baking with Mummy and also managed to cheer Chatty up.

Hopefully, everyone would be back together tomorrow and the fun would start again.

*

Back up the corridor, the visit from Lizzy Wizzy had done Chatty the world of good. It had taken her mind off the argument with Mum and put her in a much happier mood. The cookies had also done their job and the world always felt a bit better for not having to live with an angry stomach.

The emotional roller coaster she had been on today finally took its toll. As she lay in bed, the day's events started to replay through her mind. But, for once, all the negatives – Mum, Dad, Grandpa Mal and TJ - were squeezed into the background by the fun she had just had with Lizzy Wizzy.

As she drifted off to sleep, Chatty decided that the chance to spend time with Lizzy Wizzy was the only good thing left about being on holiday at the Old Girl. Mum could do what she liked; she didn't care much about her anyway. And as for TJ and all his secrets with Grandpa Mal, well that was almost as annoying.

But at least her Dad cared about her. And Lizzy Wizzy too for that matter. Yes, at least Lizzy Wizzy had been there for her tonight. Lizzy Wizzy, the little sister she never had. Lizzy Wizzy, her best friend forever…

*

The room was dark, and the red lines of the alarm clock signalled a time just after 2am. Lizzy Wizzy had been dreaming. It was a dream she was sure she had experienced before. It felt so warm and happy that she wished it had lasted forever.

But something had disturbed her, again. Now she was awake and crying, again. Just like all the times before, she couldn't explain why. Her pyjama top was wet from sweat and she was cold as well as upset. She felt so lonely, again. So *alone, again*. Not for the first time, sad to the very core of her being. As if nothing would be right in the world, ever again.

"Not again," she said dejectedly to herself, sitting upright in bed. She tried hard to remember the dream that had taken her to such a warm and happy place, but she couldn't, as usual. "Why can't you remember?" came the familiar reprimand to herself.

Lizzy Wizzy slid out of bed, forced her slippers clumsily onto her feet and put her dressing gown on. As usual, it offered a crumb of comfort, but was not sufficient to take away the feeling of being upset and alone.

Opening the door carefully, Lizzy Wizzy tiptoed down the corridor to TJ's room. She hoped it wouldn't be a repeat of the other night when she'd gone in for some company, but he wasn't there.

However, this time his bedroom door was closed. She opened it slowly and crept in, making her way over to the lump in the bed.

"TJ, it's me!" she said quietly, leaning over the lump. "Are you awake?"

There was no response.

"TJ, TJ!" she repeated, this time shaking the lump in the bed.

"Huh!" came the confused response as TJ was roused from a very deep sleep. "What?! Grandpa Mal?! *Sensei*?!" he murmured through his sleepy confused state.

"TJ! It's me, Lizzy Wizzy, wake up."

TJ began to regain his waking senses. "Lizzy Wizzy!" he exclaimed tiredly. "What do you want? What's the time?"

He propped himself up on his elbows and rubbed his eyes with one of his fists while his other hand ran through his tangled mop of blonde bed-hair.

"I think it's just gone two o'clock TJ," Lizzy Wizzy replied.

TJ groaned. "Well go back to bed then. You should be asleep, just like I was a second ago."

TJ banged his head down on his pillow and tried to roll over. He'd had quite an eventful day after all. Even though he'd spent most of the time after the Simulator resting at Christophé's, he was still feeling quite drained by everything that had happened.

Lizzy Wizzy was having none of it. "Don't go back to sleep, I need to talk to you," she said, digging her fingers into TJ's ribs and prodding him as if to reinforce the point.

TJ squirmed and groaned again.

"Alright, alright, stop it, I'm awake now," he moaned.

"Good," she said as she plonked herself down on TJ's bed, nudging him to give her some more room. "I had another one of those horrible 'lost' dreams TJ. You know, the ones I used to get. I thought perhaps you could help me find it."

"What do you mean, find it?" TJ said defensively. What did she know?

"Well, you know, I thought if we talked about it and you asked me questions then maybe I'd be able to remember it."

TJ breathed a sigh of relief. She knew nothing, of course! It was his job to ensure it stayed that way.

"Well, it's a bit difficult to help you find a dream if you don't remember anything about it," he said half-heartedly.

"Well can we at least *try*?" implored Lizzy Wizzy, immediately making TJ feel sorry for her and a little guilty at being unwilling to talk about lost dreams.

"Very well, sorry. So, how did the dream start, do you remember?"

Lizzy Wizzy thought long and hard, her index finger resting on her chin so as to emphasise the intensity of her recollection effort.

"No. Can't remember," she answered, her head and hand dropping.

TJ sighed and tried a different angle.

"Do you remember *anything* about the dream?"

Again, Lizzy Wizzy raised her head, this time stroking her chin with her fingers in an attempt to coax a memory out somehow.

"No!" she declared dejectedly. Her head dropped again. She pounded her fists into her lap and groaned in frustration.

"I'm sorry Lizzy Wizzy, but I'm not sure there's much I can do to help you remember. What's the last thing you remember then?"

Lizzy Wizzy thought for a moment, then looked pleased as she remembered something.

"I was happy that I'd cheered Chatty up and was also hoping we'd all have a better day tomorrow and some fun together. You see, Chatty and Auntie Katherine had a massive argument because Uncle Bertie dropped by. Today wasn't much fun, TJ, although at least I did get to bake some cupcakes with Mummy."

"Yes, we heard all about it when we got back," TJ said. "Auntie Katherine was not impressed. Nor was Grandpa Mal for that matter."

TJ steered the conversation back to the original subject, so they could finish it off quickly, get Lizzy Wizzy back to her own room and himself back to sleep.

"So that's the last thing you remember then?" TJ asked.

"Yes," she conceded. "Maybe having no dream though is better than the scary one I had last night."

The reply grabbed TJ's attention immediately. "You had a Scarer?" he asked quickly.

"A what?"

"Sorry, I meant a scary dream." TJ kicked himself for not being more careful.

"Yes, last night. I was riding a fairground carousel and it wouldn't stop. It was getting faster and faster, and then the horse I was on came to life and..."

"And what?"

"Then I woke up. But it was horrible TJ, it really frightened me." She reverted to her baby voice as she repeated how much it had frightened her.

TJ remained silent. He tried to remember back to the description of a Scarer in the Great Book. He could remember that it mentioned something important. He closed his eyes.

"Are you going back to sleep TJ, don't you care?"

"Shhh," TJ said. "No, I'm not going back to sleep. I do care and I'm thinking."

"About what?"

"Doesn't matter. Just be quiet, will you?"

"Charming," Lizzy Wizzy replied, feeling a bit put out.

TJ racked his brain. Then he remembered:

Scarers - mildly scary dreams – evidence that a Dreamstealer has taken some hold of, and power over, a dreamer

That was the important bit that had stuck in his mind: *'evidence that a Dreamstealer has taken some hold of, and power over, a dreamer.'*

"Are you ok TJ?" Lizzy Wizzy asked, "you've gone very quiet."

"I'm fine. I said be quiet for a moment," TJ said abruptly.

Lizzy Wizzy pulled a face and folded her arms. "Fine, no need to be so rude." She was beginning to lose patience with him.

TJ didn't respond. In his mind's eye he was back in the Inner Sanctum reading through the Great Book.

Now, in terms of bad dreams, what was next after a Scarer? Come on, he thought, before he suddenly recalled the answer. That's it, a Nightfright. He could picture it now:

Nightfrights - more sinister and threatening than Scarers; evidence that a more powerful Dreamstealer has taken even more hold over a dreamer; unless stopped could lead to the unleashing of more sinister dreams, to the great danger and detriment of the dreamer and their wellbeing

TJ tried to compose himself as he began to put the pieces together. It was all starting to make sense, even if the conclusion was far from pleasant.

For a long time now, Lizzy Wizzy had been subject to *Forgetters* and prevented from remembering parts of a particular dream. She had also been subject on more than one occasion to the theft and loss of a dream: outright *Stealers*. Then, just last night, she had been subject to a *Scarer*.

Armed with all the knowledge gained from the past few days, it was now clear to TJ: a Dreamstealer had taken hold of Lizzy Wizzy's dreams and was now exerting increasing power over them.

TJ knew what it would lead to if it was left unchallenged. It would lead to something altogether more sinister and threatening. He guessed next to come would be a Nightfright. Who knew what damage a Nightfright might inflict upon someone so young, sensitive and vulnerable as Lizzy Wizzy?

TJ tried to gain control of his train of thought which was currently hurtling down a track, dangerously gaining speed. Right under his nose, a Dreamstealer had started to torment his little sister. Up to now, he hadn't realised it. But now he did.

A righteous anger began to rise up inside of him. TJ vowed then and there he would take care of everything. TJ the Dreamguardian would take care of the filthy Dreamstealer tormenting Lizzy Wizzy.

He opened his eyes and tried to sound calm.

"They're just silly dreams," he said to his little sister. "Perhaps it's because you're missing home." He cringed at the ridiculousness of the excuse but hoped he would get away with it. "They're nothing to worry about I'm sure," he continued, doing his best to play everything down and conceal his anger at the situation. "I think the best thing you can do is go back to sleep."

"But what if the lost feeling comes again, or a bad dream comes back?"

"It won't," TJ said defiantly.

"How do you know?"

"Trust me, Lizzy Wizzy," TJ said confidently. "These will all be over soon enough. From now on you'll be safe. Just go back to sleep and concentrate on the most amazing dream you can. Something you'd really like to do."

He smiled at Lizzy Wizzy and she smiled back weakly. She wanted to believe and trust him, she really did. But she just wasn't sure. What she did know was that she was tired and scared.

TJ could sense her apprehension and fear. He made a decision then and there, although Lizzy Wizzy could never be aware of it.

"I promise, Lizzy Wizzy," he said solemnly.

Nothing was going to stand in the way of him protecting Lizzy Wizzy. After all, even *Sensei* said he'd performed well in the Simulator, before *The Cerebrum* had uncharacteristically malfunctioned.

TJ was deadly serious. He was ready for his first proper mission as a Dreamguardian. In fact, after listening to Lizzy Wizzy and seeing her emotional state and fears, he was more than ready.

He, TJ, a Dreamguardian no less, was ready to protect the safe passage of his little sister's dreams.

CHAPTER 25 – THE BALLERINA

After some further reassurance from her brother, Lizzy Wizzy reluctantly went back to her room. She pulled the duvet up around her ears and closed her eyes tightly and willed herself back to sleep. It didn't take long. The last couple of nights of broken sleep had taken their toll and she soon drifted off. She did as TJ instructed and tried to concentrate on the most amazing dream she could.

*

TJ ran through the dark room, grabbing a robe and *Dreamswick* as he went. There was no time to lose. He hoped he wouldn't be too late. For Lizzy Wizzy's sake. He reached the far end of the room and located the smooth brass doorknob. As he turned it, he exchanged the darkness of The Armoury for the light of what was to come...

*

Towering high above TJ was a spectacular glass-vaulted barrelled roof. It looked like an enormous yet elegant curved glasshouse, allowing the evening sun to stream in. The spacious room was bordered on three sides by a galleried balcony restaurant. Its elegant tables had not long been vacated and were now strewn with plates, bowls and glasses. Most of them were empty, although some bore the evidence of expensive, yet uneaten, food and drink.

The allure of being perched at a cosy table up in the gallery being supplied with exquisite food and drink was tempting, but the emptiness of the restaurant confirmed that being somewhere else was now far more important. There was no time for TJ to stop to enjoy the restaurant's culinary delights either.

He rushed across the hall, completely unnoticed by the waiting staff who above him on the balcony were far too busy clearing and preparing the tables for the next course during the first interval. TJ exited the hall, then bounded up an impressive stone staircase and then up smaller carpeted staircases.

After scaling quite a few he reached the doors at the top that led into the auditorium. He carefully edged them open and slipped inside. He was on the third balcony tier within the huge auditorium. It was dark, with the only lights in the room concentrated on the stage. Looking out from up here the stage was a long way away. From over the heads of the seated audience, he could just about make out the orchestra pit in front of the stage, soft lights within it illuminating the conductor's score and the various musicians.

The stage was empty and the orchestra was playing softly. As he slipped into the shadows at the back of the balcony, TJ accidentally banged his *Dreamswick* against the wall.

"Shhh," came the agitated response from someone within the back row of the section he had just entered.

TJ cringed, but said nothing. He needed to be careful and stay hidden. Just in case.

The music emanating from the orchestra increased in volume. A small figure dressed in a white leotard, tutu and tights appeared from the side of the stage. She moved sideways towards the centre of the stage delicately on her tiptoes, *en pointe*, elegantly moving her arms as she did so. She took bigger steps in time with the music, still on the tips of her toes, before she performed a graceful leap in the air, creating the most beautiful lines.

TJ gasped. Even from this distance he knew who it was. It was Lizzy Wizzy. Of course! She loved dancing, so it came as no great surprise to TJ that Lizzy Wizzy would dream about performing as the principal ballerina at the Royal Opera House.

He smiled as he watched his little sister on the stage, captivating the attention of the audience. He could hear them gasp as she performed the most amazing move. Whilst on the tiptoes of her right foot she leant forward and raised her left leg straight up above her head at an angle approaching one hundred and eighty degrees: an *Arabesque penché* no less.

As proud as he was, and as beautiful was the combination of music and graceful ballet, TJ forced himself to turn his attention away from Lizzy Wizzy. He needed to be on full alert to make sure her dream would not be interrupted and replaced with a Nightfright or stolen altogether. Even though she didn't know it, he had promised her after all.

TJ scanned the darkness. In some respects, although this was one of Lizzy Wizzy's lifetime dreams, she had chosen the worst place for a dream. There were so many places for a Dreamstealer to hide. TJ made his way carefully along the balcony, his *Dreamswick* clutched tightly in his hand, ready for action, just in case.

The music began to build and the stage filled with more ballerinas. For a moment TJ was mesmerised by the sight, until he thought he saw something out of the corner of his eye. In the tier beneath this one. On the left-hand side, close to the stage. In one of the private boxes. Was that something?

His heart began to beat faster, but he needed to get closer, so he could be sure. Turning on his heels quickly, he slipped out of the doors he had come through just a moment ago and ran down a short flight of stairs leading to the balcony below.

He carefully slipped through the doors leading onto the Grand Tier and made his way to the left. He crept along the wall behind the audience, quietly stalking his prey as if he were a ravenous predator.

He passed the closed curtain leading to the first private box. It wasn't this one he was interested in, but the one furthest along, closest to the stage. As he got closer his heart began to pound in his chest. The doubts began to build in his mind too.

Had he seen an actual Dreamstealer? What would it do when it was cornered? What if there was more than one? Would he be able to expel a real Dreamstealer from Lizzy Wizzy's dream? What would happen if he didn't get it right? What if he got Transfixed? What if he got trapped... lost in a void of dreamless darkness from which he couldn't escape...?

His legs began to feel like jelly and the butterflies in his stomach fluttered with alarming power. The determination and confidence he had felt earlier when talking to Lizzy Wizzy had suddenly deserted him. It had been replaced by fear.

He passed the closed curtain leading to the second and third box. As he did so, the music was starting to build into a crescendo. His legs felt heavier and heavier with each step and he could now feel his hands start to tremble. Finally, he reached the curtain of the last box which was also closed. As the music gathered pace and volume, almost mimicking his heartbeat, TJ took some deep breaths and tried to formulate a game plan.

He decided that surprise was the best form of attack. If a Dreamstealer was hiding behind the curtain, then he would have the upper hand. Despite the close proximity he hoped there would be enough time and space to generate his orb of light ahead of the Dreamstealer and expel it from Lizzy Wizzy's dream.

TJ decided he could pontificate no longer. He decided he would burst through the curtain on the count of three.

Feeling as if his heart was about to pump out of his chest, he started his count. One, two, three...

He parted the curtain slightly with his left hand and burst through, his *Dreamswick* poised in his right hand.

TJ scanned the box quickly, there was nothing there! But then he saw it. A black hooded figure was disappearing over the low carpeted partitioning wall into the box next door. It was trying to make its escape! TJ turned around quickly and made a swift exit. They both emerged from the curtains at the same time back into the small corridor that ran behind the rest of the boxes and seats.

Fortunately, as far as TJ was concerned, he had caught the Dreamstealer by surprise and it had no intention of standing around to fight. It turned left and started to run away from TJ back down the small corridor. As fast as he could TJ quickly swung his *Dreamswick*. He attained a fast spin quickly, assisted by the adrenaline pumping around his body. The white orb of light appeared, grew and intensified at a pace TJ had not experienced before. Then just as he feared the Dreamstealer was getting too far away, he threw down his right foot and powered the white orb towards the retreating figure.

The orb of light shot out of the hooped end of the *Dreamswick*. Then, just as the orchestra reached its crescendo, the orb exploded with a flash of white light, coinciding with a great crash of cymbals from the orchestra pit.

"No flash photography. Behave please, this is a serious ballet..." came a stern voice from an incredulous member of the audience.

TJ was rooted to the spot for a few moments, still holding his *Dreamswick* attacking position. He was breathing and sweating heavily. It had all happened so quickly he hadn't really had time to think. But he'd done it. At least he thought he'd done it!

Drawing himself up into his normal standing position, he edged slowly down the corridor, careful not to disturb any more members of the audience. They could obviously see and hear him to some extent within the dream, which was something he hadn't really thought about before or appreciated.

He looked for the Dreamstealer but couldn't find it. He began to relax and smile. The Dreamstealer was gone! He must have done it after all. He'd expelled his first proper Dreamstealer!

As he stood there, TJ started to chuckle quietly. He'd only gone and done it! Just like he'd promised Lizzy Wizzy he would, even without her knowing. It was a shame she'd never know. After all, what he'd just achieved was pretty epic, even if he did think so himself.

His self-congratulatory thoughts were interrupted by the sound of applause as the current scene of the ballet ended. For a split second TJ worried that the house lights were about to go up. If they did then hundreds of people in the audience of Lizzy Wizzy's dream were about to see a sweaty eleven-year boy at the ballet, clutching a funny wooden staff with a misshapen webbed hoop at one end, wearing a smart robe and a huge smile.

As it was, the lights stayed down and the music started up again. TJ looked down at the stage and saw Lizzy Wizzy dancing back onto it, ready for another scene. As he was closer to the stage than before, he could see she had the biggest smile on her face. He wondered whether he needed to gift her a different dream. After all, she seemed to be enjoying this one very much.

As his eyes scanned the stage, he froze. He noticed that something, or someone, was hiding behind the stage curtain on the opposite side of the auditorium.

"No!" he said angrily to himself, "that can't be right. I thought I'd expelled the Dreamstealer. Yet that must be it behind the curtain, down near Lizzy Wizzy."

Feeling angry and cross with himself, TJ made his way to the Grand Tier exit, then wound his way down to ground level. He followed the signs pointing towards the orchestra stalls, but then ignored one on a door that said, 'Performers Only'.

He entered a narrow corridor with peeling paint and could hear the music getting louder the closer he got. The sign on the door at the end of this corridor shouted 'Silence!' confirming he was within touching distance of being backstage.

He opened the door gingerly and peered through the crack. Ahead he could see some rickety wooden steps leading up to the wings of the stage. From his vantage point he could see that curtains created four entrances on and off the stage to his left. A troop of ballerinas suddenly appeared from somewhere to the right of the stairs, ran across the top of them and through the first entrance closest the audience and onto the stage.

TJ slipped quietly through the door. The ballerinas had not encountered anything hiding in that particular corridor, so it was safe to hide there for the time being. He climbed the wooden steps and pressed himself into the thick black drapes of the curtains in the wings, almost wrapping himself up in the process. As he peeped out, he could see Lizzy Wizzy dancing beautifully on the stage. He could also see the black outline of the audience, the grand tiers of the balcony where he had been only moments ago, some green emergency exit signs and television screens that showed the conductor.

Suddenly the troop of ballerinas were heading back towards him, making their way off the stage. TJ wrapped himself completely up in the thick black drapes, plunging his world into darkness, and held his breath. He heard the ballerinas pass by, their feet treading the boards like a herd of the daintiest elephants.

He peeped out again and the coast was clear. Lizzy Wizzy was engaged in yet another solo performance on stage, twirling and jumping like never before. Not that he could ever tell her, but her dream imagination was certainly impressive!

Within the wings he poked his head round the first curtain to check out the second corridor leading onto the stage. Satisfied there was no-one there, TJ quickly moved into that aisle and wrapped himself up in the black curtain again.

He heard more dancers go past. Then just as he was about to reappear from the curtain some of them came back. If it wasn't so serious, it would be a good game, TJ thought. When he believed the coast was clear he poked his head out again and looked round into the third corridor leading onto the vast stage.

As he looked, he saw a small bulge in the curtain. Something else was hiding, in exactly the same way as he was. TJ thought it too risky to expel the Dreamstealer so close to the stage, for fear of disturbing Lizzy Wizzy. Plus, he wasn't completely sure whether the orb of light would work through a heavy curtain.

He decided the best thing was to surprise the Dreamstealer, much in the same way he had done in the box in the Grand Tier. Only this time he would already be advanced in his attacking procedure and wouldn't miss when the Dreamstealer fled from the false security of the curtain.

Stepping out from where he was hidden, TJ tiptoed his way carefully towards the lump in the curtain. Making sure he had his back to the stage he began to spin his *Dreamswick*. The white orb of light appeared and gained in size and intensity. As he spun it with his right hand, he reached forward and grabbed the curtain with his left-hand, just above where the Dreamstealer looked to be crouched. He yanked the curtain hard and it flew open.

It was all something of a blur. The figure jumped out and looked to make its escape away from TJ and the stage. Even though he knew someone was there, the speed at which it moved still took TJ by surprise. Just as he was about to unleash his *Dreamswick* and expel the Dreamstealer, he stopped abruptly. His bottom jaw almost hit the floor.

He couldn't believe it. It wasn't a Dreamstealer.

He called out over the music that filled the stage wings.

"Stop! Stop! Don't move."

All motion stopped just as TJ had demanded.

"What on earth?" TJ exclaimed. He couldn't believe his eyes.

The figure had also been taken by surprise and was completely confused by what was happening.

"Turn around, slowly," TJ called out.

The figure did as it had been told and turned around slowly to face TJ.

Both TJ and the figure gasped.

CHAPTER 26 – WEIRDO IN THE WINGS

"**C**hatty?" he asked incredulously, even though there was no doubt it was her.

"TJ!" Chatty exclaimed, running towards him.

"What… what are you doing here?" TJ stammered, his eyes out on stalks.

"I don't know," Chatty replied. "What's going on? Where are we?"

At that moment, TJ realised that Chatty had absolutely no idea what was happening. Furthermore, not only was she shocked and confused, but TJ could also tell she was very scared.

He looked over her shoulder and as she got close to him, he dragged her into the curtain.

"We need to stay as hidden as possible, just in case," he warned.

"Ow! That hurt," she said.

"Shh!" TJ responded and covered them both with the curtain, just before another herd of dainty elephants ran past.

TJ unwrapped them from the curtain once the dance troop had gone.

"Do you mind telling me just what's going on TJ?" Chatty demanded. "I mean, where are we? Also, what *are* you wearing and what is *that* in your hand?"

"Steady on Chatty, one at a time, it's complicated," TJ replied, a little unsure himself as to precisely what was going on. Maybe Chatty was just part of Lizzy Wizzy's dream. But then again, she seemed real enough to him and her behaviour didn't indicate she was an integral part of Lizzy Wizzy's dream.

TJ didn't know how he was going to explain all this, or whether he should. He quickly formulated a plan. He would play ignorant and let on nothing. Perhaps there was a chance he could trick Chatty into not believing any of this.

"Where are we? I have no idea Chatty," he lied. The truth was quite clear: they were both in Lizzy Wizzy's dream.

Chatty was suspicious. "Are you sure you don't know what's going on TJ?" she asked. "It's almost as though we are within Lizzy Wizzy's dream. It must be a dream, as how else would Lizzy Wizzy be dancing at the Royal Opera House. But it doesn't feel like one of my dreams. After all, why would I dream about Lizzy Wizzy dancing? In some strange way it also feels quite real, even more so now that I'm stood here having a conversation with you."

TJ shrugged his shoulders. It would be difficult to throw Chatty off the scent. "I don't know Chatty. Perhaps you're right. But perhaps what's more likely is that this is your own dream? You must be dreaming about watching Lizzy Wizzy dancing and talking to me."

Chatty stopped to think. "Hmmm," she muttered. Perhaps TJ was right. Whatever was going on, it was all rather bizarre. But then again, this all seemed too real. Much more realistic than any of her own dreams, although her embarrassing piano playing dream the other night did also seem quite realistic. Hang on, she thought, TJ was in that dream too.

By now her mind was racing. She couldn't think straight. If this was her own dream, then why was Lizzy Wizzy the centre of attention? Why would she be dreaming that Lizzy Wizzy was the principal ballerina and not her? And what on earth was TJ up to again?

"I'm not sure, TJ," she concluded. "What is that ridiculous robe you're wearing and why are you carrying some weird stick?"

TJ looked down, acting as if it was the first time he'd ever seen the robe and the 'stick'.

"I have no idea," TJ lied quickly. "It's your dream, so perhaps you thought I'd look good in a robe and needed a stick."

Chatty wasn't convinced. This really didn't feel like her own dream. The conversation was far too authentic.

"I don't think this is my dream TJ. This *has* to be Lizzy Wizzy's. But I don't know what I'm doing in it. Or what you're doing in it for that matter."

She paused again and tried to make some sense of it all. As she looked over

TJ's shoulder, she could see Lizzy Wizzy pirouetting across the stage, totally engrossed in her performance. The music from the orchestra was soft and delicate, with just the flute barely audible.

Just as Chatty started to speak again, TJ saw something move a short distance away in the shadows over her right shoulder.

Then he heard it. The swish of a staff being spun through the air. A Dreamstealer stepped out from the shadows just as a red orb appeared around its fist.

TJ's heart sank. "No!" he cried, as the red orb grew in size. He tried to warn Chatty. "Watch out, it's a Dreamstealer," he shouted, but the Dreamstealer's ambush was already complete and it fired the orb towards them.

With her back to the Dreamstealer, Chatty didn't see it coming. Just as it was about to hit her, TJ dived forwards, knocking Chatty to the ground. They tumbled heavily into the thick curtain as the red orb narrowly missed them. The Dreamstealer wasn't going to give up easily. It started to spin its staff again, attempting to generate another red orb as quickly as possible.

TJ wasted no time. He jumped to his feet, span his *Dreamswick* and was pleased to see a white orb of light form quickly. Almost simultaneously, a red and white orb were released from the duelling pair. The orbs flew towards each other and exploded almost equidistant between the Dreamstealer and TJ. The pink flash it generated amongst the darkness of the stage wings was blinding. Chatty, who up to then had been observing the tussle with eyes wide open in shock, now shielded them from the light.

By the time she reopened them, TJ had resumed spinning his *Dreamswick* and had generated another white orb. Before the Dreamstealer was able to do the same, TJ fired it in the direction of his enemy. It hit the Dreamstealer square in the chest, generating a flash of pure white light and a loud bang. As soon as Chatty and TJ dropped their hands from shielding their eyes, the Dreamstealer had gone.

TJ took a few deep breaths to recover, then offered a hand down to Chatty to help her up off the floor.

"I can do it myself," she said angrily, disentangling herself from the curtain. "If you want to help, you can start by telling me just what is going on here. What was that thing? How and why was it attacking us, and what was that thing you were firing at it? Where did it go?"

Once on her feet, she moved well into his personal space. With her face almost pushed up against his, she confronted TJ.

"It's about time you started telling the truth Thomas Daniel Joseph. What's going on?"

"I don't know," TJ responded quietly, unable to look her in the eyes.

"Rubbish, you're lying. Tell me the truth," Chatty said raising her voice.

"I don't know," persisted TJ.

Chatty lost her temper.

"Tell me the truth," she bellowed.

"No," TJ replied defensively.

"Tell me!" she screamed.

"I can't," TJ said, this time looking her defiantly in the eyes. He had promised Grandpa Mal and was not about to break it.

They stared hard at each other, each willing the other to blink and determined not to crack themselves. It was a battle for control of the truth.

As it happened, they both lost when they became aware someone was running off the stage towards them.

It was Lizzy Wizzy.

"What's going on over there?" she called out.

"Don't answer her," TJ snapped at Chatty. "This is very bad. We need to go."

"Go where?" Chatty asked, somewhat alarmed at the panic that seemed to have quickly grabbed hold of TJ.

"We need to get out. If she sees us and gets suspicious, then the shock might suddenly wake her. That can't happen. It's too dangerous. Especially with us in here."

"TJ, what are you talking about? What do you mean get out and more importantly what do you mean by dangerous? Stop it, you're scaring me. It's fine, this is all just a dream, right?"

Chatty's anger at TJ had now been replaced by fear. She didn't like the way TJ was behaving. Now it wasn't just her that was scared.

"Quick we need to get out before she sees us. Hold my hand," TJ demanded.

Chatty hesitated for a split second.

"Hold my hand," TJ shouted at her, making her jump. She was now very scared.

"No. I'm not going with you," she said as she turned to run.

"Chatty, no! Come back, you don't understand!" TJ begged.

She spun back round to face him. "I don't need you TJ," she shouted back.

With his free hand, TJ made a grab for Chatty's arm. She tried to shake him off, but TJ persisted. "Please, Chatty, you need to trust me," he begged.

The urgency in his voice and fear in his eyes unsettled Chatty. "Fine," she said sharply and ended her resistance, even if was against her better judgement.

Quickly taking hold of Chatty's hand in his left hand and his *Dreamswick* in his outstretched right hand, TJ rolled his right wrist over. He faced the webbed hoop down to the floor and tried to hold the *Dreamswick* in a perfectly vertical position.

"I don't think she's seen that it's us yet," he said quickly to Chatty, "but I need to gift her a dream to try and confuse her just in case."

He paused for a second, a look of panic coming over his face.

"What's up TJ, what is it?" Chatty asked nervously. She didn't like the look on his face.

He looked directly at her, the panic visible in his eyes.

"I can't remember which one I need to gift. Is it a *Jumbler,* or a *Random,* or a *Weirdo*? Oh no! I can't remember Chatty."

"TJ!" Chatty said desperately looking over to the stage, "quickly, she's coming. I don't know what you're talking about, but you need to choose one. Quick!"

"Ok, ok," TJ said urgently, "but you need to hold on. Whatever happens, don't let go of my hand. I hope this works."

Chatty nodded. Questions were racing through her head, but clearly now was not the right time to ask any of them.

As TJ held the *Dreamswick* as vertically as he could manage, he concentrated hard. "*Weirdo, Weirdo,* please give me a *Weirdo,* and quickly," he said desperately.

Just at that point, Lizzy Wizzy reached the edge of the stage and peered into the darkness. Without warning, a white orb of light appeared from nowhere. It lit up the area, including them.

"TJ, Chatty, is that you?" Lizzy Wizzy called out. "What's going on? What are you two doing here in my dream?"

Before anything further could be said, the orb of light shot out of the end of the *Dreamswick* into the air.

The *Weirdo* came quickly.

Instantly a pure white unicorn began to float down from the ceiling onto the centre of the stage. Its huge feathery wings were outstretched, and its golden horn radiated as it reflected the stage lights. When it landed on the stage, it reared up onto its hind legs and began to slowly execute a pirouette.

As soon as it did so, a trio of clowns appeared from the opposite wings and tumbled their way onto the stage. One back-flipped, one performed cart-wheels and the other did roly-polys until they stood behind the pirouetting unicorn.

A lady in a flowing dress appeared from the far side and began to sign op-eratically. She hit dramatic high notes that pierced the air. From out of her dress emerged doves that flew out over the heads of the audience.

Then up from the orchestra pit, the instruments levitated and began play-ing by themselves. Bows of the violins and cellos moved violently back and forth over the strings, beaters pounded the timpani drums, flutes let of a shrill scream and the brass instruments punctured the air with sharp stabs of sound. It created a chaotic concerto of carnage. The conductor had been replaced by a majestic Red Deer stag which nodded its head as if directing the airborne orchestra with its huge antlers.

TJ had no idea what was going on. Things were getting out of hand. This was not going the way he had planned.

Clutching Chatty's hand tightly, he whispered "Lizzy Wizzy exit, Lizzy Wizzy exit, Lizzy Wizzy exit," under his breath. He clung on for dear life to the *Dreamswick* in his right hand too, hoping for the best.

CHAPTER 27 – TELL THE TRUTH

The next thing TJ felt was someone shaking him hard. Then he started to feel a sharp pain. As he opened his eyes and tried to fully wake up, he saw Chatty stood over him, poking him hard in the ribs.

He flinched, but before he could say anything, Chatty got in first.

"I want a word with you TJ? What are you up to?"

"Huh?" came the deliberately vague and sleepy reply.

"Don't pretend you don't know what's going on. What was that all about?" She was not happy.

"I don't know what you're talking about Chatty. Are you alright?"

Chatty huffed and gave him another poke.

"Ouch! Stop it," TJ pleaded.

Chatty was not impressed. "I won't stop until you tell me what's going on and what you're up to," she demanded.

"I don't know what you're talking about," came the reply yet again.

"Don't lie."

"I'm not Chatty, honestly."

"Liar!" she said, giving him another big poke, the hardest of them all so far.

TJ squirmed and protested at yet another dig in his ribs.

"They'll get harder if you don't tell me the truth about what's going on. I'm pretty sure you know, don't you?"

"Calm down, Chatty," he said, playing for time. "Once you've calmed down then I might be able to understand just what it is you're talking about."

TJ had no intention of helping her discover the truth of course, but he was very keen to protect his ribs before they were attacked again.

Chatty moved back enough to let TJ sit up in bed. He switched on his bedside lamp and pulled the duvet up under his armpits to protect himself against any more poking.

"We were in Lizzy Wizzy's dream, both of us, somehow." Chatty announced it as a matter of fact. She was convinced.

TJ's heart skipped a beat and he felt his forehead start to get hot. How was he going to deflect the truth and get out of this one?

"Chatty, you're mad," he tried to joke, but Chatty was in no mood for joking.

"We were watching her dance in a ballet at the Royal Opera House. You know that's one of her dreams."

"Well, yes, but I wasn't there. Well, maybe Lizzy Wizzy included me in the dream, but it was not 'me' me. If you know what I mean."

Chatty had no intention of accepting this as an explanation. "Yes, you were there. And it was 'you' you alright. Not a figment of Lizzy Wizzy's dream or imagination. You were dressed in a strange robe, with a strange stick. Then you spun it and were firing these white balls of light at something you called a Dreamstealer."

TJ gulped. He must have accidentally let that slip when they were ambushed. He began to get a sinking feeling that it would be a difficult job to convince Chatty that all this hadn't happened.

"Chatty, are you sure you're feeling ok? Do you need to see a Doctor? This all sounds a little bit weird if you ask me."

Chatty glared at him. She felt like hitting him.

"TJ, this was real. I know it was and you know it was. In fact, you know exactly what I'm talking about it and I want answers. I want answers and I want them *now!* How did this happen and what is going on?"

TJ shook his head, but deep down he knew that the game was up. Chatty was stubborn and far from stupid. She would never be convinced this was all a figment of her own imagination.

"This isn't the first time this sort of thing has happened either, is it TJ?" Chatty asked, leaning in close to TJ's face. He drew the covers in tighter to reinforce his rib protection.

"It's you, isn't it?" she said accusingly.

"What's me?"

"Why are you tormenting Lizzy Wizzy?"

"You what? Tormenting her?" TJ asked. She was so wrong. He was trying to do the opposite, before *she* showed up and almost ruined everything.

"She's been having horrible dreams. I don't know how you're doing it, but it's obvious. It's you. How dare you. To your own little sister too. What a horrible bully you are."

She glared at him again.

TJ didn't quite know quite how to respond. He tried to sound as calm as possible, but he was far from calm.

He shook his head. "You're wrong Chatty," he said, "I'm certainly not a bully and not tormenting Lizzy Wizzy either". That much was true of course. "As for all the other things you claim happened, they sound ridiculous. You must have either had a strange dream or you're just making it all up. You have been rather out of sorts lately."

Chatty had heard enough. She knew he was lying and hiding something big. She grabbed a cushion and aimed a blow at TJ's head. He saw it coming and ducked quickly under the covers.

"Liar! Coward!" she shouted as she pounded the lump in the duvet with the cushion. "Tell me the truth."

From behind her, a voice stopped her in her tracks.

"Chatty, that's enough, dear girl."

Chatty spun round, the cushion still above her head. TJ poked his head up from beneath the duvet.

"Grandpa Mal!" TJ said quickly. Even though his bedside light was not that powerful and he could barely see Grandpa Mal standing on the other side of the room in front of the now closed door, his voice was instantly recognisable.

TJ got in first. "It's not my fault Grandpa Mal. Chatty's going mad and accusing me of all sorts of things. She reckons she was in a dream and…"

Chatty interrupted. "Grandpa Mal, I'm not making it up, it's TJ, he's…"

"That's enough, that's enough," Grandpa Mal said as they both talked over each other, trying to explain to Grandpa Mal what had happened.

As they continued to bicker, getting louder and louder as they did so, an exasperated Grandpa Mal shouted for them to be quiet. It was an uncharacteristic thing for Grandpa Mal to do and it took them by surprise. They both fell silent instantly.

"Thank you," Grandpa Mal said reverting back to his normal gentle voice, "that's quite enough you two."

"Do you know what's going on Grandpa Mal?" Chatty asked. "Something weird is happening and I don't like it."

"Yes, dear girl, I do," Grandpa Mal confirmed. "But you need to listen carefully, all of you, as this is more serious than I ever could have imagined."

Chatty and TJ looked at each other and then back in the direction of Grandpa Mal.

"I took a call from one of my friends, Christophé, just a few moments ago," Grandpa Mal said.

TJ's ears pricked up at the mention of *Sensei*. What had he discovered and why was Grandpa Mal mentioning him in front of Chatty?

"He is very concerned," Grandpa Mal continued. "Some unusual and unorthodox activity was detected within the Old Girl a short time ago. Upon investigation Christophé discovered that more than one light was detected on the holographic globe, coming from the same source."

"What does that mean? What are you talking about Grandpa Mal?" Chatty asked.

"Nothing," TJ interrupted. He glared at Grandpa Mal, motioning him to be quiet. He had done just that and hadn't told Chatty anything. The secrets of the Brethren were safe with him. Chatty didn't know anything!

"TJ, please, if I may," Grandpa Mal said quietly. TJ was confused. Here he was trying to stop Grandpa Mal from saying too much in front of Chatty, but he wasn't listening.

"As I was saying, more than one light was detected on the holographic globe but from the same source. In other words, your robe TJ picked up activity from more than one Dreamguardian."

"A what?" Chatty asked, screwing up her face as she did so. "Dreamguardian?"

"Didn't TJ tell you already?" asked Grandpa Mal.

"No!" Chatty said grumpily, scowling at TJ. He *was* hiding something after all. She *knew* it. How *dare* he lie to her like that.

"No, I didn't," TJ said proudly, "I kept it a secret Grandpa Mal. Just like I promised."

"Well yes, quite so, dear boy," Grandpa Mal continued. "But I'm somewhat surprised you didn't, given what's just happened."

"Thanks!" Chatty said to TJ. Her suspicions were right. She vowed then and there that she would never trust TJ ever again.

"But Grandpa Mal...,"

"TJ, let me continue please, dear boy, this is very important". TJ's shoulders dropped at Grandpa Mal's interruption.

"A Dreamguardian," Grandpa Mal said, addressing Chatty directly, "is someone very special who is able to enter the dreams of others. They do so to protect a dreamer from coming to harm from the Dreamstealers. The Dreamstealers, dear girl, are the enemy."

TJ glanced across at Chatty who sat motionless with her mouth wide open.

"Grandpa Mal! I hadn't told her!" TJ cried, his frustration bubbling over at him for revealing what he thought were secrets that couldn't or shouldn't be shared with Chatty.

"Dear boy, you need to stop and think about what you are saying," Grandpa Mal said, almost equally as frustrated with him. "In all the apparent excitement or confusion, you have clearly missed something very important."

TJ was stung at yet another gentle reprimand. "Grandpa Mal?" he asked.

"Oh TJ, the events of the past few days have clearly taken their toll. After all, you were so astute at the beginning. What I mean is that it is evident that you were not the only person in Lizzy Wizzy's dream last night."

Suddenly it dawned on TJ. He was flabbergasted. In all the drama of the dream and trying to protect the secret of the Brethren, TJ had overlooked the single most important fact. Chatty was in Lizzy Wizzy's dream as she was one of them! She had the gift too!

"Of course," TJ exclaimed, "how stupid of me! Chatty...!"

"Yes, dear boy," Grandpa Mal chuckled. "A bit slow on the uptake this time, dear boy," he said continuing to chuckle.

"What?" Chatty asked, "will someone please explain what you're talking about?"

"Indeed, I will," Grandpa Mal said. "Chatty my dear girl, it is my honour to tell you that you are a Dreamguardian. A protector of dreams. You have the gift! Just like young TJ has and also yours truly."

"But, how...? Why...? What...?" said Chatty, struggling to string a sentence together. In fact, she was pretty much speechless for one of the very first times in her life.

TJ smiled as he knew exactly what she was feeling. "Welcome to the Dream-guardians," he said quickly. Now that she knew he felt the weight of secrecy lift from his shoulders. "There's so much to tell you Chatty,' he continued. "Wait until you see the..."

"TJ, one thing at a time, dear boy," Grandpa Mal quickly interrupted. "As you know these things can't be rushed. There is a time and a place for everything."

"Oh," TJ said, a little disappointed not to be able to share some of his recent experiences. "Of course, sorry Grandpa Mal."

"That's quite alright, dear boy. Now there is just one more thing to say. As I said, somehow *The Cerebrum* detected activity from more than one Dream-guardian tonight. More than one light was recorded here at the Old Girl..."

"Yes, you said that already Grandpa Mal," TJ interrupted excitedly. He needed to make amends for his stupidity in not actually realising Chatty was a Dreamguardian before now.

"There must have been two lights, one for me and the other for Chatty...," TJ continued.

"No, my dear boy, that's not quite right." Grandpa Mal smiled.

TJ looked puzzled. "But you just said..."

"I did indeed say there was more than one light. Yes, one was yours and the second was Chatty."

"So, I was right then…"

Grandpa Mal chuckled again.

"Not quite, dear boy. Not just two lights, but a third light. You see, somehow *The Cerebrum* detected yet another Dreamguardian in Lizzy Wizzy's dream…"

Chatty and TJ looked at each other, their eyes almost as wide as their mouths. She'd only just heard about the Dreamguardians and now there were even more being discovered.

"Who was it?" Chatty asked quickly.

"But I didn't see anyone else," TJ said. "Who was the other Dreamguardian Grandpa Mal?"

"Why, it was dear Lizzy Wizzy herself."

Grandpa Mal stepped to one side and from behind his back Lizzy Wizzy jumped out. She had been stood behind him all the time. She had succeeded, just, in suppressing her excitement and staying concealed, just like Grandpa Mal had asked her to. Like Chatty, she didn't fully understand everything that was going on either, but it all seemed so exciting.

TJ jumped out of bed. He couldn't believe it. "What?! But how?" he exclaimed.

"The threads on your robe TJ. Remember? They picked up extremely advanced brainwave activity from Lizzy Wizzy which *The Cerebrum* was somehow able to detect. None of this has ever happened before, so it is a very exciting development for us to research. Lizzy Wizzy must be very special, but then again I think we all knew that already."

He smiled at Lizzy Wizzy before turning back sternly to TJ. "But in talking to Lizzy Wizzy, TJ, she said that she saw you in her dream. You were arguing in the wings off the stage with Chatty. You really must be more careful TJ."

"But…," TJ said starting to protest, but Grandpa Mal cut him short.

"No buts," he said crossly. "You must be more careful. Listen, all of you. Being a Dreamguardian is a great honour and very serious. The consequences can be severe and…"

He stopped as he realised now was not the right time to go into all the details. He softened his tone. "Well, we'll talk about that later. Of course, I should add that one can have great fun being a Dreamguardian if you observe all the rules and do it correctly."

He smiled again at Lizzy Wizzy who was unable to contain her excitement anymore. She began to jump up and down, singing "I'm a Dreamguardian, I'm a Dreamguardian, I'm a Dreamguardian," as she did so.

Chatty also jumped up off the bed and ran over to Lizzy Wizzy. They embraced, and she started to jump up and down with her.

TJ stood there, completely stunned. He was upset that Grandpa Mal had just told him off. He was also unsure as to how he felt now that Chatty and his little sister had been revealed as Dreamguardians. How would they be able to cope? he thought.

TJ began to feel concerned for Lizzy Wizzy and Chatty. After all, as Grandpa Mal himself had stressed, being a Dreamguardian was a serious and dangerous business and not for the fainthearted. He explained his feelings of apprehension as part of being a protective older brother and cousin, rather than contemplate that some jealousy may have just crept in. It was now no longer just his and Grandpa Mal's secret.

Lizzy Wizzy felt so happy as she jumped and danced around. She hadn't understood much, apart from the very simple explanation Grandpa Mal had given to her before they had made their way to find Chatty and TJ. The main thing she had understood was that being a Dreamguardian meant she was special, a chosen one, and it was a way for her to help others too. She could think of no better combination.

Even though Chatty hadn't fully understood everything Grandpa Mal had said either, in that precise moment she felt as if she belonged again. She didn't feel quite so lonely, like she had in recent days.

As the girls continued to dance, Grandpa Mal joined in with a little jig too. Although both the girls were unaware of precisely what being a Dreamguardian meant and would require of them, he would teach them over time. He beckoned TJ over to join them, which he did, reluctantly.

As they all stood together in a circle, Grandpa Mal motioned for them to quieten down even though the excitement was palpable.

"Now, now, settle down please dear children," he said. "It is not completely surprising that you all have the gift. As I have already said to young TJ and also Lizzy Wizzy just before we came in here, you must promise to keep this secret young Chatty. Not a word to anyone."

Chatty promised immediately. There was no chance she would tell her Mum of course.

"As young TJ will testify, there is much teaching, explaining, learning and practice to undertake," Grandpa Mal continued.

"It doesn't make sense to do it now, as sunrise will be here soon enough. As I now have some important calls to make in the morning to bring people up to speed, let us reconvene this afternoon. Remember, not a word to anyone. We will need to be extremely careful so as not to upset or trigger any curiosity in young Benjamin. So, do you promise?"

"I promise," said Chatty, followed by Lizzy Wizzy.

"I don't have to ask you that question again, TJ, do I?" Grandpa Mal asked, before TJ could answer.

"Your refusal to give the game away, even though it was already up, is admirable and very commendable," Grandpa Mal continued. "Well done dear boy."

TJ smiled and felt a little bit better.

Grandpa Mal didn't stop there. "You will also play an important role dear boy in explaining the basics to young Chatty and Lizzy Wizzy. After all, you have shown such great potential already."

TJ felt his chest puff out and that he had grown a couple of inches taller at Grandpa Mal's words of encouragement. Chatty was less impressed. She thought that all of them being a Dreamguardian would put them back on level ground again. She thought there would be no more favourites.

"Right, dear Dreamguardians," Grandpa Mal said suddenly, "back to your rooms. And remember, not a word to anyone. Not young Benjy and especially not your Mothers."

With that he ruffled TJ's blonde hair and shepherded his other young protégés out of TJ's room.

*

TJ climbed back into bed but was unable to get back to sleep. He was far too preoccupied with everything that had just happened and what was to come.

The revelation that both Chatty and Lizzy Wizzy had the gift was amazing. He also realised it had completely overshadowed the fact that he had overcome his first Dreamstealer in Lizzy Wizzy dream. He had expelled his first real Dreamstealer! What an achievement!

The longer he lay awake though, the more he began to smart over the telling off from Grandpa Mal about being seen in Lizzy Wizzy's dream. That was Chatty's fault, not his, he thought to himself. The delay in gifting Lizzy Wizzy a dream after he had defeated the Dreamstealer was also Chatty's fault. In fact, *he* was the one that had kept *her* safe and saved *her* life. How unfair of Grandpa Mal to blame him!

TJ began to realise that things would be different now that he wasn't the only young Dreamguardian around. At that precise moment, he didn't quite know how he felt about that either.

He tried to put it to the back of his mind. He would just have to wait until later to see how the new dynamic would play out.

It would be an interesting afternoon.

CHAPTER 28 – AN UNEXPECTED TURN

T he two newest Dreamguardians were in high spirits and extremely excited at breakfast, as they laughed and joked along with Benjy at the table. It was if yesterday had never happened.

Both Emma, but especially Katherine, were pleasantly surprised and had asked the girls why they were in such a good mood. But they were true to their word and gave nothing away, since they had promised Grandpa Mal they would keep all things Dreamguardian secret. Although he had not appeared for breakfast, Grandpa Mal would have been proud of their discretion, for sure.

Katherine was relieved Chatty was in a much better mood after all the drama of yesterday. She had started to feel as if she was at the end of her tether with her daughter. At these low points, she wondered whether Chatty might actually be better off living with Bertie, as she tended to be a Daddy's girl. But then Katherine would snap herself out of it and chide herself for thinking such thoughts. As much as Chatty was difficult, she loved her too much to let her go.

TJ was less ebullient. He was still to work out exactly how he felt after last night. On the one hand, he was excited there were two new Dreamguardians to help in the fight against the Dreamstealers. It would also be good to talk about it with the others as he no longer had to keep secrets from them. But on the other hand, he had enjoyed the feeling of being special and the undivided attention of Grandpa Mal. Then there was the safety of the girls to think about, of course, or at least that was the way he was framing the argument. Chatty would be very upset if she suspected TJ might be thinking that being a Dreamguardian was for boys only.

As they finished their breakfast, the old-fashioned telephone rang in the kitchen. It made everyone jump, mainly because of all the years they had visited the Old Girl, they had never known it ever to ring before. In fact, the children were not even aware that it worked.

They had always thought it was quite an unusual object. It was black and had a round plastic dial on the front with numbers. Grandpa Mal had once shown them how to dial a number. A finger needed to be inserted into one of the holes over the desired number and the plastic dial turned to the left and then let go. The same motion apparently needed to be repeated for each number, rather than simply pressing one on a screen or keypad as they were used to doing now.

The children had laughed at just how long it took to dial a telephone number. Also, at the cumbersome corded curved handset that went from the ear to the mouth. It meant the user had to stand in one place when they were on the telephone. How antiquated!

Katherine got up from the table and answered the telephone in her soothing, soft, polite telephone voice. After a short exchange of pleasantries with the anonymous caller her face dropped. She took the handset from her ear and covered the mouthpiece with her hand.

"Emma, it's for you," she said softly.

"Who is it?" Emma asked, getting up quickly from the table. She didn't like the way Katherine's mood had changed so suddenly.

"It's about your Mum," came the reply.

Emma's heart was in her mouth as she quickly took the handset from Katherine. The room went silent. After a few moments, even though they could only hear one side of the conversation, everyone could tell the news was not encouraging.

"Yes, this is Mrs Joseph... Yes... what's wrong? Oh no...." She put her hand over her mouth and tears welled in her eyes.

"What is it Mummy?" Lizzy Wizzy asked, concerned, but Emma turned around and carried on the conversation.

"How bad is it?" they heard her ask down the telephone. "Is she going to be ok?"

She nodded as she listened to what was being said on the other end of the line.

"I'm away on holiday at the moment, but I'll be straight there. I should be able to make it early afternoon." She paused before she spoke again. "That won't be too late, will it?" she asked. Her voice cracked as she did so.

After a short while of more listening and agreeable noises, Mum spoke one last time.

"Yes, I understand. Well, thank you so much for the call and for everything you're doing for her. I'll see you later today. Goodbye."

She put the phone down and remained with her back to them for a little while, as she tried to compose herself. Katherine went over, offered her a handkerchief and gave her a little cuddle.

"Mummy, what is it? What's happened?" Lizzy Wizzy asked again, very concerned at this stage.

Emma turned to face them. She tried to cover up the fact she was crying.

"Lizzy Wizzy, TJ, darlings. I'm afraid it's Granny Winifred."

She went on to explain her mother had been taken into hospital and was now awaiting tests. She had been rushed there in the early hours of the morning. It was early days, but they suspected a stroke.

Lizzy Wizzy began to cry and Emma gave her a big cuddle to reassure her, although she wasn't quite sure herself what was going to happen. Even though the news had also come as a shock to TJ, he tried to be as strong as possible for the sake of his Mum and fought back his own tears. There had been too much heartache in the family already, and the prospect of more was most unwelcome.

After Emma had comforted Lizzy Wizzy, she became engaged in deep conversation with Katherine over by the Aga. As the children sat pushing around what was left of their cereal in their bowls, they could hear parts of the discussion but were unable to work out exactly what was being discussed or decided.

After their tête-à-tête ended, Emma and Katherine retook their seats at the table. The children were silent as they waited patiently for one of the Mums to speak. Emma took a deep breath and spoke softly as she addressed the children.

"As we've just heard," she said, "Granny Winifred has been rushed to hospital and I really need to be with her as soon as possible. As she lives on the other side of the country and it's all come as a bit of a shock, Auntie Katherine has kindly offered to come with me and drive me to the hospital. She'll stay with me until we know a bit more about Granny's condition."

"But what about us?" TJ asked.

come with you Mummy," Lizzy Wizzy pleaded. She was now upset only the news about Granny Winifred, but also that Mummy would have to leave them for a little while. Emma gave her a huge cuddle to try and put her mind at ease that Granny Winifred would be fine, and she would be back before she knew it. Lizzy Wizzy knew this was true, but she would miss Mummy regardless.

"I know you want to come with me sweetheart, but I think it's best if you stay here at the Old Girl with Grandpa Mal. The hospital wouldn't be a very nice place for you both to be. Nobody really knows how bad Granny Winifred is and how long she might be in the hospital. I hope and pray she will be fine of course, but we just don't know. It's best if you stay here and keep Grandpa Mal company until we return."

"As your Mum has had quite a shock," Auntie Katherine said caringly, "I'll drive her to the hospital in her car. Once we're confident that the situation is settled, I'll leave her there with Granny Winifred and get the train back home. Then your Mum will come back here when she's able to."

"Thank you, Katherine," Emma said, reaching out to hold her hand. "I really appreciate your help and support."

Then she turned to TJ and Lizzy Wizzy. "I'm sorry to have to leave you darlings," she said sincerely, "but it's best you stay here. I know it will be difficult but try not to worry. Grandpa Mal will take good care of you and of course you need to look after him too."

She tried to smile to put their minds at ease, but it was clear she was extremely upset at the news about her mother and having to leave so suddenly. She made her way over to TJ and Lizzy Wizzy and gave them a massive hug.

"Don't worry about Granny Winifred. She's a tough old cookie, I'm sure she'll be ok," Emma said unconvincingly. "I love you two, so much," she said. "Take care of each other, as well as Chatty, Benjy and Grandpa Mal. Please don't worry too much and mope about. Try and have some fun, especially now that your old Mum won't be around. It is the school holidays after all."

They all laughed, but at that moment none of them felt like having any fun. Not while they didn't know what was happening with Granny Winifred.

*

Later that morning they all gathered outside the Old Girl to wave Katherine and Emma off. TJ had helped put two suitcases in the boot of the Range Rover that would keep them clothed for a lengthy period of time, although everyone hoped that Granny Winifred would make a good recovery and they would be back before too long.

As they waved them off, the mood was sombre. Benjy and Lizzy Wizzy in particular were very sad to see their Mums leave. Although she felt guilty for such thoughts given the circumstances, Chatty felt relieved her Mum wouldn't be around for a few days. She felt even more guilty for wishing it would be longer, as that would imply Lizzy Wizzy's Granny Winifred was very sick. TJ also had mixed feelings. He was upset about Granny Winifred of course, but was also excited that the absence of both Mums would free up time for Grandpa Mal to bring Lizzy Wizzy and Chatty up to speed about the Brethren and the art of being a Dreamguardian. As the eldest and more experienced of the three children, he was fully ready to play his part in their education.

As the car disappeared from sight, Grandpa Mal broke the silence.

"Righto my dear children," he said in a deliberately jolly voice, "it's just you and me now. We shall miss your dear Mums, but there is nothing to worry about. We shall all work together as a team and help each other out. If we all pull together, then I'm sure you can still have the best holiday yet, even if we have to spend a bit more time here at the Old Girl."

TJ smiled. That wasn't such a bad thing after all, he thought.

"How does that all sound to you?" Grandpa Mal asked optimistically.

The murmured replies from the four children were underwhelming.

"Oh, come on dear children," Grandpa Mal said, "let's have a bit more excitement. You all sound terribly miserable. I know that your dear old Granny Winifred wouldn't want that, she was always up for a good laugh. So, let's make the most of a bad situation shall we? Who's up for some more fun at the Old Girl?"

They mustered a more enthusiastic response which met with Grandpa Mal's approval and he ushered them inside. As Lizzy Wizzy, Chatty and Benjy rushed back into the Grand Hall, TJ held back as he wanted to grab a private word with Grandpa Mal.

"Grandpa Mal, can I ask you something?" he enquired.

"Of course, dear boy, fire away," came the response.

"When are we going to start teaching the girls about, you know, the Brethren?" He looked carefully around him as he said it just in case anyone was eavesdropping. But there was no-one around.

"Hmm, that is indeed a good question dear boy," Grandpa Mal replied, which took TJ a little by surprise. He thought Grandpa Mal would have had it all worked out by now.

"Are we going to see the Dreamorian today or to see *Sensei* to put them on the Simulator?" TJ asked. "There's a lot they need to learn."

"Indeed, but we cannot rush these things, dear boy, and I have to say that the departure of your Mum and Auntie Katherine has complicated matters somewhat."

"Why is that?" TJ asked quickly. "Surely it helps if they're not around. We can do what we like and they're not here to interfere."

"In some ways yes, but you must not forget young Benjamin."

"Benjy? What about him?" TJ asked, feeling somewhat confused.

"My dear boy, it is going to be very difficult of course to go anywhere or spend much time with just the three of you when Benjamin is around. If we go to see the Dreamorian or *Sensei,* who's going to look after young Benjamin?"

TJ rolled his eyes. Of course, he hadn't thought about such practical matters. What a pain, he thought!

Grandpa Mal continued. "He's far too young to keep any secrets and, in any case, we can't risk telling him anything. Remember, there is no guarantee that he has the gift, even though we have just discovered the wonderful news that Chatty clearly does. As I thought I had told you, the gift can – and often does - skip generations and even siblings. The fact that both you and Lizzy Wizzy have the gift is of course marvellous but was not a given."

TJ smiled at the thought that perhaps he and Lizzy Wizzy were quite a rare species. But then his smile was replaced by frustration.

"So, we're not going to be able to do *anything* while Benjy is around?" TJ asked.

"Yes, unfortunately that's correct, dear boy," Grandpa Mal confirmed. "There can be no trips to the Dreamorian or *Sensei* until either your Mum or Auntie Katherine returns."

TJ felt his heart sink. He was impatient for the others to know all about being a Dreamguardian. Now, the earliest that could happen would be to-night, provided Benjy went to bed without a fuss and kept out of the way. That already felt a long way off. What if Grandpa Mal wanted to wait even longer?

Grandpa Mal could sense his disappointment.

"You mustn't be too disappointed, dear boy," he said reassuringly, but then his tone changed. "You must have patience, dear boy. This is so important and must not be rushed. In some ways, this isn't such a bad thing."

By now Grandpa Mal sounded quite serious. "On reflection," he continued, "I feel we took things a bit too quickly, dear boy, with your introduction to the Brethren and Dreamguardian activities."

TJ's heart dropped. "No Grandpa Mal, it was fine," he said defensively. He disagreed with Grandpa Mal. Being a Dreamguardian was dangerous if they weren't taught how to do things properly. At the same time, TJ was also excited for Lizzy Wizzy and Chatty to experience what he had over the past few days.

"That's a very commendable attitude, dear boy, but your session on the Simulator was just too much, too soon."

"It was fine Grandpa Mal," TJ insisted.

"And then last night your inexperience showed. Despite all my warnings, you were spotted by Lizzy Wizzy in her own dream. We spoke about being careless TJ. I must say you were very fortunate not to get trapped in her dream. Both you and Chatty for that matter."

TJ tried to protest. "But Grandpa Mal, it was Chatty's..."

"Now, now, you mustn't feel bad, dear boy," Grandpa Mal interrupted. "It's my fault, not yours. It's a lesson to me that we must be a lot more cautious and progress at a much slower pace going forward. After all, this is not a game and the stakes are very high, especially as it seems that *Dominus Tenebris* has come."

TJ felt the frustration build and threaten to spill out into the summer sun.

"But Grandpa Mal..." he said, unsure whether he was trying to explain, argue or object.

"It's fine my dear boy, I'm not cross. Not at you anyway. I just think I got rather carried away with all the excitement in wanting to share the Great Room and Inner Sanctum with you. I'm not saying we won't take the girls to the Great Room, or to the Dreamorian or *Sensei* at some point, but we need to tread very carefully."

Before TJ could say anymore, they heard Benjy rush back into the Grand Hall and to where they were stood at the front door.

"TJ! TJ!" Benjy said excitedly.

"What?" TJ asked, unhappy with the interruption.

"Come on!" Benjy shouted. "Let's go outside and play."

Grandpa Mal answered for TJ.

"What a good idea Benjy. TJ, why don't you and Benjy play outside. It's such a lovely day and we've finished here anyway."

With that Grandpa Mal rustled Benjy's hair and gently manoeuvred him out of the front door onto the step with TJ.

"Go and enjoy yourselves boys," Grandpa Mal said. "If you're going to wander around the grounds, then just remember that lunch will be at one o'clock. I'll be around the Old Girl this afternoon, but you won't see me. I have some important calls to make. So, have fun and be good. Remember, if you can't be good, be careful!"

Before anything more could be said, Grandpa Mal smiled and shut the door firmly behind him as he went inside the Old Girl. The conversation was well and truly over, and he left a dejected TJ stood on the front step.

TJ was extremely unhappy that Grandpa Mal thought he hadn't been able to cope with his training so far. Up to now, TJ thought that he'd done really well. In fact, everyone had thought he'd done really well, right up until the incident with the Simulator and Chatty's interference in Lizzy Wizzy's dream.

As he smarted at the injustice of it all, he decided that he would prove Grandpa Mal wrong. TJ would show Grandpa Mal that he *was* ready *and* that he'd be able to teach the girls too. After all, it was too dangerous not to teach them the basics, especially if Grandpa Mal suddenly decided that tonight was too soon or not possible. It was possible that Benjy might be missing his Mum tonight and demand to sleep in the same room as Chatty or himself.

A shove in the chest ended his scheming. "It!" cried Benjy as he turned on his heels and scarpered onto the driveway, his little feet sending small pieces of gravel flying everywhere.

"I'm not playing!" TJ shouted. But Benjy was having none of it.

"You're it," he shouted, moving closer to TJ to try and tempt him into chasing him.

The plan worked. TJ leapt into action and began chasing Benjy, firstly round the stone fountain and then off into the sunny dry fields surrounding the house.

CHAPTER 29 – HIDE AND SEEK

After yesterday's cloudy and cooler weather, the return of the summer sun was welcome even though the temperature didn't get much above twenty degrees Celsius. However, it was sufficient for the four children to be content to spend the day outside. Even though the reason for their liberation was not ideal, it was quite a treat not to have their mothers around telling them what to do, or what not to do. It would have its disadvantages as well though. One would be their attendance at the travelling fun fair that was due to arrive in the neighbouring village and set up on the green tomorrow. They had all been looking forward to its arrival and had begged their Mums to take them. Emma and Katherine had made a conditional promise to do so if they were good. However, it was unlikely they would be able to go now that the Mums had been called away to see to Granny Winifred.

Instead, the children would have to make do with the three hundred acres that the Old Girl sat within. It offered quite the playground and funfair in its own right. With untold paddocks, woodland, streams, outbuildings, wildlife and cattle, there was always something to keep them amused. They lost track of time in the great outdoors, until their rumbling stomachs told them it was lunchtime. They returned to the Old Girl to find that Grandpa Mal had left them jam and cheese sandwiches on the wooden table on the terrace to the rear of the house. Some of the sandwiches had both jam and cheese in them, a combination provided especially for Lizzy Wizzy. It divided opinion amongst the rest. There was a huge round Victoria sponge cake to keep them occupied too. The sandwiches and cake were protected by a huge square net food cover and a patterned tea towel kept the wasps off a large jug of Grandpa Mal's homemade cloudy lemonade.

The lunch itself rested in the shade of a large garden umbrella and the children were glad of its protection from the sun. They sat at the table and tucked into lunch, watching bees and butterflies flit from one flower pot to the other, attracted by the allure of the colourful floral contents. The terrace overlooked the formal walled garden, which contained hundreds of beautiful plants, some quite exotic, that no-one seemed to know the names of, as well as a small box-hedge maze. Beyond this a grass tennis court lay quiet, waiting for energetic participants to bring it to life. The court itself was bordered on three sides by a row of rose bushes and in the far corner of the walled garden an elegant timber changing room also lay empty.

After the sandwiches and generous slices of cake had been devoured, the topic of conversation turned to the afternoon's activities. TJ suggested a game of hide and seek in the grounds. Not just any old game of hide and seek in a small enclosed space, but something on a much grander scale. A serious game of hide and seek outside, with nowhere off limits. With both Mums away, this was the perfect time to play such a game. Had the Mums been here, then too many places would be off limits to them, such as the woods or some of the sheds, barns and outbuildings. Just in case someone got lost of course. But not today. Even though Grandpa Mal was meant to be looking after them, he was off somewhere in the Old Girl taking care of important business. They were on their own. Anything could happen!

In any case, TJ had an ulterior motive for suggesting such an activity. He needed some time alone with Lizzy Wizzy to talk to her about the Brethren. His plan was to send them all off to hide and then talk to Lizzy Wizzy once he'd found her. After all, she wasn't the best 'hider' in the world. He would have plenty of time to talk to her whilst Benjy and Chatty hid somewhere else. Whenever they played the game inside, Benjy bordered on being a professional hide and seeker. Perhaps it was his size. Chatty was also pretty good too, although TJ noted she didn't do such a good job hiding in Lizzy Wizzy's dream last night. He had managed to spot her from a distance after all.

Benjy was well up for an outside game of hide and seek, with nowhere out of bounds. Lizzy Wizzy was quite excited too and managed to persuade a somewhat reluctant Chatty to join in after an initial refusal.

TJ volunteered to be the seeker, which pleased everybody else. He informed them of the limited rules. The first was that once you chose a hiding place, you were not allowed to move subsequently. With three hundred acres to choose from, the odds were already stacked against TJ without people moving from place to place. However, he was confident of finding Lizzy Wizzy quickly. He had a good idea where she was likely to hide. The second rule was to not get lost and the final one was to be back well before teatime if you weren't found. TJ explained that Grandpa Mal would probably be unhappy if he found out they were all splitting up and even more so if they missed whatever culinary delight he had conjured up.

TJ said he would give them a five-minute head start, in order for them to have enough time to get away and find somewhere good to hide. Somewhere well away from the Old Girl.

By now, everyone was excited by the prospect of the game, even Chatty who had forgotten her initial reluctance. As TJ began counting down, Chatty, Lizzy Wizzy and Benjy ran off, each screaming with excitement as they did so. TJ took a quick peek to see which direction they were running in. Lizzy Wizzy and Chatty were headed south-east towards the now derelict stables and old farm buildings, beyond which lay the woods. Benjy had immediately split from the girls and was headed due south through the walled garden towards the tennis court. Beyond the tennis court, through a small archway, was a small patch of woodland and some open fields, a couple of which contained some large oak trees that TJ guessed Benjy would try to climb and hide in.

He felt bad for cheating a little, so he closed his eyes again, though it wouldn't make much difference as before long they had all disappeared through hedges and gates out of sight. TJ hoped his plan would work, otherwise he was in for a long afternoon of searching underneath the hot sun.

*

After what seemed like a long wait, TJ was on the move. He made his way south-east, following the path Lizzy Wizzy and Chatty had taken, deliberately choosing to go in the different direction to the one Benjy took. The poor little chap would remain hidden for as long as it took, TJ thought to himself.

TJ passed through a gap in the yew hedge that marked the boundary of the designed back garden of the Old Girl and into the surrounding meadow. His hunch was that Lizzy Wizzy would have headed for the disused farmyard and collection of old stables and barns. They had been expressly banned from ever going there which made them all the more attractive. In addition, Lizzy Wizzy had always loved the idea of owning a horse so was always hoping one might still live there, even though everyone always said there wasn't. Maybe she might find one there after all and would be allowed to keep it as her own.

After passing through the meadow, TJ made his way down a disused farm track towards a collection of stables and barns constructed from timber and brick. Three were arranged around the sides of a quadrangle, while an impressive Suffolk barn with the later addition of a piggery stood nearby. Some barns retained their original slate roofs, while the remainder were kept barely watertight by industrial corrugated iron.

TJ chose to investigate the stables around the quadrangle first. They were in various states of disrepair. Some of the stable doors no longer closed properly, while the top half of one of the doors had completely disappeared. TJ carefully unbolted each door and looked inside each stable. Some were completely empty, apart from the spectacular collection of dust and cobwebs that had accumulated over the years. Others no longer housed horses, but piles of wood and other discarded farm tools instead. They had lay dormant for so long that they were also engulfed in sticky silky cobwebs. On the floor of the barn with only half a door was the unmistakable black pellet droppings of a barn owl.

Satisfied that the stables were empty, TJ made his way to the Suffolk barn. At this time of year, it would have once thronged with farm workers threshing the grain ready for storage. The timber barn had two great sets of double doors either side of the building that would have been regularly opened during harvest to allow the carts laden with wheat to drive in and out. They also allowed the wind to blow through to help the threshers separate the wheat grain from the chaff. Now those doors were firmly locked closed from the inside and so TJ walked round to the entrance to the piggery.

The door was slightly ajar which made TJ smile. He was sure that once Lizzy Wizzy was satisfied no horses were secretly living in the stables, the small spaces and evidence of an army of spiders would have put her off from hiding there. He guessed she was in the much larger Suffolk barn, accessed through the piggery via this door.

Inside, the piggery was about eighteen metres long, with five concrete bays where the pigs once lived. Three of the bays were now occupied by a huge pile of logs and yet more discarded objects that were no longer required. As TJ surveyed his surroundings, he noticed one of the roof joists had collapsed and the lengths of wood that clad the underside of the roof were peeling as if shedding its skin. The place had seen better days.

As he headed towards the door to the Suffolk barn at the end of the piggery, he checked each bay as he walked past, half expecting to see Lizzy Wizzy hiding in the two that were empty. But she wasn't there. As TJ opened the wooden door into the Suffolk barn it creaked loudly. He smiled. She knows I'm coming, he thought to himself, if indeed she was in here.

As he went through the door and turned to the right, the inside of the Suffolk barn made him gasp. It was stunning. The main barn space was huge with a double height ceiling and an arched timber-frame that looked like the skeleton of a ginormous crooked whale. The rays from the mid-afternoon sun beamed through gaps in the timber cladding of the barn, lighting up areas within the dark barn like a spotlight on the stage. TJ could see the dust particles dance in the beams of light.

There were some bales of straw but little else in this section of the barn, so TJ turned around and headed the other way. He walked past an abandoned old rowing boat on his left that was clearly no longer seaworthy and a large wooden grain storage box on his right. Ahead to the right was a flight of rickety wooden steps that led to a mezzanine level. Directly opposite the steps to his left was a bay area leading to another set of huge double doors.

Beyond the steps were a couple of thick wooden posts marking the entrance to another double height room, about a third of the size of the one he had just come from. In the far corner of this room was a pile of junk and discarded farm machinery, some of it covered by tarpaulin and some old hessian feeding bags. The tarpaulin suddenly twitched even though there was no breeze in the barn. TJ smiled. "Got you," he said quietly to himself.

He crept slowly over to the covered junk pile and without too much pause quickly whipped back the tarpaulin.

"Found you!" he shouted.

Lizzy Wizzy screamed. She thought she'd heard that someone was coming but didn't expect to get a sudden shock like that.

"TJ!" she cried, "you scared me!"

"Haha! Found you. I knew you'd be over here," TJ said triumphantly.

Lizzy Wizzy was not happy. She folded her arms and shouted at him. "Why did you have to shout like that and make me jump. That wasn't very kind."

TJ said sorry, even though he wasn't really. At this precise moment, he was quite proud of his sleuthing skills and how he had deduced that Lizzy Wizzy was likely to be hiding around here somewhere.

"Don't be silly Lizzy Wizzy," TJ said. "Anyway, I'm glad I've found you as we need to talk."

"What do you mean?" a puzzled Lizzy Wizzy asked. "Now that you've found me, we've got to go and find the others surely?"

TJ smiled. "Not just yet. They can wait," he said.

"But that's mean," Lizzy Wizzy replied.

"Maybe, but that was my plan," TJ said mischievously. "I really need to talk to you Lizzy Wizzy without Benjy around. About what happened last night. You know, about this Dreamguardian stuff." He lowered his voice as he used the D-word and looked around, but he couldn't see anyone.

"I thought Grandpa Mal was going to talk to us about it," Lizzy Wizzy said.

"Well he probably will at some point, but Benjy is complicating things now that Mum and Auntie Katherine have had to leave to visit Granny Winifred. There are some important things you need to know. I thought I'd tell you now, just in case Grandpa Mal's not able to for a while. In any case, it's so exciting I can't keep it to myself for much longer. I'll simply burst."

Lizzy Wizzy smiled and giggled. She knew what he meant. Up to now Grandpa Mal hadn't really told her much apart from this mysterious fact that she was a Dreamguardian. This meant she was special and could help protect the dreams of others. But he had sworn her to secrecy and hadn't told her anything else, so she was desperate to know more.

"I know what you mean," Lizzy Wizzy said, "my head has been spinning ever since Grandpa Mal told me I was a Dreamguardian. I'd love to know what it's all about and what it all really means."

She stopped suddenly and looked a little concern. "But what about Chatty?" she continued, "shouldn't we wait until she's with us? After all, she is a Dreamguardian too isn't she? And what about Grandpa Mal?"

TJ shifted on the spot a little uncomfortably. "Well, yes, Chatty is a Dreamguardian, but she's not here now is she and I really want to tell you. Chatty can find out later from Grandpa Mal. As for Grandpa Mal, it'll be fine. You heard him earlier this morning, didn't you? He did say I would play an important role in explaining the basics to you."

"...and Chatty," Lizzy Wizzy added.

"Do you want me to tell you anything Lizzy Wizzy or not?" TJ said sharply, his frustration beginning to show.

"Yes, please," came the reply.

"Good. Don't worry about Chatty. She can wait," TJ said, still annoyed with Chatty for interrupting and interfering in Lizzy Wizzy's dream last night. It was because of her that Grandpa Mal had unfairly chided him about being careless in a dream and put his own training on the slow track as a result. She can just wait and serves her right, he thought.

"Well, that doesn't seem very fair or kind TJ," Lizzy Wizzy warned.

"Look, do you want to know or not Lizzy Wizzy?" TJ snapped again.

Lizzy Wizzy knew he wasn't going to change his mind, so she nodded. Sorry Chatty, I did try, she thought to herself.

"Good, let's get started then, take a seat," TJ said, pointing to a straw bale that was against the wall behind her. "Remember, this is our secret and no telling anyone about it."

TJ remained standing, so he could show her all the important moves once he had gone through the basics with her.

"Are you sitting comfortably Lizzy Wizzy?" he teased as she perched on the straw bale. In that moment, he felt like something between a majestic story-teller and a university professor. He would have complete command and control of his audience, even if it was just one. Lizzy Wizzy's Dreamguardian education was about to begin.

TJ began by telling Lizzy Wizzy why a Dreamguardian was so special. He explained why dreams needed to be protected and how important sleep was for the dreamer's wellbeing. Lizzy Wizzy listened intently, daring to stop TJ as he was in full flow.

He left the historical facts quite vague, only mentioning that the first people who had the gift – the first Dreamguardians – were recorded in a secret copy of Genesis. Lizzy Wizzy was not that interested by this part, until TJ mentioned that the first proper Dreamguardian was the son of Joseph. This captured Lizzy Wizzy's attention as she loved the musical. Before she got side-tracked thinking about the story of Joseph, TJ moved on to the Dreamstealers. He now had first-hand knowledge of what they were like and what the worst of them could do. It was imperative that he impress upon Lizzy Wizzy how careful she needed to be.

"Now, you need to listen carefully to the next part," TJ said to his sister.

"I am listening carefully," she replied. It was true, she hadn't taken her eyes or ears off TJ.

"Being a Dreamguardian is important and can be really exciting, especially when you get to gift a dream, but there is one thing that you need to know."

"What's that then?" asked Lizzy Wizzy, completely unprepared for what TJ was about to share with her.

"You must be extremely careful when you are within someone's dream," TJ said seriously, "because it is possible that you can get trapped."

Lizzy Wizzy looked at him puzzled. "Trapped where?" she asked.

"Inside the dream," TJ confirmed.

"Oh. How do you get out then?"

TJ shook his head. "You don't. That's the point."

"Well what happens to you then?"

Although TJ wasn't entirely sure, he could remember well the passages from the secret copy of Genesis and Grandpa Mal's warning.

"You get trapped inside someone else's dream, *forever*. Lost in a void of dreamless darkness from which you cannot escape."

Lizzy Wizzy went silent. Suddenly she felt scared and a little bit sick.

"I don't like the sound of that TJ," she said nervously, "surely you can be rescued at some point?"

"No!" exclaimed TJ. He was cross with her for not listening, although he could remember thinking exactly the same when Grandpa Mal first told him too. "You get trapped, forever. Well, probably forever."

"What do you mean, *probably*?" Lizzy Wizzy asked, picking up on some hesitation even though he had been quite unequivocal a second earlier.

"Well, there is a prophecy that the Dreamologist can rescue a Dreamguardian lost in a dream..."

"The Dreamologist?" Lizzy Wizzy repeated, "what's that then?"

TJ paused. "I don't know," he said, sounding far from convincing or convinced himself. "I'm not even sure the Dreamologist exists," he continued, "or, if it does, whether it hasn't already been defeated by the Dreamstealers."

"Oh," said Lizzy Wizzy, her initial intrigue upon hearing about the Dreamologist now tarnished by TJ's doubt. "It all sounds rather horrible TJ. In fact, I'm not sure I want to be a Dreamguardian now if something nasty is going to happen to me."

In the cool and shadows of the Suffolk barn she suddenly felt cold. She'd had that feeling before, in a dream no less.

"Don't be like that Lizzy Wizzy," TJ said, concerned that this wasn't quite going the way he planned. "Focus on the positives. It can be so much fun. I mean, on gifting my first dream to Grandpa Mal we had a Flyer and an Extravaganza."

Lizzy Wizzy looked at him strangely and pulled a face. "A what?"

TJ laughed. "Oops sorry," he said, "they're the names of some of the dreams contained in the Great Book that you can gift to a dreamer".

Before Lizzy Wizzy could ask him what the Great Book was, he continued his explanation of the dream he gifted Grandpa Mal.

"A Flyer is a dream in which you can fly. It was amazing Lizzy. Then I followed it with an Extravaganza, which was even more amazing. We slid down a giant rainbow Lizzy. It was incredible!"

At this point Lizzy Wizzy's mouth and eyes were wide open.

"You flew and slid down a rainbow?" she said jumping to her feet.

"Yep," said TJ proudly. "It was awesome!"

"Wow!" exclaimed Lizzy Wizzy, now completely captivated by TJ's story. "So how does it all work then? How do you do it?" she asked.

"Well, I'm not entirely sure how it actually works," TJ replied, "apart from the fact that you need to have the gift." He'd been trying to fathom it all out for days now, without completely putting his finger on it. "As for how you do it, well that I can help you with," he said proudly.

"Really?" Lizzy Wizzy said, "but are you sure we shouldn't wait for Grandpa Mal and Chatty?"

"No!" TJ replied quickly. "I've told you before it's too important to not share all this with you, just in case. As for Chatty, well right now she's not important and to be honest I just don't really care about her."

As soon as the words came out of his mouth TJ instantly regretted them. He didn't quite mean it as it sounded, and he hoped Lizzy Wizzy wouldn't say anything. He moved on quickly before she did.

"Now, to enter someone's dream you have to be thinking about them before you go to sleep yourself. In fact, you have to be thinking about the dreamer and repeat their name in your head at least three times. So, if you repeat my name in your head three times as you drift off to sleep, you will be able to enter my dream because you have the *gift*."

TJ and Lizzy Wizzy's eyes danced together in perfect synchronicity.

"Amazing!" she said excitedly.

"Wait, there's more," TJ said. "Before you enter my dream you have to go through a room called *The Armoury*. You need to put on a white robe – a bit like Joseph's coat – and pick up a *Dreamswick*. Before you ask, it's a type of staff with a webbed hoop at one end. You spin it round and it fires orbs of light to help you expel Dreamstealers and then gift dreams. You enter *The*

Armoury by thinking about the robe and *Dreamswick*."

"Slow down TJ!" Lizzy Wizzy pleaded, struggling to catch up. "You're going too fast!"

"Sorry," TJ responded, "but there's so much to tell you. Now that you know how to get into a dream, the most important thing is that you can get out as well, before any harm comes to you. The *Dreamswick* will help keep you safe, of course, but for now the best thing you can learn is how to exit a dream."

"How do you exit then TJ? Please tell me, I really want to know how you get out," she said, sharpening her concentration. Lizzy Wizzy had no desire to get trapped inside a dream.

"The only way to safely exit is to repeat the name of the dreamer followed by the word 'exit' at least three times. Got it?"

Lizzy Wizzy wasn't sure. "So, if I'm in your dream TJ, then all I have to do is say 'TJ exit, TJ exit, TJ exit' and that's it?"

"Yes, that's right. If you say that whilst holding your *Dreamswick* in your right hand, you'll safely exit the dream. See, it's easy."

Lizzy Wizzy wasn't convinced. That bit sounded easy enough but putting everything together it all seemed a bit complicated. Not to mention dangerous. She wasn't so sure she was cut out to be a Dreamguardian after all.

"I'm not sure about all this, TJ," she said quietly, "it seems dangerous. Is it really worth it?"

"Yes!" TJ replied enthusiastically, with a good measure of exasperation thrown in at Lizzy Wizzy's reluctance to embrace her destiny. "Grandpa Mal said that being a Dreamguardian is a great honour and privilege and he's right. We also need as many Dreamguardians as possible to stop the rise of the Dreamstealers, especially now that *Dominus Tenebris* is here."

"Who?" Lizzy Wizzy asked nervously.

"Oh, nobody, it doesn't matter," TJ said quickly. He kicked himself for letting that slip out. If Lizzy Wizzy was already faltering at the thought of being a Dreamguardian, even hearing about *Dominus Tenebris* was likely to definitively convince her to not use the gift that had been bestowed upon her.

"Hmm, really? It sounded important a moment ago TJ," Lizzy Wizzy probed.

"Not that important," TJ said, desperately trying to cover his tracks. "If it is, I'm sure that Grandpa Mal will talk about it at some point later."

As Lizzy Wizzy trusted TJ, she let it go.

TJ was happy. He'd made sure she knew how to enter a dream properly and, most importantly, exit a dream. And he hadn't just undone all his good work by suddenly scaring Lizzy Wizzy off being a Dreamguardian by accidentally mentioning *Dominus Tenebris*.

"So that's your brief introduction to being a Dreamguardian," TJ said proudly to his little sister. "What do you think then Lizzy Wizzy?"

She paused for thought. Her brain was working overtime, trying to understand, rationalise and remember everything she had just been told.

"Well..." she started slowly, "I'm not sure TJ. Some of it sounds really exciting. For instance, being able to help people by protecting their dreams, and being able to gift fantastic dreams. Like a Flying dream and the Ext... Extrav..." She struggled to recall the name.

TJ helped her out. "Flyer and Extravaganza," he said.

"Yes, that's it." Lizzy Wizzy continued. "That bit certainly sounds exciting. But I don't like the sound of Dreamstealers and especially the chance you get trapped in a dream and lost forever. That seems risky, dangerous and horrible."

"It won't be Lizzy Wizzy, I promise," TJ said, desperate to convince his little sister. "There are people, including me, to teach you everything. Then there's a Simulator for you to practice on. You'll be fine, it's so exciting. Trust me," he begged.

"Hmm," said Lizzy Wizzy. In her heart, she did trust and believe him, although her head was not yet fully won over.

"I think it will help if I talk to Chatty about it," she continued. "After all, we need to tell her how to enter a dream and then warn her about getting lost. Perhaps we could practice together and..."

TJ snapped at Lizzy Wizzy again. "Why do you need to talk to Chatty? You need to make your own mind up Lizzy Wizzy. I told you before, focus on yourself and not Chatty." He rolled his eyes and huffed heavily. Why did Lizzy Wizzy have to involve Chatty, he thought to himself. He was quite irritated that even now she was still able to interfere.

"Lizzy Wizzy," TJ said impatiently, "I'm not bothered about Chatty right now, she'll just have to wait..."

"Charming TJ," came a familiar voice from behind him, interrupting the conversation.

TJ wheeled round. Standing next to one of the wooden posts by the entrance to this section of the barn was Chatty, her arms folded tightly into her chest.

"Chatty!" TJ said uncomfortably, "what are you doing there? Why aren't you hiding?" The question he really wanted to ask was how long she had been stood there. He hoped the answer was not long.

"I *have* been hiding," Chatty said angrily, scowling at TJ for good measure. "Just over there."

She turned and pointed in the direction of the boat. As TJ looked closely through the darkness, he saw a dark opening to a small room leading off from the bay just past the boat. He hadn't noticed it before on the way in to where he stood now.

"Oh," TJ said, the wind knocked out of his sails. "So, you heard then?"

"Yes," Chatty said harshly, "all of it."

TJ fell silent. He had been quite dismissive and rude about Chatty and he knew it. Nothing he could say at this precise moment would put it right.

"Apparently, I'm not important," she hissed. "You're more than happy to tell Lizzy Wizzy how to enter and exit a dream, but apparently I can wait."

"Chatty..." TJ tried to explain, but he was immediately interrupted.

"No, I'm not interested TJ," she shouted. "I'm already well aware of what you think and how you feel about me. First off, you and Grandpa Mal were going to keep all this secret. I only found out about it by accident. Secondly, when were you going to be bothered to tell me about the danger of being trapped inside a dream and therefore how to exit one? Or were you hoping I would be lost forever?"

As well as angry, Chatty was now quite upset.

"I'm not altogether surprised though," she continued, fighting back the tears, "you've even been nasty to me in my dreams. There you were laughing at me when I couldn't play the piano and my skirt was tucked into my tights. Then you were TJ the favoured one, with Grandpa Mal sticking up for you when you sunk Benjy's boat and were an obnoxious winner of the regatta."

TJ tried to interrupt Chatty again, but she was in full flow. She was shouting, and the tears had started to reveal themselves.

"Well now I've heard it straight from the horse's mouth. I know the truth. I'm just not important and you just don't care about me. In fact, you'd be quite happy if I was lost, forever."

She burst into tears. TJ felt awful.

"Chatty, no, that's just not true," he protested, as he started to make his way over to her to try and placate her.

"No! Don't come near me," she wailed. "I'm not interested. Leave me alone!"

With that, she turned and ran, past the steps, rowing boat and large wooden grain storage box, and out into the piggery.

"TJ!" Lizzy Wizzy shouted, "look what you've done."

Before he could stop her, Lizzy Wizzy was off, running after Chatty.

"But, Lizzy Wizzy…" TJ said forlornly, but she wasn't hanging around to listen. She disappeared into the piggery, in hot pursuit of Chatty.

TJ stood rooted to the spot. It was no point chasing after Chatty. She wouldn't listen to him. He didn't blame her either. He had been cross with her and really horrible as a result. He didn't mean it. Did he? At that moment TJ wasn't sure. All he knew was that even though he had managed to teach Lizzy Wizzy the basics to keep her safe, after that it had just gone horribly wrong.

As he stood in the barn TJ felt ashamed at his behaviour. He had gone from the excitement of sharing the secrets of being a Dreamguardian with Lizzy Wizzy, to seriously upsetting Chatty. Now he was alone, feeling guilty and a bit sorry for himself in the Suffolk barn.

Only he wasn't alone.

Somebody else was still in the barn with him, up on the mezzanine level. They had been looking down from an opening in the wooden partition wall, where sacks of grain used to be lowered down to the ground floor where TJ now stood.

Unbeknown to TJ and the two girls, they had seen and heard everything.

CHAPTER 30 – WINNERS AND LOSERS

TJ traipsed dejectedly out of the Suffolk barn back into the afternoon sun. He wandered slowly over to the meadow behind the walled garden and tennis court. Although he didn't feel much like continuing with the game of hide and seek, he still had to find Benjy.

He made his way over to the huge oak tree closest to the tennis court. This was Benjy's favourite tree and the one he had been itching to climb ever since they arrived. Up to now, eagle-eyed Mums had suffocated Benjy's ambition, but as they were not around TJ guessed he would be hiding up there.

To TJ's surprise he wasn't there. He muttered crossly under his breath, his patience with the game running very thin. What was a good plan had subsequently backfired spectacularly. He felt like giving up and going to crash out on a sofa in the Old Girl, but it wasn't fair to leave Benjy hiding.

TJ hoped that his hunch was correct, and Benjy had indeed gone tree climbing in this area and not carried on into the woodland. If he'd gone in there it would take ages to find him and his appetite for hide and seek had gone.

He trudged slowly through the meadow, towards the woodland. In the next field was a much smaller oak and TJ hoped he would find a little boy safe within its embrace. He climbed the sty over the hawthorn hedge and headed for the tree.

He began to look up into the branches as he approached the huge trunk. Was he there? To his relief he saw something up in the branches. It was Benjy! He had tried hard to hide by lying across the top of one of the huge branches, pressed into the bark like a human chameleon. But his camouflage was nowhere near as successful. His attempt was betrayed by a little leg that dangled down behind the branch slightly in view.

TJ smiled. He was right, after all!

"Gotcha!" TJ shouted up into the tree.

There was no reply.

He shouted up again. "I know you're up there Benjy, I can see your leg!"

As quick as a flash the leg disappeared back onto the branch. Then came a suppressed giggle, followed by some uncontrollable laughing. If it had been an even smaller tree then the branches would have probably started shaking, but the oak remained steadfast.

A smiling face poked over the branch and beamed at TJ. "I'm not here!" he joked, and immediately TJ felt cheered by Benjy's silliness.

"Come on, down you get," TJ called up to Benjy, "game's over."

After quite a bit of protestation, Benjy carefully clambered down. His little arms and legs stretched to their limits as he felt for the branches that formed his ladder back down the tree.

As Benjy made it back down to earth from his lofty heights he gave TJ a big smile, the gap in his front teeth making it look even cheekier. His cheeks were redder than normal, and his strawberry blonde hair was damp with sweat. Must be hot work climbing and hiding in trees, TJ thought.

"Shall we go and find the others TJ?" Benjy asked excitedly.

"No need," TJ replied flatly, "I already found them."

"Oh," Benjy said, sounding slightly disappointed, "that was quick."

"Yes, I knew Lizzy Wizzy would be in the Suffolk barn," TJ said, "but it turned out Chatty was in there too."

"Well whose turn is it to be the seeker next?" asked Benjy.

"Nobody. Game's over," TJ confirmed.

"Oh, why's that?" Benjy asked.

TJ just shrugged his shoulders. It was too complicated to explain.

That was good enough for Benjy. "What are we doing next instead?"

"Nothing," was TJ's simple reply. "I'm going in."

"No," groaned Benjy. "Stay outside and play tennis with me," he pleaded.

"Sorry, I've had enough Benjy," TJ said. He still felt bad about what had happened with Chatty and wasn't in the mood.

"Really?"

"Really. I'm not much company Benjy. Sorry."

With that, TJ made his way back to the Old Girl. Undeterred, Benjy followed since he loved nothing more than to spend time with his older cousin who he idolised. Even before he could walk and talk, Benjy had tried to emulate TJ. For years, whatever TJ did, Benjy would want to do it as well. Some things never changed.

*

Dinner proved to be a subdued affair. Grandpa Mal did his best to try and rally the troops but everyone bar Benjy was preoccupied, and their thoughts were elsewhere. Chatty was intent on not even looking, let alone talking, to TJ. She had only just made up with Lizzy Wizzy, since at least she had tried to get TJ to share his secrets when Chatty was around.

In any case, Chatty needed one friend. The only good thing was that she wasn't missing her Mum. Benjy also seemed to be coping with his Mummy's absence quite well. He seemed quite excitable, which made Chatty even grumpier, which in turn made Benjy even more mischievous. He loved winding Chatty up, even if it did get him a thump every now and then from his beloved sister.

Grandpa Mal did a grand job of producing another huge steaming bowl of spaghetti and more of his special sauce. No matter how many times they would have it this summer they would never tire of it, washed down with copious amounts of his homemade cloudy lemonade. Grandpa Mal was determined that the children would feel at home here, even though both their mothers were some way away.

Dinner was followed by a rather fractious game of cards, as the tension between Chatty and TJ persisted. Benjy chose to side with TJ to ensure he caused maximum irritation to his sister. It meant he needed to be light on his feet to avoid a couple of blows from Chatty when Grandpa Mal wasn't looking.

After quite some pestering, Grandpa Mal relented and allowed some television time, in order to placate his grandchildren before bedtime. He was particularly keen to get Benjy off to bed so he could spend some time with the newest members of the Dreamguardians.

Before he could ask him to go up to bed, Benjy jumped up from the sofa where he was sprawled with TJ.

"Right, I'm off to sleep everyone," Benjy announced excitedly.

They all looked and stared at him.

"What's up with you then?" TJ asked.

"Nothing," came the cheerful reply.

"Are you feeling alright, dear boy?" Grandpa Mal asked, a little concerned Benjy wasn't feeling well or was missing his mother.

"I'm feeling fine," came another chipper reply. "Just looking forward to going to sleep," Benjy confirmed.

"Weird little boy," Chatty said unkindly without averting her gaze from the television, as she lay on one end of the largest sofa in the room.

"Now don't be like that Chatty dear," Grandpa Mal chided, but it fell on deaf ears. "Well, if you're sure you're ok dear Benjamin, then goodnight dear boy. Would you like me to tuck you in to bed?"

Benjy shook his head vigorously. "No, I'm fine, thank you Grandpa Mal. I'm a big boy now after all." He grinned mischievously.

Grandpa Mal smiled back. "Well, if you say so, dear boy. Goodnight."

Grandpa Mal had a soft spot for Benjy. After all, what wasn't there to love about such a sweet and innocent boy. Grandpa Mal had already felt very blessed to have three grandchildren, but the birth of Benjy had filled him with great joy. Although he had always hoped that all four grandchildren would get along and spend many happy times at the Old Girl, he was pleased there were at least two girls to keep each other company and two boys to do the same.

"Good night," Benjy replied as he pretty much skipped out of the room.

After a few minutes, Grandpa Mal got up from his chair and went over to the doorway to check Benjy wasn't hanging around. Satisfied he was nowhere to be seen, Grandpa Mal closed the door and returned to his chair. He turned down the volume on the television, immediately raising Chatty's hackles as she had remained engrossed in the programme.

"My dear girls and boy," Grandpa Mal began, "now Benjy has gone to bed I would like to talk to you about last night's activities, as well as my conversations today." He had been looking forward to this moment all day.

"Excellent," TJ said, trying to sound enthusiastic, although in truth he was worried what Chatty might say to Grandpa Mal about this afternoon.

Lizzy Wizzy looked nervously across at Chatty, who was doing a good job in ignoring everyone, then to Grandpa Mal.

"I'm listening, Grandpa Mal," Lizzy Wizzy said, hoping to make up for Chatty's apparent lack of interest.

"Very good, dear girl. And what about you Chatty?" Grandpa Mal asked.

Chatty heard the question but did not reply. She did not acknowledge Grandpa Mal at all.

Grandpa Mal tried again. "Chatty, dear girl, did you hear me?"

Reluctantly, Chatty looked across at Grandpa Mal. "I heard you, but I'm busy watching the television right now," she said. Chatty was quite surprised just how rude it sounded as it came out. She didn't mean it to, but there was no taking it back now.

Grandpa Mal was taken aback. "I'm sorry, what did you say Chatty?" he asked.

The reply was equally as rude.

"You heard, not now. I want to watch the end of this programme."

Lizzy Wizzy winced and TJ held his breath. He wasn't quite sure how this was going to go, but he had a feeling it was going to end badly.

"Chatty! Don't be so rude!" Grandpa Mal barked. Up to now he'd kept quiet all the times Chatty had been arguing with Katherine. But not anymore. His patience had worn thin and was now close to evaporating. Chatty had been getting more and more insolent by the day and it was about time she was told, and it stopped. He knew where she got this attitude from, and that made him all the more determined to ensure it stopped.

"If you don't turn that television off right this second, then I will," Grandpa Mal continued, his voice still raised.

"Fine," huffed Chatty as she reached down onto the floor, picked up the remote control and killed the television with one fell swoop.

"Thank you," Grandpa Mal said, "but it's about time this attitude stopped young lady."

"What attitude?" came the stubborn reply.

"The one being exhibited now," Grandpa Mal shot back. He was now getting quite riled. "You are being obnoxiously rude to everyone and anyone. I've heard it far too many times from you already this holiday with your mother and I've just about had enough. It's time it stopped. Do you hear me young Charlotte?"

The room went silent once Grandpa Mal had finished his reprimand. TJ and Lizzy Wizzy dared breathe. They had never seen Grandpa Mal this cross before.

Chatty glared at Grandpa Mal, all manner of responses running through her mind. She knew that the right response was to stand down and apologise, but something inside her prevented her from choosing it. Instead, Grandpa Mal calling her obnoxious, by her full name, and the mention of her Mum caused the red mist to descend.

Chatty exploded as she jumped to her feet.

"I am no such thing," she shouted at Grandpa Mal. "You're always on *her* side. You don't care about me, or what I'm thinking, or what I'm feeling. All you care about is *her* and all the stupid dream secrets you've been sharing with TJ."

She flashed a glare at TJ, who gulped. Chatty had really lost her temper this time, and he feared what might come next. Was she about to tell Grandpa Mal that he'd already told Lizzy Wizzy all the important things about being a Dreamguardian and deliberately excluded her?

"That's enough Charlotte," Grandpa Mal snapped, pouring even more fuel on a fire that was already raging out of control.

"No! I don't care!" she shouted, throwing the television remote control down hard onto the floor. It smashed, sending fragments flying across the room. She felt terrible instantly and wished she hadn't done it, but there was no way to turn back the clock. What was done, was done.

Before Grandpa Mal could do or say anything further, Chatty ran towards the door.

"Well, you can keep all your secrets to yourself, see if I care. I've had enough."

She slammed the door hard behind her as she exited, leaving its occupants and all the secrets she desperately wanted to know more about, behind her.

*

In his bedroom, Benjy was so excited. He had been wishing the whole evening away just for this moment. At one point, he thought the games were going to go on forever and he would never get to this stage.

But now it was time.

He'd had a brilliant afternoon playing hide and seek. He'd managed to fool TJ into thinking he'd been hiding all along in one of the oak trees behind the Old Girl. But he hadn't. Instead, he'd taken the slightly longer route to the old farmyard. He'd always wanted to go there, but it had always been off limits.

He'd slipped quietly and unnoticed into the piggery and then into the old barn. As he passed a rowing boat, he had heard some rustling and, in a panic, shot up some old wooden steps that took him to the first floor. As he'd peered out down through an opening in one of the wooden partition walls, he'd seen Lizzy Wizzy conceal herself under some tarpaulin that covered up some junk in the corner of the room below.

Benjy had sniggered quietly to himself. He'd found Lizzy Wizzy already and he wasn't even the catcher. He had also found Chatty as well when she suddenly appeared and revealed her hiding place to TJ.

As he lay in his bed, Benjy was proud of himself. He was the undisputed champion of hide and seek. After all, he'd managed to observe everything that had unfolded this afternoon, and no-one was any the wiser. He'd heard almost everything that TJ had said to Lizzy Wizzy, although he hadn't understood some of it. Nobody had known he was there, even after Chatty showed up. Then he'd managed to sprint back via the longer route, hidden from sight by the hawthorn hedge and climb the smaller oak tree before TJ had 'found' him.

Benjy hadn't heard everything, but more than enough to now be excited to try and put into practice what he'd overheard this afternoon.

He was excited as he closed his eyes and repeated a name over and over in his head. Tonight, Benjy was going to find out if he was a Dreamguardian too.

CHAPTER 31 – THE GLASSHOUSE

Grandpa Mal had been quite perturbed by Chatty's outburst. Whether it was the rush of adrenalin, anxiety or disappointment, the result was that he began to feel unwell soon after Chatty left the room.

He apologised to TJ and Lizzy Wizzy as he ushered them off to their bedrooms, as he needed to retire to bed himself. He was getting old and increasingly feeling the physical and emotional effects of the events of the past few days.

TJ wasn't too disappointed to get into bed. Running around in the sun earlier this afternoon had sapped his energy and he too was feeling the after-effects of his time yesterday with the Dreamorian and *Sensei*.

He went to sleep quickly, very careful not to think about anyone as he did so. He wasn't in the mood for any Dreamguardian activity tonight. He hoped his own dreams would be safe and he would wake up in the morning feeling refreshed and all the better for a good night's sleep.

*

TJ was in a dense forest, surrounded by trees of all shapes and sizes. Around him as far as the eye could see was a collage of green and brown: ferns, foliage, trunks of various diameter and the thick canopy of the trees. The dark grey sky above was barely visible.

Suddenly he was on the move, heading in no particular direction. He felt like he was looking for something but wasn't quite sure what. He passed an oak tree, then a sycamore, another oak, an ash, followed by another larger oak. Every now and then he stumbled over a root that was slightly exposed.

The density of the trees thinned after a while and he found himself in an open expanse. Ahead of him was a steep grass hill that young children would instinctively feel the urge to run or roll down. A gravel path led up the side of the hill and TJ made his way onto it. Each step he took up the hill produced a crunching sound as the small stones ground against each other.

As he reached the top, he saw a huge glasshouse a short distance away. It was octagonal, with glass panels set in an intricate steel frame mounted on a small course of bricks. Atop its sloping ceiling panels was a smaller octagonal roof lantern. It was an impressive building which TJ instantly recognised. He had been here before with his parents when they visited the acres of landscaped grounds and global vegetable garden which had at its heart this spectacular octagonal glasshouse. From its position perched on the apex of the hill, TJ could see for miles across the surrounding farmland and countryside.

He made his way into the vegetable garden, past the finest specimens of vegetables from around the world. The different varieties were impeccably organised and growing proudly in rows in various raised beds, each labelled with their elaborate Latin names. On the far side of the garden, rows of sweetcorn towered behind smaller lines of fennel, beetroot, and radishes.

Ordinarily the place was thronging with visitors, but TJ couldn't see a soul as he looked around.

He headed into the glasshouse, carefully closing the door behind him. Inside it was hot and humid, even though the automatic windows had fully extended open. Most of the windows were steamed up and it was difficult to see outside. A straight flagstone path headed from the door he had just entered to another one directly opposite him about twelve metres away.

The contents of the glasshouse were also impeccably arranged. Scores of varieties of pepper and chillies, as well as some citrus trees growing oranges and lemons stood in two large soil beds either side of the path. Close to the door at the other end of the glasshouse was a vine, growing melons. The weight of the fruit was supported by little hessian bags that had been attached to a bamboo cane frame.

TJ wondered why he was here. They hadn't visited here for a while, not since Dad died. It had been one of his favourite places to come as a family. It was somewhere they came for a good walk and to inhale some fresh air. Mum and Dad would admire the gardens, flowers, trees, fruit and vegetables, while TJ and Lizzy Wizzy would enjoy some of the nature trails and treasure hunts organised by the owners of the gardens. Once they had finished outside, they would all enjoy refreshments in the café. TJ would enjoy chatting with Dad while Lizzy Wizzy and Mum browsed through the gift shop.

As he wandered through the glasshouse, TJ could feel himself getting hotter and hotter. He began to feel very uncomfortable and uneasy. Something didn't feel right.

He got the sense he was being watched. But when he looked to his left, the windows were steamed up and he couldn't see anything. He did the same to his right, where the windows had less condensation on them. As he peered in the direction of the tall sweetcorn outside, he thought he saw something move over by the sweetcorn. Then he thought he caught a glimpse of someone trying to peer in through one of the windows.

Before he could work out what it was, he heard a loud bang. As he looked up out of one of the windows in the lantern roof, he saw a red orb had been fired into the air a short distance away. It was streaking up into the sky like a devilish rocket.

A Dreamstealer was present and at work.

Without warning, the doors at either end of the glasshouse blew open with great force. A violent wind surged through the glasshouse, almost knocking TJ off his feet. He leant into the wind with all his might to stop himself from being swept away by its power. As he struggled to remain standing, TJ saw what he thought was a dense black cloud moving quickly towards him. But as it got closer, he realised it was made up of hundreds of individual organisms moving quickly towards him. It was a frightening sight.

As he struggled to stand against the wind, hundreds if not thousands of bats entered the glasshouse. They flew at great speed within an inch of TJ's head and body. TJ was sure he could feel some of the wingtips brush his hair as they hurtled past him. They quickly flew out of the doors behind him, into the dark grey sky.

The wind intensified, causing TJ to stoop further into it. As he angled his face down, he noticed the earth in the two large beds begin to twitch, then move. All of a sudden, the soil was teeming with worms, cockroaches and scorpions, pushing their way up from beneath the earth. The cockroaches and scorpions quickly scurried onto the path where TJ was stood. Even though he was terrified, he remained rooted to the spot for fear of being blown away.

He tried to control his breathing as some of the creatures began to crawl onto his feet, but as they moved up his leg, he could bear it no more. As he tried to kick them off, the movement unbalanced him, and the violent wind knocked him over. The cockroaches and scorpions were quick to start to climb over the new obstacle that was now in their way. As he lay winded on the ground, they crawled all over his legs, hands and arms.

TJ writhed and thrashed his limbs about to try and get them off, but to no avail. There were just too many of them. No sooner had any been displaced then they were instantly replaced. They came in their thousands, crawling up, over and around him, trying to get to his face.

His screams were stifled by a new sound. Not above the wind, but almost in tune with it. A sound getting increasingly louder and louder. As TJ lifted his head up off the flagstone path and looked beyond his infested body, he saw a new dark swarm flying in on the wind. It was larger in size than the colony of bats and looked like a seething formation of deadly black and yellow enemy fighters.

A buzzing noise got louder and louder as a giant swarm of wasps entered and soon filled the glasshouse. As TJ lay on the ground thrashing about, they began to settle upon him, first upon his thighs and then down his legs. In a matter of moments, the wasps had completely covered them, as well as the cockroaches and scorpions that had clambered onto him.

In greater number, the wasps began to settle. As more and more landed, his chest started to be covered by a deadly blanket. He began to feel the weight of them pressing him down. He stopped thrashing his legs, for fear of agitating the wasps. He dared move, even as the cockroaches and scorpions started to move menacingly up his arms towards his face. He flailed his arms around to try and throw them off and prevent any wasps from settling.

TJ began to panic as he realised he was becoming increasingly engulfed by the creatures he feared the most. He was to be mummified by wasps, cockroaches and scorpions. His breathing became very erratic as he felt the tiny movements of thousands of bristly legs over his bare arms and an increasing number of pin pricks through his jeans as the wasps began to sting.

Suddenly, he became aware of a deep rumbling sound. It started off barely audible above the angry swarm of the wasps, and within a few seconds the ground was shaking. Then, as the rumbling got louder, the ground shook more violently and gained even more strength. The glasshouse started to rattle. It started slowly at first, but as TJ looked up, he could see the metal structure of the glasshouse vibrating quicker and quicker.

The rumbling, shaking and power of the wind intensified. As TJ looked on in horror, the glasshouse could withstand it no more. One by one, every pane of glass shattered with a deafening explosion. Shards of glass rained down onto the beds and path below. As TJ put his arms over his head to shield himself from falling glass, cockroaches dropped onto his head. A scorpion landed and clung onto his left cheek.

Before the glass landed, a great rush of wind ripped into the glasshouse and lifted TJ off the floor. He found himself rising quickly and shot through one of the holes in the top of the glasshouse where a window stood only a few seconds ago. In just a matter of moments, TJ had shot thousands of feet vertically into the sky.

As he looked down, TJ realised he was now at quite some height. The glasshouse with all its unwelcome occupants was but a tiny dot below. TJ was relieved to see that most of the creatures had been shaken off his body as he'd climbed in altitude. His relief, however, was short-lived.

Without warning, he was falling. Picking up speed and hurtling towards the ground. He could feel the wind battering him, aggressively slapping his cheeks. His eyes started to water.

Beneath him, the glasshouse was getting bigger and bigger as he plummeted towards it. His heart was racing as he realised he was not going to stop. Fear suddenly gripped him as the ground got closer and closer. But then, from the corner of his blurry eyes, he saw someone cowering just outside the glasshouse.

As he got closer, the figure looked up. As he continued to freefall at great velocity, the noise of the wind suddenly died.

He heard a desperate high-pitched cry from beneath him.

"TJ!"

But he was falling too quickly to do anything about it.

As he fell through the frame of the glasshouse, TJ saw the flash of strawberry blonde hair and a freckled face full of fear.

TJ's senses were overloaded, and everything was happening too quickly. Only metres from the ground, TJ realised who it was.

But before he could do anything, TJ woke up with a start, just as he was about to hit the ground at great speed.

He sat bolt upright, drenched with sweat and his heart racing. He began to process what had just happened as he tried to bring his heavy breathing under control.

His first realisation was that a Dreamstealer had infiltrated and corrupted his dream with some deadly combination of Nightfright, Multiplier and Faller.

His second realisation was what he had seen in the last split seconds of his dream just now.

"Benjy, no!" he cried out desperately.

He scrambled out of bed and ran to Benjy's room. He barged in, flicked the main light on and rushed over to the bed. Benjy was there, sleeping soundly with his strawberry blonde hair just visible over the duvet cover.

"Benjy, Benjy," TJ shouted.

But there was no response.

TJ tried again. "Benjy, Benjy, wake up, it's me, TJ."

Again, there was no response.

TJ shook him anxiously through the duvet cover.

"Benjy, please, wake up," he cried.

Benjy still didn't move.

"No, please, no, Benjy," he said through his tears, continuing to shake him as hard as he could.

But it was no use. He couldn't wake him up.

Although he kept shaking him, he knew it was hopeless.

TJ understood exactly what had just happened. In that moment, he felt something he had only ever experienced once before. The sense of sorrow, loss and emptiness was overwhelming, and he felt sick to his stomach.

Benjy had the gift and somehow had found his way into a dream.

But now he was trapped. Trapped inside someone else's dream. His dream.

Little Benjy was lost; lost in a void of dreamless darkness from which he was unable to escape.

TJ put his arms around the sleeping boy, his one true friend in the world, and wept bitterly.

CHAPTER 32 – A TALE OF TWO DREAMS

Down the corridor, Chatty was deep in REM sleep. She was sitting in a huge upholstered wingback chair, opposite another larger one covered in leather. To her right was a primitive fireplace, from which came the comforting sound and smell of a crackling fire.

In between them was an ornate games table, inlaid with the squares of a chessboard as well as a backgammon board. Strangely, Chatty noticed that the backgammon checkers had been replaced by the chess pieces which were laid out on the Inner and Outer table of the backgammon board. Except for an extra piece per side, the chess pieces had been set up almost identically to the starting position for backgammon.

The white King and Queen replaced the two white checkers that started the game on Black's Inner Table, while on the opposite side the black King and Queen had done the same to the two black checkers on White's Inner Table. Five pawns of white were lined up on the sixth triangle of White's Inner Table, while the remaining three white pawns were on the eighth triangle of White's Outer Table. Opposite, the eight black pawns were a mirror image on the Black side.

On either side of the twelfth triangle of the Outer Table stood the remaining six chess pieces: two rooks, two bishops and two knights. The white pieces were placed on Black's Outer Table while the black pieces had been set up on White's Outer Table. Two pairs of dice, one black with white dots and the other white with black dots, sat next to two leather dice boxes.

Chatty was confused by the juxtaposition of the two games. Next to each chair was a side-table, upon which stood a lamp and books. On the table next to the leather chair was a ceramic phrenology head. Black lines marked out different areas of varying sizes around the cranium and the closed left eye. Chatty didn't know what it was, other than distinctive and odd.

She had no idea where she was. To her left the entire length of the wall was covered by books, neatly organised within vast bookcases. They were so large that two sets of wooden wheeled library stairs were attached to the cases to allow access to every single book on the numerous shelves. Old books were piled high around the room on an eclectic array of tables, while many stuffed animals stared out from behind glass domes and tanks.

As Chatty looked beyond the empty large leather chair in front of her she saw a stag's head mounted on the wall. Further along was a wild boar's head and an array of mounted animal skulls. In front of the wall were various display cabinets and bookcases. She could see a collection of anatomical models and figures in the cabinet, including a white plaster arm that hung down from a chain. On one of the bookcases was a plaster bust of a striking bearded gentleman, mounted on a wooden plinth.

Then she noticed the ceiling, covered with intricate paintings and ornate gilded cornicing. She gasped at its beauty. Above her she saw different painted panels of people asleep. In one, to the side of a sleeping couple were figures dressed in white, while dark shadowy figures loomed menacingly on the other. In another, the person sleeping was accompanied by a figure in white, while it was just a figure in black in another scene.

Her eyes were then drawn to five larger and more prominent panels: an old man sleeping at the foot of a rising spiral stairway, upon which figures of light ascended and descended; a young man asleep in a farmer's field as the sun, moon, eleven stars and wheat sheaves bowed down to him; a man on the ramparts of a castle; a figure of intense light on its knees, trapped in a cage and surrounded by shadowy figures; and a figure surrounded by intense light, towards which figures of light were escaping from opening cages.

"What is this place?" Chatty whispered.

"Good question, *girl*," came the deep and sinister reply from within the large leather chair.

It made her jump, since the chair had been empty just before she looked up at the ceiling.

Sat opposite her was a figure dressed in a full-length black hooded robe, with a monastic scapular hung from its shoulders. She couldn't see its face, if indeed it had one. A staff was gripped tightly in its left hand. At the top, a carved demonic looking creature with fangs and pointed ears grinned over its shoulder at her.

Chatty wasn't quite sure what to think or do. She felt a little nervous, but also somewhat intrigued by the figure in front of her. It wouldn't frighten her. After all, she was tough. Wasn't she?

"Who are you and where are we?" Chatty asked, as nonchalantly as she could manage.

Dominus Tenebris emitted a deep growled laugh. "We shall come to this soon enough, *girl*. But it would seem that in your asking of these questions, it is clear that the old man and foolish *boy* have kept many secrets from you."

"What do you mean?" Chatty said, her curiosity pricked. "Do you mean that TJ knows what this place is and who you are?"

"What does it matter to you, *girl*?" *Dominus Tenebris* hissed, the staff twitching in the gloved left hand. "You are clearly not important *girl*. Even those two *fools* see no reason to tell you the intricate details and secrets of their filthy Brethren."

Chatty was quick to interrupt him. "The what?" she asked.

The patronising laugh was quick to come. "You don't even know that, *girl*?" *Dominus Tenebris* sneered. "They haven't told you anything at all, have they?"

As *Dominus Tenebris* laughed at her, Chatty could feel herself getting angry. Not necessarily angry at this 'thing', whatever it was, but the reason it was laughing at her.

Dominus Tenebris could sense her anger rising and took great delight in it.

"You don't know much about anything, do you, *girl*?"

"Shut up," she said angrily, "yes, I do. I'm a Dreamguardian. According to Grandpa Mal that makes me special and a protector of dreams."

Dominus Tenebris laughed sarcastically in the chair. As the hood tilted back slightly, Chatty caught sight of two red eyes, boring into her.

"Yes, I was told you had the filthy gift, *girl*. Which is why I am here. Now is the time for introductions. After all, if I don't start to tell you things, I doubt anyone else will. Certainly not the old man and that *silly little boy*." The last three words were dragged out for emphasis. *Dominus Tenebris* sensed the weaknesses in Chatty's character. They would become strengths in the right hands.

"Do you mean TJ?" a curious Chatty asked, hoping the reply would be yes.

It was. "Of course," replied *Dominus Tenebris*, "the *silly little boy*. But you do know that the *silly little boy* is the old man's favourite, don't you?"

Chatty was stung. Although she was increasingly suspecting this, she had hoped it wasn't true. But everything was starting to point to it being true. Wasn't it?

Dominus Tenebris could sense the uncertainty running through her mind.

"The *boy* doesn't want you to be a Dreamguardian. Nor does the old man. But I don't need to tell you that, *girl*. You already know that, don't you?"

Chatty paused. She was getting confused and didn't know what to think. She knew TJ didn't want her to be a Dreamguardian. After all, he had said very clearly to Lizzy Wizzy that he didn't care about her and didn't want to share the secrets with her. But she wasn't so sure about Grandpa Mal.

Detecting the doubt and knowing what would work, *Dominus Tenebris* continued.

"Have you ever seen this room before, girl?"

Chatty shook her head and muttered "no".

"This is the Great Room of the Brethren of the Dreamguardians. Somewhere here is where *all* the secrets are kept. When did the old man say he would bring you here, *girl*?"

Chatty hung her head. "He didn't," she said quietly, "not yet".

"Not yet!" *Dominus Tenebris* shouted incredulously. "Perhaps you are as foolish as the others after all," he laughed, and Chatty bristled at the suggestion she was a fool.

"You have too much faith and belief in the old man. He was only too quick to bring the silly little boy here. To show and tell him all the secrets that they are desperate to withhold from you."

"What? No..."

Another sinister laugh punctuated the air.

"Yes... They are devious. The *boy* in particular. Sly, devious and dangerous. Before you know it, he will try and trick you. Trick you and then trap you in a dream. Did they warn you about that yet, girl?"

"Sort of," Chatty replied weakly.

"Sort of..." *Dominus Tenebris* repeated mockingly and then roared with laughter.

Although she did know about the dangers of being a Dreamguardian and getting trapped inside a dream, it was only by accident when she had overheard TJ telling Lizzy Wizzy in the Suffolk barn.

"What a sorry, sad, pathetic state of affairs," *Dominus Tenebris* spat out, getting up from the chair. Chatty looked up at the imposing figure as it walked towards her and towered over her.

"Now is the time for proper introductions, *girl*. I am *Dominus Tenebris*, the Master of Darkness and leader of the Dreamstealers." The staff twirled theatrically, and the demonic creature danced before Chatty's eyes.

"You must understand that we Dreamstealers are the rightful heirs of the gift that the Dreamguardians now claim as their own." The staff slammed down into the floor, making Chatty jump. "You will find the story very familiar *girl*: one unrighteous child favoured over the more deserving one by a foolish old man. Ring any bells, *girl*?"

Chatty hesitated before nodding and *Dominus Tenebris* was quick to continue.

"I think you need to think very carefully, *girl*. After all, the people you thought cared about you have been selfish, scheming behind your back, keeping secrets, lying to you, putting you down. Before long, they will abandon you, in one way or the other."

Chatty tried to stay strong and hold herself together. But *Dominus Tenebris* was right. TJ and Grandpa Mal had been keeping secrets and lying to her. Mum was always quick to blame her for everything and even Grandpa Mal was now siding against her. Her Mum had been selfish by choosing to send Dad away and now she'd just abandoned her. Left her here all alone.

Her thoughts were interrupted by *Dominus Tenebris*.

"You should join *us*, Chatty. We have great need for someone with your skill and ability. Join us, before TJ and Grandpa Mal can trap you in a dream so you are no longer an irrelevance to them and the filthy Brethren of the Dreamguardians."

The staff twirled effortlessly and elaborately, before being held out horizontally in front of Chatty's face. *Dominus Tenebris* was inviting her to take hold of it and help her out of her chair.

"Now you are in possession of the truth, *girl*," *Dominus Tenebris* hissed. "The Dreamstealers are the rightful heirs of the gift, before it was stolen from us. The Dreamstealers are rising again and gaining in power. Join us before the *boy* and the *old man* silence you forever. We will be victorious Chatty. You can be one of the greatest Dreamstealers ever to have graced the line of Manasseh. Join us, Chatty, before it's too late."

At that moment, a log in the fire cracked. Chatty looked over to see what the noise was.

When she turned back to the leather chair in front of her, *Dominus Tenebris* was gone.

*

Down the corridor, Lizzy Wizzy was sprawled out in bed, sound asleep. One leg was stuck outside of the covers to keep her cool.

In her dream, she was in her prettiest pink dress, with matching pink shoes and handbag covered with material roses. It was the height of summer and she was dancing in the walled garden of the Old Girl. It was dusk, and the light was beginning to fade. She glided through the maze, around the small square pond with the stone peacock standing proudly at the far end, and then out amongst the rose bushes. Every so often she would stop, cup a rose in both hands and take a deep breath. The scent was intoxicating. Then she would skip and dance to the next constellation of roses and do the same.

Sticking up out of the immaculate grass was a pretty wooden sign. The word 'Wedding' had been beautifully scribed, and a large arrow underneath pointed towards the archway in the end wall.

This was one of Lizzy Wizzy's favourite dreams; a very special day. It had been the wedding of the daughter of a good friend of Grandpa Mal. The Joseph family, all four of them, had been invited to share in the celebrations. She remembered the evening fondly. There had been pretty lights and dancing. What more could she wish for?

The specially crafted wooden door within the archway had been propped open and Lizzy Wizzy danced through into the meadow behind. It had been left to grow and was full of delicate wildflowers, disturbed only by a winding path that had been cut through the long grass. At random intervals were bamboo torches to guide guests to and from the next field. The soft orange flames and light emanating from them flickered in the gentle breeze.

In the next field stood a huge rectangular marquee that had been pitched especially for the wedding. The perimeter of the roof of the marquee was illuminated with a string of fairy lights which ascended at various points and joined up at the twin peaks in the roof.

Long chains of lanterns hung from the trees nearby and swung gently in the warm breeze, while a crowd of people queued for drinks at a camper van that had been converted into a very small bar.

The sound of folk music spilled out from within the marquee and drifted on the breeze. Lizzy Wizzy heard it and hurried herself towards the festivities. After all, she wanted to dance. As she entered the marquee, she saw a small band of men and women at the far end, playing a variety of instruments including a guitar, accordion, double bass, violin and pared back drum kit.

The band had set up in front of a large black and white chequered temporary dance floor, fully revealed now that all the chairs and tables from the wedding breakfast had been moved. The dance floor was packed with people country dancing.

A pretty young lady in a floral dress at the front of the band was playing the violin energetically, while next to her a rotund elderly gentleman with ruddy cheeks, a tweed waistcoat and black bowler hat was calling the dance steps.

As Lizzy Wizzy approached the dance floor, she saw Daddy dancing with Mummy and TJ. She smiled as she saw them enjoying themselves. After a minute, the song ended with a flourish from the accordion. The men faced the women and bowed, and the ladies curtseyed to the gentlemen. Then they all applauded the band.

"Grab your partners for the next dance, please, ladies and gentlemen," the caller announced down the microphone. "Into groups of four and in pairs within the group. This is a good one ladies and gentlemen, lots of fun for everyone..."

Daddy spotted Lizzy Wizzy and quickly beckoned her over to join in the dancing with them. She would be Daddy's partner for this next dance, within their family group of four.

The caller slowly ran through the steps for the next dance and they walked through each part of it. It would be a lively number, involving a lot of promenading, swinging your partner around, do-si-do-ing and walking under arches of arms created by the coming together of the pairs and more than one group.

This was so much fun thought Lizzy Wizzy. No wonder she often remembered this night in her dream.

The rotund gentlemen took a swig from a hip flask, checked the band was ready and spoke again into the microphone. "If you're ready then ladies and gents, grab your partners by the hand. Swing them round and all be grand..."

With that the band started up again. The violin and accordion took turns to play the melody and then joined together in unison.

Daddy and Lizzy Wizzy in one pair, and Mummy and TJ in another followed the instructions of the caller and soon the dance was well underway. They all laughed and joked as they spun each other around and then came together as a group of four to dance around in a circle. After a do-si-do it was time to join with the other groups to create a tunnel with their partners for the couple at the bottom of the line to dance down the tunnel to the top. Lizzy Wizzy stretched as high as she could on tiptoes to touch Daddy's fingertips, so as to leave just enough room for the bottom couple to skip together down the middle.

The dance went on and on in order to give each couple the opportunity to skip down the tunnel of arms. This was Lizzy Wizzy's favourite part of the dance and she loved to remember how Daddy had beamed as they danced down the tunnel, beads of sweat forming on his brow from all the exertion, and then how fast he had swung her round. They leaned back as far as they dared, their spin getting faster and faster.

The caller shouted out again, "Spin your partner by the…"

Suddenly, without warning, the music stopped, and the lights went out. Just some faint light from large candles within huge glass jars remained.

Lizzy Wizzy didn't know what was going on. She looked around her, but everyone was frozen. They were not moving. Reluctantly, she let go of Daddy's hands which were still held out in front of him in order to swing her round. He was still leaning slightly backwards but was now defying the laws of gravity.

From out of the shadows came a figure. It walked slowly and menacingly towards her. It was wearing a full-length black hooded robe, with a monastic scapular hung from its shoulders. She couldn't see its face, if indeed it had one. A staff was gripped tightly in its left hand. At the top, a carved demonic looking creature with fangs and pointed ears grinned over its shoulder at her.

Lizzy Wizzy was petrified.

"Who… who… who are you?" she asked.

"I am your worst nightmare, *little girl*," the figure growled in a deep voice.

Lizzy Wizzy instinctively started to back away. She wanted to run, but her legs felt like jelly.

"Don't waste your time trying to escape, you will never get away from me, *little girl*," the sinister figure continued.

Lizzy Wizzy froze and the figure got closer to her. She began to shake with fright.

"I will keep this very simple for you, *little girl*. I am *Dominus Tenebris*, the Master of Darkness and ruler of the Dreamstealers. I understand that you, *little girl*, are a Dreamguardian. A Dreamguardian is a Dreamstealer's sworn enemy, ever since you took something that didn't belong to you."

Through quivering lips, Lizzy Wizzy tried to speak. She managed to, just.

"I'm sorry, I don't understand what you mean. I didn't take anything, I promise."

Dominus Tenebris laughed and was now within touching distance of her.

"It is too late for apologies, *little girl*. Thousands of years too late in fact."

The staff held in *Dominus Tenebris'* left hand twirled round quickly and the demonic creature danced menacingly in front of Lizzy Wizzy's face. She flinched and closed her eyes.

"Open your eyes, *little girl*," shouted *Dominus Tenebris* and Lizzy Wizzy did it immediately. They filled with tears easily.

"Good," *Dominus Tenebris* continued. "You will do very well to listen to me carefully, *little girl*. I come with two messages, one for you and the other for the old man and foolish little brother of yours."

Lizzy Wizzy looked in horror at the figure in front of her.

"Grandpa Mal? TJ?" she asked nervously.

"Indeed. But this first message is for *you*. Understand it very well, *little girl*."

Lizzy Wizzy nodded her compliance and *Dominus Tenebris* continued. The voice terrified her.

"If you carry on with this Dreamguardian folly, then I will come and find you again, *little girl*. The next time you are in someone's dream, I will see to it personally that you become trapped."

Dominus Tenebris reached out and touched her cheek with a gloved right hand. She flinched at the touch from the devilish figure in front of her and closed her eyes, wishing it would end.

"Do you know what that means, *little girl*? You will be lost... Forever... There will be no more pretty Lizzy Wizzy."

She took a sharp intake of breath at the thought. She had never been so scared in her life.

Dominus Tenebris let go of Lizzy Wizzy's face and walked round all the people close to her, poking some of them with the staff and gently tapping the faces of others with the free right-hand. But the human statues didn't respond. They couldn't see, hear or feel anything.

Dominus Tenebris walked up behind Lizzy Wizzy and whispered into her left ear. "You do realise that none of this is real," *Dominus Tenebris* said, taunting Lizzy Wizzy. "It is all a figment of your imagination. Apart from me that is. Be under no illusion. I am very real..."

Dominus Tenebris paused, walked back around in front of Lizzy Wizzy and towered over her. As the cavernous black hood was bent down to complete the sentence, she saw two red eyes pierce through the darkness and stare at her without blinking. She shivered.

"And I will be watching," *Dominus Tenebris* said menacingly before standing up straight again.

"Your job now is to give this message to old man Grandpa Mal and foolish TJ. Understand?" *Dominus Tenebris* barked.

Lizzy Wizzy nodded frantically.

"Good. Tell them this is their last warning. The game is almost over. I am advancing and *will* be victorious. The Dreamstealers will not rest until our dominion has authority over the night and the Brethren of the Dream-guardians is no more.

"Tell them, they have a choice. If the Brethren ceases in its folly, then many can and will be saved. If not, then many Dreamguardians will be lost. This is their choice to make. If they choose to ignore my warning, then they are responsible for all the losses. And mark my words, those losses will include people you love *little girl*. People such as your dear old Grandpa Mal and wretched brother, and also *you* if you ignore my rather generous advice from earlier."

"Yes, I will tell them, I promise," Lizzy Wizzy said as the tears streamed down her face. "But please, not Grandpa Mal or TJ, please don't hurt them."

Dominus Tenebris sneered. "Well, you know what you need to tell them. You must convince them in what they must do: lay down and surrender their

Dreamswick and accept the unadulterated rule and line of Manasseh. Then all will be saved."

Dominus Tenebris took a few steps back and looked around at the disgusting scene: people enjoying themselves, families and friends together, celebrating love and enjoying each other's company. How pathetic!

But now they were frozen in time and space.

"Say goodbye to your lovely little dream, *little girl*," *Dominus Tenebris* jeered as the demonic creature atop the staff began to spin. "When you wake, you will remember only my visit, our conversation and the warnings you need to pass on."

"No... please no," Lizzy Wizzy begged. She wanted to remember the happy parts of this dream forever. The day she danced with her Daddy. She would never be able to do it again.

"Daddy...," she cried, wishing he would come back to life and somehow rescue her. But he didn't and couldn't.

A red orb appeared around *Dominus Tenebris'* gloved left hand. An evil laugh pierced the air as it fired and tore through the white cotton canvas roof of the marquee. "Say goodbye to your Daddy too, *little girl*..."

"NO... DADDY...," Lizzy Wizzy cried, trying to grab hold of him for one last time. For one last cuddle. But before she could, he dissolved before her eyes. One by one, all the family and friends, old and new, disappeared from around her.

Until there was nothing left. Except for darkness. And the giant teardrops falling from her chin.

Not for the first time, Lizzy Wizzy felt cold and alone.

CHAPTER 33 – THE FALLOUT

They were all gathered around Benjy's bed, crying. Chatty was distraught as she lay across her little brother's body. Other than the gentle rise and fall of his chest confirming he was still breathing, Benjy lay lifeless in his bed.

When he had been unable to wake Benjy, TJ had raced to Grandpa Mal's room for help. The old man had rushed as quickly as his old legs could manage to Benjy's room, hoping that TJ was somehow mistaken. But he'd sobbed uncontrollably as his attempts to wake Benjy also failed and his worst nightmare was confirmed. His beloved little Grandson was lost.

Grandpa Mal's heart could barely withstand the pain. His mind had been conflicted between the confusion of how it had all happened and the guilt he now felt that he hadn't somehow stopped it. But he just didn't know! In all his years involved with the Brethren he had only even known one person as young as Benjy to have the gift, and that was believed to be an anomaly. But that was little consolation now. How would he ever forgive himself? And more importantly, how would he ever explain all this to his dear Katherine? All he could now do was look on, devastated at what had happened to Benjy.

Lizzy Wizzy had been next to discover the awful news about Benjy. She had woken soon after her frightening encounter with *Dominus Tenebris*. The soft sound of her own crying had soon been overwhelmed by the haunting wails from Grandpa Mal and TJ a little way down the corridor, which had chilled her to the bone. She had run as quickly as possible to find out what was wrong. At first, she thought that Benjy was dead, but her relief that he wasn't was short lived as Grandpa Mal explained that he might as well be. Once she had understood what had happened, her tears came easily and flowed rapidly. Her heart had been broken again, and she thought her tears would never cease.

Chatty had burst through the door only a few moments ago. Before then, she had been enjoying the state between sleep and wakefulness. As she drifted through her hypnagogia, she replayed in her mind the events of her dream and visit from *Dominus Tenebris*. She had not been overly disturbed by her encounter with the intriguing being, dressed all in black with a fascinating creature on the end of a wooden staff. In fact, it had left her with more questions than answers.

In many ways, the leader of the Dreamstealers had made quite a lot of sense and sounded strangely convincing. The story of one undeserving child favoured over another certainly resonated with her situation, and *Dominus Tenebris* understood the selfish scheming that had been going on behind her back. But she still wasn't quite sure. TJ would never trap her in a dream to get rid of her, would he? As she contemplated what her response would have been if *Dominus Tenebris* had not disappeared so quickly and silently, she had also become aware of uncontrollable crying down the corridor. It sounded like Lizzy Wizzy, but someone else too.

Intrigued, she had rushed down the corridor and was surprised to hear it was coming from Benjy's room. As she had entered his bedroom, she too discovered the devastating truth about her baby brother. Grandpa Mal, his face wracked with the pain of immeasurable loss, had immediately scooped her up into an embrace and whispered the painful truth into her ear. Benjy had been trapped inside a dream. He was lost...

Chatty had refused to believe him at first and shouted for Benjy. She struggled to break free of Grandpa Mal as he tried to hold her tightly and give her a reassuring cuddle that everything would be alright. Although he knew it wouldn't. How could it be? The world had changed for the worse, yet again.

Chatty had finally broken free and was now distraught as she lay across Benjy's body. She buried her tearful face into his strawberry blonde hair, which still smelt like it always did.

"Benjy, wake up, please," she pleaded through her tears, "it's me Chatty. Come on, wake up Benjy... please..." She broke down again as Benjy made no response. Although they had had their arguments and fought like cat and dog at times, Benjy was her little brother. And she loved him more than she had ever told him or shown him.

Grandpa Mal could barely take it as he watched Chatty reach the heart-breaking realisation that Benjy was indeed gone. Yes, his body was still breathing and alive, but his mind was elsewhere. He wouldn't respond to her. Not now, not ever. He was lost; lost in a void of dreamless darkness from which he was unable to escape.

After sobbing for her little brother, Chatty eventually lifted her head from Benjy and turned to Grandpa Mal.

"Where is he Grandpa Mal?" she just about managed to ask through her grief.

Grandpa Mal paused and swallowed hard, as he tried to speak.

"I... I don't know, my dear Chatty," came the devastating, but truthful, answer.

But it wasn't good enough for Chatty. "You must know where he is Grandpa Mal," Chatty shouted back through her tears, "you need to get him back!"

Grandpa Mal took a sharp intake of breath, which splintered into multiple shudders in his distress.

"I know my dear, but I can't. I don't know where he is. I'm sorry." He broke down again and as he did his legs gave way. He fell heavily onto the end of Benjy's bed, squashing the little boy's favourite teddies.

"Grandpa Mal! Are you alright?" asked TJ, concerned for Grandpa Mal's health. The last thing they needed now was for anything bad to happen to Grandpa Mal. He couldn't bear that, especially not after the loss of Benjy, his brother in all but name.

Grandpa Mal nodded softly as he sat slouched on the bottom of the bed, his shoulders shuddering as he cried softly to himself.

Chatty turned to TJ. "Grandpa Mal? What about Benjy?!" she shouted at TJ. Her poor little brother was lying here, as good as dead, and all he was worried about was Grandpa Mal!

"Don't you care TJ?" she barked at him. After all, what had happened to Benjy wasn't fair. She needed someone to blame.

"Of course I care," TJ shot back and glared at her through eyes red raw from trying to rub away his tears with his palms. "Benjy was like the little brother I never had..." he said, aware that his tears were about to reappear too.

"No!" shouted Chatty angrily. "He was MY little brother. It's not about *you* this time TJ. All you care about is yourself and those most precious to you. But we all know that doesn't include Benjy, or me..."

She glared at him. At least shouting at TJ made her feel a little bit better.

TJ was stung by an accusation he thought grossly unfair. He looked forlornly across at Grandpa Mal for some support, but his head was still bowed and shoulders still shaking. TJ knew Chatty was upset and he would just have to take her barrage of abuse.

"So, what about you then TJ?" Chatty asked. TJ looked at her puzzled but didn't respond.

"Aren't you meant to be the clever one?" she continued, her voice getting louder all the time. "The one with all the secrets? The one with all the answers? So, TJ the great," she mocked, "where's Benjy?"

"I don't know," came his muted reply, "I didn't know he was there. I only saw him at the last minute, but it was too late. I didn't have time to expel him from the dream. It was just too late."

Chatty went silent as she stared hard at TJ. Her brow twitched as she analysed carefully what TJ had just said.

"Say that again," she demanded.

"What?" TJ asked, still puzzled.

"Say what you just said *again!*" Chatty shouted angrily.

"I said I didn't know where Benjy is," TJ replied.

"No, the bit after that," came the impatient reply.

"I said I only saw him at the last minute..."

"Stop," shouted Chatty. "Saw who?"

"Benjy," TJ replied quickly.

"Where?"

"In my dream," TJ said.

"Your dream?"

"Yes," TJ confirmed, still unsure where Chatty was going with her line of questioning.

But Chatty knew exactly where she was going and what was happening. A rage was beginning to rise up within her.

"So, what you've been trying to hide is the fact that Benjy was in your dream?" she said accusingly.

"Well, yes, but I'm not trying to hide anything…"

"So, when I asked if you knew where Benjy was, you lied to me, didn't you…?"

"No…," TJ just about managed to say before Chatty interrupted again.

"You said you didn't know where Benjy was. But you do! You knew all along. He was in your dream."

"Yes, but…"

"So, he must still be in your dream."

"No! That's not the way it works Chatty…" TJ tried to explain, but he was quickly shouted down by Chatty.

"He's right, dear girl," Grandpa Mal tried to interject.

"Shut up, both of you!" bellowed Chatty. "I don't believe you!" She paused to try and think for a moment. Nothing made sense anymore. If no-one knew where Benjy was now, she decided to focus on why and how he had been trapped in the first place.

"Why didn't you get him out of your dream then TJ? I know that can be done."

"I told you, I didn't see him until it was too late," TJ said exasperatedly.

"Liar!" Chatty shouted.

"No!" TJ said as gently as he could, imploring Chatty to believe him.

She looked round at Benjy and then whirled round to face TJ again. Her eyes blazed with hatred.

"It was YOU!" she shouted at TJ. "YOU trapped Benjy in a dream. YOUR dream. You did it on purpose!"

"No!" TJ said desperately. She was so wrong and far from the truth.

But Chatty was in no mood to listen or believe him as she maintained her verbal assault on TJ.

"You just couldn't stand it, could you? All the rest of us being Dreamguardians. Getting in the way of your secrets and special time with Grandpa Mal. So, you decided to do something about it."

"No Chatty, you're wrong. That's not how it happened," TJ said defensively.

"There was a Nightfright, and a Multiplier, and a Faller. I didn't see Benjy until I was about to hit the ground in the glasshouse, and by then it was too late…"

"LIAR!" screamed Chatty.

"NO!" TJ shouted back, trying again to explain. "I couldn't do anything Chatty, I wish I could go back and change it, but I can't."

But Chatty was no longer listening to him. In her head, she was replaying her conversation with *Dominus Tenebris* in her dream. TJ's voice was drowned out by the voice of the hooded figure dressed in black with the fascinating creature on the end of a wooden staff:

"They are devious. The boy in particular. Sly, devious and dangerous. Before you know it, he will try and trick you. Trick you and then trap you in a dream…You should join us, Chatty… Join us, before TJ and Grandpa Mal can trap you in a dream so you are no longer an irrelevance to them and the filthy Brethren of the Dreamguardians…Join us before the boy and old man silence you forever…Join us, Chatty, before it's too late."

*

After the shock and sadness of discovering Benjy, and once Chatty's fury at TJ had subsided, Grandpa Mal suggested they all go downstairs for a drink. Chatty refused and stayed with Benjy. TJ and Lizzy Wizzy did as they were instructed but neither fancied eating or drinking anything. Their minds were occupied by a little boy sleeping soundly upstairs but lost. Somewhere…

Chatty spent hours with Benjy, experiencing a range of emotions. One moment she was upset, the next angry, then suspicious, then vengeful, then full of grief again. After hours of endless crying and shouting, at no-one and everyone, she lay down next to Benjy. She felt exhausted. As she started to drift off to sleep, she planned to enter TJ's dream to find Benjy. But as TJ was awake downstairs, nothing happened. She would have to wait.

Then she had an idea. Why hadn't she thought about it earlier? Even though Grandpa Mal and TJ said it wouldn't work, what was to stop her from entering Benjy's dream right now? She would just go in there and bring him back from wherever he was. Benjy would listen to Chatty. If he didn't, she would just drag him back anyway!

Before she got too excited at the prospect of rescuing Benjy from wherever he was, she settled herself down and tried to drift off to sleep. As she did so, she said Benjy's name in her head, over and over. She also thought about a white robe and some weird staff with a webbed hoop at one end, since she had overheard TJ tell Lizzy Wizzy to do exactly that in the Suffolk barn yesterday.

The emotional trauma of the morning had taken its toll on her. Before long she was asleep and finally the REM stage she was waiting for kicked in.

*

Chatty found herself in a large, dark room. In front of her hung row after row of white robes, stretching out into the blackness ahead. Next to each robe, a wooden staff was sticking up out of a wicker basket.

She approached the nearest robe and took it off the wooden hanger with the letters 'DG' intricately carved into it. She put the robe on, but no matter how many times she adjusted it, she still felt uncomfortable. She picked up the *Dreamswick*, revealing the intricate web woven across the misshaped hoop. As she looked at it, it struck her that it was nowhere near as impressive as the staff that *Dominus Tenebris* had offered to her.

All of a sudden, from behind her, a figure quickly rushed past, closely followed by another. They both grabbed robes from a nearby rail and *Dreamswicks* from the adjacent baskets and continued on into the darkness of the room that stretched out in front of her. As their footsteps faded, a door opened at the far end of the room. A large block of blinding light entered the dark room before the door slammed shut. A few seconds later the door opened again, and the light returned momentarily, before the room was plunged into darkness again when the door slammed shut.

Chatty made her way towards where the light had appeared, passing hundreds if not thousands of robes and *Dreamswicks*. As she reached the end of the room she put her arms out and felt for the opening she had seen and knew was there. After some fumbling, she found a smooth brass doorknob. With some trepidation, she turned it and pushed the door open.

But there was no light, just darkness. Even darker than the room she had just been in. It was so black she couldn't see anything. She stepped carefully through the doorway, her arms outstretched just in case she hit something. After a few steps, she stopped to wait for her eyes to adjust to the darkness and focus in on the smallest source of light. But it was pointless: there was no light. Just the deepest black of empty darkness.

All of a sudden, the door behind her slammed shut. She jumped as the bang echoed and reverberated out into the darkness. Wherever she was, it was vast, black and empty.

Nervously, she called out for Benjy.

"Benjy... Benjy... Benjy... Benjy... Benjy... Benjy..." echoed out into the darkness.

"Are you there...? there...? there...? there...? there...? there...?"

The echo of her own voice was the only reply to her question.

She tried one last time.

"Where are you..? you...? you...? you...? you...? you...?"

It was no use. This should have been Benjy's dream, but there was nothing here. Nothing, except for a void of darkness.

Up until now, Chatty had been sure that Grandpa Mal and TJ were wrong. She thought she would be able to enter Benjy's dream and find him pretty quickly. She was his big sister and knew everything about him after all. All the good things, as well as the annoying things. But right here, right now, there was no sign of little Benjy. No sign of anything, except extreme darkness.

The sudden realisation of what had happened to Benjy hit her hard. Her first reaction was one of intense sorrow, the second fear, and then finally an overwhelming sense of panic. Chatty didn't like this place one little bit. She needed to get out, just in case... She didn't want to be trapped here. She couldn't be trapped here. What would happen to her if she was?

She turned around quickly and reached out for the door she had just come through. But she couldn't feel anything. She took a few steps forward and reached out again, but there was nothing there. Her panic started to rise.

"Please, I need to get out," she said quietly to herself, so as not to hear the panic in her voice repeated back to her. "I have to get out!"

But no matter how far forwards she shuffled, she never reached a doorway.

As she spun around feeling for an exit, she became disorientated. Where was it, where was she, and how would she get out?

As the panic set in, Chatty was no longer thinking straight and had forgotten the rest of TJ's lesson to Lizzy Wizzy in the Suffolk barn.

"No...! No...! No...! No...! No...! No....!" came her desperate cry, echoing out once again into the darkness.

She began to hyperventilate, and her mind flooded with negative thoughts: she was never going to escape, she was stuck, she was lost, forever.

"No, no, no, no," she said quietly to herself, trying to regain some composure, "this can't be right. Pull yourself together," she said, starting to get cross with herself. "Think, Chatty, think."

She wracked her brain, but nothing came quickly enough for her liking.

"Where's the exit?" she said impatiently to herself, "think, stupid girl, think."

In her frustration, she yelled out into the darkness.

"Benjy where's the exit...? exit ...? exit ...? exit...? exit ...? exit ...?"

As she heard the echo, she remembered.

"Thank you, Benjy," she whispered quietly, before shouting back defiantly into the darkness.

"I will find you and bring you back, I promise... promise... promise... promise... promise..."

Then she closed her eyes and said, "Benjy exit" three times.

The darkness disappeared and Chatty woke up with a start, heartbroken to still be lying next to her silently sleeping brother who hadn't moved an inch.

Chatty stroked his hair gently. She hadn't found him, but she would. She was sure she would.

In any case, she'd promised him...

CHAPTER 34 – TELL ME YOUR DREAMS

I t was one of the worst days ever, on par with the fateful day they had been told that Dad had died on a mountain in Switzerland. TJ and Lizzy Wizzy spent most of it in a daze, wishing neither of these events had happened. But, for some reason, they had. Grandpa Mal had done his best to try and support them, but he was taking the loss of Benjy particularly hard and had disappeared for most of the afternoon to make some calls. TJ guessed there were a number of issues within the Brethren that needed to be addressed. The loss of a Dreamguardian, not to mention one so young, would prompt a great deal of soul searching.

Before then, Grandpa Mal had been on the receiving end of another outburst from Chatty when she had demanded that Benjy be taken to the hospital. Grandpa Mal had told her that no such intervention was required and that he and the Brethren would take care of Benjy. Chatty had replied angrily that the Brethren hadn't done much to protect Benjy before now, especially from TJ's deviousness and his deliberate entrapment of Benjy in his own dream. She hadn't let on to Grandpa Mal, but she was fully intent on finding where Benjy was later tonight.

TJ had spent the afternoon going over and over what had happened in his dream. Perhaps Chatty was right, he had thought to himself. Not that he had trapped Benjy on purpose, but that he could have done more. He began to dwell on all the alternative scenarios that might have been: if only a Dreamguardian had been there to protect his own dream from the Dreamstealer; if only the Dreamstealer hadn't corrupted his dream with such an effective Multiplier and Faller; if only TJ had seen Benjy earlier and expelled him before he woke up. But it was no use. There were just too many 'what ifs' and none of them counted for anything. What was done, was done.

TJ had felt a whole range of emotions. At one point, he was full of hope. He made a solemn vow to Benjy that he would search and find him in one of his dreams. Then, one day, the Dreamologist – whoever that was - would somehow come and rescue him. But then, all of a sudden, his faith had disappeared, only to be replaced with despair. After all Grandpa Mal himself had admitted to him there had been no recorded case where a lost Dreamguardian had been saved in the past four thousand years. He desperately wanted to believe but remembered the doubts he'd had at the Dreamorian's cottage. Perhaps the 'prophecy' of the Dreamologist that was spoken about in Genesis was nothing other than a dying man's hallucinations or simply some empty promises in a dusty old book. Or even assuming the prophecy was indeed true, there was also the possibility that the Dreamologist had already come but been beaten by a more powerful being and was lost forever.

The end result was that TJ just didn't know what to think any more. Other than life could be, and so often was, so cruel.

At the end of the day he laid down to sleep determined at least to try and find Benjy. He had no idea how he would do it and doubted it would ever work, but in spite of his scepticism, he would never forgive himself if he didn't at least try.

TJ went to bed thinking about his dream the previous night. The one where it had all gone horribly wrong. He repeated 'The Glasshouse' three times in his head as he drifted off to sleep…

*

TJ was in a dense forest, surrounded by trees of all shapes and sizes. Around him as far as the eye could see was a collage of green and brown: ferns, foliage, trunks of various diameter and the thick canopy of the trees. The dark grey sky above was barely visible.

Suddenly he was on the move, heading in no particular direction. He felt like he was looking for something but wasn't quite sure what. He passed an oak tree, then a sycamore, another oak, an ash, followed by another larger oak. Every now and then he stumbled over a root that was slightly exposed.

The density of the trees thinned after a while and he found himself in an open expanse. Now that he was out of the trees, he could see the sun was shining brightly in the royal blue sky. Ahead of him was a steep grass hill, which some young children were taking great delight in rolling down. The whole area was packed with young children and families. A gravel path led up the side of the hill and TJ made his way onto it. Each step he took up the hill produced a crunching sound as the small stones ground against each other.

As he reached the top, he saw a huge glasshouse a short distance away. It was octagonal, with glass panels set in an intricate steel frame mounted on a small course of bricks. Atop its sloping ceiling panels was a smaller

octagonal roof lantern. It was an impressive building which TJ instantly recognised. He had been here before. From its position perched on the apex of
the hill, TJ could see for miles across the surrounding farmland and countryside.

He made his way into the vegetable garden, past the finest specimens of
vegetables from around the world. On the far side of the garden, rows of
sweetcorn towered behind smaller lines of fennel, beetroot, and radishes.

The place was thronging with visitors. He headed into the glasshouse, carefully closing the door behind him. Inside it was hot and humid, even though
the automatic windows had fully extended open. There were quite a few
people admiring the contents of the glasshouse that had been impeccably
arranged: peppers, chillies, as well as some orange and lemon trees.

Most of the windows were steamed up and it was difficult to see outside. A
straight flagstone path headed from the door he had just entered to another
one directly opposite him about twelve metres away.

TJ knew why he was here. He was looking for Benjy. As he wandered through
the glasshouse, TJ could feel himself getting hotter and hotter.

He got the sense he was being watched. But when he looked to left, the
windows were steamed up and he couldn't see anything. He did the same to
his right, where the windows had less condensation on them. As he peered
in the direction of the tall sweetcorn outside, he thought he saw something
move over by the sweetcorn. Then he thought he caught a glimpse of someone trying to peer in through one of the windows.

His heart leapt. He'd had this dream before, so he knew who it would be…
Benjy! He'd found him! As quick as he could he pushed past the visitors in
the glasshouse and made his way out of the door he'd entered just a few
moments ago. He called out to Benjy excitedly as he turned to the right and
made his way round the outside perimeter of the glasshouse. "Benjy, Benjy!
I'm so pleased to see…"

He stopped in his tracks when he saw who had really been looking at him
through the window of the glasshouse.

It wasn't Benjy after all.

In front of him stood Chatty. She was wearing a Dreamguardian's white robe
and clutched a *Dreamswick* in her left hand.

"Chatty! What are you doing here?" he barked. He was so cross at her. She
had got his hopes up that he'd found Benjy. He really thought he'd just
found Benjy, but he was nowhere to be seen.

"Do I really need to answer that question?" Chatty barked back. "I'm looking for Benjy. Remember him? The seven-year old boy you trapped in your dream on purpose. Just so you could get rid of him. That's right, Benjy, my poor little brother who is now lost."

"Yes, I know what happened Chatty, but I didn't trap Benjy on purpose. It was a Dreamstealer."

"Whatever," came the sarcastic reply. It was quite clear: she'd made up her mind about what had happened. She'd come to her own conclusions about TJ. "So where is he then?" she demanded.

"I don't know," snapped TJ, confused by what was happening. "I thought you were him," he continued. "This was the place that it happened. Well it's almost the same, but not quite. Something's not quite right."

"Well put it right so I can get Benjy back," said an irritated Chatty.

TJ sighed. He was at a loss what to do now. He thought if he came back to the glasshouse then Benjy would be here. But even though it was the same place, it wasn't the same dream. Maybe it was Chatty's fault because she'd gate-crashed it, but then again Grandpa Mal had warned him in the Inner Sanctum that a Dreamguardian could search *forever* through the same dreamer's dream but *never* find someone lost to bring them back. Maybe it was useless after all.

"I don't think I can Chatty," TJ said flatly, the fight going out of him but stoking it in Chatty. Benjy's not here."

"No!" shouted Chatty, "that's not good enough. There must be something you can do TJ. Give him back!" As she started to walk towards TJ she screwed up her face angrily and raised her *Dreamswick* as if she was about to strike him with it. "I want Benjy," she yelled, "and I'm not going until you've given him up and I've got him back."

Realising the situation was hopeless, TJ decided to take drastic action. If Chatty struck him in his dream, then the shock might be sufficient to wake him suddenly. This would in all likelihood trap Chatty in his dream, as TJ doubted she was either aware of this risk or in any mood to exit his dream until she had done some damage to him.

One Willow trapped in his dream was disastrous enough, thought TJ. Two would be too much, even though he thought Chatty did deserve it sometimes. It was time for him to act. He'd only ever seen it done once before; when he had been discovered in Grandpa Mal's dream in a log cabin somewhere in the snowy mountains.

It was time for the process grandly referred to as *Ex-Post Permissionary Expulsion* in the Great Book that Grandpa Mal had explained to him at some length in the Great Room. In other words, it was time to automatically force Chatty to exit his dream. He closed his eyes and said, "Chatty exit" three times in his head. When he opened them, Chatty and the dream he was just in had gone.

*

As Chatty had approached TJ in his dream, she intended to give him a jolly hard whack about the head with the stupid stick thing she had in her hand. She'd had enough of him and his scheming and lying. He would pay the price for trapping Benjy, somewhere.

Instead, just as she was about to clobber him, TJ and the glasshouse had disappeared. With that she'd returned to her own sleeping consciousness.

"Coward!" she said angrily to herself, "wait until I see you in the morning TJ, then you'll be sorry."

Then, as she entered her own REM sleep, she had the most fantastically bizarre dream ever. The scenes played out vividly before her eyes, one by one. It was the most amazing, yet weirdest thing she'd ever experienced.

When the reel of dream scenes had ended, it was all she could think about and remember. She had completely forgotten about her failed attempted to find Benjy in TJ's dream.

But what did it all mean?

*

Breakfast the next morning started off as a subdued affair. TJ was keen to keep his distance from Chatty, and even though they weren't talking, she had yet to mention anything about being involuntary expelled from his dream last night just as she was about to hit him with her *Dreamswick*. TJ thought it best not to bring any of it up, even though he was annoyed that she would go trawling through his dreams to find Benjy. Would she ever listen and accept that it wasn't his fault? Maybe one day. But in the meantime, TJ thought the best thing to do was to keep quiet and out of her way as much as possible. Just in case she felt the urge to fulfil her desire to thump him as hard as she could.

They were all still in their pyjamas, dressing gowns and slippers. None of them looked great, but Grandpa Mal in particular looked awful. Lizzy Wizzy had given him a great big cuddle when she had first entered the kitchen and seen him sitting at the table all alone with his head in his hands. For one of the first times in her life, his usually slicked back grey hair was not immaculately in place and grey stubble peppered his chin. His eyes were puffy, a sure sign that he hadn't gotten much sleep. Quite simply, he looked as broken as he was. He was grateful for Lizzy Wizzy's affection, but in some way, it made him feel worse. He would never be able to cuddle Benjy in the same way again and the loss of such a young, caring and sensitive soul, so full of life, was just unbearable.

As he sat there, Grandpa Mal punished himself again. Given his position in the Brethren, how could he have allowed such a thing could happen? Even more so when they were right under his nose at the Old Girl. He should have known. He blamed himself. If only he could put it right.

Now they were sat in silence at the breakfast room table. Lizzy Wizzy and Grandpa Mal next to each other in the middle, while TJ was down one end and Chatty down the other, as far away from each other as possible, in more ways than one.

Lizzy Wizzy couldn't stand it any longer. She needed to break the silence. Benjy wouldn't want everyone to be upset and cross at each other. He'd always be the one to try and cheer someone up if they were down.

"Did you manage to get any sleep?" Lizzy Wizzy asked her brother. She was a bit scared to ask Chatty anything, so hoped that the conversation would flow and Chatty would have no choice but to be swept up and engaged by it.

"Not really," TJ replied, glancing nervously towards Chatty at the other end of the table, "bit interrupted really." He took a massive spoonful of his cereal and shovelled it into his mouth. End of conversation.

"Oh," Lizzy Wizzy replied. That didn't go so well she thought to herself. She took a deep breath and asked Chatty the same question.

"Some, but not much," came the gruff reply. She didn't feel like engaging in conversation with anyone, but before she could stop herself, she found herself carrying on. "I had the weirdest dreams though."

They all looked up at her in surprise. The last person they expected to be talking about dreams was Chatty, especially so soon after what had happened to Benjy.

Grandpa Mal bowed his head and shook it sadly from side to side. "I'm not sure it's such a good idea to be talking about such matters, my dear girl. Not in view of the circumstances…"

"Yes, I'm well aware Grandpa Mal," Chatty said, unusually calmly for a change, "but I've never experienced anything like these before. They were just so strange."

TJ wasn't interested one little bit. "I've heard enough about dreams," he said flatly, "let's change the subject."

But Lizzy Wizzy had no intention of letting that happen. She'd done it! Somehow, she'd managed to get Chatty talking and was intrigued to hear all about her weird dreams.

"No!" Lizzy Wizzy said quickly to TJ, "I don't want to change the subject." Then, turning to Chatty, she said, "tell me your dreams."

So Chatty did just that.

She said to Lizzy Wizzy, "in my first dream I saw a game of Mousetrap. There were four mice on the loop that helps determine the end of the game. The largest blue mouse was on the "turn crank" square. The second largest mouse was pink and two squares behind it on a green square. A third smaller pink mouse was in between the other two, on a white square. A fourth mouse was behind them all on the cheese square. This mouse was blue and the smallest of all of them.

"Suddenly the handle cranked, rotated some gears and a lever pushed a stop sign against a shoe. The shoe kicked over the bucket and a red orb rolled down the stairs into a drainpipe. After it had rolled to the other end of the drainpipe, it knocked a post with a hand at the top. In turn, this pushed a larger glowing red orb through a bathtub onto a diving board, catapulting a figure dressed all in black into a washtub. This caused an octagonal glass cage to fall from the top of the post, trapping the unsuspecting smallest blue mouse.

*

"In my second dream I was sitting on my Dad's left knee and Benjy was perched on the other. We were in our pyjamas and Dad was reading us a bedtime story. It was one of "The Adventures of Wensley and Dale" books, you know the two mice who used to go on different adventures. Dad read it to us slowly, acting out all the voices:

" *'One day, Wensley and Dale were hungry.*

They went to the fridge, but it was empty. There was no more cheese!

"Oh dear," squeaked Wensley.

"What shall we do?" eeked Dale.

"Let's ask Mummy Mouse where all the cheese has gone," squeaked Wensley.

"Good idea," eeked Dale.

They found Mummy Mouse and asked her where all the cheese had gone.

"Why, in your tummies, Wensley and Dale," said Mummy Mouse.

"Where can we get some more?" asked Wensley and Dale.

"Speak to Daddy Mouse," said Mummy Mouse.

So they did.

When they found Daddy Mouse, they asked him where all the cheese had gone.

"Why, in your tummies, Wensley and Dale," said Daddy Mouse.

"Where can we get some more?" asked Wensley and Dale.

"There is a place full of cheese," said Daddy Mouse, "A cave with as much cheese as you can eat."

"We should go there," squeaked Wensley.

"Good idea," eeked Dale.

And so they set off in search of the cave with as much cheese as they could eat. ' "

*

"In my third dream, I was outside, at the bottom of a stone staircase going steeply uphill, cutting through the trees. On either side of the staircase were metal handrails. At the very top I could see a Lookout Tower.

"Then suddenly the ground at the base of the staircase opened up and a new staircase appeared, leading underground. As I looked down the new staircase, it was very steep and went deep underground. I felt a strange urge to descend the staircase, even though it was so dark I couldn't see the end.

*

"In my final dream, I saw a dark cave. It was huge with many rock chambers and formations, some vast and some very small. It was cold, wet, dark and damp and I could hear a sound like the dripping of water. Stalactites hung down from the ceilings and stalagmites protruded from the floor of the caves, as if trying to escape from an even deeper chamber.

"Within one of the small caves I thought I saw something shining. When I looked closely, it was the top of a small silver cup and pieces of silver, all sitting in the mouth of a sack full of food.

*

"And that was it," Chatty said, throwing her hands up in the air. "Those were my dreams."

After a long silence and feeling brave, TJ spoke. "Do you know what the dreams mean, Chatty?" TJ asked.

"No," Chatty replied, "but they felt important."

"They are," said Lizzy Wizzy, barely able to control herself.

"What is it dear girl?" asked Grandpa Mal. His thoughts were very much elsewhere, and he had barely been able to concentrate on what Chatty had been saying, let alone decipher what all her dreams meant.

"I know what they mean," Lizzy Wizzy said excitedly.

"You what?" TJ said, puzzled.

"Chatty's dreams, I know what they mean," Lizzy Wizzy said proudly.

All eyes around the table were now firmly fixed upon Lizzy Wizzy.

"What?" said TJ and Chatty, almost in unison.

"Go on, dear girl," said Grandpa Mal, a flicker of hope daring to spark in his eyes.

"They're about Benjy," Lizzy Wizzy said confidently, her mouth breaking into a wide smile as she spoke her little cousin's name. "I think I know where he is too."

Open-mouthed, they stared at Lizzy Wizzy. TJ was the first to articulate what he was thinking. "What do you mean you know where he is? How?"

"Chatty's dreams. It's obvious," Lizzy Wizzy replied, as if it was a matter of fact. But it was far from obvious to the rest of them.

Once the shock had passed, Chatty smiled for the first time in days. She jumped up from her seat and rushed over and hugged Lizzy Wizzy.

"Well done Lizzy Wizzy. I knew my dreams were important somehow, but I just didn't know what they meant."

TJ was quick to interrupt. "Hang on a minute," he said, "let's not get ahead of ourselves. We still don't know what they mean. I don't mean to spoil things, but... are you sure Lizzy Wizzy?"

"Yes," she replied confidently, "they're definitely about Benjy and I think they tell us where he is."

"Remarkable, dear girl," Grandpa Mal exclaimed, daring to believe. "Please explain for the rest of us."

By now, Lizzy Wizzy was almost bouncing with excitement in her chair.

"This is what I think they all mean," she said to them. "In the first dream, the mice represent us four children. Benjy is the smallest blue mouse on the cheese square. The largest mouse on the "turn crank" square is TJ, since Benjy was trapped inside his dream. Red orbs have replaced the balls in the game and confirms the involvement of Dreamstealers in the dream. An octagonal glasshouse has replaced the cage and trapped the unsuspecting smallest blue mouse. This dream signifies the very place where Benjy be-came trapped.

"The second dream refers to one of our favourite adventures of Wensley and Dale, the two little mice. Uncle Bertie used to read this book to us when we were all on holiday together at the dairy farm in Somerset. The place where all the cows used to block the country lane when they were brought in from the meadows. Do you remember?

"This particular Wensley and Dale adventure was our favourite one, as at the time we really did believe the caves down the road from that dairy farm were full of as much cheese as we could eat. It was called Cheddar Gorge after all. Cheddar Gorge is where Wensley and Dale went to find the cheese. I believe this is the first clue about where Benjy might be trapped within a dream.

"The second clue was hidden within Chatty's third dream. The stone stair-case she saw is known as Jacob's ladder: a climb of 274 steps up the side of Cheddar Gorge, then a few more up to a Lookout Tower at the top. I remem-ber we walked up them all."

TJ was quick to interrupt. "Jacob's ladder! That's the picture in the Great Room Grandpa Mal, the one taken from the story within Genesis."

"Good grief, yes, that's right and extremely important in the events leading up to the establishment of the Brethren," Grandpa Mal said.

"Yes, yes, thank you TJ," Lizzy Wizzy said, not overly impressed with the interruption. She was quick to continue.

"The third clue is also here too. Jacob's ladder leading deep underground, into the caves…"

Just then, TJ felt he would burst if he didn't say something. He couldn't stop himself from blurting out.

"Grandpa Mal! It's from the original text of the true book of Genesis that I read with the Dreamorian. Where it said that a new stairway appeared, and its bottom reached down into hell. It said angels of darkness were ascending and descending on it and they carried cages of trapped figures of light down the steps."

"TJ! Stop interrupting!" Lizzy Wizzy said, rolling her eyes, although she couldn't find fault with the accuracy of TJ's intervention. "Hopefully we'll never find out whether there is actually a stairway that leads down into hell. But you must let me finish TJ, please!"

"Sorry," TJ muttered, wondering just how Lizzy Wizzy knew what all these dreams meant.

"Which then brings us on to Chatty's final dream," Lizzy Wizzy announced, smiling as she did so. "The small silver cup, in the mouth of a sack of food, hidden in a small cave. Let's go back to Genesis and the story of Joseph. He hid a silver cup in his youngest brother's sack as his brothers left Egypt to return home. This was to test the loyalty of his other brothers when Joseph accused the youngest of stealing. What was Joseph's youngest brother called?"

She paused for dramatic effect and to give the others a chance to catch up with her.

Then, excitedly, she shouted out "Benjamin!" at the top of her voice.

The others around the table gasped.

"Dear girl!" Grandpa Mal exclaimed.

TJ looked wide-eyed at Lizzy Wizzy and she beamed at him. He looked both stunned but also a little confused.

"So, there you have it," Lizzy Wizzy said. "Chatty's dreams are a clear indication that after being trapped in TJ's dream at the glasshouse, Benjy is now lost in a dream somewhere deep within the caves at Cheddar Gorge."

"Why, that is quite remarkable, dear girl," Grandpa Mal said.

"Excellent work Lizzy Wizzy," Chatty said, still smiling.

TJ was speechless for a change.

"Thank you," Lizzy Wizzy continued. "Thanks to your dreams Chatty, we now have some hope. And we now know what we need to do."

"We do?" asked TJ, still struggling to piece everything together and to plot the next course of action. "What's that then?"

"We need to go to back to the glasshouse TJ, in your dream," Lizzy Wizzy replied.

TJ wasn't convinced. "What? No, I've tried that," he said. Then he glanced nervously at Chatty, before correcting himself. "Well, we tried that, but it was no use. There was nothing there."

Suddenly, Grandpa Mal banged his fist down on the table, making them all jump.

"No!" he shouted. "Much as I admire your ability to interpret Chatty's dreams, dear girl, this is all far too dangerous. And most likely futile. After all, even in the unlikely event that you find Benjy, how are you going to bring him back? This can only be done in the presence of the Dreamologist after all."

Lizzy Wizzy went quiet. She didn't quite know how to respond.

"I do not wish to be negative, dear girl," Grandpa Mal continued, "but you do realise that none of the dreams said anything about how to bring Benjy back, or actually foresaw Benjy being rescued. I say this not to upset you, but to highlight the futility of it all."

Despite saying he didn't wish to upset anyone, Grandpa Mal had succeeded in upsetting himself. With that, he gingerly got to his feet, looking every bit as old as his years.

"Dear children," he sighed, "it is understandable that you want to find Benjy and bring him back. But the sad truth we have to accept is that he has been lost and there is nothing you can do to bring him back. So, listen to me carefully please dear children. I insist. There can be no more Dreamguardian activity from any of you from now on. Do you understand me?"

The three of them stayed quiet.

Grandpa Mal repeated himself, even more forcefully. "I said do you understand?"

Three heads nodded unconvincingly.

"Good," said Grandpa Mal. "I am feeling quite weak, so I need to rest. Please, *please*, be good. I just couldn't bear it if anything happened to you all as well." With that he tucked his chair under the table and left the kitchen.

As soon as she heard Grandpa Mal shuffle his way down the corridor, Lizzy Wizzy picked up the conversation that had been interrupted a few moments ago.

"TJ, how many mice were in Chatty's dream?"

"Eight," he replied quickly.

Lizzy Wizzy pulled a face. "No, the first dream, in the game."

TJ pulled a face back. "Four then," he replied.

"Exactly," said Lizzy Wizzy. Chatty saw three other mice on the board game when the smallest mouse was trapped. I think this is significant. Let's try going back to your glasshouse dream again TJ, but this time with the three of us."

Chatty was not so keen on the idea of doing anything with TJ. But she relented from her initial protests when Lizzy Wizzy convinced her to do it for Benjy's sake.

"So, we're all agreed then," Lizzy Wizzy said. "We meet again tonight in Benjy's room. It makes sense to try in there, just in case." She didn't know what she meant by that, but she didn't like the idea of Benjy being alone, even though he was already lost in a dream, possibly in a cave somewhere deep underground.

"This is what we'll do," TJ said, trying to regain some of the initiative from Lizzy Wizzy. After all, it was his dream they would be going into. "You two meet me in my dream and we'll go from there."

"Yes, that's what Lizzy Wizzy has already said," Chatty said impatiently. "We're not stupid you know TJ."

"I didn't say you were," TJ replied, trying to stay focused on the task in hand. He looked seriously at Lizzy Wizzy. "You must remember to bring me a robe and *Dreamswick* from *The Armoury*. You mustn't forget. Is that clear?

Lizzy Wizzy nodded.

"Oh, one other thing," TJ continued. "Best bring another robe and *Dreamswick* for Benjy, just in case…".

The girls agreed. Indeed, they all hoped the fourth robe and *Dreamswick* would be needed.

"Roll on tonight," TJ said with as much optimism as he could muster, "because that's when we're going to find Benjy and get him back."

If only he believed it himself.

CHAPTER 35 – DREAM-HOPPING

T he rest of the day was unremarkable and seemed to drag on forever, as it always did when forced to wait patiently for a certain time to arrive. Lizzy Wizzy and Chatty spent most of it together in their bedrooms, while TJ commandeered the television in the family lounge and watched nothing in particular. He had contemplated venturing outside, but everything to do out there either reminded him of Benjy or required his companionship. Hide and seek, climbing a tree, a game of cricket or throwing a ball just wasn't the same without his little cousin. How he wished they could get him back, but he still wasn't convinced, even if Lizzy Wizzy sounded sure enough with her incredible interpretation of Chatty's dreams.

After what seemed like the longest day ever, Grandpa Mal had sent them off to bed with yet another warning that any Dreamguardian activity was forbidden. TJ wondered whether the Brethren could actually physically prevent a Dreamguardian from entering a dream, maybe by locking the door leading out of *The Armoury*. But he had no idea whether that could be done, despite the millions of Swiss francs Christophé claimed he had invested into *The Cerebrum*. There were already signs that *The Cerebrum* didn't quite work as Christophé had either expected or intended. TJ seriously hoped that all the time, effort and money invested had been spent on encouraging Dreamguardian activity rather than preventing it.

Although Grandpa Mal had been extremely weary and looked very weak when he'd sent them off to bed quite early, the three of them had agreed to wait until 11pm before rendezvousing in Benjy's bedroom. By then Grandpa Mal would be fast asleep and getting some well needed rest, rather than expending energy he didn't have on any Dreamguardian activity himself.

When the time was right and satisfied the coast was clear, they entered Benjy's room one by one. It was dark in there, but they could see the outline of Benjy's sleeping body in his bed, in exactly the same position as before.

Chatty lay down next to Benjy, while Lizzy Wizzy and TJ took the other end of the bed.

Although nobody else was around, TJ was the first to whisper, just in case.

"Are you two feeling tired then?"

"Tired of some things, yes," Chatty said sarcastically, while Lizzy Wizzy simply nodded and yawned. It was way past her bedtime and she had already been struggling to stay awake for the past hour and a half.

TJ let Chatty's comment go and ran through the plan again, much to Chatty's ire. He was to go to sleep first, followed by Lizzy Wizzy and Chatty who were to go to sleep thinking about TJ and meet him in his dream. They were to bring with them two spare robes and *Dreamswicks* from The Armoury. One for him and the other for Benjy. Just in case.

Satisfied everyone understood what was to happen, TJ pulled the blanket he had brought in with him up around his ears. It was time. He tried hard to get comfortable, but it took him a while to settle down. He drifted off to sleep when he least expected to.

*

TJ stood in the middle of a deserted pedestrian area. The only company he could see was just behind him to his left: a bronze statue of a man holding a Bible on a granite pedestal in front of a huge Celtic Cross. Although it was night-time, the place was lit up on all sides by the neon glow from huge signs, billboards and giant outdoor electronic screens. The area was flanked to his left and right by tall buildings that stretched up into the dark sky. To his left beyond the statue was a deserted road, while a short distance behind him was a tower of yet more gigantic electronic screens. One showed a game of American Football deep into the fourth quarter, another a game of baseball, while a third glowed red and white, advertising something. As he looked in front of him, the buildings appeared to get closer together as they stretched out into the distance and seemed to converge on the horizon to form another tall skyscraper: One Times Square.

Although he thought he was alone, the glow from the screens and neon signs gave him some comfort, but it was eerily quiet. But he wasn't alone. Lizzy Wizzy and Chatty emerged from behind the statue, gazing up and around at their surroundings as they did so. They were both dressed in white robes and carried two *Dreamswicks* each, while two spare robes were slung over their right forearms. The girls made the short way over to TJ.

"Why have you brought us here?" Chatty asked sharply and TJ took a step back just in case she decided to make full use of one of the *Dreamswicks* she was holding in either hand.

"I have no idea," TJ replied nervously. This was the truth; he had no idea why he had come here in his dream. He had seen it before on the television but had never been here before.

"Where are we?" asked Lizzy Wizzy.

"Times Square," TJ replied quickly, "in New York."

"Oh," Lizzy Wizzy said, somewhat confused. "What are we doing here TJ? Where's Benjy?"

"Well he's not *here*, that's for sure," Chatty said crossly. "What are you up to TJ? Are you trying to trick us?" Suddenly she was very suspicious.

"No!" TJ said defensively, "I'm not trying to trick you. As I just said, I don't know why we've come here. This isn't the right dream, as you're well aware Chatty."

He walked over to Lizzy Wizzy, took the Dreamguardian robe she had brought for him and slipped it on. Then he took the *Dreamswick* from her left hand with his right hand. The wooden handle fitted snugly into his palm as he wrapped his fingers around it. He felt a bit safer now.

"Thank you, Lizzy Wizzy, TJ said genuinely. "Chatty has seen the *Dreamswick* in action, but you'll have to watch and learn how to use it as we go along. Hopefully there will be no need for it tonight, but in any case, I am here to keep you safe."

Chatty huffed from behind him and muttered "yeah, right," under her breath.

"I think I can take care of myself, TJ," she said. "It can't be that difficult if you can do it," she added.

TJ thought better of arguing with her, even though he wanted to. There were more important things to do.

TJ held his *Dreamswick* aloft, turned his wrist so that the webbed hoop faced the ground, and began to think hard.

"What are you doing TJ?" Chatty demanded to know, but TJ ignored her.

All of a sudden, the neon lights and electronic screens flickered for a few moments. They almost went out, but then recovered and flickered back to life. Then they heard a noise. It started off quietly, before getting louder. As they looked across to the far side of the Square, they could see the pedestrian area begin to fill up with people. Ordinary people going about their ordinary business.

"Come on, let's go, just in case...," TJ said, making his way past the statue towards the road.

"Just in case what?" Lizzy Wizzy asked, shouting after TJ.

As Chatty looked in the opposite direction to which TJ was headed, people were appearing from everywhere.

"Wait for me!" Chatty shouted nervously, not quite sure what was happening.

TJ waited momentarily for the two girls to catch him up. As he did, he noticed a crowd of people getting closer and closer to them.

"Come on, let's go!" he said as the two girls reached him. They walked quickly towards the edge of the pedestrian area before breaking into something of a run. They were convinced some of the people crossing the square towards them were chasing them. People continued appearing from everywhere, including from the shadows.

As the three figures in white approached the road they looked quickly to the right. There was no car in sight, so they ran out into the road. A loud noise to their left punctured the air and stopped them dead in their tracks. They wheeled round, just in time to see a yellow taxi cab swerve from the lane they were stood in to the adjacent one. TJ felt the car brush him as it went past, its tyres squealing from the sudden skid of the brakes and change of direction.

Lizzy Wizzy screamed. They had been lucky not to be hit by the first car, but there were another two yellow taxi cabs behind it, riding side by side. There was nowhere for the cab in their lane to go and it sounded its horn frantically.

Beep, beep, beeeeep... beep beeeeep...

Lizzy Wizzy screamed again and a voice from within the crowd shouted a warning.

"TJ!" shouted Chatty, "do something! It's your dream!"

The yellow cab showed no sign of stopping and was now headed straight for them, its horn now permanently sounding.

Instinctively TJ held his *Dreamswick* aloft, closed his eyes as he turned his wrist, and concentrated.

Just as the taxi cab was about to hit them, everything around them disappeared...

*

It was quite a dream-hop. Within an instant, they were on top of one of the peaks of a mountain range. A snowstorm was raging, and their white robes flapped violently as the wind howled through them. The snow beneath their feet was thick and powdery, and swirled around them in the wind. Through the blizzard they could just about make out a small wooden cottage in the distance below them. A good place to hide from the raging storm. Beyond them they could see the majestic sight of the Matterhorn, overlooking all that it surveyed.

The howling wind and cold was unbearable and the three children dropped to their knees to avoid being blown off the mountainside. Chatty looked across at TJ who was fighting the wind.

"TJ!" she yelled, but her voice was instantly lost amongst the rush of the wind and the inhalation of cold air took her breath away. Once she had recovered it, she tried again, but with no success.

She crawled through the deep snow towards TJ, then when she came within striking distance of him managed to poke him with her *Dreamswick*. TJ looked across at her, his face screwed up to protect himself from the driving snow.

"WHAT?!" he shouted, as his voice was carried off into the snowstorm.

"WHAT ARE WE DOING HERE?!" Chatty shouted back, losing the fight against the wind that continued to rage all around her. "DO SOMETHING TJ...!"

TJ looked beyond Chatty to Lizzy Wizzy. She had curled herself up into a ball to try and protect herself, but it looked ineffectual against the relentless storm. The conditions were inhospitable and unbearable, and resistance was futile.

"HOLD ON!" TJ bellowed back as he lifted himself up onto one knee. He put his left arm over his eyes to try and keep the blizzard out. Leaning into the wind, he got to his feet but was immediately blown off them. He tumbled backwards into the snow and muttered crossly under his breath.

Gathering himself up, he leant once more into the wind and got up onto one knee. He forced his *Dreamswick* forward with the webbed hoop touching the snow to give him some extra stability. Then leaning even further into the power of the storm he got to his feet.

TJ tried to clear his mind and think properly this time. He needed to go back to one particular dream. Back to that fateful dream at the glasshouse where Benjy had been trapped. But it was so difficult in these conditions. He could barely stand. He could barely concentrate.

TJ let out a frustrated shout as he battled the storm. As he fought against it, he pictured Benjy peering in through the glasshouse window. As he did so, he hardened his resolve and tried to block out the wind, the blizzard and the cold. He focused on Benjy peering in through the glasshouse window. He needed to get him back. He gripped the *Dreamswick* even tighter until his whole arm hurt.

TJ focused one more time on Benjy peering in through the glasshouse window.

They dream-hopped again, and the blizzard and the mountain had gone…

*

They were in a dense forest, surrounded by trees of all shapes and sizes. Around them as far as the eye could see was a collage of green and brown: ferns, foliage, trunks of various diameter and the thick canopy of the trees. The dark grey sky above was barely visible.

Suddenly they were on the move, heading in no particular direction. They felt like they were looking for something but were not quite sure what. They passed an oak tree, then a sycamore, another oak, an ash, followed by another larger oak. Every now and then the three of them stumbled over a root that was slightly exposed.

The density of the trees thinned after a while and they found themselves in an open expanse. Ahead of them was a steep grass hill that young children would instinctively feel the urge to run or roll down. A gravel path led up the side of the hill and they made their way onto it. Each step they took up the hill produced a crunching sound as the small stones ground against each other. Ordinarily the place was thronging with visitors, but they couldn't see a soul as he looked around.

As they reached the top, they saw a huge glasshouse a short distance away. It was octagonal, with glass panels set in an intricate steel frame mounted on a small course of bricks. Atop its sloping ceiling panels was a smaller octagonal roof lantern.

TJ and Chatty recognised it straight away.

"This is it!" TJ said excitedly, looking across at Chatty and Lizzy Wizzy.

"I know," Chatty replied, "but is he here?" she asked.

"Where would he be if he was?" asked Lizzy Wizzy. She had been to the glasshouse before, with her parents, but it was the first time she had seen it in TJ's dream.

"On the other side of the glasshouse," TJ pointed. "Come on, let's see if we can find him. Let's go around the back."

They made their way into the vegetable garden, past the finest specimens of vegetables from around the world.

As they made their way around a circular brick path, they tried to look inside the glasshouse, but the windows were steamed up. They couldn't see anything inside, but if they could they would have seen TJ from the original dream. He was inside, getting hotter and hotter, very uncomfortable and uneasy that something didn't feel right.

As the three children reached the back doors of the glasshouse, they saw something move over by where the sweetcorn was planted. Then, from out behind the tall rows of sweetcorn came Benjy. As quick as a flash, he scurried over to the glasshouse and peered inside.

Chatty was overcome with emotion upon seeing her little brother. Before TJ could stop her, Chatty called out to him.

"Benjy! Benjy! It's me! Over here!"

But he didn't acknowledge her. He just kept peering into the glasshouse.

"Chatty, no!" TJ said, not quite sure what would happen if Benjy saw them. If truth be told, he wasn't actually expecting to find Benjy in this dream. He'd tried that before but failed. But then again, this dream did seem almost identical to the one he'd had when Benjy was trapped.

Chatty turned and glared at TJ. "Shut up!" she said aggressively to him, "we've got to get him out now!"

Before TJ could explain his concerns about interfering in the dream playing out before them, he heard a loud bang. As he looked up, he saw a red orb had been fired into the air a short distance away. It was streaking up into the sky like a devilish rocket.

A Dreamstealer was at work.

TJ knew what was about to happen. What was coming. They didn't have much time!

"Quick, we need to move," TJ said.

"Why?" asked Lizzy Wizzy.

Without explaining, TJ hauled Lizzy Wizzy out of the way of the back doors.

"Ow!" she complained.

"Sorry," TJ said, "but any time now…"

Before he could finish his sentence, the doors at the back of the glasshouse where they had stood just a few moments ago blew open with great force and a violent wind surged through. They weren't able to see in, but inside the glasshouse, it almost knocked the other TJ off his feet. He leant into the wind with all his might to stop himself from being swept away by its power.

"What's going on?" asked Lizzy Wizzy, starting to feel a little scared. Before TJ could answer, Chatty had her own question.

"What's *that*?" she asked, pointing to the front of the glasshouse, with some panic evident in her voice. She thought it was a dense black cloud, moving quickly towards the glasshouse. But as it got closer, she realised it was made up of hundreds of individual organisms moving quickly towards them. It was a frightening sight, as hundreds if not thousands of bats entered the glasshouse and quickly flew out of the doors they were stood next to, into the dark grey sky.

Round the back of the greenhouse, Lizzy Wizzy grabbed hold of TJ's hand and squeezed it tightly. She hated bats and knew TJ did too. She had no idea that inside the glasshouse, the other TJ was sure he could feel some of the wingtips brush his hair as they hurtled past him but was about to encounter something even more terrifying. Outside of the glasshouse, TJ squeezed Lizzy Wizzy's hand back and told her it would be alright. As he turned back to talk to Chatty, she was no longer next to them. She'd gone.

"Chatty," TJ said as loudly as he dared, "where are you?"

As he edged his way round the glasshouse, he saw the back of her. She was heading towards Benjy, who was still looking into the glasshouse through the window.

"Benjy! Benjy! It's me! Chatty," she called out as she approached Benjy. But he didn't flinch. She tried again. "Benjy, it's me, Chatty, we've come to take you home," she said with a bit more urgency. But there was no response as he continued to peer through the window. She tried tapping him on the shoulder, but he didn't respond. He could neither hear, see or feel her.

All Benjy could see and hear was the other TJ inside the glasshouse, screaming as he lay on the ground, his body being quickly covered by cockroaches and scorpions. They were crawling all over his legs, hand and arms. TJ was writhing and thrashing his limbs about to try and get them off, but to no avail. There were just too many of them. They were coming up from the earth in their thousands, crawling up, over and around him, trying to get to his face.

Chatty was heartbroken as she came to the realisation that Benjy did not know she was there. Her cries though were stifled by a sound getting increasingly louder and louder. Benjy could hear it too. He suddenly turned his head away from the glasshouse and Chatty. Even though Benjy didn't know Chatty was there, they could both see it: a new dark swarm flying in on the wind, like a seething formation of deadly black and yellow enemy fighters. A buzzing noise got louder and louder as a giant swarm of wasps entered and soon filled the glasshouse.

Benjy turned back to the window to see the other TJ being covered by a deadly blanket of wasps inside the glasshouse. As Chatty continued looking at Benjy, in the distance she saw the Dreamstealer responsible, its plain staff held aloft in its left hand.

As Chatty realised there was nothing she could do to save Benjy from being lost in this dream, the tears began to form in her eyes. It almost felt as if she was about to lose him for the second time. Unable to watch anymore, Chatty ran back to TJ and Lizzy Wizzy positioned outside the back of the glasshouse.

"It's useless, he can't see me or hear me," Chatty spluttered through her tears. "Why did we come here anyway, just to watch Benjy get lost again? Just to make the pain stronger and more real, was that your plan TJ?"

Before he could defend himself against Chatty's accusations, they became aware of a deep rumbling sound. It started off barely audible above the angry swarm of the wasps within the glasshouse. Within a few seconds the ground was shaking. Then, as the rumbling got louder, the ground shook more violently and gained even more strength. The glasshouse started to rattle. It started slowly at first, but as they looked up they could see the metal structure of the glasshouse vibrating quicker and quicker. The rumbling, shaking and power of the wind intensified.

"We need to get back, now!" shouted TJ as he yanked them away from the glasshouse. Then, as they looked on in horror, the glasshouse could withstand it no more. One by one, every pane of glass shattered with a deafening explosion. Shards of glass rained down onto the other TJ inside the glasshouse. Suddenly a great rush of wind ripped into the glasshouse and a body shot up through the top of the frame.

TJ stood open-mouthed as he watched a different version of himself shoot vertically thousands of feet into the sky. It was the most surreal experience of his life.

He became aware of someone nudging him. It was Lizzy Wizzy. "TJ... TJ...," she said, "concentrate. How long have we got?"

TJ stopped watching himself shooting up in the air and tried to focus again on what was happening around him now.

"What?" he asked.

"How long have we got?" Lizzy Wizzy repeated.

"Not long. I will start falling any minute now," TJ confirmed. "Then just as I'm about to re-enter the glasshouse I see Benjy." He turned to Chatty. "But as I've told you before, by then it was too late to do anything about it. I wake up just as I'm about to hit the ground and..." He chose not to finish the sentence though. Everyone knew what had happened as a result.

"It's hopeless," said Chatty, dreading the thought of seeing Benjy lost in front of her eyes. "We can't do anything."

"Right, listen up" said Lizzy Wizzy quickly and assertively. TJ and Chatty looked at her quizzically.

"We might not be able to save Benjy right now, but we know where he goes, don't we?" she continued.

"We do?" asked Chatty.

"Yes, remember your dreams Chatty? They all point to Benjy somehow ending up lost inside TJ's dream, somewhere within the caves beneath Cheddar Gorge."

"But..." started TJ.

"Enough! We need to concentrate," Lizzy Wizzy said quickly. Out of the corner of her eye she had seen TJ start to fall.

"I can't watch," said Chatty, not wanting to see Benjy trapped.

"Nor can I," said TJ, not wanting to see that but also himself hurtle to the ground.

"Huddle in then," Lizzy Wizzy said, pulling the other two in so close that even their *Dreamswicks* were touching. "Now concentrate."

"On what?" said TJ.

"Close your eyes and think about Cheddar Gorge caves, three times, quickly..."

Above them, the other TJ was picking up speed and hurtling towards the ground. Beneath him, the glasshouse was getting bigger and bigger as he plummeted towards it. His heart was racing as he realised he was not going to stop. Fear suddenly gripped him as the ground got closer and closer. But then, from the corner of his blurry eyes, he saw someone cowering just outside the glasshouse.

As he got closer, the figure looked up. As he continued to freefall at great velocity, the noise of the wind suddenly died.

He heard a desperate high-pitched cry from beneath him.

"TJ!"

But he was falling too quickly to do anything about it.

As he fell through the frame of the glasshouse, the other TJ saw the flash of strawberry blonde hair and a freckled face full of fear. Only metres from the ground, the other TJ realised who it was.

Just as he was about to hit the ground, that dream ended.

When TJ, Lizzy Wizzy and Chatty reopened their eyes, the glasshouse and its surroundings had disappeared.

It was dark and felt cold.

"Where are we?" asked Chatty nervously, "did we make it or are we lost ourselves?"

Neither TJ nor Lizzy Wizzy knew the answer to that question.

As TJ spun his *Dreamswick*, he generated a small white orb which illuminated their immediate surroundings.

They immediately knew the answer to Chatty's first question, but not yet the second.

CHAPTER 36 – THE CHAMBER

The soft white glow emitted from the orb gave them just enough light to see that they were perched on a small ledge, high up in a cave. Beneath them, a cavernous chamber stretched out into the distance as far as they could see. Small burning torches in iron holders were dotted along the rock walls beneath them, throwing mysterious and sinister shadows across the rock formations. As they peered out over the edge of the ledge, they gasped at the extent of the drop below them.

The chamber itself, with its cathedral-like dimensions, was vast. At various points, large holes in the rock walls indicated the presence of further chambers and formations out of view from their current position. To the far side, a pool of perfectly still water mirrored the rock formation above it, creating a beautifully confusing kaleidoscopic reflection.

The cave system they were within was at least half a million years old, the result of river water gradually dissolving the rock through the ages. It was cold and damp, and its silence was broken only by the faint sound of dripping water. The three children stared open-mouthed at the size of the stalactites that hung down from various points, as well as the stalagmites that protruded from the floor of the caves, as if escaping from an even deeper chamber.

The place was mesmerising. Its beauty was both captivating and oppressively sinister.

"This is it," whispered Chatty, "the main cave I saw in my dream." She paused as she surveyed the vastness sprawled out beneath her. "It's even more amazing now that we're actually here," she said breathlessly, struck by the enchanting beauty of the place.

"Well I disagree," Lizzy Wizzy whispered back, her voice shaking as she shivered from the cold. "It's damp, dark and creepy. I don't like it one little bit." She pulled her arms together to her chest and held on to her *Dreamswick* tightly.

"Sorry Lizzy Wizzy, I'm with Chatty on this one," TJ said quietly as he scanned all around whilst maintaining a small white orb with his *Dreamswick*. "This place is quite incredible, whether it's in real life or within a dream." He could remember his fascination with these caves when the two families had visited them a few years ago. In the good old days, before the world had cruelly changed for them all.

"So, what do we do now?" Lizzy Wizzy asked quietly. All she could see in front and either side of her was a sheer drop off the ledge, while behind her she could make out some huge boulders in front of a seemingly impenetrable wall of rock.

"We need to get down there," TJ said, pointing to the floor of the cave, "and see if we can find Benjy."

"Obviously," Chatty said, "but how are we going to manage that maestro?"

"I have an idea," TJ replied calmly. He walked over to one side of the ledge, still swinging his *Dreamswick* as he did so. He'd already asked himself the same question but quickly formulated a plan. When they'd looked over the edge the first time, TJ thought he could just about make out a small path through the layers of rocks that fell away from the ledge to the floor of the main chamber. "Down there," he said, motioning over to the side.

"What, down the rock face?" Lizzy Wizzy asked incredulously, "you're mad TJ! We'll fall and die!"

"Yes, great idea Einstein," Chatty chipped in. She was desperate to find Benjy but falling from a great height was not a great idea, irrespective of whether it was in a dream or not. However, as she took a moment to ponder the consequences, she came to the realisation that falling in a dream would be much better than doing it in real-life.

In a dream, she would simply wake up, just like she always did when she had a dream about falling. Falling from this height when awake would lead to certain injury or death. But just when she thought she had convinced herself it would be safe, she came to another realisation. Even though she was in a dream, if she fell now then she would wake and her hunt for Benjy would be over. After all, how would she ever find her way back here again? She still wasn't quite sure how they got here in the first place.

"Well it doesn't look like there's any other way down. Not with that in the way," TJ said pointing to the rock wall behind them, "or that there," motioning to the sheer drop over the ledge.

Even TJ had to admit it looked perilous. It was extremely narrow and looked slippery in places. It would be even more be difficult to navigate without some light from a *Dreamswick* orb. However, now was not the time to sound concerned or worried.

"Hang on a minute TJ," Chatty said, sounding a little irritated. "Before we take your crazy risky route, let's just take a look around and make sure there's no other way down."

"Look, there's no time," TJ said as non-combatively as he could manage. He could feel his irritation rise too but tried to be as positive as he could. "It'll be fine, I promise. But in any case, it's the only way down and we need to find Benjy, before it's too late."

"What do you mean, too late?" snapped Chatty.

"Well, we're not going to be in REM sleep forever, are we?" TJ replied. "We need to find him before we wake up."

Although Chatty would never admit it, TJ had a point.

"Well, if you say so, then let's go," Chatty said. She was scared too, but the fear of leaving without Benjy drove her on.

Lizzy Wizzy was less convinced.

"We can't go down there," she said nervously, fear quickly entering her mind, "we'll fall."

"No, you won't," TJ replied, "but in any case, all you'll do is wake up."

"Really?" Lizzy Wizzy asked. "Are you sure?"

TJ's pause gave him away. "Err, yes, you should do."

"What do you mean, *should*?" Lizzy Wizzy shot back quickly. "That doesn't sound very convincing. You're not sure, are you?" she asked again.

"No, I'm not sure," TJ said. "I think so, but then I don't know if this is a normal dream or not. So, I just don't know."

Lizzy Wizzy froze. She was getting more scared by the minute. First it had been the darkness and sheer size and scale of the cave, now it was the fear of falling and whether she would wake or not.

"I can't do it," she said as her bottom lip started to quiver.

"Come on Lizzy Wizzy, you'll be fine. We'll do it together," Chatty said, grabbing her arm. TJ's warning about limited time had rattled her and there was no way she was leaving without Benjy. She wouldn't allow it.

"No..." Lizzy Wizzy said, trying to back away from the edge of the ledge, but Chatty stopped her.

"Yes, you can do it," Chatty encouraged, "do it for Benjy."

Lizzy Wizzy sniffed and nodded. "Ok, I'll do it," she said softly. The emotional blackmail had worked. How could she be so selfish and not try? Benjy was down there somewhere, she was sure of that. After all, she'd interpreted Chatty's dream perfectly. The silver cup in a small cave was Benjy. They just needed to find that small cave and the treasure.

"That's the spirit, Lizzy Wizzy," TJ smiled, before his serious face returned. "Follow me and be careful," he said, before carefully stepping off the side of the ledge onto a large smooth rock slightly below it. He steadied himself with his left hand against a rock as he tried to spin the *Dreamswick* sufficiently in his right hand to maintain some light without dropping it. Ahead of him, he saw the route down through the rocks more clearly than before. It would be harder than he thought.

Carefully he pressed on, slowly trying to navigate a narrow path through the giant rock formation. Before he made each small drop to another layer of rock, he turned to check how the girls were doing. They were moving at an incredibly slow pace as Lizzy Wizzy clung on to every rock she could, for fear of falling.

"TJ! Don't go so far ahead," Lizzy Wizzy called out. TJ could immediately tell from her voice she was terrified. "If we lose your light, then we'll fall. This is too dangerous," she complained, her voice shaking.

Try walking and climbing down these rocks whilst spinning a *Dreamswick*, TJ thought!

"Come on," he encouraged nonetheless, "you're doing well, we're getting there." He looked down. They had a long way to go at this pace... And it was about to get harder.

Up ahead of him, the already slim rock path narrowed even further until it formed an incredibly narrow ledge stretching along the side of the cave wall. To the right of it was a sheer drop to the cave floor below. The margin for error was very slim indeed.

TJ stopped at the start of the narrow ledge and waited nervously for the girls to join him. When they did, he asked Chatty to spin her *Dreamswick* to generate an orb. Reluctantly, she handed over Benjy's *Dreamswick* to Lizzy

Wizzy and tried spinning her own. After a few false starts she managed to generate an orb with sufficient power to light up the narrow path ahead.

Unable to carry two *Dreamswicks* and cling onto the rock face, Lizzy Wizzy passed Benjy's *Dreamswick* to TJ, who accepted it reluctantly. Ideally, he would have liked one hand free to steady himself as he went across the path, but having light was more important, and at least Chatty had the dexterity and nerve to provide it.

Placing his back up against the cold and damp rock face, TJ started to move sideways slowly onto the narrow ledge, a *Dreamswick* in each hand for balance. It was slippery underfoot and TJ tried hard not to look down further than his feet. But he couldn't help it. Beyond them it was a long way down to the hard rock floor of the chamber.

He moved slowly and carefully, and beads of sweat began to form on his forehead. He wanted to mop them with his sleeve, but he dared move his arms from by his side. One trickled down the side of his temple and another annoyingly down his nose. He tried blowing it off but succeeded only in knocking it into his mouth. It tasted salty on his lips. Another bead of sweat started to roll down his face and TJ began to feel agitated.

Lizzy Wizzy and Chatty watched on in silence, daring to breathe in case their exhalation would generate the faintest of air that would push TJ off the ledge. By the time he had got halfway across the ledge, TJ was drenched in sweat and his back muscles were aching from the tension of pressing himself backwards into the rock. His legs were feeling wobbly too and the left one that was gingerly feeling its way across was starting to cramp.

But there was no way back now. He had to dig deep, persevere and carry on. He stiffened his resolve and, despite all the distractions, focused on moving the last few metres to the much wider rock on the other side.

As he neared the end of the ledge, without warning it all went wrong. As his left foot made contact with the small rock ledge, it gave way and crumbled under his weight. Unbalanced, TJ felt himself start to fall as the ledge disintegrated and plummeted into the darkness below. As quickly as he could, he swung the right side of his body round and propelled himself forward, aiming for the wider rock on the other side.

He landed heavily, his upper body sprawled on the rock but his legs dangling over the edge into the empty void below. He had made it, just. But the rock upon which he had landed was slippery, and he felt himself start to slide backwards.

He let go of the *Dreamswick* in his left hand to try and grab hold of the rock. But his fingers failed to achieve any purchase on a surface smoothed by millions of years of trickling water. Then he saw it out of the corner of his eye. A thick stalagmite protruding from a nearby rock. Although it had formed randomly from material deposited from the ceiling, it was almost as if it had been deliberately put there to assist TJ.

He quickly threw out his right arm and hooked the webbed hoop of the *Dreamswick* in his right hand over the top of the stalagmite. He hoped it would hold his weight. It did. As TJ hung onto the handle of the *Dreamswick* with both hands and with all his strength, he was relieved by the realisation he was no longer slipping back down the rock.

Behind him, back on the other side, Chatty and Lizzy Wizzy's hearts were still in their mouth. It had all happened so quickly.

"TJ, are you alright?" Lizzy Wizzy called out agitatedly, once she had swallowed her heart back into place.

"Yes, just," TJ said, trying to haul himself up and get all parts of his body back onto the rock. But as he pulled his weight onto the *Dreamswick*, part of the webbing tore. He lurched back suddenly and let out a scream which echoed out into the chamber. The girls also screamed and Lizzy Wizzy closed her eyes. Fortunately, the wooden hoop of the *Dreamswick* clattered into the stalagmite, but neither broke. TJ was secure again.

He scrambled onto the safety of the wider rock and lay on his back, breathing heavily.

"TJ," Chatty called out, "are you still there?"

"Yes," he replied, sitting up to face them, "see, no problem," he joked.

But it was no laughing matter really. As he looked across to them, his heart sunk. A large section of the ledge had gone. Although Chatty might have been able to make the jump over, he knew instantly there was no way Lizzy Wizzy would make it. And he knew that neither him nor Chatty would be willing to leave Lizzy Wizzy behind on her own. Not here, not now.

"Ha ha, very funny, you idiot," Chatty said crossly. "I told you it was too risky and dangerous, but you didn't listen, did you? So much for all your promises that it would be fine."

"Shut up, Chatty," TJ responded, "this was the only way down and was a risk we had to take. You'll have to take Lizzy Wizzy back up to where we started on the higher ledge."

"Then what?" Chatty asked, but TJ didn't know what to answer. He didn't know. Being separated was the last thing they needed, but there was nothing they could do about it now.

"I'll think of something," he said, mainly for Lizzy Wizzy's benefit since he was devoid of much hope. "You go back to the ledge and wait there. Be careful," he continued, getting to his feet and picking up Benjy's *Dreamswick* which had come perilously close to falling off the rock he was now stood on.

"Be careful too, TJ," Lizzy Wizzy replied as they started to make their tentative way back the way they came.

Chatty said nothing. She was furious.

*

TJ's body ached, and he still felt slightly winded as he made his way down the rock formation. He was pleased to discover that the route to the cave floor was much easier. He was even able to navigate one steep section by sliding down on his bottom. After one tricky lower section and after much time and effort, TJ finally planted his feet onto the cave floor. He looked back up towards where they had started but couldn't see anything beyond the darkness. There was no sign of any light up there. Where were they? he thought.

As TJ turned back to look out into the chamber, he was struck once more by the awesome sight ahead of him. He marvelled again at the vast cathedral-like vaulted ceiling and the way the light from the burning torches emphasised the nooks and crannies of the incredible rock formation in front of him. It was only then that he realised that the torches seemed to be lighting a path further into the cave system, inviting him to a particular point perhaps. Intrigued, TJ made his way around the edge of the mirror pool, marvelling at its stillness and the beauty of its reflection.

TJ followed the torches further and further into the chamber, ignoring all the dark holes that flanked him on either side. They seemed to appear from nowhere and maybe led nowhere too. But the torches must lead to somewhere, TJ thought. After all, surely they had been put there and lit for a reason.

After some walk, the walls of the chamber narrowed. Then at the end there were two openings. A fork in his journey. One went to the left, the other to the right. They were just about big enough for a large person to walk through. A red glow emanated from deep within both tunnels.

Decision time. Left, or right?

His deliberation was interrupted by a noise behind him which took him by surprise. As quick as he could, he spun his *Dreamswick*. He would use it to either defend himself or attack, whichever was required first.

As he wheeled round, ready to do battle, his surprise was complete. Marching towards him was Chatty and Lizzy Wizzy.

"How on earth did you two..." TJ began, before Chatty finished his sentence for him.

"...get down here?" she snapped. "Well, remember earlier when I said, 'let me try and find a way down from the ledge', and you said, 'no, there's no time, let's take the ridiculously dangerous route that might actually kill us?'"

She paused for a nanosecond for breath.

"Well, once we finally made it back to the ledge, we did take a closer look around. And guess what Mr Know It All? Yes, that's right. Hidden between two of those giant boulders was a super-safe, wide and solid stone staircase, which brought us down here. Would you believe it, Mr I Don't Listen to Anyone but Myself?"

By now, Chatty was really going for it.

"So, while you nearly killed us on that idiotic walk down the rock face, all we needed to do was simply do as I suggested in the first place. Great work, Einstein."

The sarcastic criticism stung TJ, even more so because it was true. But how was he to know there had been a stone staircase behind them?

"Alright, there's no need to be so sarcastic," TJ replied. "I was only doing what I thought was best. Anyway, my route worked too. And let's face it, it was the much more adventurous one, wasn't it?"

He smiled, trying to defuse Chatty's anger with some light humour. He should have known from experience it would have the opposite effect. Before Chatty could thump TJ with her *Dreamswick*, Lizzy Wizzy interrupted.

"Well, we're all back together again now, that's the main thing," she said diplomatically. Then pointing to the two tunnels ahead, she asked the obvious question, "Now, which way are we going to go? Left, or right?"

"Right," Chatty said, at the same time as TJ called out "Left".

Lizzy Wizzy let out a groan of frustration. "Oh, come on you two, why do you both have to be so difficult?" she asked exasperatedly.

"I'm not," they both said together, and this time Lizzy Wizzy laughed.

"Why don't you two take the right tunnel and I'll take the left one," TJ proposed. "It doesn't make much sense for us all to go down the same one. If you don't find Benjy then come back down and find me, unless the two tunnels meet up somewhere further into the cave."

Chatty nodded her approval. "I'll take Benjy's *Dreamswick* with me," she said, holding out her hand expectantly to TJ.

"Err, no," TJ said, "I'll take it with me."

"No!" Chatty complained.

"Yes," TJ countered.

"Oh, for goodness sake you two, pack it in," Lizzy Wizzy exclaimed, much in the same way her mother said to her and TJ when they were bickering. "You're like a couple of little children. Chatty, you will keep hold of Benjy's robe, and TJ will keep hold of Benjy's *Dreamswick*. I think that's fair, don't you?"

Reluctantly TJ and Chatty both agreed, although they disputed acting like little children. Once that was settled, they turned their attention to investigating their respective tunnels to see if either one got them any closer to finding Benjy.

Wishing each other well, they set off towards the red glow within the passageways: TJ to the left, and Chatty and Lizzy Wizzy to the right.

"Hang in there, I'm coming for you Benjy," TJ said loudly, to anyone who might be listening, as he walked down the left tunnel, gripping both *Dreamswicks* tightly.

In the passage next door, Chatty was saying the same thing as she and Lizzy Wizzy made their way deeper into the right tunnel.

They thought they were ready for anything.

CHAPTER 37 – OUT OF THE SHADOWS

The tunnel TJ took sloped down as it turned first to the left then to the right, taking him further and deeper into the cave system. Just when TJ feared it would never lead anywhere, it opened out into another chamber. With fewer torches burning around this cave, TJ guessed it was smaller than the one he had left a short while ago, although it still looked sizeable and was geologically impressive. From what he could see, it was certainly no less spectacular in terms of its rock formations, mirror pools and natural wonders.

As he looked around, some of the rocks appeared to make hideous faces that either mocked or snarled at him. Others formed what looked like intricately carved sculptures. The first part of the chamber had a low ceiling, before it opened spectacularly above him as he walked further in.

The vivid shapes, sizes and colours of the red, orange and yellow textured rock that hung down from the ceiling made TJ feel as if he had entered the body of a giant human, via knobbly stalagmite tonsils. As he gazed up, TJ saw a number of ledges and openings dotted either side of the vast walls at various heights. They looked like nesting platforms or nesting holes, only big enough for giant birds.

When he reached the middle of the chamber, to his right was a large hole in the floor that fell into darkness. A small rock stairway was on the other side of the hole, tucked up against the cave wall. It appeared to lead down into darkness. TJ peered hard into the semi-darkness of the far-right corner of the cave where there were fewer torches, anxious for any clues as to Benjy's whereabouts. There didn't appear to be any there. In the far-left corner of the chamber opposite it was pitch black.

Aside from the echoes of the occasional drips from the chamber roof into the small mirror pools down the left side of the chamber, it was eerily silent. The small drops would momentarily break the silence, as well as shatter the mesmerising reflections of the pools of water.

As TJ made his way towards the back of the chamber, he heard it. Softly and slowly at first, before it got faster and louder. It was behind him, up to his right. He turned to look and immediately spotted a red orb illuminate one of the holes high up in the rock wall with a deadly glow. These openings weren't for giant nesting birds. They were for Dreamstealers.

The red orb gained in size and intensity, before streaking down towards TJ. He dived and rolled quickly to his right to evade the orb. It exploded into the ground behind where he had just been standing. As he looked back up, he saw another red orb being generated. Then his attention was distracted as he saw another Dreamstealer emerge onto one of the lower ledges further along to the right. Another red orb started to generate, revealing another silhouetted figure dressed in black with a staff.

"Great, more than one, just what I need," TJ said, jumping to his feet and spinning his *Dreamswick* with his right hand. He held Benjy's Dreamswick tightly into his chest, so it didn't get in the way. He had to be quick. He had a lot of work to do.

As his eyes darted all around the chamber, he saw more and more Dreamstealers emerge from the shadows, not only on the wall he was facing but also the one behind him. He generated a white orb quickly and fired it up towards the first Dreamstealer who had taken aim at him first, just as the red orb from the second Dreamstealer he had seen came hurtling down towards him. TJ dived and rolled again, and then rolled again as a third red orb came streaking in his direction.

In an instant he was on his feet again, spinning his *Dreamswick*. As he did so, he saw an incoming red missile out of the corner of his eye. There was no time to jump clear or execute the proper defensive move. Instead, TJ swung round and connected his attacking spin with the red orb, sending it hurtling back the way it came. It exploded into the chest of the Dreamstealer and darkness returned to that particular platform in the cave.

The rest of the chamber was now alight with red orbs raining down upon TJ. He needed some cover, and fast. The orbs exploded on either side of TJ as he scrambled for a huge rock formation amongst the mirror pools that ran down the left-hand side of the chamber. As he ducked behind one of the huge rock columns there, an orb exploded on the other side of it. Even though he had just made it to cover in time, TJ could feel the intensity of the explosion through the thick rock.

As he tried to regain his breath, an orb unexpectedly exploded just a few metres away from him, slamming him hard into the rock he thought he had been hiding behind.

"What…?!" TJ exclaimed, immediately looking up to see where the orb had come from. High up above him, two Dreamstealers were leaning out from one of the openings in the wall. The first had discharged its staff, while the other was about to do the same. TJ mobilised his *Dreamswick* as quickly as possible and fired a white orb vertically, just as the red orb came down. They met in the middle and exploded in a flash of blinding pink light.

As TJ shielded his eyes, he saw something off to his right, in the furthest corner of the chamber. A small dark opening. The mouth of a small cave perhaps. On either side of the opening stood a Dreamstealer. They looked like ordinary Dreamstealers, apart from one important difference. Their staffs had a small carved demonic creature crouching on the end, grinning at anyone with the misfortune to look at it. Although smaller, it was almost identical to the one on *Dominus Tenebris'* staff.

TJ's heart, already pounding, beat faster and his mind began to race as he tried to process too many thoughts. First things first though. He spun his *Dreamswick* hard and fired it quickly above his head again, before the Dream-stealers above him mounted another attack. He was pleased to see his orb explode into them and darkness returned above his head. His relief was short-lived as another red orb exploded into the other side of the rock he was hiding behind. Then another, and another.

He really didn't have any time to think, although he had already worked out he was badly outnumbered. He wasn't sure Chatty or Lizzy Wizzy could offer much help either.

"Stop it, focus," he said sternly to himself. "Why is that opening being guarded?" he asked himself quickly, as another explosion lit up the area close to where he was hiding. He started to smile as he asked himself another question.

"What's in that cave?"

Then he grinned.

"Yes," he said quietly to himself, "it must be! Benjy… Found you! Coming, ready or not!"

As TJ laughed, something inside him stirred. His resolve to somehow not only get to the cave, but into it, strengthened. It didn't matter how many of them he would fight. He would take them all on! Nothing was going to stop him getting to Benjy.

TJ was on the move, stealthily but quickly, weaving in and out of rocks and around the back of the mirror pools. He was trying to stay as close to the rock wall down the left-hand side of the chamber as he could, in order to remain as hidden as possible. The fact that the red orbs were continuing to home in on where he had been just a few moments ago was a good sign. They thought he was still hiding back there. "Stupid Dreamstealers!" he whispered to himself.

As he reached the darkest corner of the chamber and the last decent piece of rock that would provide cover, he peered around it. It was dark in this corner, although every time a wasted red orb exploded further up the cave behind him, he could just about make out the small opening about fifteen metres away.

He would need to be quick with his ambush, since as soon as he started to generate a white orb it would give him away. Not only would it give him away to the two guards a short distance away, but also to the countless number of Dreamstealers that had crawled out from where they had been hiding.

TJ ended his reconnaissance and crouched with his back up against the rock. This was it. It was do or die time. This was for Benjy.

He took some deep breathes to calm his nerves, carefully got to his feet and maintained his starting position behind the rock. He clutched Benjy's *Dreamswick* tightly in his left hand and held it close to his chest.

Then, determined, he spun his own *Dreamswick* as quick as he could. The white orb appeared quickly and continued to expand as TJ spun his *Dreamswick* furiously. The red orb explosions around his old hiding place stopped and new ones started getting closer to where he was now.

They had seen him. This was it. Now or never time.

TJ peeled around the last rock. The strength of the white orb lit up the whole corner and helped TJ aim his attack.

Having already been alerted to his presence, the two guards were almost ready to fire at him, but TJ was quicker.

"FOR BENJY!" came his war-cry and he threw forward his *Dreamswick* with every fibre of his being. The force with which the bright white orb left the end of his *Dreamswick* was incredible. Unlike anything he had experienced before. It traced the short distance towards where the guards stood and slammed into the first one. The force of the strike threw the guard backwards and up into the rock face above the cave mouth. The guard disappeared in a flash of light. Undeterred, the orb streaked on and smacked into the second guard, filling the cave with an almighty explosion and incredible flash of light.

When TJ took his arm away from shielding his eyes, both the guards were gone. It was silent all around him too. TJ walked into the centre of the chamber to quickly scan it, from left to right, and floor to ceiling. But he couldn't see any Dreamstealers. They'd gone!

"Whoo, yes!" TJ yelled in triumphant relief, clenching his left fist and looking down at his *Dreamswick* almost in disbelief. It looked no different to what it did before. But what power lay within the simple misshaped webbed hoop at the end of a plain wooden stick!

He turned and made the short walk towards the opening of the small cave where he hoped Benjy was being held captive.

Just as TJ got within a couple of metres of the cave, a deep dark voice filled the chamber and shattered the silence.

"Stop, *boy*," came the unmistakable growled shout from some way back over TJ's right shoulder.

TJ froze instantly, but his stomach turned.

"Yes, that's it. Stop right where you are, *boy*," the voice growled. "Face me," it demanded.

Slowly, TJ turned around. Not that he needed to see who the voice belonged to. He knew that from the first word that had been growled from within the dark hood.

It was *Dominus Tenebris*.

TJ stood tensely, daring to breathe, as the hooded figure wearing a black monastic scapular walked slowly from the top of the rock stairway and around the top edge of the large black hole in the chamber floor. The demonic creature on the end of the staff danced deliberately slowly in the gloved left hand, almost as if it was mocking TJ.

Dominus Tenebris stopped about ten metres away from TJ.

"How *dare* you enter the Terror of the Dreamstealers, *boy*," spat *Dominus Tenebris*. The venomous hatred in the voice was tangible and sent a shiver down TJ's spine. "How did you get here, *boy*?" the voice boomed.

TJ said nothing.

"I said how did you get here, *boy*?" came the ferocious shout, but TJ stayed silent. He thought it was a rather odd question to ask, almost as if *Dominus Tenebris* was surprised to see him. TJ felt a flicker of hope inside. Had he just detected the first sign of confusion, or, dare he think, the first sign of weakness in the leader of the Dreamstealers?

Dominus Tenebris spoke again, although in a much more composed manner. The staff, and its demonic creature, turned gently.

"Not in the mood for talking then, *boy*? Cat got your tongue, perhaps? Well that could be arranged one night, I'm sure. So, the foolish *boy* decided to ignore all my warnings and persisted in his *folly* after all. And now, we meet again, *boy*. Somehow you have made it here..."

Dominus Tenebris paused for a moment, as if still thinking how it had happened, before continuing.

"Tell me, are you alone, *boy*, or did you bring the decrepit *old man* with you for company? Or maybe that delicate, gentle, innocent little sister of yours perhaps. Or perhaps the other girl, the spirited and interesting one. Young Chatty."

TJ swallowed hard. "Yes, I'm alone, it's just me," he lied. He needed to keep Lizzy Wizzy and Chatty as safe as can be.

"Are you *sure*, *boy*?" came the sceptical reply.

TJ nodded.

"That's a shame indeed, *boy*. It would have given me great pleasure to subject both you and the *old man* to *Transfixation* here, at the same time. Your little sister could have watched, just like she saw you all freeze and disappear the other night. But as for the other young girl, Chatty, well she's quite different. An interesting one for sure. She was quite fascinating when we met."

TJ raised his eyebrows. "You've met Chatty?" he asked. Surely not, he thought to himself. "She didn't tell me..."

A deep, sinister, laugh from within the hood interrupted TJ.

"Why should she tell you, *boy*?" *Dominus Tenebris* sneered, "are you her *keeper*?"

"No, but..."

"We had a very interesting chat by the fireside in the Great Room," *Dominus Tenebris* continued. "Chatty was very surprised to learn about some of the secrets you and the *old man* had been keeping from her."

"But... but...." TJ stammered. Now it was TJ's turn to be confused and on the backfoot. How did *Dominus Tenebris* know about the Great Room and what lies had *Dominus Tenebris* spun Chatty?

"She also seemed rather intrigued by the Dreamstealers, and my staff in particular," *Dominus Tenebris* teased, toying with TJ's confusion.

TJ shook his head quickly, as if trying to clear the fog of confusion being created by *Dominus Tenebris* from his mind.

"Stay away from Chatty," TJ said, "and Lizzy Wizzy. Or..."

"Or what...?" *Dominus Tenebris* sneered, followed by another laugh.

"This," TJ shouted. He had decided it was time for the talking to stop. In a flash he threw Benjy's *Dreamswick* as far behind him as he could and started to spin his *Dreamswick* in his right hand. Given his surprise attack, he needed both hands for some defensive moves and needed to be sure the spare *Dreamswick* was well out of the reach of *Dominus Tenebris*. Benjy's *Dreamswick* slid into the darkness inside the mouth of the small cave behind him.

Within a fraction of a second, TJ had generated a small orb and fired it off towards *Dominus Tenebris*, who deflected it easily off towards the mirror pools running down the left side of the chamber.

TJ used both hands to spin the Dreamswick defensively, awaiting an attack from *Dominus Tenebris*. Instead, a red orb appeared on one of the upper ledges and a previously hidden Dreamstealer fired it down quickly towards TJ. As it entered TJ's orbit, his *Dreamswick* easily deflected it. It too exploded over by the mirror pools, where his own white orb had detonated a few moments ago.

Dominus Tenebris was outraged. The demonic creature on the staff spun with great power and speed, generating an intense fiery ball around the gloved left hand. Just as it was about to released, *Dominus Tenebris* turned and fired it up towards the upper ledge near the roof of the chamber. The Dreamstealer was engulfed in a ball of flames as the evil orb struck its chest. Then it was gone.

"The boy is *mine*," yelled *Dominus Tenebris*, wheeling around to ward off any other predatory Dreamstealers still hiding in the shadows. "Do you hear me? The boy is *MINE*!" The voice thundered around the chamber.

TJ was rooted to the spot. He was stunned by what he had just witnessed, even though he shouldn't have been. He shouldn't have been at all surprised by the callousness of someone or something that would think nothing of turning on one of its own.

Dominus Tenebris turned back to TJ and raised a gloved right hand.

"Enough, *foolish boy*, if you know what's good for you."

"No," shouted TJ, beginning to spin his *Dreamswick* once more. "I've come for Benjy," he announced in the strongest, bravest voice he could muster.

Dominus Tenebris laughed and span the demonic creature on his staff hard.

"What makes you think Benjy is here?" *Dominus Tenebris* sneered, another intense red fiery orb building in size and volume around the gloved left hand.

"Chatty's dreams all pointed to here," TJ said, stalling for time so he could produce a light orb that might have at least some chance of matching the fiery orb that *Dominus Tenebris* was cultivating. "A small mouse trapped by the octagonal glasshouse, Uncle Bertie reading a bedtime story about Wensley and Dale's adventure to a cave with all the cheese they could eat, Jacob's ladder leading deep underground into a system of caves, and a small silver cup hidden in a sack within a cave. Lizzy Wizzy interpreted them and worked it all out. Benjy trapped within a dream and taken to a small chamber buried somewhere deep in the caves beneath Cheddar Gorge."

Dominus Tenebris laughed mockingly. "It would seem the *girls* are the ones with a superior gifting. What do *you* have to offer, *boy*?" Another laugh emerged from the hood. "You have *nothing* to offer to *anyone, boy*. The world has no need for such a *silly little boy*."

TJ clenched his teeth and *Dominus Tenebris'* red eyes blazed brighter from within the depths of the hood. By now, the orbs they were each creating were crackling with the intensity of the energy being produced.

"Throw down your *Dreamswick, boy*," *Dominus Tenebris* yelled. "If not, then I hope you like it here, because you will *never, ever, leave*."

TJ furrowed his brow and narrowed his stare. He had no intention of throwing down his *Dreamswick* and had every intention of leaving, with Benjy and the others too.

Without warning, TJ let out a scream. He slammed his right foot forward and threw his right arm out, trying to channel the same aggression and intensity through his *Dreamswick* that he had used to expel the guards. The white orb flew out at lightning speed straight towards *Dominus Tenebris'* hood.

It hit something with a flash of light and TJ shielded his eyes. When he looked back, *Dominus Tenebris* was still standing there. The demonic creature on the staff was spinning so fast it was barely discernible. It had easily deflected TJ's attack and the red orb around the gloved left hand was now a seething, hissing mass of unbridled energy.

"*Foolish boy*," *Dominus Tenebris* said slowly, the words dripping with disdain. Then with an almighty shout, an orb filled with what looked like the deepest crimson of swirling blood was discharged.

As TJ dived for cover, the orb hit his *Dreamswick*. It catapulted from his hand and TJ slid away from it across the floor. The *Dreamswick* clattered onto the chamber rock floor, rattled a couple of times before becoming still. It was steaming from the strike.

Before TJ could do anything, *Dominus Tenebris* had moved with terrifying speed, grabbed the *Dreamswick* from the floor and taken a few paces backwards.

"Get up, *boy*," *Dominus Tenebris* said slowly and deliberately.

TJ hung his head as he lay on the floor. His body hurt from the fall and he intended to remain where he was. He would never take orders from this 'thing'.

"GET UP, *BOY!*" *Dominus Tenebris* boomed. It echoed and swirled around the chamber.

Gingerly, TJ got to his feet, holding the right arm he had landed heavily on. He could taste blood on his lip. He stared hard at *Dominus Tenebris*, who was only a few paces away. TJ was determined he would show him no fear.

"It didn't have to be this way, *boy*," *Dominus Tenebris* said, almost with an unusual tinge of regret, before the usual demeanour returned.

"I already have one little *boy* trapped here in the darkness, but *you* will be different.

There was only one part of the sentence that TJ latched onto and cared about. The bit which confirmed that *Dominus Tenebris did* have Benjy.

Benjy was definitely here! He'd found him!

However, no sooner had the flicker of excitement entered TJ's heart, it was quickly extinguished. There was no chance of getting Benjy out. Not TJ, anyway. And the others were highly unlikely to succeed too. *Dominus Tenebris* was too strong. Too powerful. Too evil. TJ hoped Chatty and Lizzy Wizzy would be able to escape before anything happened to them too. Wherever they were right now...

Dominus Tenebris derailed his train of thought.

"Are you listening *boy*?" came the impatient sneer.

TJ nodded.

"Something tells me that you've always thought you were something special. Isn't that right, *boy*?"

TJ shook his head in disagreement but said nothing.

"You always thought you were better than everybody else, didn't you?"

TJ shook his head again.

"Well, now you *will* be special. Because I have something that I have been saving for you. You see, you deserve nothing better than to suffer the glorious, torturous indignity of *Transfixation*, you *silly... ordinary... little... boy...*"

TJ went cold at the thought.

Dominus Tenebris emitted a shallow laugh and pointed a gloved finger at TJ, the staff remaining firmly clutched by the others.

"So, you *will* be special after all, *boy*, since you will soon be trapped within your own dream. You will never wake. You will get to spend eternity *here*, in this very chamber, on this very spot. Think about it. Able to see everything around you, yet unable to move.

"Then, one by one, I will see to it personally that I trap everybody you love. Bring them here for you to see. But you will never be able to talk to them, touch them, or feel the warmth of their embrace. How does that sound to you, *boy*?"

Dominus Tenebris laughed cruelly, turned away from TJ and took a few steps forward, before turning back to face him. The black hood shook slowly from side to side.

"You were warned, and on more than one occasion. First, when I met you at the monastery in your dream, and then again, as I have been informed, within that wretched Simulator. Why, I believe it even gave you a foretaste of what this moment would feel like. Yet still you persisted."

TJ heard *Dominus Tenebris* take a deep inhalation of breath and saw the body within the full-length black robe straighten.

"Yes, I was very pleased to hear that even *The Cerebrum* understands and recognises the power of *Dominus Tenebris*. You see, we are very real, *boy*. We are everywhere, *boy*. Wherever you turn, you will see that the Dreamstealers are rising and multiplying, while you *filthy… unrighteous…* Dreamguardians… are *dying…*"

With that, *Dominus Tenebris* started to spin the staff and the demonic creature danced in front of TJ's eyes. The speed increased until it was going so fast it formed a ring of evil. Then, in *Dominus Tenebris'* right hand, TJ's *Dreamswick* was spun powerfully.

An orb appeared in each hand, just like it had happened in the Simulator. One bright white and the other dark red. The perfect representation of purity and corruption. As they grew bigger and more powerful, lightning streaked between the two. They clashed in front of *Dominus Tenebris'* body, each orb seeming to fight, yet absorb, the power of the other, as if part of some frightening, yet powerful, paradox. The chamber lit up with the energy of the newly created orbs.

The thought of closing his eyes crossed TJ's mind. But then he decided he would never give *Dominus Tenebris* the satisfaction of knowing he was scared. He would keep them open and watch what was coming as a final show of defiance.

*

Over by the mirror pools, Chatty and Lizzy Wizzy were crouched by the huge rock column TJ had taken refuge behind during the Dreamstealer attack. Their passageway had led eventually to a dead end, and so they had made the long walk back and taken the tunnel TJ chose. They had arrived at the entrance to the chamber just as TJ had decided to take on a Dreamstealer army single-handedly. They had waited there until they heard the huge explosion and saw the cave lit up by a huge flash of light. At that point they'd sprinted as hard as they could into the chamber and hidden themselves down the left-hand side amongst the mirror pools.

From there, they'd seen *Dominus Tenebris* come up the stone stairway from beneath the chamber floor and challenge TJ after he'd let out some weird celebratory whoop. Lizzy Wizzy had been too scared to move, but Chatty had made her creep as far as the huge rock column so they could get a better view. They'd almost got hit twice, the first time by the small white orb TJ had fired towards *Dominus Tenebris*, and the second by the red orb TJ had deflected their way.

As they had listened and watched from their hidden position, they had experienced contrasting emotions. Lizzy Wizzy was close to tears as she overheard what *Dominus Tenebris* was planning to do TJ. *Transfixation* would be horrendous. She remembered only too well her dream and encounter with

Dominus Tenebris on the dance floor at the wedding reception in the marquee. How everyone had been frozen in time, and then disappeared one by one, including her precious and special Daddy.

Chatty on the other hand was elated to hear that Benjy was alive, even if he was still trapped down here somewhere. She also felt strangely pleased to hear *Dominus Tenebris* describe her as 'interesting' and 'fascinating'. She'd thought the same about the mysterious figure she had encountered in her dream in the Great Room. *Dominus Tenebris* was right; she had indeed been intrigued by the demonic creature on the end of the staff. And by *Dominus Tenebris* too.

As she had listened, she couldn't believe the audacity of TJ, telling *Dominus Tenebris* to stay away from her. She would do what she wanted, whether TJ liked it or not. Who did he think he was?!

Now, as she watched *Dominus Tenebris* simultaneously spinning the demonic creature on the staff and TJ's *Dreamswick*, she felt a strange sense of curiosity for what was about to happen. TJ had been annoying her for some time now, and although she knew she probably shouldn't, she felt almost pleased to see TJ being tormented by *Dominus Tenebris*.

Lizzy Wizzy pulled Chatty's sleeve hard and leant over to her.

"Chatty, we need to get out," she whispered as loudly as she dared in her ear.

"What? No!" Chatty mouthed back.

Lizzy Wizzy was in no mood to take no for an answer. "Yes, we need to get out," she whispered again, "don't you realise?"

"Realise what?"

"If in the process of suffering *Transfixation*, TJ suddenly wakes, then we might all get trapped in this dream. I know we don't know if this is still TJ's dream or not, but it probably is, isn't it?"

Chatty started to try and make sense of what Lizzy Wizzy had just said but couldn't.

"Yes, but if he doesn't and this *Transfixation*-thing works, then he won't wake up at all, will he?" Chatty said coldly. "Then we'll have more time to find Benjy."

Lizzy Wizzy didn't know if she was being serious or not. "Chatty! How can you say such a thing?" she said, looking shocked.

Chatty ignored her. She had more important things on her mind.

"But what about Benjy?" Chatty asked, "we haven't found him yet, so we can't leave. We're so close Lizzy Wizzy. I'm not leaving Benjy here."

"Sorry," Lizzy Wizzy said, "but I don't think we should take the risk. We'll have to come back another time. If we both go now, we can wake TJ up in a matter of seconds before *Dominus Tenebris* hurts him."

"No!" Chatty said, "I'm not going."

"But Chatty, if you don't come then when I wake TJ then there's a good chance you'll be trapped here instead."

"Fine," Chatty said harshly. "It's down to you then. Are you going to choose TJ, or me and Benjy? Your choice."

With that, she turned her head away from Lizzy Wizzy and back to see what would happen next.

*

The lightning spitting from the new orb was almost uncontrollable as it continued to absorb energy from the red and white orbs. *Dominus Tenebris* felt the intensity of the power generated by the demonic staff and the righteous *Dreamswick*. A feeling of invincibility. A deep laugh thundered from within the hood.

"You can see the power I possess, *boy*. The Dreamstealers will be victorious and the Dreamguardians will be no more. So, last chance, boy. Bow at my feet and serve me or feel the full force of *Transfixation* and be trapped here, forever."

"No! Never! I will *never* serve you," shouted TJ. He was determined that his last act would be one of defiance in the face of this monster, whoever, or whatever, it was.

A sinister laugh emerged from within the hood.

"FOOL!" *Dominus Tenebris* shouted, rocking back in preparation for firing the deadly lightning orb at TJ. "Prepare to spend eternity like this then, *boy*."

Without warning, a giant dome of white light appeared from the shadows from behind *Dominus Tenebris*, causing TJ to squint. It was unlike anything he'd seen before, and infinitely stronger than the impressive orb he had himself generated during his attack on the two Dreamstealer guards.

"Cease!" came a familiar voice from within the light.

Dominus Tenebris wheeled around, startled by the intrusion, and watched on as the giant dome of white light moved slowly towards them.

Within it, TJ could just about make out someone spinning what looked like an ordinary *Dreamswick*, although he had never seen anything as spectacular as this from one before.

The figure of light stopped and held the *Dreamswick* aloft, above its head.

TJ gasped as he saw who the figure was within the dome of light.

It was Grandpa Mal.

CHAPTER 38 – IT ALL MAKES SENSE

An immense roar of frustration, irritation, resentment, anger, aggression, loathing and intense hatred thundered from *Dominus Tenebris*. TJ shuddered at the sound.

"How *dare* you come here to interfere and interrupt *me, old man*," roared *Dominus Tenebris*. "This is Dreamstealer territory. How *dare* you *defile* it with the presence of an unrighteous Elder from your filthy Brethren."

Grandpa Mal remained motionless, encapsulated within the dome of light from the power of his *Dreamswick*.

"Let the boy go," Grandpa Mal shouted weakly. "This can be between you and me."

Dominus Tenebris looked back at TJ, sneered at him and turned back to Grandpa Mal.

"Very well. The *boy* can wait a bit longer," *Dominus Tenebris* spat. "It's about time I dealt with you, *old man*. In many ways, it is quite fitting. The *boy* can see his dear Grandpa Mal subjected to *Transfixation*, right before suffering the same fate himself."

Dominus Tenebris drew out a laugh, before continuing.

"There was I thinking that your sudden arrival, however it has happened, was an inconvenience. However, now I see its advantage to me."

The laugh returned and *Dominus Tenebris* looked down at the lightning that was still crackling powerfully between the two staffs.

"In fact, it's perfect. Both of you will be lost here forever, leaving the Brethren seriously weakened and the Terror of the Dreamstealers even stronger. In fact, without you both around, we will be unstoppable."

As *Dominus Tenebris* turned again to direct a laugh in TJ's direction, Grandpa Mal took his opportunity.

"Never!" Grandpa Mal shouted, as he fired a huge white dome of light out of his protective shield and down towards *Dominus Tenebris*. The force of it leaving his *Dreamswick* pushed Grandpa Mal backwards.

The dome was much more powerful than *Dominus Tenebris* expected. As it thundered into the lightning orb between the staffs, it exploded, knocking *Dominus Tenebris* backwards to the floor and within touching distance of TJ, who took evasive action. The power of Grandpa Mal's strike dislodged TJ's *Dreamswick* from *Dominus Tenebris'* grasp. It went spinning through the air and high over TJ's head. TJ heard it clatter to the floor and the sound of wood sliding along the rock, but when he turned to recover it, he couldn't see it.

Almost immediately, *Dominus Tenebris* sprung back up athletically. Another roar reverberated throughout the chamber, followed by a shout for more Dreamstealers. They began to reappear quickly from the holes and ledges in the cavern walls.

The rage that followed from *Dominus Tenebris* was unlike anything TJ had ever witnessed. Raw, unadulterated and intense. The demonic creature on the staff became a blur almost instantaneously and fired red orb after red orb in the direction of Grandpa Mal who stood encapsulated in his dome of pure white light. The newly gathered Dreamstealer army joined in the assault.

As the orbs hit the dome of pure white light, they deflected off indiscriminately. The chamber was soon filled with red missiles, streaking in all directions. Many orbs exploded into the rocks, creating giant balls of flames. Some orbs hit Dreamstealers on the ledges around the chamber, while others fizzled as they entered the mirror pools and exploded beneath the surface, spraying water high into the air and over the surrounding rock.

TJ stood rooted to the spot, helpless and almost in a daydream as he surveyed the sight before him. By now the cave was lit up with red as the orbs rained down on Grandpa Mal and were deflected randomly around the chamber. It was a scene of deadly chaos.

TJ came to his senses when he noticed an orb heading directly for his face. He ducked and was relieved to see it explode a few metres behind him, especially when he felt the heat and force of its power. He was exposed here. A sitting duck. It was time to move!

He crouched down and as the orbs continued to fall, made his way carefully over to the mouth of the small cave in the far-left corner of the chamber. He hoped it would offer some protection and he would be safe there. But then he had a horrible thought. What if it was a passageway to another chamber full of Dreamstealers, or there were some in there already, waiting patiently for him to walk right into their hands? As he approached the opening cautiously, TJ wished he knew where his *Dreamswick* had landed.

As he reached the opening, he heard movement from the darkness within. TJ's heart froze. As the orbs continued exploding around him, he had nowhere to go. He was unarmed, vulnerable and about to be captured – or worse - by a Dreamstealer. If he tried to escape by waking himself up, he ran the risk of trapping Lizzy Wizzy and Chatty. Where were they anyway? He hoped they were safe. He could probably expel them all safely from his dream, but that would mean leaving without Benjy and he dared to think how they would all cope with the failure. As for TJ right now, he was cornered.

As a feeling of dread and resignation came over TJ, something suddenly appeared from the mouth of the cave.

"Argh," cried TJ, taken by surprise.

But it didn't harm him. It was suspended in the air and appeared to float in front of his eyes.

It was the unmistakable misshaped webbed hoop of his *Dreamswick*.

"What on earth...?" TJ exclaimed, relieved it wasn't something sinister or threatening, at least to him.

He looked at the *Dreamswick* and peered again into the darkness of the opening before him.

"How on earth...?" he questioned again, moving slowly towards the floating *Dreamswick*, his right arm outstretched ready to grab it.

Suddenly it twitched and moved towards him, making him jump.

"Lost something?" came a squeaky and excitable voice.

Then, from out of the darkness of the mouth of the cave, walked Benjy. His strawberry blonde hair was ruffled and untidy, but in spite of his ordeal he was beaming his toothy little grin at TJ. He waved TJ's *Dreamswick* at him in one hand and clutched his own in the other.

"Benjy!" TJ shouted, rushing forward to greet him. He picked him up and gave him the biggest squeeze he could. "Benjy, we found you!" he said, tears of relief rolling down his face. "We've missed you so much. Are you ok?"

"Yes, I'm fine," Benjy replied, grinning. "What took you so long?"

TJ laughed through his tears. "It's a long story," he said. "Come on, let's get you out of here."

Benjy looked at the chaos in the chamber.

"Good idea, but how?"

TJ paused. "I'm not quite sure yet," he said, surveying the scene. The onslaught against Grandpa Mal continued, but he remained protected within his dome of light, taking the opportunity every now and then to fire upon the surrounding Dreamstealers. TJ wondered how long he would be able to sustain the bombardment.

"We need to find Lizzy Wizzy and Chatty first, though," TJ informed Benjy.

"They're here?" he asked.

"Yes, somewhere, they went down a different tunnel. Come on, let's..."

From behind them, a girl's scream pierced the air. It was Lizzy Wizzy. As the two boys looked towards the mirror pools, Chatty and Lizzy Wizzy appeared from behind the rock TJ had used to hide himself before launching his ambush on the two guards.

Both of them were flanked on either side by Dreamstealer guards. The four guards half-marched, half-dragged Lizzy Wizzy and Chatty, such was the girls' struggle against them.

"Benjy!" shouted Chatty as she saw her little brother for the first time. She struggled hard against the guards to free herself, so she could be reunited with him. But they held her firm.

"Chatty! Lizzy Wizzy!" Benjy shouted, excited to see them both. The guards stopped, unsure what to do. Then, two stepped forwards, leaving the other two clutching the girls tightly to prevent their escape.

"Don't worry," TJ whispered to Benjy who was a few paces away to his right. "Leave this to me. Watch and learn." As Benjy watched on, TJ began to spin his *Dreamswick* and a small white orb appeared quickly.

As he was about to fire it towards the two guards in front of the girls, an incoming red orb from elsewhere landed within a whisker of TJ's left side. The force of the explosion from the orb hitting the floor knocked TJ diagonally backwards. He landed heavily, up against the rockface next to the opening of the small cave. He was dazed. "Do something Benjy," TJ said sluggishly, struggling to move himself.

Benjy sprang into action. He'd picked up the *Dreamswick* for the first time when it had come sliding into the entrance of the mouth of the small cave he had been kept in. He'd been curious at first, but then felt an overwhelming attachment to it. Then he'd watched from the shadows as TJ had confronted the thing that seemed to control everything that happened in these caves.

Benjy spun his *Dreamswick* quickly and adeptly, first in his right hand, then passed it momentarily into his left hand, and back into his right. The speed which he had already generated was astounding. Smiling, he spun the *Dreamswick* expertly above his head, then around his back, the *Dreamswick* passing from one side of his body to the other until it was circling him effortlessly. TJ gasped as he looked on. He'd seen *Sensei* do some of these moves in the Japanese temple within the Simulator, but even those looked clumsy now compared to the way Benjy was executing them.

"Ha!" Benjy exclaimed as two white orbs appeared in the middle of his *Dreamswick*. He moved forward slowly, twisting and spinning himself, as well as the *Dreamswick*, as he did so. TJ sat open-mouthed watching Benjy handle the *Dreamswick* with all the movement and skill of the most accomplished warrior. The most incredible and nimble *Dreamswick* ninja.

By this time, the two orbs around Benjy's *Dreamswick* had multiplied into four. Their strength and brightness were undeniable. Then, with a flurry of legs, arms and *Dreamswick,* Benjy fired off two of the orbs into the first two guards. He let out a warrior-like cry as he did so.

The power and speed with which the orbs moved was breath-taking. No sooner had Benjy fired them, they had exploded into the Dreamstealer guards and they were gone.

"Wow..." TJ exclaimed, watching from where he sat against the cave wall. But he still didn't know how Benjy was going to release the girls from the other two guards.

Chatty and Lizzy Wizzy continued to struggle against their captors. The guards stood behind them and held them tightly, using the girls as a shield to protect themselves from Benjy's advance.

Benjy paused and assessed the situation, glancing all around him as he did so. The guards were much taller than his sister and cousin, but it would still require precision and skill. His pause proved momentary. He spun the *Dreamswick* around his body a few more times and the two remaining orbs multiplied again, this time into eight.

Without any warning, Benjy flicked his *Dreamswick* forward. Six orbs streaked off, in multiples of two, towards the Dreamstealers holding Lizzy Wizzy and Chatty. Lizzy Wizzy screamed. The first two orbs hit the guards in the head and they disappeared in a flash of light. Behind them four more Dreamstealer guards had been running to provide reinforcements. The remaining orbs slammed into the four Dreamstealers and they disappeared as quickly as they had arrived.

With a flick of the wrist, Benjy sent the final two orbs streaking to the left, where he had seen two Dreamstealer guards closing in on an unsuspecting TJ. They hit their targets precisely and expelled the Dreamstealers in a flash of light.

Benjy faced TJ and performed some more elaborate and advanced moves, as if he was engaged in hand-to-hand combat. He finished with the *Dreamswick* vertical in his hands in front of his face, the webbed hoop still facing up. Symbolically his right hand finished above his left. TJ had seen something similar before, only with Benjy it looked much more natural, graceful, beautiful and powerful.

Suddenly, someone grabbed Benjy. They held him so tightly he couldn't move.

It was Chatty.

"Benjy, you're alive!" she said, squeezing him with all her strength. She had missed him more than she would ever tell him. Lizzy Wizzy joined the cuddle briefly from behind, creating a 'Benjy sandwich', before she went over to help TJ up and give him a cuddle of his own.

"Are you ok? Are you hurt Benjy?" Chatty asked. She hoped he was unharmed, otherwise TJ would have even more to answer for.

"I'm fine Chatty," Benjy said, trying to pull himself away so he could breathe properly. He'd missed her more than he would ever tell her.

After Chatty could feel Benjy wriggling, trying to break free from her embrace, she let him go. He looked cheekily up at her. How she'd missed him, she thought to herself. Then, quick as a flash, Benjy grabbed the robe that Chatty had tied loosely around her waist. "For me? Thanks, big sis,'" he said, then ran over to TJ and Lizzy Wizzy, putting the robe on as he went. "Benjy!" Chatty said crossly. Some sense of normality had resumed she thought as she made her way quickly over to the other three, calmly sidestepping red orbs that continued to fly uncontrollably and explode around the chamber.

*

Inside his dome of light, Grandpa Mal was weakening and the defensive properties of his shield were fading fast. In all his years of devotion to the Brethren, he had only ever read about such a defensive procedure. He had found it after a long and, at times, arduous search within the Brethren, in an ancient leather-bound book hidden away amongst the thousands of other books in the Great Room. Very few people throughout history would have known about the book's existence, let alone been privileged enough to have touched it, or even read it. Grandpa Mal was one of those chosen ones, deciphering some almost impenetrable clues hidden in the Great Book as to its whereabouts. But even then, he was surprised he'd been able to perform the defensive procedure. Not even *Sensei*, Master of *The Armoury*, was aware of the move.

Prophecy, rumour and wild stories of the book's existence and precise whereabouts had circulated for centuries. Its contents were too sacred to be lost, or worse, stolen. If it ever fell into the hands of the Dreamstealers, and *Dominus Tenebris* in particular, it would likely lead to the downfall and destruction of the Dreamguardians. As a result, it now lay on the altar table within the Inner Sanctum.

Sustaining the defence was taking even more concentration and power than Grandpa Mal expected, and the constant barrage of red orbs was taking its toll on his strength. As the red orbs thundered into his shield, creating muffled thuds inside, Grandpa Mal looked out through the translucent light shield towards the back of the chamber.

His heart had leapt when he had seen Benjy emerge from the cave and then he'd watched in amazement at Benjy's prowess and skill with the *Dreamswick*. The sight of Benjy had given him a small boost of energy and hardened his resolve to buy them as much time as possible. Now that the four of them were huddled together within the relative safety of the mouth of the small cave, he hoped they would hurry and find some way to exit the dream before his defensive last-stand was breached. Once it was, it would probably be over quickly, and then *Dominus Tenebris'* attention would swiftly return to TJ and the others. Even if it meant he was trapped here as soon as TJ awoke, then so be it. His time had come.

Irrespective of which outcome it was, he didn't have much time. He wanted to see them clearly, perhaps for one last time, and he needed to tell them all to go without him.

*

The four of them huddled just inside the mouth of the small cave Benjy had emerged from a short while ago. They were together for the first time as Dreamguardians, looking resplendent in their flowing robes and holding their *Dreamswicks* in their right hands.

As they looked out into a chamber that rained blood-red orbs of fury, their feelings of elation and joy at finding and being reunited with Benjy had been replaced by anxiety, concern and fear as to the plight of Grandpa Mal.

"What are we going to do?" Lizzy Wizzy asked, getting increasingly distressed by the minute.

"Let's go fight them and rescue Grandpa Mal," Benjy said excitedly. Even though he'd been trapped down here in the darkness for some time, he still hadn't fully grasped it wasn't just part of some epic harmless game.

After what he'd just witnessed Benjy do with his *Dreamswick*, TJ seriously considered it for a moment, before Chatty rudely got in first.

"Too risky Benjy. Let's just leave. Get out of this place." Chatty said coldly.

TJ gave her a hard stare. "What, and leave Grandpa Mal? Don't you get it? If I exit before him, then he'll more than likely be trapped."

"Yes, I know that," Chatty snapped. "I was talking about the rest of us. You'll have to stay here until all of us have gone. Grandpa Mal included. Last man standing and all that. If you're half as clever and brave as you think you are, you'll be fine. You think you can do everything yourself and you don't need anyone else, so now's your chance to shine. Your chance for a bit of glory. TJ the man."

Lizzy Wizzy and Benjy looked at each other and put their heads down. They'd seen this happen before.

"Now hang on a minute Chatty," TJ said, fed up of her sniping. "That's not fair. I don't know what lies you've been fed, but *Dominus Tenebris* is the enemy. Not me. Now's not the time for us to turn on each other. We need to stick together."

Before the argument progressed further, their attention was grabbed by shouting from Grandpa Mal. As they looked out, they saw he was trying to get closer to them. In doing so, he had provoked an even stronger assault from the Dreamstealers.

"What's he saying?" Lizzy Wizzy asked.

"I don't know, we need to get closer," TJ said. "Benjy, you come with me. You two stay here."

"What?! No," Chatty protested. "What's to say that as soon as my back's turned you'll be heading for the exit and I'll be trapped here. Just like you already tried with Benjy."

"Oh, give it a rest, Chatty," TJ complained. "We don't have time for this. Benjy and I are going out there, whether you like it or not."

Chatty huffed and barged her way past TJ. "Fine," she said, "I'm going out there with you then."

"Are you going out there too?" Lizzy Wizzy asked Benjy. He grinned and nodded eagerly.

"Right, let's go then," TJ said, following Chatty out into the chamber. Benjy followed them both.

Lizzy Wizzy looked around at the dark cave. "Well, I'm not staying in here on my own, wait for me," she called out after them.

As they all emerged from the cave, Grandpa Mal had made it to the middle of the chamber. He was stood with his back to the rock column by the mirror pool, where TJ and the girls had all hidden earlier.

Grandpa Mal looked across and saw them stood a stone's throw away from him.

"Go!" he shouted over to them, hoping they would hear above the explosions from the Dreamstealer's heavy artillery. *Dominus Tenebris* looked across and roared. They had found the little boy. But much as *Dominus Tenebris* loathed the older boy, the old man would be the prize and was now within reach. The leader of the Dreamstealers continued pounding the dome of light, desperate to break through its defence and get to the old man.

"What did Grandpa Mal say?" Lizzy Wizzy asked anxiously, half hiding behind TJ.

"I'm not sure," TJ replied. He cupped his left hand to the side of his mouth and bellowed "Grandpa Mal," hoping the shout would travel above the chaos.

Grandpa Mal heard the shout and offered a weak wave towards them with his left hand. His right arm which was holding the *Dreamswick* above his head was tiring. He could only manage a few more minutes at most.

"He's seen us and can hear us!" a relieved TJ said to the others. He cupped his hand back to his mouth and shouted again. "We didn't hear you. What did you say? What should we do?"

Grandpa Mal could feel his energy draining and his right arm began to shake as he struggled to keep it raised above his head.

"You need to go," he shouted back, as loudly as he could muster. "I have been with you since Times Square. It was me shouting out when you nearly got run over by the taxi cab. But we need to separate now. I will hold *Dominus Tenebris* off. YOU NEED TO GO. NOW...!"

Despite all the commotion in the chamber, the clarity of the last command was crystal clear and heard by them all.

They all looked at each other.

"But... but what about Grandpa Mal?" Lizzy Wizzy said quickly. "If we all go, but especially you TJ, he'll be trapped here. Forever."

"No, that can't happen," Chatty said anxiously, starting to get upset. Even though she had been cross with him the past few days, she loved Grandpa Mal very much. She didn't want to lose him.

"TJ?" asked Benjy, his lower lip starting to quiver as he picked up on what the others were saying and the rare show of emotion from Chatty.

"He said we needed to go. He'll be fine," TJ said, with no apparent display of emotion or concern for what might happen to Grandpa Mal.

"How do you know?" snapped Chatty.

"Think about it," TJ said smiling. "Grandpa Mal is the Dreamologist..."

The two girls gasped.

"The what?" asked Benjy quickly. He had no idea what they were talking about.

"The most powerful Dreamguardian ever," TJ replied. "A Dreamguardian so special that he can find lost Dreamguardians and save them. A Dreamguardian so incredible that he can do something like that, I guess." He pointed to Grandpa Mal who after all this time was still within a dome of light, engaged in a ferocious battle with *Dominus Tenebris* and the dark army of Dreamstealers.

"Think about it," TJ continued, "Grandpa Mal just said he's been with us since the beginning at Times Square. So, he's the one that has brought us here to rescue Benjy. And it'll be because of him that we'll be able to get Benjy out too."

Lizzy Wizzy, Chatty and Benjy all looked at TJ and then across at each other.

"Are you sure?" Chatty asked.

TJ nodded. "I'm positive. It all makes sense. I had my suspicions from the first moment I heard about the Dreamologist." He looked over at Grandpa Mal with great pride. "Just look at him," TJ beamed. "There's the special one. There's the Dreamologist." He took one more lingering look at Grandpa Mal within the dome of light, and then turned his focus back to the others. "Come on then, let's do as the Dreamologist says, we really do need to go."

"How are we going to do it?" asked Lizzy Wizzy.

Before TJ could answer, they suddenly came under attack. A red orb hit the face of the small cave just above their heads and exploded. Then another one landed a short distance from them.

"What's happening?" yelled Chatty.

"He's weakening," said TJ. "Up to now he's been able to protect us as well as himself, but he's getting weak. Plus, if you look, you'll see there's more and more Dreamstealers coming up from that stairway. Where are they all coming from? We don't have long."

"Leave it to me," Benjy said, stepping forward further into the chamber.

"Benjy, what are you doing?" Chatty said concerned. They'd already lost him once, she didn't want it to happen again. Twice would be really careless.

But Benjy wasn't listening. He was concentrating like never before. He spun his *Dreamswick*, quickly right from the beginning, then faster and faster. Within a few moments it became a blur, as it was spun all around his body. Then a small translucent purple orb appeared, and Benjy smiled. He maintained his power of concentration and continued spinning his Dreamswick.

The translucent purple orb moved down to the webbed hoop end of his Dreamswick and expanded. The centre of the orb appeared to be glowing with intense energy. With a shout, Benjy lifted his right arm above his head, adopting the same position Grandpa Mal had taken at the start of his battle with *Dominus Tenebris* and the Dreamstealer army. A giant translucent dome, tinged with purple, rose up out of Benjy's *Dreamswick* and formed a protective perimeter around them. It was almost as if they were inside a Portuguese Man O'War jellyfish.

TJ, Chatty and Lizzy Wizzy looked up in awe as the translucent walls of the dome covered them. As they did, a red orb came straight at them from up on high. It hit the dome and exploded with a muted thud. Intrigued, TJ put his left hand out to touch the wall, but it went straight through the dome of light.

Dominus Tenebris could do nothing but watch as the four children became enclosed within the safety of another protective dome. The rage and fight against Grandpa Mal intensified and *Dominus Tenebris* instructed another new rank of Dreamstealers to join in the attack against the old man. Within the fading safety of his white dome of light, Grandpa Mal dropped to his knees, his right arm and Dreamswick barely above his head.

Through the translucent walls of the dome of purple light, Chatty could see Grandpa Mal was in trouble. She held her *Dreamswick* high above her head, turned her wrist so that the webbed hoop faced the ground and concentrated hard.

Everything outside of their protective domes in the chamber froze. Dreamstealer statues were dotted around the cave, red orbs were suspended in mid-air and permanently but statically exploding, while the intense energy and power from *Dominus Tenebris'* demonic staff was neutered.

TJ's eyes widened as he surveyed what now looked like a three-dimensional painting in front of them. "How did you do that Chatty?" he whispered, daring to disturb the calm and serenity that had replaced the chaotic noise of the battle from a few moments ago.

"Just be quiet for a change TJ, and go get Grandpa Mal," Chatty said. She had no time to explain, neither could she. She had just wanted everything to stop, so someone could help Grandpa Mal.

TJ walked through the wall of their dome and cautiously passed the nearest Dreamstealers. Just in case they suddenly jumped back to life. But they were harmless, frozen in time. As TJ approached Grandpa Mal's dome, he saw him on his knees. Then without warning the *Dreamswick* dropped from Grandpa Mal's hand and he fell to the floor. The white dome around him disappeared and he lay prostrate on the cold cave floor.

"Grandpa Mal!" TJ cried out and rushed over to him. He was alive, but very weak.

"Help... me... up.... please... dear... boy...," he just about managed to splutter.

"Come on, Grandpa Mal, you can do it," TJ responded, helping the old man to his feet.

Within the dark hood, *Dominus Tenebris* was fighting Chatty's intervention hard and watching everything play out through static red eyes. This is what I'd do, the girl is special just as I suspected, *Dominus Tenebris* thought, unable to move. As *Dominus Tenebris* fought hard against Chatty's Stopper, the fingers around the demonic staff begin to twitch slightly.

TJ and Grandpa Mal staggered the short distance back into the one remaining defensive dome that Benjy was sustaining.

"Quickly... we don't... have much... time...," Grandpa Mal wheezed, now fading fast.

"Don't speak, Grandpa Mal, save your energy," TJ said quickly. "Now, listen to me, I need to expel you all from my dream..."

"No...," Grandpa Mal said, wearily wagging his left index finger to make TJ stop. "No... we need to... we need to do it... ourselves. Trust me... I know..."

He looked at them all, one by one, and then smiled weakly.

"Circle... hold hands... now..." he continued, as he started to sway. He was beginning to lose consciousness.

Benjy lowered his *Dreamswick* to his side and Chatty righted hers. As they stood in a circle, they all grabbed the hand of the person next to them. The protective wall of the dome began to disintegrate, and *Dominus Tenebris* fought even harder against the paralysis. Movement was being regained, fast. It needed to. Soon they would be gone, and this opportunity lost.

"Grandpa Mal, stay with us," Chatty said firmly.

"Quite so... dear... girl...," came the reply. "Now close... your eyes... You must say... '*Dreamologist rescustorum*'... in your head... three times. I will... and you must... do... the same..."

With that, Grandpa Mal's head slumped down and his grey lightly stubbled chin rested on his chest.

The children all looked around. Had he passed out? Was he able to say '*Dreamologist rescustorum*' himself?

"Grandpa Mal?" asked a concerned Lizzy Wizzy, and she saw his head nod slightly in faint acknowledgement.

"He's awake and doing it! Let's go!" Lizzy Wizzy exclaimed.

They all stood in a circle, holding hands, each saying '*Dreamologist rescustorum*' three times just as Grandpa Mal had instructed.

As they were doing so, *Dominus Tenebris* broke free from the paralysis. The power and ferocity instantly returned to the demonic staff. The rage exploded.

Just as Grandpa Mal was saying his final *'Dreamologist rescustorum'*, one of *Dominus Tenebris'* fearsome fiery red orbs exploded right behind him.

CHAPTER 39 – DID IT WORK?

Lizzy Wizzy and Chatty both woke with a start in Benjy's room. They sat bolt right up and looked at each other from either end of Benjy's bed, both unsure whether what they had just experienced had actually taken place.

TJ woke noisily and animatedly a few seconds after them, making both the girls jump.

"...exit... urgh!" he cried, his body jumping as he awoke. As he sat up his chest was rising and falling rapidly as he panted for breath.

"Did you just have the same dream as me?" Lizzy Wizzy asked quickly. Although her interactions with them had felt real enough, she wasn't sure if she hadn't just imagined the whole thing. But then again, she doubted whether she would have ever generated a dream as imaginative and out of control as that one.

Chatty beat TJ to the response, starting to list the locations of their dream-hops. "Times Square," she said, "followed by mountain top blizzard, glass-house and..."

"Cave," they all called out in unison.

"That'll be a yes then," Lizzy Wizzy said.

"Can you believe what just happened?" TJ said from the bottom of the bed. "That was intense. Are we all back?" he asked anxiously. "Did it work?"

Chatty looked down at Benjy. He lay in precisely the same position as he did before they went to sleep. He hadn't moved.

"Oh no!" Chatty said forlornly, "he hasn't moved. She started to shake him. "Benjy, Benjy, wake up!" she cried. But there was no response.

TJ was devastated. "No, how can that be?" he shouted as his tears came quickly. "I don't understand. Grandpa Mal is the Dreamologist. He knew where to find Benjy, which is why he was so insistent we didn't do any Dreamguardian activity tonight. He took us to those dreams to find and rescue Benjy. What went wrong?"

It was all too much for Lizzy Wizzy. She started to sob for Benjy. Everything they had just been through had been for nothing. The more she thought about Benjy stuck in those cold, dark, damp caves, held captive by all those Dreamstealers and *Dominus Tenebris,* the more she sobbed.

Chatty stopped shaking Benjy and sat staring at his motionless body. It was no use. He hadn't moved. A tear trickled down her face. If only they'd got to spend some more time with Benjy before they'd exited. Inside, she was in turmoil. She felt an overwhelming sense of loss, but also anger. This was all TJ's fault.

"Boo...!" Benjy shouted, opening his eyes and sitting up quickly. "Tricked you...!" he teased, beaming from ear to ear.

Chatty cried "Benjy!" as Lizzy Wizzy screamed.

TJ sat open-mouthed and watched in shock as Chatty flung her arms around her brother. "You're back!" she exclaimed, squeezing him tightly. He hugged her back and then began struggling to free himself from Chatty's embrace.

"Miss me?" Benjy asked, as he wriggled free.

Chatty wiped her tears from her face and gave him a gentle thump on the arm. "Don't ever do that to me again," she said. Of course she'd missed him, even though she would never admit that to him.

"Very much," TJ said smiling, "welcome back!" He bounced up the bed and gave Benjy the biggest hug he could. Benjy reciprocated. He'd missed them all, but especially TJ.

"I've missed you so much," an emotional Lizzy Wizzy said, bursting into tears as she gate-crashed the manly hug. She couldn't wait any longer

Already tired of the hugging, Benjy wriggled free and got to his feet. "I'm back," he shouted repeatedly as he bounced on the bed. TJ and Lizzy Wizzy got to their feet and started bouncing too. Lizzy Wizzy didn't know whether to laugh or cry, so she did both, and TJ gave off a celebratory whoop.

Chatty remained seated on the bed. She was experiencing a mixture of emotions: excitement, relief, happiness, familial love, anger and bitterness. It was so, so good to have Benjy back. But he should never have been lost in the first place. She knew who was to blame. He would pay for this.

After they had gone crazy for a few minutes, TJ, Benjy and Lizzy Wizzy collapsed onto the bed in a fit of giggles.

TJ suddenly sat up again with a glint in his eye.

"We need to tell Grandpa Mal that Benjy's back!" he said excitedly, dismounting from the bed. "Come on, let's go," he said, holding out his hand to help Benjy off the bed. Before Benjy could take it, Chatty grabbed hold of Benjy's arm.

"I want a word with you first Benjy," Chatty said firmly.

"Later," Benjy said, trying unsuccessfully to wriggle free.

"Come on Chatty," TJ said, "let him go. Talk to him later."

"No, I want to talk to him now. In private." She glared at TJ, who knew the face well. Now was not the time to argue with Chatty.

"Ok, well we're going now," TJ said, helping Lizzy Wizzy from the bed. "Join us when you're finished," he shouted as they both rushed out of the door.

*

TJ and Lizzy Wizzy shouted jubilantly as they raced each other through the corridors of the Old Girl to Grandpa Mal's bedroom. They knew where it was but didn't go to that part of the East Wing very often. Grandpa Mal rarely heated the section which contained his bedroom, as he always maintained that he never felt the cold.

They took it in turns to grab one another in an attempt to slow each other down. They both wanted to be the first to give Grandpa Mal the good news that he had been successful in getting Benjy back.

TJ won the race and burst through the door into Grandpa Mal's bedroom. He instantly noticed the cold. He saw a Grandpa Mal-shaped lump tucked well down beneath the covers in the bed in the middle of the far wall. He wasn't surprised: how could anyone sleep in this temperature?

"You did it, Grandpa Mal, you did it! Benjy's back, Benjy's back," TJ shouted excitedly as he raced over to one side of the bed. Behind him Lizzy Wizzy sang, "Benjy's back, Benjy's back."

TJ waited for Grandpa Mal to stir and then jump for joy with them at the news. But there was no stirring or jumping.

There was no movement at all.

"Grandpa Mal!" TJ said anxiously, giving him a little shake.

"What's wrong TJ?" Lizzy Wizzy asked, realising something wasn't quite right.

"Grandpa Mal, wake up!" TJ said, increasing the volume and shaking him harder.

"Grandpa Mal," said Lizzy Wizzy, joining in with the shaking. "What's happened?" she asked TJ, looking across at him?

"I don't know," TJ said anxiously. "He was very weak from fighting *Dominus Tenebris*, but he acknowledged you when you checked how he was. You know, just before we all had to make our exit…"

TJ stopped speaking suddenly. He went white.

"Oh no," he said.

"What?" asked Lizzy Wizzy. She was getting scared.

"What if Grandpa Mal was so weak that he wasn't able to say *"Dreamologist rescustorum"* three times. What if he passed out before he'd said it?"

"TJ, stop it, you're scaring me," Lizzy Wizzy said, clutching her fists to her cheeks. "What are you trying to say?"

TJ bowed his head. "I don't think Grandpa Mal made it," he said softly, fully aware of the magnitude of what he was saying.

Lizzy Wizzy started to cry.

"I'm sorry Lizzy Wizzy," TJ said sombrely. "I don't think Grandpa Mal made it out from the cave. I think he's trapped."

*

Chatty sat cross-legged on the bed, talking to Benjy. He was desperate to join TJ and Lizzy Wizzy, so he could pounce on Grandpa Mal and show him he was indeed free and back from his dark imprisonment. But Chatty wasn't letting him go. She wanted to talk. Her initial emotion at being reunited with Benjy had subsided rapidly. She was preoccupied by something else.

"Benjy, are you sure you're ok?" Chatty asked.

"Yes, yes, I'm fine Chatty," Benjy said impatiently. He rolled his eyes. He'd already said it a million times to her already.

"Nobody hurt you down there?"

"No, I was just kept in that little cave."

Chatty was inquisitive. "Did you see *Dominus Tenebris* down there?" she asked.

"Yes," Benjy said hesitantly.

"What did *Dominus Tenebris* say to you?"

"I don't want to talk about it," Benjy said defensively.

"Don't be like that, tell me," Chatty requested. She needed to know. "*Dominus Tenebris* visited me in one of my dreams," she confided, hoping that would encourage Benjy to open up to her.

"Really?" Benjy said, "what happened?" Her plan was working.

"*Dominus Tenebris* said to me that TJ and Grandpa Mal have been keeping secrets from us. There's so much they haven't told us Benjy, about this Brethren Dreamguardian thing."

Benjy sat unusually still and quiet, listening intently.

"*Dominus Tenebris* said TJ doesn't want us to be Dreamguardians. *Dominus Tenebris* said TJ is sly, devious and dangerous and will try and trick us. Trick us and then trap us in a dream."

Benjy shook his head. "*Dominus Tenebris* said the same to me too, but you don't believe that do you?"

Chatty stared hard at him.

"Chatty, TJ would never do that. He's like our big brother."

Chatty ignored him. She'd seen him in action and knew what TJ was really like.

"Ok then Benjy, how did you get into TJ's dream in the first place?" Chatty asked.

There was no answer.

"Answer me Benjy," Chatty said starting to get annoyed with Benjy for sticking up for TJ. Benjy was meant to be on her side, not his. "Who told you how to enter a dream?"

Benjy thought about it for a moment before replying.

"Well, it was TJ..."

Chatty exploded. *Dominus Tenebris* was right, TJ did do it on purpose to get Benjy. "See I told you," she shouted, "he tricked you and trapped you in a dream..."

"No, it wasn't like that Chatty," Benjy insisted, but Chatty was in no mood to listen. She was full of anger and rage again.

But just as Benjy was about to explain that, just like Chatty, he had overheard TJ tell Lizzy Wizzy all about being a Dreamguardian in the Suffolk barn, Lizzy Wizzy burst through the door...

"Quick, come quickly," she panted, out of breath. She had run as fast as she could from Grandpa Mal's bedroom after TJ had sent her to get them.

Benjy and Chatty whirled round to face her.

"What is it?" Benjy asked, although he knew straight away from Lizzy Wizzy's face that it was bad news.

"It's Grandpa Mal," Lizzy Wizzy said. "Come quickly..."

*

Once Lizzy Wizzy had left the room, TJ let go of his emotions. He lay slumped over Grandpa Mal's body in the bed, sobbing.

"I'm so sorry I let you down Grandpa Mal," he wept.

As he lay there thinking about what must have happened his heart ached. Grandpa Mal must have been too weak to exit properly. He must have remained in the cave. But he was far too weak to fight *Dominus Tenebris*.

TJ's mind started to run away with itself as he pictured *Dominus Tenebris* picking up Grandpa Mal's *Dreamswick* and spinning it together with that evil demonic staff. TJ could hear the lightning crack, spark and spit as the two orbs fought against each other and produced a new orb. He could see *Dominus Tenebris* torment Grandpa Mal one last time before it shot towards him at unnatural speed.

He could see Grandpa Mal being thrown back and lying on the rock floor of the cave. Paralysed. Unable to move. Inside his brain would be telling him to move his arms and legs.

Quickly! Get up! Danger! Move!

He could hear the deep growled laugh get louder as *Dominus Tenebris* would have approached Grandpa Mal and stood over his motionless body.

He knew exactly how Grandpa Mal would have felt. He'd felt it himself within The Simulator.

Even though Grandpa Mal was still alive within Transfixation, he couldn't move.

It was a horrible way to effectively die.

TJ couldn't bear to think about it anymore. He continued sobbing until Chatty burst through the door, followed by Benjy and Lizzy Wizzy.

"Grandpa Mal! NO!" Chatty yelled, running over to the bed. "It's all your fault, TJ" she shouted at him, as she stood staring over Grandpa Mal's motionless body.

TJ didn't respond. He didn't have the energy to, and he didn't care what Chatty thought. She could think what she liked. It didn't matter anymore. Nothing mattered anymore. His most favourite person in the world was no longer here. He could see him and touch him, but he would never get to talk, laugh and joke with him anymore. He had gone.

*

As the four children stood crying over Grandpa Mal's body, Lizzy Wizzy gasped suddenly.

"He moved!" she said, her voice full of shocked excitement.

"Stop it, Lizzy Wizzy!" TJ shouted back at her, "he can't have, he's gone."

"He did, I'm sure he did," Lizzy Wizzy said.

They all stared hard at Grandpa Mal, hoping and praying Lizzy Wizzy was right.

Just then, Grandpa Mal's body beneath the duvet twitched.

"There, see! Did you see that?" Lizzy Wizzy shouted.

"Yes!" Chatty replied, "I saw it."

"It was nothing, stop it you two," TJ said, "I know it's hard to accept what's happened, but we have to. He's gone."

The duvet twitched again.

"It moved! I saw it too," Benjy shouted.

TJ had seen it too. He dared to believe.

"Grandpa Mal!" TJ exclaimed, as he put the side of his face within a few centimetres of Grandpa Mal's face. "Can you hear me, Grandpa Mal?" he said, full of hope and anticipation.

They all held their breath.

"Well?" Chatty snapped, unable to bear the suspense.

"Shhh!" TJ demanded and pressed in even further. So much so that he was almost touching Grandpa Mal's face with the side of his.

Then, from Grandpa Mal's mouth came a mumbled whisper. TJ's heart leapt. He was here! He was alive!

"He said something! He made it back!" TJ shouted, turning up to look at the others crowded around. They all exhaled and let out cries of relief. As the three onlookers hugged each other in response to the fantastic news, TJ shushed them loudly again.

Grandpa Mal let out another mumble and TJ strained to hear.

"What did he say TJ?" Lizzy Wizzy asked. TJ looked up from Grandpa Mal and simply shook his head.

"I don't know, I can't hear him. He's not talking properly."

Just then, Grandpa Mal murmured and mumbled for a third time.

"TJ... I am... so... very... weak," Grandpa Mal mumbled and slurred. TJ struggled to hear and understand.

"I... must... tell you... something..." Grandpa Mal continued. There was a long pause between his words. He was quite breathless, and his words were still very slurred.

"What is it Grandpa Mal?" TJ whispered, as the others looked on.

"Come... closer... I don't.... think.... I can..."

As he stopped, TJ got right up close to Grandpa Mal's face again. Grandpa Mal continued, but as he did so his words got softer and more slurred.

"My... dear... boy..., I need... to tell you.... that I... am the..."

With that, Grandpa Mal went quiet. He had fallen unconscious.

"Grandpa Mal! Grandpa Mal!" TJ said quickly, urgently shaking him. "Wake up! Wake up!"

But he didn't.

"Is he still alive?" Lizzy Wizzy asked quickly, her heart in her mouth.

As TJ checked, he could feel a faint pulse and could feel Grandpa Mal's breath on the back of his hand.

"Yes, he is, but he's unconscious," TJ said, more relived that he was still alive than he was concerned about his loss of consciousness.

"What did he say TJ?" Benjy asked.

"He said he needed to tell me that he was the...."

"The what?" Benjy asked, once he realised TJ was not going to finish the sentence.

"I don't know, he didn't finish," TJ said.

"Oh," Benjy said disappointed.

"But I know what he was about to say," TJ replied. He knew what Grandpa Mal was about to tell him. He'd already worked it out anyway. It was just as TJ had said in the cave.

"I think Grandpa Mal was about to tell us that he is the Dreamologist... Just like I told you all in the cave. Grandpa Mal is the Dreamologist".

"Wow...," Benjy said, not fully understanding the significance of it all.

There then followed a long pause as they let those words and TJ's revelation sink in.

Finally, Chatty broke the silence. As she stood watching her poor, dear Grandpa Mal lie motionless in his bed, she could not suppress the feelings inside her any longer.

"That's all very well," she said softly at first, "but look what you've done to him TJ."

TJ turned to her with a surprised look on his face. "What do you mean, what I've done to him?" he asked.

"He wouldn't be like this if he hadn't needed to rescue Benjy," Chatty shot back, her voice getting louder all the time.

"But that wasn't me," TJ protested, "it was *Dominus Tenebris*. The fight must have taken nearly all of Grandpa Mal's strength."

"No!" Chatty shouted. "It was your fault that Benjy got trapped in the first place. You did that to him," she shouted, pointing at Grandpa Mal's unconscious body in the bed.

"No! No! it was *Dominus Tenebris*," TJ insisted.

But Chatty was in no mood to listen.

"NO!" she screamed. "It's all your fault, TJ. I'm never going to forgive you. I HATE YOU..."

Then she turned and ran out of the room.

CHAPTER 40 – THE RED DEER STAG

I t was the middle of the night and there was nothing anyone could do for Grandpa Mal. He lay perfectly still in bed, unresponsive but alive.

TJ had managed to convince Lizzy Wizzy not to call for help. After all, Grandpa Mal was stable, and who would look after them if he was suddenly taken to hospital?

He had confused Lizzy Wizzy by asking how they would ever explain the events leading up to Grandpa Mal's unconscious state, even though they wouldn't have had to. The irony was that nobody would have believed the truth anyway.

Finally, TJ placated his sister by saying he would try and contact Grandpa Mal's friend Christophé in the morning. He had no idea how, but Lizzy Wizzy wasn't to know that.

So having sent Benjy and Lizzy Wizzy back to bed sometime earlier, TJ was now slumped in the comfy old armchair in Grandpa Mal's bedroom. Just in case Grandpa Mal woke suddenly in the night, or the situation turned more serious and he became distressed.

The mental exertion and emotional rollercoaster of the night finally got the better of him. Although he hadn't planned to, TJ fell asleep.

*

He was in a clearing within a forest. As he looked around, he saw something moving slowly against the green and brown of the trees and ferns. It was making its way towards him, purposefully, on all fours. From out of the safety of the forest strode a huge Red Deer Stag. It looked straight at TJ and seemed to give him a sad smile. A tear rolled from a large brown eye down its face. TJ dared move. He had never seen an animal with such beauty, but as he observed the creature he was filled with an overwhelming sense of sadness.

After a short stand-off, the Red stag turned slowly and walked away from him. Just as it was about to be swallowed up by the forest, it turned its head. With a flick of its impressive antlers it appeared to beckon TJ to follow him.

"Do you want me to follow?" TJ called out, but the animal simply turned and walked into the forest. "I think you do," TJ said quietly to himself, and set off in pursuit of the Red stag.

He kept a short distance from the Red stag, as it expertly weaved its way through the forest. After a while the forest began to thin, and they found themselves walking through the countryside. Every now and then the Red stag would turn its head, as if to check TJ was still there.

TJ followed diligently, quite unsure where the Red stag was taking him, if that was indeed the animal's intention. As they walked over hill and dale, the fields gave way to a cart track which led to a crossroads. An old wooden arrowed signpost pointed to the right and read 'London – this way'. The Red stag duly followed the cart track to the right. Without warning, its pace and urgency quickened, and it started to run. TJ quickened his own pace as the Red stag began to put more distance between them.

"Slow down!" TJ called out. He still had no idea why he was following the creature and where it might be taking him. The Red stag simply looked round, offered another flick of the antlers and pressed on ahead. As they pressed on, the landscape gradually changed from rural countryside to that of London in the late 1600s.

Far off in the distance, TJ saw a hill leading up to a large imposing dome. As they got closer to the top of the hill, TJ could see it was a grand Cathedral. A number of horse and carriages were outside, some stationary and some moving. As one went past him, TJ noticed a couple of people dressed in old fashioned clothes inside. The driver perched at the front of the carriage tipped his top hat to TJ, before whipping the black horses ahead of him to go faster.

Undeterred by the activity around it, the Red stag continued up the hill to the Cathedral. It climbed the bank of stone steps outside and entered the Cathedral through its giant ornate doors. TJ bounded up the stairs and carefully slipped inside. As soon as he entered, TJ saw that the vast building was still under construction. However, there was already sufficient evidence that once completed the Cathedral would be incredibly beautiful and ornate. As he looked around for the Red stag, TJ realised he had lost sight of it.

Up ahead in the middle of the building, a group of men stood around a quite severe looking gentleman. He looked important, and his height was enhanced by a large hair wig that rose up and then parted to fall either side onto his shoulders. In one hand he clutched some giant scrolls of paper and with the other pointed to some drawings on another scroll that two other men had rolled out before him. After stabbing a figure at the drawings, he then did the same at the corresponding points of the building.

Convinced they hadn't seen him, TJ crept a bit closer to hear what was being said. However, as he approached the group, the severe looking gentleman in the middle of the group looked straight at him. TJ froze, but the gentleman didn't acknowledge him. He simply returned to the drawings in front of him. Suddenly he spoke, his voice echoing around the vast building.

"Look up!" he said, deliberately loudly to the men around him. He looked over quickly at TJ, and then back to the men. "Look up!" he repeated. It was then that TJ realised the man wasn't just talking to the men, he was talking to him!

TJ immediately looked up. Above him was the giant dome of the Cathedral. He was sure he had seen it before, somewhere, but he couldn't remember. Around the circumference of the dome, about one hundred feet up, was a gallery. As he strained his eyes to look, TJ thought he saw something move on it.

"The Red stag," TJ whispered to himself, "what's it doing up there?"

He quickly made his way to the side of the building, careful not to disturb the working party of men who remained underneath the middle of the dome. They continued looking at the hand-drawn plans before them, directed by the severe looking wigged gentleman.

TJ managed to find a staircase that he hoped led to the gallery and began to climb. After passing two hundred steps he stopped counting. His thighs began to hurt, but he needed to carry on. After a lengthy and arduous ascent, he found himself out on the gallery. It ran all around the interior of the dome, about one hundred feet above the Cathedral floor. A stone seat ran around the wall and a continuous inner iron railing prevented a substantial and deadly plummet to the floor below.

As he looked down over the railing, he heard a whisper from behind him.

"Find him...!"

TJ wheeled around, but there was no-one there.

As he faced the wall, he heard it again, as if was being spoken right in front of him.

"You need to find him...!" came the whispered voice. TJ thought it sounded familiar but couldn't quite place it through the whisper.

As he turned away from the Dome wall to face back inside, TJ thought he saw something on the opposite side of the gallery to him. A figure in the shadows. But before he could see who it was, it disappeared.

When TJ looked over the railings, the men on the Cathedral floor and their drawings were gone. In their place, he saw the Red stag looking up at him. It flicked its antlers and was off again, its hooves clattering rhythmically on the stone floor as it went.

"Wait!" TJ shouted, as he headed for the staircase. He ran down as quickly as he could, his thighs ready to ignite by the time he reached the bottom.

He exited the Cathedral just in time to see the Red stag had turned left and was headed further into the City. The animal stopped momentarily and looked behind. Satisfied that TJ had resumed following, it turned its head back and kept on walking.

In an instant, TJ's surroundings had changed. The Cathedral behind him had gone and he was approaching an isolated fluted stone column mounted on a huge stone plinth. The column reached some two hundred feet into the sky. Atop the column, TJ could just about make out a viewing gallery and a sculptured gilded urn of fire. The Red stag was stood by the base of the column. It nodded its head, as if pointing out the stone column to TJ. Then it disappeared into the stone plinth via a door on the East side.

TJ sprinted to the column and made his way through the door. He thought he would find a circular staircase inside, leading them up the inside of the column. Instead, as he went through the door, his surroundings changed again.

TJ and the Red stag stood next to each other on the bank of a wide, fast-flowing river. On the opposite side were two separate majestic L-shaped buildings, each a mirror image of the other. A dome towered above the entrance to each building. They were set some way in front of a classical grand house, which had been precisely situated so that it was in the middle of the space between the two other buildings. On the sunny blue skyline behind the house was a steep hill. On the top of it, TJ could make out a statue, while a strange domed building was just about visible to the right, poking out of the top of some trees.

"What is this place?" TJ asked aloud, immediately feeling foolish. The Red stag looked at him as if it had understood the question but being an animal, it said nothing.

"Is this place important?" TJ asked, having taken some comfort, if not surprise, that the Red stag appeared to understand what he was saying. The Red stag nodded its head, offering another perspective of the architecture of its beautiful antlers.

TJ looked across the water at the buildings. The domes looked familiar.

"Do I need to go here?" TJ asked the Red stag. But when he looked back to where the creature was a moment ago, it had gone.

Puzzled, TJ looked all around him, but he was alone with just the fast-flowing river for company. Where had the Red stag gone? As he stood looking out across the river a voice called out from down below him, over the edge of the bank.

"*'ello, me'ansum*," came a familiar country lilt, "Are you *awright dear*?" TJ knew who the voice belonged to immediately. It was the Dreamorian. As he peered over the edge of the riverbank, the Dreamorian was sat in a wooden rowing boat. She had on the same pink fluffy slippers, green crochet tights, blue denim skirt and thick grey knitted jumper that she was wearing when they first met.

Next to the old lady was the little pale red-haired girl that TJ had met in the school playground, in what felt like a lifetime ago. They bobbed up and down in the boat as the water swelled around it.

TJ was speechless, and his eyes were like saucers.

Before he could say anything, the Dreamorian spoke.

"You look a bit *betwaddled,* my boy," the old lady said. "Let me *'elp you* dear. *You's needs* to remember what *I's says* to you the first time we met."

With that, she let out a deep sigh, closed her eyes and remained quiet and motionless. TJ had seen this before. After some time had passed, the old lady started to speak, her eyes still firmly closed:

"You will see a cottage,
An old lady will be inside.
Tell her your fears and where you are going,
She will ask you for your dreams,
Give them to her.

Trust the red deer,
Who will take you to the river.
There could be a ferryman,
Offering to take you across the water,

But do not be fooled,
For the demon of the deep is no longer sleeping."

After she had stopped talking, the Dreamorian opened her eyes. She looked first at TJ and then at her companion in the boat.

The pale red-haired girl smiled at TJ. "You need to remember what I told you too," she said. "Do you remember?"

TJ nodded. How could he ever forget?

"You said I was one of them," TJ shouted down to the girl. "What did you mean?"

Before she could reply, and TJ could ask the Dreamorian what her strange poem meant, dark clouds began to form and roll in above them. The water began to get choppier. A look of worry came over the Dreamorian's face and she began to row the boat out into the river.

The wind began to pick up and the waves got rougher. The little wooden boat began to pitch violently in the ever-increasing swell of the water.

"What did you mean, what does it all mean?" TJ shouted over the rush of the wind. But by now they had rowed some distance and they were unable to hear TJ's desperate pleas.

"Find him...!" came a whisper from behind his back, but when TJ turned to see who had spoken, there was no-one there.

Then he heard a bang. As he turned back, he saw it. A red orb fired into the air over the right dome of the building in front of him.

Without warning, a large sea creature burst out of the river near to the boat. A huge giant scaly sea serpent erupted from the deep. The stuff of nightmares. Full of fear, the Dreamorian and little pale red-haired girl screamed.

TJ woke up screaming too.

*

Once TJ had convinced her to go back to bed, Lizzy Wizzy had fallen asleep quite quickly. She didn't think she would because of all the excitement and exertion in finding Benjy. However, although she was still very worried about Grandpa Mal, TJ had put her mind at rest that he would contact one of Grandpa Mal's friends for help in the morning. Even though she had wanted to, they couldn't call an ambulance. How would they ever be able to explain the events leading up to Grandpa Mal's unconsciousness?

She had got back into bed concerned for Grandpa Mal, but relieved Benjy was back. It had been quite a night…

*

She was in a snowy clearing within a forest. As she looked around, she saw something moving slowly against the snow-covered pine trees. It was making its way towards her, purposefully, on all fours. From out of the safety of the white forest strode a huge Red stag. It looked straight at Lizzy Wizzy and seemed to give her a sad smile. A tear rolled from a large brown eye down its face. Lizzy Wizzy dared move. She had never seen an animal with such beauty. As she observed the creature she was filled with an overwhelming sense of excitement.

After a short stand-off, it turned slowly and walked away from her. Just before it was swallowed up into the forest, it turned its head.

"I'll follow you!" Lizzy Wizzy called out. With an affirming flick of its impressive antlers, the Red stag turned and walked into the forest. Lizzy Wizzy followed.

After a while, the forest began to thin and the snowy terrain beneath their feet got steeper and steeper, and the snow deeper and deeper. The Red stag started pulling ahead as it climbed more adeptly than Lizzy Wizzy up the snow-covered mountainside. Lizzy Wizzy was getting slower and colder with every step. Every now and then the Red stag would turn its head, as if to check Lizzy Wizzy was still there.

Up ahead, Lizzy Wizzy saw an old wooden arrowed sign. It read 'Zermatt – this way'. Without warning the Red stag's pace and urgency quickened and it started to run. Lizzy Wizzy quickened her pace as the animal began to put more distance between them.

"Slow down please!" Lizzy Wizzy called after the Red stag. The Red stag looked round, offered another flick of the antlers but pressed on.

Up ahead, Lizzy Wizzy saw a wooden cabin, tucked away on the hillside. The Red stag stopped at the door, looked back at Lizzy Wizzy, then entered the cabin. When she reached the door, it was closed. She looked behind her and saw the town some distance below in the valley. From up here, it looked like a model village.

Lizzy Wizzy knocked on the door to the cabin, but there was no reply. She opened it cautiously and stepped inside. Her eye caught the light from a small window on the other side of the room, looking out in the direction of the mountain range. Snow was dusted on the top. In the distance was the unmistakable sight of the Matterhorn, majestically overlooking all that it surveyed. In the corner of the small room, the logs in the woodburner were already well ablaze. The burner was generating plenty of heat to warm the cabin and provided a lovely orange glow. On the top of it stood a well-worn copper kettle that had clearly seen better days. A wooden table took up most of the room.

Suddenly, Lizzy Wizzy heard something outside. Concerned that the Red stag was leaving without her, she turned and went back out of the front door.

The brightness was blinding. When she lowered her arm from shielding her eyes, she found herself admiring the spectacular view of the Chinese valley from her vantage point. The battlements to either side of Lizzy Wizzy were tall, and she struggled to see over them. However, through the gaps she was able to ascertain she was high up and well above the canopy of the surrounding trees and dense woodland. A large section of the Mutianyu section of the Great Wall upon which she now stood snaked out ahead of her as it climbed and slithered over the mountainous terrain and across the landscape.

Up ahead of her, she saw the Red stag. It looked back at her, nodded its large antlers and began walking away from her again. Lizzy Wizzy followed. After a short while they approached a Watchtower, its ramparts protruding high above the Wall. The Red stag disappeared inside, and Lizzy Wizzy hurried and entered through the narrow single door.

Her surroundings changed instantly. She was in a square courtyard, one of a number within a vast walled palace complex. It was surrounded by beautifully carved wooden Chinese palatial architecture. Towers sat at the four corners of the city walls, each topped with an intricate roof containing a multitude of ridges. Lizzy Wizzy walked across the square, towards one of the huge Gates separating one courtyard from another.

As she followed the Red stag through the Gate, she was no longer walking through the Forbidden City. She was on the decks of a huge wooden ship - a tea clipper - which was just setting sail from the docks of Shanghai port. Beneath her, the docks were buzzing with people talking and shouting to each other in a language Lizzy Wizzy didn't understand. They were wearing clothes typical of the early 1870s.

She gazed up and saw three giant masts towering above her. Smaller wooden beams ran perpendicular to the masts and from these hung a myriad of ropes. Casting her eye down the wooden splendour of the deck, she saw the Red stag at the bow of the clipper. Ahead of it the ship's figurehead of a bare-breasted Nannie Dee clutching a horse's tail stretched out, as if urging the boat on and pointing the way home. The Red stag stood facing out, waiting to feel the rush of the wind and splash of the waves as the clipper cut through the water, racing her cargo of tea from China back to Britain.

As the clipper gained speed, it began to rise and fall on the waves and Lizzy Wizzy began to feel seasick. She made her way over to one of the wooden cabins situated in the centre of the deck, close to the huge wooden spoked ship's wheel that was taller than a man and guided the clipper through treacherous seas to safe harbour.

As Lizzy Wizzy slumped into one of the small bunks inside the cabin, she felt the room spin and closed her eyes for a few moments. When she opened them, she was no longer in the cabin aboard the clipper.

Now she lay on a wooden floor in a room with eight walls. Some sections of the wall were covered with wood panelling, while the remaining parts were painted white. The domed ceiling was also white and decorated with elaborate plasterwork, as was the cornice. Thirteen-foot tall windows filled five of the walls, while a further two walls were dominated by separate doorways. Above one door hung two large oil paintings of men from a different century, wearing fine silk robes.

The room itself was sparse, aside from an eclectic selection of timepieces and astronomical instruments. These included a grandfather and grandmother clock that seemed to keep each other company. Leant up against one of the large windows was a wooden ladder that supported the end of a primitive telescope. It was made from a long wooden beam, supported at the other end by a simple wooden frame.

Lizzy Wizzy looked out of one of the windows and saw the Red stag on a grassy hill. As it looked straight at Lizzy Wizzy, it nodded its head. With a flick of its impressive antlers it appeared to beckon Lizzy Wizzy to follow it once again. Then it turned and ran towards a classical grand house that had been precisely set before, but aesthetically between, two majestic L-shaped buildings, each a mirror image of the other. The shorter end of those buildings each had a dome that faced the other.

Lizzy Wizzy raced to the doorway to try and get outside to follow the majestic Red stag. However, as she exited the room, she found herself instead at the start of an underground stone tunnel that stretched out before her. It was gloomy, cold and smelt damp. Although it was dark, she thought she could see wooden doorways down both sides of the corridor.

Suddenly a voice whispered up ahead from the shadows.

"Find him!"

Lizzy Wizzy jumped. Although she thought the voice sounded familiar, she couldn't place it. As she peered into the gloomy darkness ahead, she thought she saw a figure in the shadows. But before she could see who it was, it disappeared.

Just then, a red glow appeared further down the corridor in front of her, illuminating her stone surroundings. It did indeed have wooden doorways down each side, just as she suspected.

Within seconds of a red orb being fired, Lizzy Wizzy heard trickling water either side of her. As she looked around her, she saw water trickling down two stone staircases on either side of her. It started slowly at first, before the volume of water increased. The water flowed past her feet and seemed to be going downhill. Then the water level began to rise. It must have hit a dead-end further up the tunnel. Within no time at all, the water had risen above her ankles and then above her knees. She started to panic. But no matter how hard she tried to move, she was unable to reach the stone staircase.

The water continued to pour down the steps. By now the water level was above her waist. First Lizzy Wizzy tried to wade, then swim. But for some reason she couldn't coordinate her arms and legs. Her anxiety was rising as fast as the water. After a few more seconds she found herself lifted off her feet and started to tread water furiously. Her relief at being able to keep her head above the water disappeared quickly as she noticed the stone ceiling getting closer and closer as the water continued to pour down the steps into the tunnel.

As the water poured in, she began to struggle to keep her chin above the water. As she tired, her head dipped under the water momentarily. She swallowed a mouthful of water and panicked. As she came back up coughing and spluttering, there was just enough room between the water level and the ceiling for her to breath. A small air pocket that was closing by the second. Lizzy Wizzy strained her chin upwards, fighting for air, as the water continued its relentless march towards filling every gap in the tunnel.

As she struggled, Lizzy Wizzy inhaled more and more water. She was now straining her neck upwards to try and grab the last remaining mouthfuls of air before it was eliminated by the marauding water. It was frightening. In a moment, all the air in the tunnel would be gone. She would drown...

As she fought to stay above the water one last time, she swallowed a mouthful of water again. Then another, and another...

She woke up just as she was about to drown, coughing and spluttering.

*

Lizzy Wizzy rushed to Grandpa Mal's room where TJ was sat in the chair.

"TJ! Are you awake?" Lizzy Wizzy said as she burst through the door.

"Yes, just as well," TJ replied, trying to sound calm. But the truth was he'd been awake a while now. Ever since he'd had that nightmare with the giant scaly sea creature bursting out of the river near the boat. He swore he could still hear the screams of the Dreamorian and pale red-haired girl.

"Very funny," Lizzy Wizzy said, pulling a face. "I need to tell you what just happened," she said, "in my dreams just now." From the tone of her voice and speed with which she was talking, TJ realised it was important.

TJ sat listening intently as Lizzy Wizzy went on to recount her dreams. She went through them, one by one, about the places where she had followed the Red stag.

A Red stag thought TJ, but he said nothing and let Lizzy Wizzy continue. However, the more she spoke, the more TJ became convinced that Lizzy Wizzy's dreams were somehow connected to the ones he had experienced a little while earlier.

Lizzy Wizzy ended by recalling the nightmare about nearly drowning in a stone tunnel. By the time she had recounted it all, she was very upset.

TJ put a caring arm around her shoulders and gave her a little reassuring squeeze.

"Lizzy Wizzy," TJ said slowly, "try not to focus on the last part of the dream. That was only due to the presence of a Dreamstealer. Focus instead on the first bits. They must have been the work of a Dreamguardian. Did you see anyone?"

Lizzy Wizzy shook her head, sniffed and cuffed her nose.

"There was definitely someone in the tunnel, but I couldn't see who it was," she said somewhat dejectedly. She paused as she suddenly remembered what had been whispered to her. "Whoever it was TJ, they whispered 'find him' to me. But I don't know who said it, or who I need to find."

TJ's mind started to whir. "There was a Red stag in my dream too, Lizzy Wizzy," TJ said. "A voice whispered 'find him' to me too, but when I looked they were gone."

Suddenly, Lizzy Wizzy was intrigued. "What does it all mean TJ?"

"I'm not completely sure, but I think I know where we need to go," TJ replied, giving Lizzy Wizzy a little smile.

"Where?" Lizzy Wizzy asked quickly.

"Come on, you'll see. Let's go," TJ said.

With that, he grabbed Grandpa Mal's dressing gown from the back of the door, then Lizzy Wizzy's hand. Together, they headed quickly through the corridors to the West Wing of the Old Girl.

CHAPTER 41 – DELIGHT, DESPAIR, DETERMINATION

TJ and Lizzy Wizzy negotiated many twists and turns around the Old Girl, as TJ tried hard to remember his way back to the Great Room.

He was convinced that the stone tunnel Lizzy Wizzy had seen in her dream was the one he had walked down with Grandpa Mal on two previous occasions. The stone tunnel that led to that special curiosity room with the painted ceiling and home to the most amazing secrets.

Having unsuccessfully checked a number of empty rooms, they approached a door much like any other in the house. TJ tried the handle, but it was locked. He fumbled in the pocket of Grandpa Mal's dressing gown and pulled out a key. To his relief he heard the door click open as he turned the key in the lock. Inside was the sparse, windowless room, illuminated by the single bulb hanging from the end of a long, woven cord. They made their way over to the wooden desk, and opened the top drawer using another key from the dressing gown pocket. TJ grabbed the ornate iron key that was inside the drawer and slipped behind the faded tapestry that hung on the far side of the wall, taking Lizzy Wizzy by surprise.

She heard a rattle of the iron key in the iron lock, then a creak and loud bang as the heavy door swung open.

TJ called out for Lizzy Wizzy to join him and she too slipped behind the tapestry. TJ had Grandpa Mal's small torch in his hand and was shining it down the steep stone staircase. He motioned for her to follow him and they held on tightly to the iron rail as they descended the steps. When they reached the bottom, TJ shone the torch down the tunnel and turned to Lizzy Wizzy.

"See, this is it," he said, his voice bouncing off the stone walls.

Lizzy Wizzy looked around her. It certainly was cold and damp, but this wasn't the same tunnel she had seen. The one in her dream could be accessed via two staircases on either side, not by this one steep stone staircase.

"No, it isn't TJ," she said, shaking her head as if to emphasise the point.

"It must be," TJ insisted.

But Lizzy Wizzy was sure.

"Sorry, very similar TJ, but not the same tunnel," she replied.

A dejected TJ made his way down the increasingly sloping tunnel, counting the wooden doors as they passed. They stopped at door eleven and TJ flicked up the cover, revealing the soft glow of the keypad for the steel door.

"Do you know the code?" Lizzy Wizzy asked.

TJ's response was to punch in a long stream of numbers. He had watched Grandpa Mal closely twice and prided himself on remembering numbers. The sound of steel bolts sliding was his reward. After much clunking, a beep signalled that the door was unlocked.

"Welcome to Grandpa Mal's special place," TJ said swinging open the door and resurrecting the soft lighting in the room with the flick of a switch. "Welcome to the Great Room, the home of the Brethren of the Dreamguardians."

Lizzy Wizzy's reaction upon seeing the Great Room for the first time was much the same as TJ's. She gasped and stood open mouthed as she gazed up at the painted ceiling, then at the impressive bookcase, and then at all the curiosities around the room.

As she wandered around, TJ made his way to the bookcase and to the row of books slightly to the left of the centre of the room. He reached his hands deep into the shelf behind the top of the books and fumbled about, just like Grandpa Mal had done as he'd looked on. Just as TJ was about to lose patience, he heard two clicks. He turned the handles he had been looking for and pushed the released section of bookshelf, books and all, back into the void behind it.

TJ walked into the recessed doorway and slid to the left. A speechless Lizzy Wizzy followed close behind. With the help of the torch and some matches that had been left on the altar table, TJ and Lizzy Wizzy lit the vast array of candles, revealing the primitive splendour of the Inner Sanctum.

The three, large leather-bound books lay untouched on the large altar table covered in white cloth. TJ could vividly remember how excited he had been to read an extract of the dreams that could be gifted from the Great Book. So much had happened since then, and there were still so many more things to discover and unearth.

Lizzy Wizzy finally found her voice.

"What is this place?" she asked TJ, awestruck.

"This is the Inner Sanctum," TJ replied proudly, "Grandpa Mal said this is the most sacred and important place for any Dreamguardian. I think he's right."

Lizzy Wizzy spotted the items on the wall behind the table and covered her mouth in shock.

"Joseph's coat," she exclaimed, pointing to the ancient robe mounted in the glass frame.

"Yes, and the first *Dreamswick*," TJ said excitedly, pointing to the now familiar long wooden staff with a misshaped webbed hoop at one end. He had seen it for the first time himself only a few days ago, but now it was a prominent and familiar ally in the fight against the Dreamstealers.

"This is quite incredible, but what exactly are we doing here?" Lizzy Wizzy asked TJ. "What does this have to do with the dreams we had?"

TJ shrugged his shoulders. He just didn't know. He was sure that the stone tunnel Lizzy Wizzy had seen was the one that led to the Great Room and Inner Sanctum, but she was adamant that it was not.

They stood gazing at the three books displayed on the altar table, trying to think of some connection with their dreams involving a Red stag. They were so preoccupied that they didn't hear someone creep in behind them.

Suddenly, a voice rang out behind them.

Lizzy Wizzy screamed, loudly, from the shock, and they both spun around.

They couldn't believe their eyes.

It was Auntie Katherine...

*

"TJ, Lizzy Wizzy, what are you doing in here?" Auntie Katherine asked sharply. She was wearing her dressing gown and her long red hair was ruffled as if she had just woken up.

Both TJ and Lizzy Wizzy immediately noticed that Auntie Katherine looked a little perturbed.

"Auntie Katherine, you frightened the life out of us. When did you get back?" TJ asked, trying to avoid her question with one of his own.

"A few hours ago," she replied quickly. "The good news was your Granny Winifred had suffered only a mini-stroke. As she's on the road to recovery your Mum was keen for me to come back and help Grandpa Mal look after you four. Just as well I did it would seem. As it was a long journey back on the train and there wasn't much sign of life in the Old Girl when I returned, I went straight to bed. I thought I would catch up with everyone in the morning. But then I knew something serious was up."

"We can explain..." TJ started to say, but Auntie Katherine interrupted him.

"I'm not sure you can," she said. "I'm not sure anyone other than Grandpa Mal can..." She trailed off and held her hand up to her face, as if trying to compose herself and hold back the tears.

"I take it that you know about all this then?" Auntie Katherine asked, motioning at the Inner Sanctum in general. TJ and Lizzy Wizzy nodded.

"Do you?" Lizzy Wizzy asked.

Auntie Katherine gave off an exasperated laugh and nodded her head in resignation.

"Yes," she replied, "but I've never seen this room before. The truth is I've never wanted to see this room before. You see, even though some like my father are convinced that having the gift is the most important life you can lead and the greatest honour, the truth is that the risks are just too great. Trust me when I say that the costs of being a part of the Brethren, for being a Dreamguardian, can be high."

TJ nodded. He had already experienced first-hand the risks and costs of being a Dreamguardian. Then his eyes widened. Hang on, he thought. If Auntie Katherine knew all about the Brethren and the gift, that could only mean one thing. Auntie Katherine must have the ability to be a Dreamguardian too.

"I know what you're thinking, TJ," Auntie Katherine continued, noticing the penny drop in TJ's eyes, "and yes, you're right. I have ... no, sorry... I should say, *had* the gift, but I chose not to exercise it..." She stopped in mid-sentence as her mind wandered off to some faraway place.

"Why not?" TJ asked, but Auntie Katherine ignored the question.

"So here we are," Auntie Katherine continued, "in the most sacred of sacred places. You have no idea what some people would do to get in here. It just doesn't bear thinking about..."

TJ and Lizzy Wizzy looked at each other. They had no idea what she was talking about.

Lizzy Wizzy plucked up the courage to speak.

"We came in here because we both had strange dreams..." she ventured.

"About a Red stag by any chance?" Auntie Katherine asked.

"Yes... but... how do you know that?" TJ stammered, before Lizzy Wizzy could do the same.

"Because I had a dream about a Red stag too," Auntie Katherine said. "In my dream, the stag was grazing on park grassland. In the distance I saw a large domed building on top of a hill. The stag was majestic and clearly the leader of its herd. As it grazed it was joined by the most beautiful hind and two calves.

"Then without warning a Fallow Deer Buck arrived, with a deep dark brown coat. It was aggressive and challenged the Red stag. But this was not rutting season and transcended anything to do with the typical mating ritual of a stag. This was about territory and authority. The Fallow buck threatened the offspring of the Red stag. Sensing danger, the calves emitted a high-pitched squeal and the hind barked in alarm.

"I saw the Red stag being chased by the aggressive Fallow buck. The Red stag was chased into the mouth of a deep, dark, black cave. But the Fallow buck stopped outside, as if keeping guard. When it was satisfied the Red stag wasn't returning, the Fallow buck left."

TJ and Lizzy Wizzy looked at each other, puzzled.

Auntie Katherine took a deep breath and appeared to steady herself.

"Then, from out of the opening of the same cave that the Red stag entered, walked Daniel. My brother and your father."

Tears began to well up in all their eyes as they each dared comprehend and believe what Auntie Katherine had seen in her dream.

"What are you trying to say ...?" TJ just about managed to ask.

"In my dream, the Red stag must have turned into your father." She looked at them through tearful eyes and her voice began to crack with emotion. "You see, TJ, Lizzy Wizzy, I believe the dream is trying to tell me that your dear Daddy - my dear brother Daniel - might still be alive."

"What? Daddy, still alive?" Lizzy Wizzy exclaimed bursting into tears. In an instant she was overcome with shock, disbelief, reticent happiness and confusion.

"No...! How can you say that? He's dead," TJ exclaimed, even though he desperately wanted to believe her. "How can that be? How?" he asked, choking up with the same emotions as his little sister.

"I don't know exactly," Auntie Katherine said, "but I saw Grandpa Mal in my dream. He made sure that I saw him. He had his robe on. He was kneeling and putting down his *Dreamswick*."

The two children let out an incredibly confused gasp. "What does that mean?" TJ asked.

"I'm not sure," Auntie Katherine said. "That's why I'm here. We need to look in the Great Book. I presume it's one of those books over there. I heard many stories about the Great Book, but never physically saw it myself."

TJ was confused. Why had Grandpa Mal never shown Auntie Katherine the Great Book? But those questions would have to wait for later.

"Yes, it's the middle one on the altar table," TJ replied, quickly making his way over to the Great Book clutching a candle with shaking hands. When he reached the Great Book, he noticed it had been opened on different pages to those he had viewed the other night.

As he scanned down the list of dreams in front of him, he stopped at the heading named 'Futures'. He read its description aloud:

"Futures - *a prophecy within a dream, potentially very significant; WARNING: it is essential these dreams are protected and saved, but to do so risks the Dreamguardian's own health; as a result the **Futures** must only be performed by an experienced and physically strong Dreamguardian; the bravest and most willing Dreamguardian must empty their hand of the Dreamswick and kneel to perform a **Futures** to signify acceptance of their own potential sacrifice for the sake of the prophecy; a **Futures** dream automatically expels any Dreamstealers so the dream itself is protected and ensures the Dreamguardian is protected from the 'unbearable consequence'; the Dreamguardian will also be automatically expelled from the dream; the adverse impact on the Dreamguardian's strength and health from performing a **Futures** should not be taken lightly".*

They stood in silence once TJ had finished reading the description of the 'Futures' dream. As they did so, TJ carried on reading to himself the next dream beneath the description of a 'Futures'.

Revealers – use to impart and reveal some particular knowledge to the dreamer; should only be used by experienced Dreamguardians as can have a regressive and negative effect on a dreamer.

Lizzy Wizzy broke the silence. "What does it all mean Auntie Katherine?" she asked.

"I believe your dear Grandpa Mal just gifted me a Futures dream," Auntie Katherine explained. "That is, effectively a prophecy that your father – as represented by the Red stag – will one day emerge from his current state and location, whatever they may be, and return to us." She began to cry. "Return to us alive and well."

It was all too much for Lizzy Wizzy to take as well, and she buried herself into the arms of Auntie Katherine who cuddled and tried to comfort her.

"As soon as I woke from this dream," Auntie Katherine continued after she had sufficiently calmed both herself and Lizzy Wizzy, "I went to Grandpa Mal's room to check on him. He's alive, but unconscious and not in a good way. It would appear that gifting the 'Futures' has indeed left him extremely weak and vulnerable."

A tear rolled down her cheek, but she continued bravely.

"I knew straight away that I needed to come to the Great Room to try and find some answers. But when I looked for his dressing gown that contained the keys to get here – he always kept them in there – it was missing. It was then that I knew someone had got hold of them. I admit I feared the worse. But I have to say I'm quite relieved, if not very surprised, to see you two here."

TJ nodded. There was so much he needed to tell Auntie Katherine. He needed to tell her all about Benjy and how Grandpa Mal had come to his rescue and helped him escape. But that would have to wait too, for his eyes had strayed to the third and final book on the table. The book had been deliberately left open on this page.

The handwritten text was very difficult to read, just like within the Great Book. But TJ's attention had been captured by the heading written in large letters at the top of the page.

The Rescape Creed

"What's this?" he asked Auntie Katherine, and the three of them gathered round the third book on the altar table.

Using her index finger to guide her through the elaborate handwriting,

Auntie Katherine read the page aloud, holding Lizzy Wizzy's hand reassuringly with her other hand.

"The Rescape Creed

We believe in the Order of the Brethren of the Dreamguardians, the Defenders of the safe passage of dreams, through the all-powerful protection of the Dreamswick, and the rightful inheritance of the Gift through the line of Ephraim.

We believe in the vision of our father Ephraim, that the Dreamologist will come, with the power to defeat the Stealer of Dreams, and end the great struggle against the evil of Dominus Tenebris, for all eternity.

We believe in the power of the Dreamologist, the ability to acquire, retrieve and interpret dreams like no other, with all-encompassing authority and power within the Dreamswick to Rescape a lost Dreamguardian, by reuniting a slumbering body with dream-captured mind, even those at the deepest depths, at the place where the ladder touches hell.

We affirm our belief in the Gift, the all-powerful protection of the Dreamswick, and the Order of the Brethren of the Dreamguardians, the Defenders of the safe passage of dreams. Amen."

"What does it mean Auntie Katherine?" Lizzy Wizzy asked in a scared voice. It was all too much for her to take in.

"A 'creed' is like a formal statement of belief, Lizzy Wizzy," Auntie Katherine said gently. "It looks like this is a believer's statement written by some ancient forefathers of the Brethren of the Dreamguardians."

Wedging his finger in the spine of the book to keep the page, TJ gently turned to the front cover of this third book on the altar table. He knew what the other two books were. One was the Great Book and the other the only surviving original language version of the one true book of Genesis. But he didn't know what this one was.

On the front cover, the title of the book was embossed into the leather with fading gold leaf:

LEGENDS, PROPHECIES AND EXALTATIONS OF THE DREAMOLOGIST

It was all about the Dreamologist.

TJ was amazed. He wondered what stories and secrets were contained within the book. His curiosity could wait no more.

"So, how much do you know about the Brethren then?" TJ asked Auntie Katherine.

"I knew enough to put me in danger," Auntie Katherine replied, and TJ and Lizzy Wizzy froze. Undeterred, Auntie Katherine continued. "I saw the Great Room once, and came to realise that my own dear father, the person we simply know as Grandpa Mal, was someone very special within the Brethren. Once I saw and understood the risks, that was enough."

"The risk of getting trapped?" Lizzy Wizzy asked.

"Well, yes, that was one of the risks," Auntie Katherine.

Lizzy Wizzy jumped in again before TJ could probe further.

"I know what you mean. It all seems too dangerous and scary. I don't know how Benjy managed to cope with it all ..."

"Benjy?" Auntie Katherine interrupted. "What about Benjy?"

Lizzy Wizzy looked up at Auntie Katherine with glassy eyes.

"He got trapped in TJ's dream. I just don't know how he managed to cope being lost in the darkness and held prisoner in the caves."

Auntie Katherine went white as a ghost. She looked alarmed and then angrily at TJ.

"TJ, what's been going on? What's happened to Benjy?" By this point she was extremely agitated. "Is Benjy ok? Please tell me he's ok TJ."

"Benjy's fine," TJ reassured Auntie Katherine, "he's safe and sound up in the East Wing."

Auntie Katherine let out a huge sigh of relief.

"Thank goodness for that," she said, but then a look of confusion spread across her face. "Wait, how is that possible? That must mean that the… Right," she said suddenly, "I want to know everything that's been going on in my absence. I suggest you start talking now TJ. And leave nothing out."

TJ did as he was told. He began to tell Auntie Katherine everything that had happened over the past couple of days. He started tentatively at first, before it all came flooding out. He mentioned nothing about his meeting with the Dreamorian and *Sensei*, as strictly speaking Auntie Katherine was still around at the time. He focussed mainly on how the four of them had come to realise they had the gift and what had happened as a result.

Auntie Katherine listened intensely, shaking her head and muttering under her breath at various points. She held her hands to her mouth and whispered, "oh, please, no," as TJ had informed her that both Chatty and Benjy had the gift. She looked both heartbroken and angry. TJ wasn't sure at who or why.

Then Auntie Katherine had shaken her head solemnly as TJ recounted the circumstances that had led to Benjy being trapped. She got angry when she realised that Grandpa Mal had deliberately not told her that Benjy had been lost. She had called him in the morning to let him know she would be home soon. She thought he had sounded a bit distant and tired but put that down to the exhaustion and preoccupation of looking after four lively children.

She calmed down when she realised there was no point blaming TJ or Lizzy Wizzy. It wasn't their fault. To TJ's relief, Auntie Katherine believed him when he said that Benjy had eavesdropped to find out about how to be a Dreamguardian and there was nothing he could do to avoid trapping him in his dream.

Lizzy Wizzy jumped in to tell Auntie Katherine all about Chatty's dreams and how she had worked out where Benjy was hidden, before TJ reassumed control of the storytelling. He described their dream-hopping, their search for Benjy through the caves and yet another near-deadly encounter with the evil creature called *Dominus Tenebris*.

As Auntie Katherine listened, she felt the weight and realised the significance of what she was being told. To anyone else the story would have seemed preposterous, but she was only too aware of the incredible mystery and power that came from having, and exercising, the gift.

Finally, TJ got on to the last part of the story. He described how, just as he was about to suffer Transfixation at the hands of Dominus Tenebris, Grandpa Mal had appeared in the cave within a protective dome of light.

At that point, Auntie Katherine looked like she had been subject to Transfixation herself.

"Grandpa Mal?" she asked, either not hearing or believing.

"Yes, it was Grandpa Mal," TJ said smiling. "It was him. He rescued Benjy, and all of us for that matter. Without him, I think *Dominus Tenebris* would have got us all."

"No, that can't be right," Auntie Katherine said, shaking her head.

"Yes, it is," said TJ. "Grandpa Mal is the Dreamologist."

Auntie Katherine stared long and hard at TJ. "No, it can't be," she said again.

"Yes," insisted TJ. "We were worried he had been trapped there, but he spoke to me when we had all escaped from the cave and woke up safe and sound in the Old Girl. He definitely made it back."

"But what did he say to you?" Auntie Katherine asked.

"Well, he was very weak, but he managed to whisper a few mumbled words."

"What were they?" Auntie Katherine asked quickly, "sorry, but this is very important, TJ."

"He said he was very weak, but he needed to tell me something. He said he needed to tell me that he was the Dreamologist. But I'd already worked it out in the cave anyway."

"Are you sure that's what he said TJ?"

TJ nodded. He knew exactly what Grandpa Mal was going to say just before he lost consciousness. Given what had already happened in the cave before then, it was obvious.

As he finished his story, Auntie Katherine looked shell-shocked. She put her head in her hands.

"Are you ok, Auntie Katherine?" Lizzy Wizzy asked.

"I'm not sure, Lizzy Wizzy," she replied. "To be honest with you, I'm worried."

"Why?" asked TJ. "What's there to be worried about?"

Auntie Katherine let out a sigh. "Well, from what you've just described TJ, this 'thing' - *Dominus Tenebris* - is extremely powerful. I would say it's a threat to not only you, but every single Dreamguardian, including my two children. From what you say, the Brethren has encountered its greatest enemy and is now facing its greatest existential threat for thousands of years."

"I agree," TJ said nodding, "but you've forgotten the most important thing Auntie Katherine."

A look of confusion came over her face.

"The Dreamologist has come, just like it was promised by Ephraim and in these books. How can we be defeated if we have the Dreamologist on our side?"

"TJ!" shouted Auntie Katherine, "wake up."

Both Lizzy Wizzy and TJ jumped at the sudden shout, and Auntie Katherine immediately felt bad.

"TJ," she said softly, "if Grandpa Mal is indeed the Dreamologist, as you say he is, he's an old man. A very unwell old man, lying unconscious upstairs. And you know why?"

A chastened TJ shook his head. "No," he said quietly.

"Because I think Grandpa Mal might have just sacrificed himself. Not just in getting Benjy back, but by gifting me the Futures dream to tell me that, somehow, somewhere, your Dad might still be alive."

Suddenly TJ understood. He'd felt so stupid that he hadn't seen it before now. A huge wave of despair rose up inside him and swallowed him whole.

"What do you mean Auntie Katherine?" Lizzy Wizzy asked. In reality she already knew, but she didn't want it to be true.

"There's a chance that it's no use Lizzy Wizzy," TJ said sorrowfully. "Grandpa Mal can't do anything in his current state. And if Grandpa Mal doesn't recover then it doesn't matter whether Dad is alive or not."

"No, that can't be right," Lizzy Wizzy said.

"You don't understand, Lizzy Wizzy," TJ replied. "Grandpa Mal must have known he was weakening and that his health was failing. That's why his last act was to sacrificially gift the Futures to Auntie Katherine."

"Lizzy Wizzy," TJ continued gravely, "Grandpa Mal might not recover. And without Grandpa Mal we won't be able to find and rescue Dad, from wherever he is."

He paused and hung his head.

"That's bad enough, of course," he continued, "but without Grandpa Mal, there is no Dreamologist. And if there is no Dreamologist, then the Dreamstealers will continue their advance. Without the Dreamologist there is no hope."

As he finished his grave assessment, he couldn't fight them back anymore. He was determined not to make any sound that would indicate defeat. But the tears rolled down his cheeks.

"No," cried Lizzy Wizzy through her tears at TJ. "How can you say that? We can't give up TJ. Grandpa Mal might recover. And whatever happens, I need to see Daddy again. Even if it is to give him one last kiss goodbye if Grandpa Mal can never Rescape anyone again. We need to find him. We need to find Daddy, TJ. Please..."

With that, she broke down into sobs.

"There, there, dear girl" Auntie Katherine said softly, trying to pull Lizzy Wizzy into an embrace to comfort her.

Lizzy Wizzy struggled and pulled free.

"No, I'm not giving up, and neither are you Thomas Daniel Joseph," she shouted. "We must try. Not only must we find Daddy, but we must also hold on to the hope that one day Grandpa Mal will be well enough to rescue him and bring him back to us. Just like he did with Benjy."

TJ hung his head and tried to block out what Lizzy Wizzy was saying. In his mind he had concluded that the situation was hopeless. What was the point?

However, the more he tried to ignore Lizzy Wizzy, the more she penetrated his heart.

She continued shouting at him, her voice full of passion and emotion.

"But more than that TJ, we must *fight*. We must *fight* to find Daddy. We must *fight* those disgusting Dreamstealers. We need to *fight* for the sake of the Brethren."

TJ's heart stirred at her impassioned speech. Slowly, he looked up at her.

She smiled at him, her blonde hair damp and tousled, and her eyes glistening from the tears and fight burning within.

"We need to do this TJ. After all, the Dreamguardians needs our protection. That 'thing' - *Dominus Tenebris* - can never be allowed to win."

She clenched her fists and stared hard into TJ's eyes.

"TJ, we need to do two things. First, find Daddy. Second, secure the future of the Brethren of the Dreamguardians," Lizzy Wizzy said determinedly. "That way, we can honour Grandpa Mal, no matter what happens. We need to do it. We need to find Daddy and defend the safe passage of dreams. And we need to do it together."

CHAPTER 42 – TEMPTATION

After they had securely locked up the Inner Sanctum and Great Room, they made their weary way back to the East Wing, whereupon Auntie Katherine sent TJ and Lizzy Wizzy back to bed. It had been a very long night. They would talk more in the morning. Then she rushed to Benjy's room.

As he lay there sleeping, she stroked his hair and gently woke him. She held him tightly, kissed his forehead and told him how much she loved him. Then she told him off and forbid him from ever getting trapped in a dream again.

Benjy promised through his yawns. He was pleased to see his Mummy again. After telling him they would talk more about it in the morning, she let him go back to sleep. She would make sure he got a good night's rest.

She made her way quickly to Chatty's bedroom and perched herself on the edge of her bed. She stroked her hair, just like she did when she was younger and gave her a gentle kiss on the forehead. Chatty stirred and slowly opened one eyelid.

"Mum?" she said sleepily.

"Yes, it's me darling. I'm home."

Chatty smiled. She had missed her after all, really, although she would never tell her that.

"Welcome home, Mum," Chatty said, through a big yawn.

"Thank you, not a moment too soon from what TJ and Lizzy Wizzy told me," Mum said smiling. "Still, at least Benjy is safe now, tucked up like a bug in a rug in his bed. Let's talk in the morning sweetheart. Hopefully Grandpa Mal will be awake in the morning too."

With that, she kissed her on the cheek and closed the bedroom door on the way out.

Chatty closed her eyes. Without warning, a small jealous thought appeared in her mind. Why was she the last person that Mum had been in to see and why had she spoken to TJ before her? Why had TJ, of all people, got to tell her what had been happening? Benjy was her brother, not TJ's. And after all, it was all TJ's fault. Why was she not cross with him about Benjy and Grandpa Mal? She should have been cross with him, because all the problems were because of TJ, TJ, TJ...

As she drifted off to sleep, her thoughts watered the small seed of jealousy in her mind until it had grown into a wild and uncontrollable tree of anger and resentment.

*

Chatty strode through The Armoury, picking up a *Dreamswick* as she headed through the darkness to the door at the far-end of the room. She opened the door and stepped into the light on the other side.

*

Even though his mind was whirring and racing when he got back into bed, it hadn't taken TJ long to get back to sleep. He was reassured that Auntie Katherine was home and he was no longer the eldest and responsible for Grandpa Mal. Would Grandpa Mal ever regain consciousness? TJ certainly hoped so. After all, a lot rested on it.

As he entered REM sleep, TJ found himself replaying bits of the dreams he and Lizzy Wizzy had discussed earlier. He was on a moor in winter, watching a Red stag in the distance. It was majestic; a creature of great beauty. As he looked to his left, Lizzy Wizzy was there as part of his dream, and his Mum to his right. There were no Dreamguardians around, or so he thought.

The Red stag looked over at TJ, Lizzy Wizzy and Mum and nodded its head and antlers in acknowledgement and recognition.

TJ dared believe Auntie Katherine that the Red stag represented his Dad, and that he was still alive.

The Red stag roared in their direction, as if trying to answer TJ's doubts. Then it began to run towards them.

The three of them started to run through the bracken and grass too, towards the stag.

The three humans met the Red stag with an embrace. TJ put his arms around the stag's neck and buried his face into the warm brown fur. It offered some warm respite from the chill on his face.

The animal snorted, its breath visible against the cold air.

"Dad, is it you, are you really alive?" TJ said to the animal.

*

On the high ground some way away behind TJ, Chatty crouched behind a medium-sized boulder, watching and wondering what was happening beneath her. She looked around. Apart from TJ, Lizzy Wizzy and Auntie Emma below, there was no sign of life for miles. No Dreamguardians. No Dreamstealers. What on earth was TJ dreaming about? And what were they all doing hugging a Red stag?

At first Chatty found the scene below her strangely moving and touching. But she brushed those feelings aside almost as quickly as they came. She then unequivocally decided she found the scene pathetic and nauseating. Much like TJ himself.

As she crouched on the damp grass watching a strange reunion of three humans and a large Red stag, Chatty felt alone. The more she observed, the angrier and more vengeful she became.

She looked at the *Dreamswick* in her right hand. When she had used it last, she had both felt and witnessed its power in delivering a Stopper.

She tried not to, but couldn't help but wonder what she would be able to achieve with a staff like the one that belonged to *Dominus Tenebris*. One with a beautifully ugly demonic creature dancing on her left fist.

As she looked between TJ below her and the *Dreamswick*, she felt a strong urge inside her.

She stood slowly and adopted the starting position. She passed the *Dreamswick* from her right hand to her left hand. She began to spin it slowly. It felt wrong, but good.

In her mind, she started to think what she could do to TJ in his dream. To embarrass him, to scare him, to hurt him maybe.

She thought an Embarraser ought to do it, or maybe a Stresser. Perhaps a Multiplier, just like the one he'd experienced at the glasshouse, although she would need to exit quickly before he woke. She grinned mischievously to herself. Or perhaps she should give him a Scarer, or something a bit nastier.

He did think he was a man after all.

She knew she shouldn't, but deep down she felt excited. Even though she knew what she was about to do was wrong, no-one would ever know.

But then, with a sudden pang of conscience, she stopped spinning the *Dreamswick*.

She held the *Dreamswick* in both hands and stared at it long and hard.

Inside, she was conflicted.

She closed her eyes, took some deep breaths and tried to empty her mind of everything that had happened in the past few days.

After some time, Chatty smiled enigmatically and opened her eyes.

She knew exactly what she was going to do...

TJ, Lizzy Wizzy, Chatty and Benjy will return...

ABOUT THE AUTHOR

N. R. Matthews

N. R. Matthews is a first-time author. His debut novel The Dreamguardians was written during a rare quiet period in his professional life and provided a wonderful journey of discovery, as the complex and secret world inhabited by Dreamguardians and Dreamstealers emerged. He is a big believer in the underlying themes of The Dreamguardians: family, friendship, love, hope, creativity, adventure, endeavour and having big dreams.

Printed in Great Britain
by Amazon

49261856R00234